OFF ON A COMET

OR

HECTOR SERVADAC

TRAVELS AND ADVENTURES
THROUGH THE SOLAR SYSTEM

The Crisis of Peril was close at hand.

Off on a Comet

or

Hector Servadac

TRAVELS AND ADVENTURES
THROUGH THE SOLAR SYSTEM

BY

JULES VERNE

ILLUSTRATED

ILLUSTRATED WORKS OF JULES VERNE
PUBLISHED BY

SEAWOLF
PRESS

EDITION INFORMATION
The original title was *Hector Servadac* but was released in the United States as *Off on a Comet*. The illustrations are from the French edition by Paul Philippoteaux. The translation from French is by Ellen Frewer.

SeaWolf Press
P.O. Box 961
Orinda, CA 94563
Email: support@seawolfpress.com
Web: http://www.SeaWolfPress.com

CONTENTS

PART I

I.	A CHALLENGE	3
II.	CAPTAIN SERVADAC AND HIS ORDERLY	8
III.	INTERRUPTED EFFUSIONS	13
IV.	A CONVULSION OF NATURE	17
V.	A MYSTERIOUS SEA	18
VI.	THE CAPTAIN MAKES AN EXPLORATION	29
VII.	BEN ZOOF WATCHES IN VAIN	37
VIII.	VENUS IN PERILOUS PROXIMITY	46
IX.	INQUIRIES UNSATISFIED	53
X.	A SEARCH FOR ALGERIA	60
XI.	AN ISLAND TOMB	68
XII.	AT THE MERCY OF THE WINDS	75
XIII.	A ROYAL SALUTE	83
XIV.	SENSITIVE NATIONALITY	92
XV.	AN ENIGMA FROM THE SEA	102
XVI.	THE RESIDUUM OF A CONTINENT	111
XVII.	A SECOND ENIGMA	118
XVIII.	AN UNEXPECTED POPULATION	128
XIX.	GALLIA'S GOVERNOR GENERAL	139
XX.	A LIGHT ON THE HORIZON	147
XXI.	WINTER QUARTERS	157
XXII.	A FROZEN OCEAN	165
XXIII.	A CARRIER-PIGEON	172
XXIV.	A SLEDGE-RIDE	179

PART II

I.	THE ASTRONOMER	191
II.	A REVELATION	198
III.	COMETS, OLD AND NEW.	207
IV.	THE PROFESSOR'S EXPERIENCES	217
V.	A REVISED CALENDAR	228
VI.	WANTED: A STEELYARD	239
VII.	MONEY AT A PREMIUM	247
VIII.	GALLIA WEIGHED.	254
IX.	JUPITER SOMEWHAT CLOSE.	263
X	MARKET PRICES IN GALLIA.	272
XI.	FAR INTO SPACE	280
XII.	A FÊTE DAY	287
XIII.	THE BOWELS OF THE COMET.	296
XIV.	DREARY MONTHS	305
XV.	THE PROFESSOR PERPLEXED.	314
XVI.	A JOURNEY AND A DISAPPOINTMENT.	324
XVII.	A BOLD PROPOSITION	335
XVIII.	THE VENTURE MADE.	344
XIX.	SUSPENSE.	354
XX.	BACK AGAIN	360

HECTOR SERVADAC

TRAVELS AND ADVENTURES

THROUGH THE SOLAR SYSTEM

"Here is my card—And mine."

BOOK I.

CHAPTER I.

A CHALLENGE

"Nothing, sir, can induce me to surrender my claim."

"I am sorry, count, but in such a matter your views cannot modify mine."

"But allow me to point out that my seniority unquestionably gives me a prior right."

"Mere seniority, I assert, in an affair of this kind, cannot possibly entitle you to any prior claim whatever."

"Then, captain, no alternative is left but for me to compel you to yield at the sword's point."

"As you please, count; but neither sword nor pistol can force me to forego my pretensions. Here is my card."

"And mine."

This rapid altercation was thus brought to an end by the formal interchange of the names of the disputants. On one of the cards was inscribed:

Captain Hector Servadac,
Staff Officer,
Mostaganem.

On the other was the title:

Count Wassili Timascheff,
On board the Schooner "Dobryna."

It did not take long to arrange that seconds should be appointed, who would meet in Mostaganem at two o'clock that day; and the captain and the count were on the point of parting from each other, with a salute of punctilious courtesy, when Timascheff, as if struck by a sudden thought, said abruptly: "Perhaps it would be better, captain, not to allow the real cause of this to transpire?"

"Far better," replied Servadac; "it is undesirable in every way for any names to be mentioned."

"In that case, however," continued the count, "it will be necessary to assign an ostensible pretext of some kind. Shall we allege a musical dispute? a contention in which I feel bound to defend Wagner, while you are the zealous champion of Rossini?"

"I am quite content," answered Servadac, with a smile; and with another low bow they parted.

The scene, as here depicted, took place upon the extremity of a little cape on the Algerian coast, between Mostaganem and Tenes, about two miles from the mouth of the Shelif. The headland rose more than sixty feet above the sea-level, and the azure waters of the Mediterranean, as they softly kissed the strand, were tinged with the reddish hue of the ferriferous rocks that formed its base. It was the 31st of December. The noontide sun, which usually illuminated the various projections of the coast with a dazzling brightness, was hidden by a dense mass of cloud, and the fog, which for some unaccountable cause, had hung for the last two months over nearly every region in the world, causing serious interruption to traffic between continent and continent, spread its dreary veil across land and sea.

After taking leave of the staff-officer, Count Wassili Timascheff wended his way down to a small creek, and took his seat in the stern of a light four-oar that had been awaiting his return; this was immediately pushed off from shore, and was soon alongside a pleasure-yacht, that was lying to, not many cable lengths away.

At a sign from Servadac, an orderly, who had been standing at a respectful distance, led forward a magnificent Arabian horse; the captain vaulted into the saddle, and followed by his attendant, well mounted as himself, started off towards Mostaganem. It was half-past twelve when the two riders crossed the bridge that had been recently erected over the Shelif, and a quarter of an hour later their steeds, flecked with foam, dashed through the Mascara Gate, which was one of five entrances opened in the embattled wall that encircled the town.

At that date, Mostaganem contained about fifteen thousand inhabitants, three thousand of whom were French. Besides being one of the principal district towns of the province of Oran, it was also a military station. Mostaganem rejoiced in a well-sheltered harbor, which enabled her to utilize all the rich products of the Mina and the Lower Shelif. It was the existence of so good a harbor amidst the exposed cliffs of this coast that had induced the owner of the *Dobryna* to winter in these parts, and for two months the Russian standard had been seen floating from her yard, whilst on her mast-head was hoisted the pennant of the French Yacht Club, with the distinctive letters M. C. W. T., the initials of Count Timascheff.

Having entered the town, Captain Servadac made his way towards Matmore, the military quarter, and was not long in finding two friends on whom he might rely—a major of the 2nd Fusileers, and a captain of the 8th Artillery. The two officers listened gravely enough to Servadac's request that they would act as his seconds in an affair of honor, but could not resist a smile on hearing that the dispute between him and the count had originated in a musical discussion. Surely, they suggested, the matter might be easily arranged; a few slight concessions on either side, and all might be amicably adjusted. But no representations on their part were of any avail. Hector Servadac was inflexible.

"No concession is possible," he replied, resolutely. "Rossini has been deeply injured, and I cannot suffer the injury to be unavenged. Wagner is a fool. I shall keep my word. I am quite firm."

"Be it so, then," replied one of the officers; "and after all, you know, a sword-cut need not be a very serious affair."

"Certainly not," rejoined Servadac; "and especially in my case, when I have not the slightest intention of being wounded at all."

Incredulous as they naturally were as to the assigned cause of the quarrel, Servadac's friends had no alternative but to accept his explanation, and without farther parley they started for the staff office, where, at two o'clock precisely, they were to meet the seconds of Count Timascheff. Two hours later they had returned. All the preliminaries had been arranged; the count, who like many Russians abroad was an aide-de-camp of the Czar, had of course proposed swords as the most appropriate weapons, and the duel was to take place on the following morning, the first of January, at nine o'clock, upon the cliff at a spot about a mile and a half from the mouth of the Shelif. With the assurance that they would not fail to keep their appointment with military punctuality, the two officers cordially wrung their friend's hand and retired to the Zulma Cafe for a game at piquet. Captain Servadac at once retraced his steps and left the town.

For the last fortnight Servadac had not been occupying his proper lodgings in the military quarters; having been appointed to make a local levy, he had been living in a gourbi, or native hut, on the Mosta-

ganem coast, between four and five miles from the Shelif. His orderly
was his sole companion, and by any other man than the captain the enforced exile would have been esteemed little short of a severe penance.

On his way to the gourbi, his mental occupation was a very laborious effort to put together what he was pleased to call a rondo, upon a
model of versification all but obsolete. This rondo, it is unnecessary to
conceal, was to be an ode addressed to a young widow by whom he had
been captivated, and whom he was anxious to marry, and the tenor of
his muse was intended to prove that when once a man has found an
object in all respects worthy of his affections, he should love her "in
all simplicity." Whether the aphorism were universally true was not
very material to the gallant captain, whose sole ambition at present
was to construct a roundelay of which this should be the prevailing
sentiment. He indulged the fancy that he might succeed in producing
a composition which would have a fine effect here in Algeria, where
poetry in that form was all but unknown.

"I know well enough," he said repeatedly to himself, "what I want
to say. I want to tell her that I love her sincerely, and wish to marry
her; but, confound it! the words won't rhyme. Plague on it! Does nothing rhyme with 'simplicity'? Ah! I have it now:

> 'Lovers should, whoe'er they be,
> Love in all simplicity.'

But what next? how am I to go on? I say, Ben Zoof," he called aloud
to his orderly, who was trotting silently close in his rear, "did you ever
compose any poetry?"

"No, captain," answered the man promptly: "I have never made
any verses, but I have seen them made fast enough at a booth during
the fête of Montmartre."

"Can you remember them?"

"Remember them! to be sure I can. This is the way they began:

> 'Come in! come in! you'll not repent
> The entrance money you have spent;
> The wondrous mirror in this place
> Reveals your future sweetheart's face.'"

"Bosh!" cried Servadac in disgust; "your verses are detestable trash."

"As good as any others, captain, squeaked through a reed pipe."

"Hold your tongue, man," said Servadac peremptorily; "I have
made another couplet.

'Lovers should, whoe'er they be,
Love in all simplicity;
Lover, loving honestly,
Offer I myself to thee.'"

Beyond this, however, the captain's poetical genius was impotent to carry him; his farther efforts were unavailing, and when at six o'clock he reached the gourbi, the four lines still remained the limit of his composition.

The two officers listened gravely enough to Servadac's request.

CHAPTER II.

CAPTAIN SERVADAC AND HIS ORDERLY

At the time of which I write, there might be seen in the registers of the Minister of War the following entry:

SERVADAC (*Hector*), born at St. Trelody in the district of Lesparre, department of the Gironde, July 19th, 18—.

Property: 1200 francs in rentes.

Length of service: Fourteen years, three months, and five days.

Service: Two years at school at St. Cyr; two years at L'Ecole d'Application; two years in the 8th Regiment of the Line; two years in the 3rd Light Cavalry; seven years in Algeria.

Campaigns: Soudan and Japan.

Rank: Captain on the staff at Mostaganem.

Decorations: Chevalier of the Legion of Honor, March 13th, 18—.

Hector Servadac was thirty years of age, an orphan without lineage and almost without means. Thirsting for glory rather than for gold, slightly scatter-brained, but warm-hearted, generous, and brave, he was eminently formed to be the protege of the god of battles.

For the first year and a half of his existence he had been the foster-child of the sturdy wife of a vine-dresser of Medoc—a lineal descendant of the heroes of ancient prowess; in a word, he was one of those individuals whom nature seems to have predestined for remarkable things, and around whose cradle have hovered the fairy godmothers of adventure and good luck.

In appearance Hector Servadac was quite the type of an officer; he was rather more than five feet six inches high, slim and graceful, with dark curling hair and mustaches, well-formed hands and feet, and a clear blue eye. He seemed born to please without being conscious of the power he possessed. It must be owned, and no one was more ready to confess it than himself, that his literary attainments were by no means of a high order. "We don't spin tops" is a favorite saying amongst artillery officers, indicating that they do not shirk their duty by frivolous pursuits; but it must be confessed that Servadac, being naturally idle, was very much given to "spinning tops." His good abilities, however, and his ready intelligence had carried him successfully through the curriculum of his early career. He was a good draughtsman, an excellent rider—having thoroughly mastered the successor to the famous "Uncle Tom" at the riding-school of St. Cyr—and in the records of his military service his name had several times been included in the order of the day.

Ben Zoof

The following episode may suffice, in a certain degree, to illustrate his character. Once, in action, he was leading a detachment of infantry through an intrenchment. They came to a place where the side-work of the trench had been so riddled by shell that a portion of it had actually fallen in, leaving an aperture quite unsheltered from the grapeshot that was pouring in thick and fast. The men hesitated. In an instant Servadac mounted the side-work, laid himself down in the gap, and thus filling up the breach by his own body, shouted, "March on!"

And through a storm of shot, not one of which touched the prostrate officer, the troop passed in safety.

Since leaving the military college, Servadac, with the exception of his two campaigns in the Soudan and Japan, had been always stationed in Algeria. He had now a staff appointment at Mostaganem, and had lately been entrusted with some topographical work on the coast between Tenes and the Shelif. It was a matter of little consequence to him that the gourbi, in which of necessity he was quartered, was uncomfortable and ill-contrived; he loved the open air, and the independence of his life suited him well. Sometimes he would wander on foot upon the sandy shore, and sometimes he would enjoy a ride along the summit of the cliff; altogether being in no hurry at all to bring his task to an end. His occupation, moreover, was not so engrossing but that he could find leisure for taking a short railway journey once or twice a week; so that he was ever and again putting in an appearance at the general's receptions at Oran, and at the fêtes given by the governor at Algiers.

It was on one of these occasions that he had first met Madame de L——, the lady to whom he was desirous of dedicating the rondo, the first four lines of which had just seen the light. She was a colonel's widow, young and handsome, very reserved, not to say haughty in her manner, and either indifferent or impervious to the admiration which she inspired. Captain Servadac had not yet ventured to declare his attachment; of rivals he was well aware he had not a few, and amongst these not the least formidable was the Russian Count Timascheff. And although the young widow was all unconscious of the share she had in the matter, it was she, and she alone, who was the cause of the challenge just given and accepted by her two ardent admirers.

During his residence in the gourbi, Hector Servadac's sole companion was his orderly, Ben Zoof. Ben Zoof was devoted, body and soul, to his superior officer. His own personal ambition was so entirely absorbed in his master's welfare, that it is certain no offer of promotion—even had it been that of aide-de-camp to the Governor-General of Algiers—would have induced him to quit that master's service. His name might seem to imply that he was a native of Algeria; but such was by no means the case. His true name was Laurent; he was a native of Montmartre in Paris, and how or why he had obtained his patronymic was one of those anomalies which the most sagacious of etymologists would find it hard to explain.

Born on the hill of Montmartre, between the Solferino tower and the mill of La Galette, Ben Zoof had ever possessed the most unreserved admiration for his birthplace; and to his eyes the heights and district of Montmartre represented an epitome of all the wonders of the world. In all his travels, and these had been not a few, he had never beheld scenery which could compete with that of his native home. No cathedral—not even Burgos itself—could vie with the church at Montmartre. Its race-course could well hold its own against that at Pentelique; its reservoir would throw the Mediterranean into the shade; its forests had flourished long before the invasion of the Celts; and its very mill produced no ordinary flour, but provided material for cakes of world-wide renown. To crown all, Montmartre boasted a mountain—a veritable mountain; envious tongues indeed might pronounce it little more than a hill; but Ben Zoof would have allowed himself to be hewn in pieces rather than admit that it was anything less than fifteen thousand feet in height.

Ben Zoof's most ambitious desire was to induce the captain to go with him and end his days in his much-loved home, and so incessantly were Servadac's ears besieged with descriptions of the unparalleled beauties and advantages of this eighteenth arrondissement of Paris, that he could scarcely hear the name of Montmartre without a conscious thrill of aversion. Ben Zoof, however, did not despair of ultimately converting the captain, and meanwhile had resolved never to leave him. When a private in the 8th Cavalry, he had been on the point of quitting the army at twenty-eight years of age, but unexpectedly he had been appointed orderly to Captain Servadac. Side by side they fought in two campaigns. Servadac had saved Ben Zoof's life in Japan; Ben Zoof had rendered his master a like service in the Soudan. The bond of union thus effected could never be severed; and although

Ben Zoof's achievements had fairly earned him the right of retire-
ment, he firmly declined all honors or any pension that might part
him from his superior officer. Two stout arms, an iron constitution, a
powerful frame, and an indomitable courage were all loyally devoted to
his master's service, and fairly entitled him to his *soi-disant* designa-
tion of "The Rampart of Montmartre." Unlike his master, he made no
pretension to any gift of poetic power, but his inexhaustible memory
made him a living encyclopaedia; and for his stock of anecdotes and
trooper's tales he was matchless.

Thoroughly appreciating his servant's good qualities, Captain Servadac endured with imperturbable good humor those idiosyncrasies,
which in a less faithful follower would have been intolerable, and from
time to time he would drop a word of sympathy that served to deepen
his subordinate's devotion.

On one occasion, when Ben Zoof had mounted his hobby-horse, and
was indulging in high-flown praises about his beloved eighteenth arrondissement, the captain had remarked gravely, "Do you know, Ben
Zoof, that Montmartre only requires a matter of some thirteen thousand feet to make it as high as Mont Blanc?"

Ben Zoof's eyes glistened with delight; and from that moment Hector Servadac and Montmartre held equal places in his affection.

CHAPTER III.

INTERRUPTED EFFUSIONS

COMPOSED of mud and loose stones, and covered with a thatch of turf and straw, known to the natives by the name of "driss," the gourbi, though a grade better than the tents of the nomad Arabs, was yet far inferior to any habitation built of brick or stone. It adjoined an old stone hostelry, previously occupied by a detachment of engineers, and which now afforded shelter for Ben Zoof and the two horses. It still contained a considerable number of tools, such as mattocks, shovels, and pick-axes.

Uncomfortable as was their temporary abode, Servadac and his attendant made no complaints; neither of them was dainty in the matter either of board or lodging. After dinner, leaving his orderly to stow away the remains of the repast in what he was pleased to term the "cupboard of his stomach." Captain Servadac turned out into the open air to smoke his pipe upon the edge of the cliff. The shades of night were drawing on. An hour previously, veiled in heavy clouds, the sun had sunk below the horizon that bounded the plain beyond the Shelif.

The sky presented a most singular appearance. Towards the north, although the darkness rendered it impossible to see beyond a quarter of a mile, the upper strata of the atmosphere were suffused with a rosy glare. No well-defined fringe of light, nor arch of luminous rays, betokened a display of aurora borealis, even had such a phenomenon been possible in these latitudes; and the most experienced meteorologist would have been puzzled to explain the cause of this striking illumination on this 31st of December, the last evening of the passing year.

But Captain Servadac was no meteorologist, and it is to be doubted whether, since leaving school, he had ever opened his "Course of Cosmography." Besides, he had other thoughts to occupy his mind. The prospects of the morrow offered serious matter for consideration. The captain was actuated by no personal animosity against the count;

though rivals, the two men regarded each other with sincere respect; they had simply reached a crisis in which one of them was *de trop;* which of them, fate must decide.

At eight o'clock, Captain Servadac re-entered the gourbi, the single apartment of which contained his bed, a small writing-table, and some trunks that served instead of cupboards. The orderly performed his culinary operations in the adjoining building, which he also used as a bed-room, and where, extended on what he called his "good oak mattress," he would sleep soundly as a dormouse for twelve hours at a stretch. Ben Zoof had not yet received his orders to retire, and ensconcing himself in a corner of the gourbi, he endeavored to doze—a task which the unusual agitation of his master rendered somewhat difficult. Captain Servadac was evidently in no hurry to betake himself to rest, but seating himself at his table, with a pair of compasses and a sheet of tracing-paper, he began to draw, with red and blue crayons, a variety of colored lines, which could hardly be supposed to have much connection with a topographical survey. In truth, his character of staff-officer was now entirely absorbed in that of Gascon poet. Whether he imagined that the compasses would bestow upon his verses the measure of a mathematical accuracy, or whether he fancied that the parti-colored lines would lend variety to his rhythm, it is impossible to determine; be that as it may, he was devoting all his energies to the compilation of his rondo, and supremely difficult he found the task.

"Hang it!" he ejaculated, "whatever induced me to choose this meter? It is as hard to find rhymes as to rally fugitive in a battle. But, by all the powers! it shan't be said that a French officer cannot cope with a piece of poetry. One battalion has fought—now for the rest!"

Perseverance had its reward. Presently two lines, one red, the other blue, appeared upon the paper, and the captain murmured:

"Words, mere words, cannot avail,
Telling true heart's tender tale."

"What on earth ails my master?" muttered Ben Zoof; "for the last hour he has been as fidgety as a bird returning after its winter migration."

Servadac suddenly started from his seat, and as he paced the room with all the frenzy of poetic inspiration, read out:

"Empty words cannot convey
All a lover's heart would say."

"Well, to be sure, he is at his everlasting verses again!" said Ben Zoof to himself, as he roused himself in his corner. "Impossible to sleep in such a noise;" and he gave vent to a loud groan.

"How now, Ben Zoof?" said the captain sharply. "What ails you?"

"Nothing, sir, only the nightmare."

"Curse the fellow, he has quite interrupted me!" ejaculated the captain. "Ben Zoof!" he called aloud.

"What on earth ails my master?" muttered Ben Zoof.

"Here, sir!" was the prompt reply; and in an instant the orderly was upon his feet, standing in a military attitude, one hand to his forehead, the other closely pressed to his trouser-seam.

"Stay where you are! don't move an inch!" shouted Servadac; "I have just thought of the end of my rondo." And in a voice of inspiration, accompanying his words with dramatic gestures, Servadac began to declaim:

> "Listen, lady, to my vows—
> O, consent to be my spouse;
> Constant ever I will be,
> Constant...."

No closing lines were uttered. All at once, with unutterable violence, the captain and his orderly were dashed, face downwards, to the ground.

CHAPTER IV.

A CONVULSION OF NATURE

WHENCE came it that at that very moment the horizon underwent so strange and sudden a modification, that the eye of the most practiced mariner could not distinguish between sea and sky?

Whence came it that the billows raged and rose to a height hitherto unregistered in the records of science?

Whence came it that the elements united in one deafening crash; that the earth groaned as though the whole framework of the globe were ruptured; that the waters roared from their innermost depths; that the air shrieked with all the fury of a cyclone?

Whence came it that a radiance, intenser than the effulgence of the Northern Lights, overspread the firmament, and momentarily dimmed the splendor of the brightest stars?

Whence came it that the Mediterranean, one instant emptied of its waters, was the next flooded with a foaming surge?

Whence came it that in the space of a few seconds the moon's disc reached a magnitude as though it were but a tenth part of its ordinary distance from the earth?

Whence came it that a new blazing spheroid, hitherto unknown to astronomy, now appeared suddenly in the firmament, though it were but to lose itself immediately behind masses of accumulated cloud?

What phenomenon was this that had produced a cataclysm so tremendous in effect upon earth, sky, and sea?

Was it possible that a single human being could have survived the convulsion? and if so, could he explain its mystery?

CHAPTER V.

A MYSTERIOUS SEA

VIOLENT as the commotion had been, that portion of the Algerian coast which is bounded on the north by the Mediterranean, and on the west by the right bank of the Shelif, appeared to have suffered little change. It is true that indentations were perceptible in the fertile plain, and the surface of the sea was ruffled with an agitation that was quite unusual; but the rugged outline of the cliff was the same as heretofore, and the aspect of the entire scene appeared unaltered. The stone hostelry, with the exception of some deep clefts in its walls, had sustained little injury; but the gourbi, like a house of cards destroyed by an infant's breath, had completely subsided, and its two inmates lay motionless, buried under the sunken thatch.

It was two hours after the catastrophe that Captain Servadac regained consciousness; he had some trouble to collect his thoughts, and the first sounds that escaped his lips were the concluding words of the rondo which had been so ruthlessly interrupted;

> "Constant ever I will be,
> Constant...."

His next thought was to wonder what had happened; and in order to find an answer, he pushed aside the broken thatch, so that his head appeared above the *debris*. "The gourbi leveled to the ground!" he exclaimed, "surely a waterspout has passed along the coast."

He felt all over his body to perceive what injuries he had sustained, but not a sprain nor a scratch could he discover. "Where are you, Ben Zoof?" he shouted.

"Here, sir!" and with military promptitude a second head protruded from the rubbish.

"Have you any notion what has happened, Ben Zoof?"

"I've a notion, captain, that it's all up with us."

"Nonsense, Ben Zoof; it is nothing but a waterspout!"

"Very good, sir," was the philosophical reply, immediately followed by the query, "Any bones broken, sir?"

"None whatever," said the captain.

"Here, sir!" . . . from the rubbish.

Both men were soon on their feet, and began to make a vigorous clearance of the ruins, beneath which they found that their arms, cooking utensils, and other property, had sustained little injury.

"By-the-by, what o'clock is it?" asked the captain.

"It must be eight o'clock, at least," said Ben Zoof, looking at the sun, which was a considerable height above the horizon. "It is almost time for us to start."

"To start! what for?"

"To keep your appointment with Count Timascheff."

"By Jove! I had forgotten all about it!" exclaimed Servadac. Then looking at his watch, he cried, "What are you thinking of, Ben Zoof? It is scarcely two o'clock."

"Two in the morning, or two in the afternoon?" asked Ben Zoof, again regarding the sun.

Servadac raised his watch to his ear. "It is going," said he; "but, by all the wines of Medoc, I am puzzled. Don't you see the sun is in the west? It must be near setting."

"Setting, captain! Why, it is rising finely, like a conscript at the sound of the reveille. It is considerably higher since we have been talking."

Incredible as it might appear, the fact was undeniable that the sun was rising over the Shelif from that quarter of the horizon behind which it usually sank for the latter portion of its daily round. They were utterly bewildered. Some mysterious phenomenon must not only have altered the position of the sun in the sidereal system, but must even have brought about an important modification of the earth's rotation on her axis.

Captain Servadac consoled himself with the prospect of reading an explanation of the mystery in next week's newspapers, and turned his attention to what was to him of more immediate importance. "Come, let us be off," said he to his orderly; "though heaven and earth be topsy-turvy, I must be at my post this morning."

"To do Count Timascheff the honor of running him through the body," added Ben Zoof.

If Servadac and his orderly had been less preoccupied, they would have noticed that a variety of other physical changes besides the apparent alteration in the movement of the sun had been evolved during the atmospheric disturbances of that New Year's night. As they descended the steep footpath leading from the cliff towards the Shelif, they were unconscious that their respiration became forced and rapid, like that of a mountaineer when he has reached an altitude where the air has become less charged with oxygen. They were also unconscious that their voices were thin and feeble; either they must themselves have become rather deaf, or it was evident that the air had become less capable of transmitting sound.

The weather, which on the previous evening had been very foggy, had entirely changed. The sky had assumed a singular tint, and was soon covered with lowering clouds that completely hid the sun. There were, indeed, all the signs of a coming storm, but the vapor, on account of the insufficient condensation, failed to fall.

The sea appeared quite deserted, a most unusual circumstance along this coast, and not a sail nor a trail of smoke broke the gray monotony of water and sky. The limits of the horizon, too, had become much circumscribed. On land, as well as on sea, the remote distance had completely disappeared, and it seemed as though the globe had assumed a more decided convexity.

At the pace at which they were walking, it was very evident that the captain and his attendant would not take long to accomplish the three miles that lay between the gourbi and the place of rendezvous. They did not exchange a word, but each was conscious of an unusual buoyancy, which appeared to lift up their bodies and give as it were, wings to their feet. If Ben Zoof had expressed his sensations in words, he would have said that he felt "up to anything," and he had even forgotten to taste so much as a crust of bread, a lapse of memory of which the worthy soldier was rarely guilty.

As these thoughts were crossing his mind, a harsh bark was heard to the left of the footpath, and a jackal was seen emerging from a large grove of lentisks. Regarding the two wayfarers with manifest uneasiness, the beast took up its position at the foot of a rock, more than thirty feet in height. It belonged to an African species distinguished by a black spotted skin, and a black line down the front of the legs. At night-time, when they scour the country in herds, the creatures are somewhat formidable, but singly they are no more dangerous than a dog. Though by no means afraid of them, Ben Zoof had a particular aversion to jackals, perhaps because they had no place among the fauna of his beloved Montmartre. He accordingly began to make threatening gestures, when, to the unmitigated astonishment of himself and the captain, the animal darted forward, and in one single bound gained the summit of the rock.

"Good Heavens!" cried Ben Zoof, "that leap must have been thirty feet at least."

"True enough," replied the captain; "I never saw such a jump."

Meantime the jackal had seated itself upon its haunches, and was staring at the two men with an air of impudent defiance. This was too

much for Ben Zoof's forbearance, and stooping down he caught up a
huge stone, when to his surprise, he found that it was no heavier than
a piece of petrified sponge. "Confound the brute!" he exclaimed, "I
might as well throw a piece of bread at him. What accounts for its being as light as this?"

The jackal perched on the top of the rock.

Nothing daunted, however, he hurled the stone into the air. It
missed its aim; but the jackal, deeming it on the whole prudent to de-
camp, disappeared across the trees and hedges with a series of bounds,
which could only be likened to those that might be made by an india-
rubber kangaroo. Ben Zoof was sure that his own powers of propelling

must equal those of a howitzer, for his stone, after a lengthened flight through the air, fell to the ground full five hundred paces the other side of the rock.

The orderly was now some yards ahead of his master, and had reached a ditch full of water, and about ten feet wide. With the intention of clearing it, he made a spring, when a loud cry burst from Servadac. "Ben Zoof, you idiot! What are you about? You will break your back!"

In his ascent he passed Ben Zoof, who had already commenced his downward course.

And well might he be alarmed, for Ben Zoof had sprung to a height of forty feet into the air. Fearful of the consequences that would attend the descent of his servant to *terra firma*, Servadac bounded forwards, to be on the other side of the ditch in time to break his fall. But the muscular effort that he made carried him in his turn to an altitude of thirty feet; in his ascent he passed Ben Zoof, who had already commenced his downward course; and then, obedient to the laws of gravitation, he descended with increasing rapidity, and alighted upon the earth without experiencing a shock greater than if he had merely made a bound of four or five feet high.

Ben Zoof burst into a roar of laughter. "Bravo!" he said, "we should make a good pair of clowns."

But the captain was inclined to take a more serious view of the matter. For a few seconds he stood lost in thought, then said solemnly, "Ben Zoof, I must be dreaming. Pinch me hard; I must be either asleep or mad."

"It is very certain that something has happened to us," said Ben Zoof. "I have occasionally dreamed that I was a swallow flying over the Montmartre, but I never experienced anything of this kind before; it must be peculiar to the coast of Algeria."

Servadac was stupefied; he felt instinctively that he was not dreaming, and yet was powerless to solve the mystery. He was not, however, the man to puzzle himself for long over any insoluble problem. "Come what may," he presently exclaimed, "we will make up our minds for the future to be surprised at nothing."

"Right, captain," replied Ben Zoof; "and, first of all, let us settle our little score with Count Timascheff."

Beyond the ditch lay a small piece of meadow land, about an acre in extent. A soft and delicious herbage carpeted the soil, whilst trees formed a charming framework to the whole. No spot could have been chosen more suitable for the meeting between the two adversaries.

Servadac cast a hasty glance round. No one was in sight. "We are the first on the field," he said.

"Not so sure of that, sir," said Ben Zoof.

"What do you mean?" asked Servadac, looking at his watch, which he had set as nearly as possible by the sun before leaving the gourbi; "it is not nine o'clock yet."

"Look up there, sir. I am much mistaken if that is not the sun;" and as Ben Zoof spoke, he pointed directly overhead to where a faint white disc was dimly visible through the haze of clouds.

"Nonsense!" exclaimed Servadac. "How can the sun be in the zenith, in the month of January, in lat. 39 degrees N.?"

"Can't say, sir. I only know the sun is there; and at the rate he has been traveling, I would lay my cap to a dish of couscous that in less than three hours he will have set."

Hector Servadac, mute and motionless, stood with folded arms. Presently he roused himself, and began to look about again. "What means all this?" he murmured. "Laws of gravity disturbed! Points of the compass reversed! The length of day reduced one half! Surely this will indefinitely postpone my meeting with the count. Something has happened; Ben Zoof and I cannot both be mad!"

The orderly, meantime, surveyed his master with the greatest equanimity; no phenomenon, however extraordinary, would have drawn from him a single exclamation of surprise. "Do you see anyone, Ben Zoof?" asked the captain, at last.

"No one, sir; the count has evidently been and gone." "But supposing that to be the case," persisted the captain, "my seconds would have waited, and not seeing me, would have come on towards the gourbi. I can only conclude that they have been unable to get here; and as for Count Timascheff—"

Without finishing his sentence. Captain Servadac, thinking it just probable that the count, as on the previous evening, might come by water, walked to the ridge of rock that overhung the shore, in order to ascertain if the *Dobryna* were anywhere in sight. But the sea was deserted, and for the first time the captain noticed that, although the wind was calm, the waters were unusually agitated, and seethed and foamed as though they were boiling. It was very certain that the yacht would have found a difficulty in holding her own in such a swell. Another thing that now struck Servadac was the extraordinary contraction of the horizon. Under ordinary circumstances, his elevated position would have allowed him a radius of vision at least five and twenty miles in length; but the terrestrial sphere seemed, in the course of the last few hours, to have become considerably reduced in volume, and he could now see for a distance of only six miles in every direction.

Meantime, with the agility of a monkey, Ben Zoof had clambered to the top of a eucalyptus, and from his lofty perch was surveying the country to the south, as well as towards both Tenes and Mostaganem. On descending, be informed the captain that the plain was deserted.

"We will make our way to the river, and get over into Mostaganem," said the captain.

The Shelif was not more than a mile and a half from the meadow, but no time was to be lost if the two men were to reach the town before nightfall. Though still hidden by heavy clouds, the sun was evidently declining fast; and what was equally inexplicable, it was not following the oblique curve that in these latitudes and at this time of year might be expected, but was sinking perpendicularly on to the horizon.

As he went along, Captain Servadac pondered deeply. Perchance some unheard-of phenomenon had modified the rotary motion of the globe; or perhaps the Algerian coast had been transported beyond the equator into the southern hemisphere. Yet the earth, with the exception of the alteration in its convexity, in this part of Africa at least, seemed to have undergone no change of any very great importance. As far as the eye could reach, the shore was, as it had ever been, a succession of cliffs, beach, and arid rocks, tinged with a red ferruginous hue. To the south—if south, in this inverted order of things, it might still be called—the face of the country also appeared unaltered, and some leagues away, the peaks of the Merdeyah mountains still retained their accustomed outline.

Presently a rift in the clouds gave passage to an oblique ray of light that clearly proved that the sun was setting in the east.

"Well, I am curious to know what they think of all this at Mostaganem," said the captain. "I wonder, too, what the Minister of War will say when he receives a telegram informing him that his African colony has become, not morally, but physically disorganized; that the cardinal points are at variance with ordinary rules, and that the sun in the month of January is shining down vertically upon our heads."

Ben Zoof, whose ideas of discipline were extremely rigid, at once suggested that the colony should be put under the surveillance of the police, that the cardinal points should be placed under restraint, and that the sun should be shot for breach of discipline.

Meantime, they were both advancing with the utmost speed. The decompression of the atmosphere made the specific gravity of their bodies extraordinarily light, and they ran like hares and leaped like chamois. Leaving the devious windings of the footpath, they went as a crow would fly across the country. Hedges, trees, and streams were cleared at a bound, and under these conditions Ben Zoof felt that he could have overstepped Montmartre at a single stride. The earth seemed as elastic as the springboard of an acrobat; they scarcely touched it with their feet, and their only fear was lest the height to which they were propelled would consume the time which they were saving by their short cut across the fields.

The shore of a tumultuous ocean.

It was not long before their wild career brought them to the right bank of the Shelif. Here they were compelled to stop, for not only had the bridge completely disappeared, but the river itself no longer existed. Of the left bank there was not the slightest trace, and the right bank, which on the previous evening had bounded the yellow stream, as it murmured peacefully along the fertile plain, had now become the shore of a tumultuous ocean, its azure waters extending westwards far as the eye could reach, and annihilating the tract of country which had hitherto formed the district of Mostaganem. The shore coincided exactly with what had been the right bank of the Shelif, and in a slightly curved line ran north and south, whilst the adjacent groves and meadows all retained their previous positions. But the river-bank had become the shore of an unknown sea.

Eager to throw some light upon the mystery, Servadac hurriedly made his way through the oleander bushes that overhung the shore, took up some water in the hollow of his hand, and carried it to his lips. "Salt as brine!" he exclaimed, as soon as he had tasted it. "The sea has undoubtedly swallowed up all the western part of Algeria."

"It will not last long, sir," said Ben Zoof. "It is, probably, only a severe flood."

The captain shook his head. "Worse than that, I fear, Ben Zoof," he replied with emotion. "It is a catastrophe that may have very serious consequences. What can have become of all my friends and fellow-officers?"

Ben Zoof was silent. Rarely had he seen his master so much agitated; and though himself inclined to receive these phenomena with philosophic indifference, his notions of military duty caused his countenance to reflect the captain's expression of amazement.

But there was little time for Servadac to examine the changes which a few hours had wrought. The sun had already reached the eastern horizon, and just as though it were crossing the ecliptic under the tropics, it sank like a cannon ball into the sea. Without any warning, day gave place to night, and earth, sea, and sky were immediately wrapped in profound obscurity.

CHAPTER VI.

THE CAPTAIN MAKES AN EXPLORATION

HECTOR SERVADAC was not the man to remain long unnerved by any untoward event. It was part of his character to discover the why and the wherefore of everything that came under his observation, and he would have faced a cannon ball the more unflinchingly from understanding the dynamic force by which it was propelled. Such being his temperament, it may well be imagined that he was anxious not to remain long in ignorance of the cause of the phenomena which had been so startling in their consequences.

"We must inquire into this to-morrow," he exclaimed, as darkness fell suddenly upon him. Then, after a pause, he added: "That is to say, if there is to be a to-morrow; for if I were to be put to the torture, I could not tell what has become of the sun."

"May I ask, sir, what we are to do now?" put in Ben Zoof.

"Stay where we are for the present; and when daylight appears—if it ever does appear—we will explore the coast to the west and south, and return to the gourbi. If we can find out nothing else, we must at least discover where we are."

"Meanwhile, sir, may we go to sleep?"

"Certainly, if you like, and if you can."

Nothing loath to avail himself of his master's permission, Ben Zoof crouched down in an angle of the shore, threw his arms over his eyes, and very soon slept the sleep of the ignorant, which is often sounder than the sleep of the just. Overwhelmed by the questions that crowded upon his brain, Captain Servadac could only wander up and down the shore. Again and again he asked himself what the catastrophe could portend. Had the towns of Algiers, Oran, and Mostaganem escaped the inundation? Could he bring himself to believe that all the inhabitants, his friends, and comrades had perished; or was it not more probable that the Mediterranean had merely invaded the region of the mouth of the Shelif? But this supposition did not in the least explain the other physical disturbances. Another hypothesis that presented itself to his mind was that the African coast might have been suddenly transported to the equatorial zone. But although this might get over the difficulty of the altered altitude of the sun and the absence of twilight, yet it would neither account for the sun setting in the east, nor for the length of the day being reduced to six hours.

"We must wait till to-morrow," he repeated; adding, for he had become distrustful of the future, "that is to say, if to-morrow ever comes."

Although not very learned in astronomy, Servadac was acquainted with the position of the principal constellations. It was therefore a considerable disappointment to him that, in consequence of the heavy clouds, not a star was visible in the firmament. To have ascertained that the pole-star had become displaced would have been an undeniable proof that the earth was revolving on a new axis; but not a rift appeared in the lowering clouds, which seemed to threaten torrents of rain.

It happened that the moon was new on that very day; naturally, therefore, it would have set at the same time as the sun. What, then, was the captain's bewilderment when, after he had been walking for about an hour and a half, he noticed on the western horizon a strong glare that penetrated even the masses of the clouds.

"The moon in the west!" he cried aloud; but suddenly bethinking himself, he added: "But no, that cannot be the moon; unless she had shifted very much nearer the earth, she could never give a light as intense as this."

As he spoke the screen of vapor was illuminated to such a degree that the whole country was as it were bathed in twilight. "What can this be?" soliloquized the captain. "It cannot be the sun, for the sun set in the east only an hour and a half ago. Would that those clouds would disclose what enormous luminary lies behind them! What a fool I was not to have learnt more astronomy! Perhaps, after all, I am racking my brain over something that is quite in the ordinary course of nature."

But, reason as he might, the mysteries of the heavens still remained impenetrable. For about an hour some luminous body, its disc evidently of gigantic dimensions, shed its rays upon the upper strata of the clouds; then, marvelous to relate, instead of obeying the ordinary laws

of celestial mechanism, and descending upon the opposite horizon, it
seemed to retreat farther off, grew dimmer, and vanished.

The darkness that returned to the face of the earth was not more
profound than the gloom which fell upon the captain's soul. Everything was incomprehensible. The simplest mechanical rules seemed
falsified; the planets had defied the laws of gravitation; the motions of
the celestial spheres were erroneous as those of a watch with a defec-
tive mainspring, and there was reason to fear that the sun would never
again shed his radiance upon the earth.

"Come, wake up!" said Servadac, shaking him by the shoulder.

But these last fears were groundless. In three hours' time, without any intervening twilight, the morning sun made its appearance in the west, and day once more had dawned. On consulting his watch, Servadac found that night had lasted precisely six hours. Ben Zoof, who was unaccustomed to so brief a period of repose, was still slumbering soundly.

"Come, wake up!" said Servadac, shaking him by the shoulder; "it is time to start."

"Time to start?" exclaimed Ben Zoof, rubbing his eyes. "I feel as if I had only just gone to sleep."

"You have slept all night, at any rate," replied the captain; "it has only been for six hours, but you must make it enough."

"Enough it shall be, sir," was the submissive rejoinder.

"And now," continued Servadac, "we will take the shortest way back to the gourbi, and see what our horses think about it all."

"They will think that they ought to be groomed," said the orderly.

"Very good; you may groom them and saddle them as quickly as you like. I want to know what has become of the rest of Algeria: if we cannot get round by the south to Mostaganem, we must go eastwards to Tenes." And forthwith they started. Beginning to feel hungry, they had no hesitation in gathering figs, dates, and oranges from the plantations that formed a continuous rich and luxuriant orchard along their path. The district was quite deserted, and they had no reason to fear any legal penalty.

In an hour and a half they reached the gourbi. Everything was just as they had left it, and it was evident that no one had visited the place during their absence. All was desolate as the shore they had quitted.

The preparations for the expedition were brief and simple. Ben Zoof saddled the horses and filled his pouch with biscuits and game; water, he felt certain, could be obtained in abundance from the numerous affluents of the Shelif, which, although they had now become tributaries of the Mediterranean, still meandered through the plain. Captain Servadac mounted his horse Zephyr, and Ben Zoof simultaneously got astride his mare Galette, named after the mill of Montmartre. They galloped off in the direction of the Shelif, and were not long in discovering that the diminution in the pressure of the atmosphere had precisely the same effect upon their horses as it had had upon themselves. Their muscular strength seemed five times as great as hitherto; their hoofs scarcely touched the ground, and they seemed transformed from ordinary quadrupeds into veritable hippogriffs. Happily, Servadac and his orderly were fearless riders; they made no attempt to curb their steeds, but even urged them to still greater exertions. Twenty minutes sufficed to carry them over the four or five miles that intervened between the gourbi and the mouth of the Shelif; then, slackening their speed, they proceeded at a more leisurely pace to the southeast, along what had once been the right bank of the river, but which, although it still retained its former characteristics, was now the boundary of a sea, which extending farther than the limits of the horizon, must have swallowed up at least a large portion of the province of Oran. Captain Servadac knew the country well; he had at one time been engaged upon a trigonometrical survey of the district, and consequently had an accurate knowledge of its topography. His idea now was to draw up a report of his investigations: to whom that report should be delivered was a problem he had yet to solve.

During the four hours of daylight that still remained, the travelers rode about twenty-one miles from the river mouth. To their vast surprise, they did not meet a single human being. At nightfall they again encamped in a slight bend of the shore, at a point which on the previous evening had faced the mouth of the Mina, one of the left-hand affluents of the Shelif, but now absorbed into the newly revealed ocean. Ben Zoof made the sleeping accommodation as comfortable as the circumstances would allow; the horses were clogged and turned out to feed upon the rich pasture that clothed the shore, and the night passed without special incident.

At sunrise on the following morning, the 2nd of January, or what, according to the ordinary calendar, would have been the night of the 1st, the captain and his orderly remounted their horses, and during the six-hours' day accomplished a distance of forty-two miles. The right bank of the river still continued to be the margin of the land, and only in one spot had its integrity been impaired. This was about twelve miles from the Mina, and on the site of the annex or suburb of Surkelmittoo. Here a large portion of the bank had been swept away, and the hamlet, with its eight hundred inhabitants, had no doubt been swallowed up by the encroaching waters. It seemed, therefore, more than probable that a similar fate had overtaken the larger towns beyond the Shelif.

In the evening the explorers encamped, as previously, in a nook of the shore which here abruptly terminated their new domain, not far from where they might have expected to find the important village of Memounturroy; but of this, too, there was now no trace. "I had quite reckoned upon a supper and a bed at Orleansville to-night," said Servadac, as, full of despondency, he surveyed the waste of water.

Their hoofs scarcely touched the ground, and they seemed transformed from ordinary quadrupeds into veritable hippogriffs.

"Quite impossible," replied Ben Zoof, "except you had gone by a boat. But cheer up, sir, cheer up; we will soon devise some means for getting across to Mostaganem."

"If, as I hope," rejoined the captain, "we are on a peninsula, we are more likely to get to Tenes; there we shall hear the news."

"Far more likely to carry the news ourselves," answered Ben Zoof, as he threw himself down for his night's rest.

Six hours later, only waiting for sunrise, Captain Servadac set himself in movement again to renew his investigations. At this spot the shore, that hitherto had been running in a southeasterly direction, turned abruptly to the north, being no longer formed by the natural bank of the Shelif, but consisting of an absolutely new coast-line. No land was in sight. Nothing could be seen of Orleansville, which ought to have been about six miles to the southwest; and Ben Zoof, who had mounted the highest point of view attainable, could distinguish sea, and nothing but sea, to the farthest horizon.

Quitting their encampment and riding on, the bewildered explorers kept close to the new shore. This, since it had ceased to be formed by the original river bank, had considerably altered its aspect. Frequent landslips occurred, and in many places deep chasms rifted the ground; great gaps furrowed the fields, and trees, half uprooted, overhung the water, remarkable by the fantastic distortions of their gnarled trunks, looking as though they had been chopped by a hatchet.

The sinuosities of the coast line, alternately gully and headland, had the effect of making a devious progress for the travelers, and at sunset, although they had accomplished more than twenty miles, they had only just arrived at the foot of the Merdeyah Mountains, which, before the cataclysm, had formed the extremity of the chain of the Little Atlas. The ridge, however, had been violently ruptured, and now rose perpendicularly from the water.

On the following morning Servadac and Ben Zoof traversed one of the mountain gorges; and next, in order to make a more thorough acquaintance with the limits and condition of the section of Algerian territory of which they seemed to be left as the sole occupants, they dismounted, and proceeded on foot to the summit of one of the highest peaks. From this elevation they ascertained that from the base of the Merdeyah to the Mediterranean, a distance of about eighteen miles, a new coast line had come into existence; no land was visible in any direction; no isthmus existed to form a connecting link with the territory of Tenes, which had entirely disappeared. The result was that Captain Servadac was driven to the irresistible conclusion that the tract of land which he had been surveying was not, as he had at first imagined, a peninsula; it was actually an island.

Strictly speaking, this island was quadrilateral, but the sides were so irregular that it was much more nearly a triangle, the comparison of the sides exhibiting these proportions: The section of the right bank of the Shelif, seventy-two miles; the southern boundary from the Shelif to the chain of the Little Atlas, twenty-one miles; from the Little Atlas to the Mediterranean, eighteen miles; and sixty miles of the shore of the Mediterranean itself, making in all an entire circumference of about 171 miles.

"What does it all mean?" exclaimed the captain, every hour growing more and more bewildered.

"The will of Providence, and we must submit," replied Ben Zoof, calm and undisturbed. With this reflection, the two men silently descended the mountain and remounted their horses. Before evening they had reached the Mediterranean. On their road they failed to discern a vestige of the little town of Montenotte; like Tenes, of which not so much as a ruined cottage was visible on the horizon, it seemed to be annihilated.

On the following day, the 6th of January, the two men made a forced march along the coast of the Mediterranean, which they found less altered than the captain had at first supposed; but four villages had entirely disappeared, and the headlands, unable to resist the shock of the convulsion, had been detached from the mainland.

The circuit of the island had been now completed, and the explorers, after a period of sixty hours, found themselves once more beside the ruins of their gourbi. Five days, or what, according to the established order of things, would have been two days and a half, had been occupied in tracing the boundaries of their new domain; and they had ascertained beyond a doubt that they were the sole human inhabitants left upon the island.

"Well, sir, here you are, Governor General of Algeria!" exclaimed Ben Zoof, as they reached the gourbi.

"With not a soul to govern," gloomily rejoined the captain.

"How so? Do you not reckon me?"

"Pshaw! Ben Zoof, what are you?"

"What am I? Why, I am the population."

The captain deigned no reply, but, muttering some expressions of regret for the fruitless trouble he had taken about his rondo, betook himself to rest.

CHAPTER VII.

BEN ZOOF WATCHES IN VAIN

In a few minutes the governor general and his population were asleep. The gourbi being in ruins, they were obliged to put up with the best accommodation they could find in the adjacent erection. It must be owned that the captain's slumbers were by no means sound; he was agitated by the consciousness that he had hitherto been unable to account for his strange experiences by any reasonable theory. Though far from being advanced in the knowledge of natural philosophy, he had been instructed, to a certain degree, in its elementary principles; and, by an effort of memory, he managed to recall some general laws which he had almost forgotten. He could understand that an altered inclination of the earth's axis with regard to the ecliptic would introduce a change of position in the cardinal points, and bring about a displacement of the sea; but the hypothesis entirely failed to account, either for the shortening of the days, or for the diminution in the pressure of the atmosphere. He felt that his judgment was utterly baffled; his only remaining hope was that the chain of marvels was not yet complete, and that something farther might throw some light upon the mystery.

Ben Zoof's first care on the following morning was to provide a good breakfast. To use his own phrase, he was as hungry as the whole population of three million Algerians, of whom he was the representative, and he must have enough to eat. The catastrophe which had overwhelmed the country had left a dozen eggs uninjured, and upon these, with a good dish of his famous couscous, he hoped that he and his master might have a sufficiently substantial meal. The stove was ready for use, the copper skillet was as bright as hands could make it, and the beads of condensed steam upon the surface of a large stone alcaraza gave evidence that it was supplied with water. Ben Zoof at once lighted a fire, singing all the time, according to his wont, a snatch of an old military refrain.

"Veal ! veal ! is there any veal,
Enough to make a stew?
Salt! salt! is there any salt,
To season what we do.

Ever on the lookout for fresh phenomena, Captain Servadac watched the preparations with a curious eye. It struck him that perhaps the air, in its strangely modified condition, would fail to supply sufficient oxygen, and that the stove, in consequence, might not fulfill its function. But no; the fire was lighted just as usual, and fanned into vigor by Ben Zoof applying his mouth in lieu of bellows, and a bright flame started up from the midst of the twigs and coal. The skillet was duly set upon the stove, and Ben Zoof was prepared to wait awhile for the water to boil. Taking up the eggs, he was surprised to notice that they hardly weighed more than they would if they had been mere shells; but he was still more surprised when he saw that before the water had been two minutes over the fire it was at full boil.

"By jingo!" he exclaimed, "a precious hot fire!"

Servadac reflected. "It cannot be that the fire is hotter," he said, "the peculiarity must be in the water." And taking down a centigrade thermometer, which hung upon the wall, he plunged it into the skillet. Instead of 100 degrees, the instrument registered only 66 degrees.

"Take my advice, Ben Zoof," he said; "leave your eggs in the saucepan a good quarter of an hour."

"Boil them hard! That will never do," objected the orderly.

"You will not find them hard, my good fellow. Trust me, we shall be able to dip our sippets into the yolks easily enough."

The captain was quite right in his conjecture, that this new phenomenon was caused by a diminution in the pressure of the atmosphere. Water boiling at a temperature of 66 degrees was itself an evidence that the column of air above the earth's surface had become reduced by one-third of its altitude. The identical phenomenon would have occurred at the summit of a mountain 35,000 feet high; and had Servadac been in possession of a barometer, he would have immediately discovered the fact that only now for the first time, as the result of experiment, revealed itself to him—a fact, moreover, which accounted for the compression of the blood-vessels which both he and Ben Zoof had experienced, as well as for the attenuation of their voices and their accelerated breathing. "And yet," he argued with himself, "if our en-

campment has been projected to so great an elevation, how is it that
the sea remains at its proper level?"

Once again Hector Servadac, though capable of tracing consequences, felt himself totally at a loss to comprehend their cause; hence
his agitation and bewilderment!

The instrument registered only 66 degrees.

After their prolonged immersion in the boiling water, the eggs
were found to be only just sufficiently cooked; the couscous was very
much in the same condition; and Ben Zoof came to the conclusion that
in future he must be careful to commence his culinary operations an
hour earlier. He was rejoiced at last to help his master, who, in spite

of his perplexed preoccupation, seemed to have a very fair appetite for breakfast.

"Well, captain?" said Ben Zoof presently, such being his ordinary way of opening conversation.

"Well, Ben Zoof?" was the captain's invariable response to his servant's formula.

"What are we to do now, sir?"

"We can only for the present wait patiently where we are. We are encamped upon an island, and therefore we can only be rescued by sea."

"But do you suppose that any of our friends are still alive?" asked Ben Zoof.

"Oh, I think we must indulge the hope that this catastrophe has not extended far. We must trust that it has limited its mischief to some small portion of the Algerian coast, and that our friends are all alive and well. No doubt the governor general will be anxious to investigate the full extent of the damage, and will send a vessel from Algiers to explore. It is not likely that we shall be forgotten. What, then, you have to do, Ben Zoof, is to keep a sharp lookout, and to be ready, in case a vessel should appear, to make signals at once."

"But if no vessel should appear!" sighed the orderly.

"Then we must build a boat, and go in search of those who do not come in search of us."

"Very good. But what sort of a sailor are you?"

"Everyone can be a sailor when he must," said Servadac calmly.

Ben Zoof said no more. For several succeeding days he scanned the horizon unintermittently with his telescope. His watching was in vain. No ship appeared upon the desert sea. "By the name of a Kabyle!" he broke out impatiently, "his Excellency is grossly negligent!"

Although the days and nights had become reduced from twenty-four hours to twelve, Captain Servadac would not accept the new condition of things, but resolved to adhere to the computations of the old calendar. Notwithstanding, therefore, that the sun had risen and set twelve times since the commencement of the new year, he persisted in calling the following day the 6th of January. His watch enabled him to keep an accurate account of the passing hours.

In the course of his life, Ben Zoof had read a few books. After pondering one day, he said: "It seems to me, captain, that you have turned into Robinson Crusoe, and that I am your man Friday. I hope I have not become a negro."

"No," replied the captain. "Your complexion isn't the fairest in the world, but you are not black yet."

Ben Zoof, keeping a sharp lookout.

"Well, I had much sooner be a white Friday than a black one," rejoined Ben Zoof.

Still no ship appeared; and Captain Servadac, after the example of all previous Crusoes, began to consider it advisable to investigate the resources of his domain. The new territory of which he had become the monarch he named Gourbi Island. It had a superficial area of about nine hundred square miles. Bullocks, cows, goats, and sheep existed in considerable numbers; and as there seemed already to be an abundance of game, it was hardly likely that a future supply would fail them. The condition of the cereals was such as to promise a fine ingathering of wheat, maize, and rice; so that for the governor and his population, with their two horses, not only was there ample provision, but even if other human inhabitants besides themselves should yet be discovered, there was not the remotest prospect of any of them perishing by starvation.

From the 6th to the 13th of January the rain came down in torrents; and, what was quite an unusual occurrence at this season of the year, several heavy storms broke over the island. In spite, however, of the continual downfall, the heavens still remained veiled in cloud. Servadac, moreover, did not fail to observe that for the season the temperature was unusually high; and, as a matter still more surprising, that it kept steadily increasing, as though the earth were gradually and continuously approximating to the sun. In proportion to the rise of temperature, the light also assumed greater intensity; and if it had not been for the screen of vapor interposed between the sky and the island, the irradiation which would have illumined all terrestrial objects would have been vivid beyond all precedent.

But neither sun, moon, nor star ever appeared; and Servadac's irritation and annoyance at being unable to identify any one point of the firmament may be more readily imagined than described. On one occasion Ben Zoof endeavored to mitigate his master's impatience by exhorting him to assume the resignation, even if he did not feel the indifference, which he himself experienced; but his advice was received with so angry a rebuff that he retired in all haste, abashed, to résumé his watchman's duty, which he performed with exemplary perseverance. Day and night, with the shortest possible intervals of rest, despite wind, rain, and storm, he mounted guard upon the cliff—but all in vain. Not a speck appeared upon the desolate horizon. To say the truth, no vessel could have stood against the weather. The hurricane raged with tremendous fury, and the waves rose to a height that seemed to defy calculation. Never, even in the second era of creation, when, under the influence of internal heat, the waters rose in vapor to descend in deluge back upon the world, could meteorological phenomena have been developed with more impressive intensity.

But by the night of the 13th the tempest appeared to have spent its fury; the wind dropped; the rain ceased as if by a spell; and Servadac, who for the last six days had confined himself to the shelter of his roof, hastened to join Ben Zoof at his post upon the cliff. Now, he thought, there might be a chance of solving his perplexity; perhaps now the huge disc, of which he had had an imperfect glimpse on the night of the 31st of December, might again reveal itself; at any rate, he hoped for an opportunity of observing the constellations in a clear firmament above.

The night was magnificent. Not a cloud dimmed the luster of the stars, which spangled the heavens in surpassing brilliancy, and several nebulae which hitherto no astronomer had been able to discern without the aid of a telescope were clearly visible to the naked eye.

By a natural impulse, Servadac's first thought was to observe the position of the pole-star. It was in sight, but so near to the horizon as to suggest the utter impossibility of its being any longer the central pivot of the sidereal system; it occupied a position through which it was out of the question that the axis of the earth indefinitely prolonged could ever pass. In his impression he was more thoroughly confirmed when, an hour later, he noticed that the star had approached still nearer the horizon, as though it had belonged to one of the zodiacal constellations.

The pole-star being manifestly thus displaced, it remained to be discovered whether any other of the celestial bodies had become a fixed center around which the constellations made their apparent daily revolutions. To the solution of this problem Servadac applied himself with the most thoughtful diligence. After patient observation, he satisfied himself that the required conditions were answered by a certain star that was stationary not far from the horizon. This was Vega, in the constellation Lyra, a star which, according to the precession of the equinoxes, will take the place of our pole-star 12,000 years hence. The most daring imagination could not suppose that a period of 12,000 years had been crowded into the space of a fortnight; and therefore the captain came, as to an easier conclusion, to the opinion that the earth's axis had been suddenly and immensely shifted; and from the fact that the axis, if produced, would pass through a point so little removed above the horizon, he deduced the inference that the Mediterranean must have been transported to the equator.

Lost in bewildering maze of thought, he gazed long and intently upon the heavens. His eyes wandered from where the tail of the Great Bear, now a zodiacal constellation, was scarcely visible above the waters, to where the stars of the southern hemisphere were just breaking on his view. A cry from Ben Zoof recalled him to himself.

"It is not the moon," again affirmed the captain.

"The moon!" shouted the orderly, as though overjoyed at once again beholding what the poet has called:

"The kind companion of terrestrial night;"

and he pointed to a disc that was rising at a spot precisely opposite the place where they would have expected to see the sun. "The moon!" again he cried.

But Captain Servadac could not altogether enter into his servant's enthusiasm. If this were actually the moon, her distance from the earth must have been increased by some millions of miles. He was rather disposed to suspect that it was not the earth's satellite at all, but some planet with its apparent magnitude greatly enlarged by its approximation to the earth. Taking up the powerful field-glass which he was accustomed to use in his surveying operations, he proceeded to investigate more carefully the luminous orb. But he failed to trace any of the lineaments, supposed to resemble a human face, that mark the lunar surface; he failed to decipher any indications of hill and plain; nor could he make out the aureole of light which emanates from what astronomers have designated Mount Tycho. "It is not the moon," he said slowly.

"Not the moon?" cried Ben Zoof. "Why not?"

"It is not the moon," again affirmed the captain.

"Why not?" repeated Ben Zoof, unwilling to renounce his first impression.

"Because there is a small satellite in attendance." And the captain drew his servant's attention to a bright speck, apparently about the size of one of Jupiter's satellites seen through a moderate telescope, that was clearly visible just within the focus of his glass.

Here, then, was a fresh mystery. The orbit of this planet was assuredly interior to the orbit of the earth, because it accompanied the sun in its apparent motion; yet it was neither Mercury nor Venus, because neither one nor the other of these has any satellite at all.

The captain stamped and stamped again with mingled vexation, agitation, and bewilderment. "Confound it!" he cried, "if this is neither Venus nor Mercury, it must be the moon; but if it is the moon, whence, in the name of all the gods, has she picked up another moon for herself?"

The captain was in dire perplexity.

CHAPTER VIII.

THE light of the returning sun soon extinguished the glory of the stars, and rendered it necessary for the captain to postpone his observations. He had sought in vain for further trace of the huge disc that had so excited his wonder on the 1st, and it seemed most probable that, in its irregular orbit, it had been carried beyond the range of vision.

The weather was still superb. The wind, after veering to the west, had sunk to a perfect calm. Pursuing its inverted course, the sun rose and set with undeviating regularity; and the days and nights were still divided into periods of precisely six hours each—a sure proof that the sun remained close to the new equator which manifestly passed through Gourbi Island.

Meanwhile the temperature was steadily increasing. The captain kept his thermometer close at hand where he could repeatedly consult it, and on the 15th he found that it registered 50 degrees centigrade in the shade.

No attempt had been made to rebuild the gourbi, but the captain and Ben Zoof managed to make up quarters sufficiently comfortable in the principal apartment of the adjoining structure, where the stone walls, that at first afforded a refuge from the torrents of rain, now formed an equally acceptable shelter from the burning sun. The heat was becoming insufferable, surpassing the heat of Senegal and other equatorial regions; not a cloud ever tempered the intensity of the solar rays; and unless some modification ensued, it seemed inevitable that all vegetation should become scorched and burnt off from the face of the island.

In spite, however, of the profuse perspirations from which he suffered, Ben Zoof, constant to his principles, expressed no surprise at the unwonted heat. No remonstrances from his master could induce him to abandon his watch from the cliff. To withstand the vertical beams of that noontide sun would seem to require a skin of brass and a brain of adamant; but yet, hour after hour, he would remain conscientiously scanning the surface of the Mediterranean, which, calm and deserted, lay outstretched before him. On one occasion, Servadac, in reference to his orderly's indomitable perseverance, happened to remark that he thought he must have been born in the heart of equatorial Africa; to which Ben Zoof replied, with the utmost dignity, that he was born at Montmartre, which was all the same. The worthy fellow was unwilling to own that, even in the matter of heat, the tropics could in any way surpass his own much-loved home.

This unprecedented temperature very soon began to take effect upon the products of the soil. The sap rose rapidly in the trees, so that in the course of a few days buds, leaves, flowers, and fruit had come to full maturity. It was the same with the cereals; wheat and maize sprouted and ripened as if by magic, and for a while a rank and luxuriant pasturage clothed the meadows. Summer and autumn seemed blended into one. If Captain Servadac had been more deeply versed in astronomy, he would perhaps have been able to bring to bear his knowledge that if the axis of the earth, as everything seemed to indicate, now formed a right angle with the plane of the ecliptic, her various seasons, like those of the planet Jupiter, would become limited to certain zones, in which they would remain invariable. But even if he had understood the *rationale* of the change, the convulsion that had brought it about would have been as much a mystery as ever.

The precocity of vegetation caused some embarrassment. The time for the corn and fruit harvest had fallen simultaneously with that of the haymaking; and as the extreme heat precluded any prolonged exertions, it was evident "the population" of the island would find it difficult to provide the necessary amount of labor. Not that the prospect gave them much concern: the provisions of the gourbi were still far from exhausted, and now that the roughness of the weather had so happily subsided, they had every encouragement to hope that a ship of some sort would soon appear. Not only was that part of the Mediterranean systematically frequented by the government steamers that watched the coast, but vessels of all nations were constantly cruising off the shore.

In spite, however, of all their sanguine speculations, no ship appeared. Ben Zoof admitted the necessity of extemporizing a kind of parasol for himself, otherwise he must literally have been roasted to death upon the exposed summit of the cliff.

Meanwhile, Servadac was doing his utmost—it must be acknowledged, with indifferent success—to recall the lessons of his school-days. He would plunge into the wildest speculations in his endeavors to unravel the difficulties of the new situation, and struggled into a kind of conviction that if there had been a change of manner in the earth's rotation on her axis, there would be a corresponding change in her revolution round the sun, which would involve the consequence of the length of the year being either diminished or increased.

Independently of the increased and increasing heat, there was another very conclusive demonstration that the earth had thus suddenly approximated towards the sun. The diameter of the solar disc was now exactly twice what it ordinarily looks to the naked eye; in fact, it was precisely such as it would appear to an observer on the surface of the planet Venus. The most obvious inference would therefore be that the earth's distance from the sun had been diminished from 91,000,000 to 66,000,000 miles. If the just equilibrium of the earth had thus been destroyed, and should this diminution of distance still continue, would there not be reason to fear that the terrestrial world would be carried onwards to actual contact with the sun, which must result in its total annihilation?

The continuance of the splendid weather afforded Servadac every facility for observing the heavens. Night after night, constellations in their beauty lay stretched before his eyes—an alphabet which, to his mortification, not to say his rage, he was unable to decipher. In the apparent dimensions of the fixed stars, in their distance, in their relative position with regard to each other, he could observe no change. Although it is established that our sun is approaching the constellation of Hercules at the rate of more than 126,000,000 miles a year, and although Arcturus is traveling through space at the rate of fifty-four miles a second—three times faster than the earth goes round the sun,—yet such is the remoteness of those stars that no appreciable change is evident to the senses. The fixed stars taught him nothing.

Far otherwise was it with the planets. The orbits of Venus and Mercury are within the orbit of the earth, Venus rotating at an average distance of 66,130,000 miles from the sun, and Mercury at that of 35,393,000. After pondering long, and as profoundly as he could, upon these figures, Captain Servadac came to the conclusion that, as the earth was now receiving about double the amount of light and heat that it had been receiving before the catastrophe, it was receiving about the same as the planet Venus; he was driven, therefore, to the estimate of the measure in which the earth must have approximated to the sun, a deduction in which he was confirmed when the opportunity came for him to observe Venus herself in the splendid proportions that she now assumed.

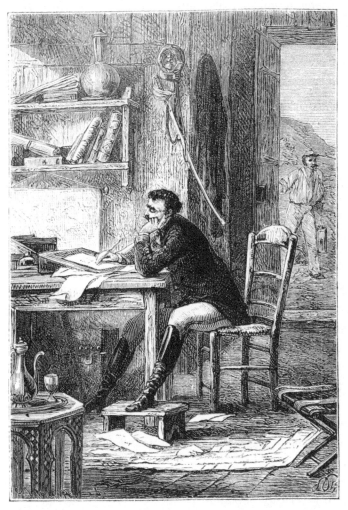

He would plunge into the wildest speculations.

That magnificent planet which—as Phosphorus or Lucifer, Hesperus or Vesper, the evening star, the morning star, or the shepherd's star—has never failed to attract the rapturous admiration of the most indifferent observers, here revealed herself with unprecedented glory, exhibiting all the phases of a lustrous moon in miniature. Various indentations in the outline of its crescent showed that the solar beams were refracted into regions of its surface where the sun had already set, and proved, beyond a doubt, that the planet had an atmosphere of her own; and certain luminous points projecting from the crescent as plainly marked the existence of mountains. As the result of Servadac's computations, he formed the opinion that Venus could hardly be at a greater distance than 6,000,000 miles from the earth.

"And a very safe distance, too," said Ben Zoof, when his master told him the conclusion at which he had arrived.

"All very well for two armies, but for a couple of planets not quite so safe, perhaps, as you may imagine. It is my impression that it is more than likely we may run foul of Venus," said the captain.

"Plenty of air and water there, sir?" inquired the orderly.

"Yes; as far as I can tell, plenty," replied Servadac.

"Then why shouldn't we go and visit Venus?"

Servadac did his best to explain that as the two planets were of about equal volume, and were traveling with great velocity in opposite directions, any collision between them must be attended with the most disastrous consequences to one or both of them. But Ben Zoof failed to see that, even at the worst, the catastrophe could be much more serious than the collision of two railway trains.

The captain became exasperated. "You idiot!" he angrily exclaimed; "cannot you understand that the planets are traveling a thousand times faster than the fastest express, and that if they meet, either one or the other must be destroyed? What would become of your darling Montmartre then?"

The captain had touched a tender chord. For a moment Ben Zoof stood with clenched teeth and contracted muscles; then, in a voice of real concern, he inquired whether anything could be done to avert the calamity.

"Nothing whatever; so you may go about your own business," was the captain's brusque rejoinder.

All discomfited and bewildered, Ben Zoof retired without a word.

During the ensuing days the distance between the two planets continued to decrease, and it became more and more obvious that the earth, on her new orbit, was about to cross the orbit of Venus. Throughout this time the earth had been making a perceptible approach towards Mercury, and that planet—which is rarely visible to the naked eye, and then only at what are termed the periods of its greatest eastern and western elongations—now appeared in all its splendor. It amply justified the epithet of "sparkling" which the ancients were accustomed to confer upon it, and could scarcely fail to awaken a new interest. The periodic recurrence of its phases; its reflection of the sun's rays, shedding upon it a light and a heat seven times greater than that received by the earth; its glacial and its torrid zones, which, on account of the great inclination of the axis, are scarcely separable; its equatorial bands; its mountains eleven miles high;—were all subjects of observation worthy of the most studious regard.

But no danger was to be apprehended from Mercury; with Venus only did collision appear imminent. By the 18th of January the distance between that planet and the earth had become reduced to between two and three millions of miles, and the intensity of its light cast heavy shadows from all terrestrial objects. It might be observed to turn upon its own axis in twenty-three hours twenty-one minutes—an evidence, from the unaltered duration of its days, that the planet had not shared in the disturbance. On its disc the clouds formed from its atmospheric vapor were plainly perceptible, as also were the seven spots, which, according to Bianchini, are a chain of seas. It was now visible in broad daylight. Buonaparte, when under the Directory, once had his attention called to Venus at noon, and immediately hailed it joyfully, recognizing it as his own peculiar star in the ascendant. Captain Servadac, it may well be imagined, did not experience the same gratifying emotion.

On the 20th, the distance between the two bodies had again sensibly diminished. The captain had ceased to be surprised that no vessel had been sent to rescue himself and his companion from their strange imprisonment; the governor general and the minister of war were doubtless far differently occupied, and their interests far otherwise engrossed. What sensational articles, he thought, must now be teeming to the newspapers! What crowds must be flocking to the churches! The end of the world approaching! the great climax close at hand! Two days more, and the earth, shivered into a myriad atoms, would be lost in boundless space!

These dire forebodings, however, were not destined to be realized. Gradually the distance between the two planets began to increase; the planes of their orbits did not coincide, and accordingly the dreaded catastrophe did not ensue. By the 25th, Venus was sufficiently remote to preclude any further fear of collision. Ben Zoof gave a sigh of relief when the captain communicated the glad intelligence.

Their proximity to Venus had been close enough to demonstrate that beyond a doubt that planet has no moon or satellite such as Cassini, Short, Montaigne of Limoges, Montbarron, and some other astronomers have imagined to exist. "Had there been such a satellite," said Servadac, "we might have captured it in passing. But what can be the meaning," he added seriously, "of all this displacement of the heavenly bodies?"

"What is that great building at Paris, captain, with a top like a cap?" asked Ben Zoof.

"Do you mean the Observatory?"

"Yes, the Observatory. Are there not people living in the Observatory who could explain all this?"

"Very likely; but what of that?"

"Let us be philosophers, and wait patiently until we can hear their explanation."

Servadac smiled. "Do you know what it is to be a philosopher, Ben Zoof?" he asked.

"I am a soldier, sir," was the servant's prompt rejoinder, "and I have learnt to know that 'what can't be cured must be endured.'"

The captain made no reply, but for a time, at least, he desisted from puzzling himself over matters which he felt he was utterly incompetent to explain. But an event soon afterwards occurred which awakened his keenest interest.

About nine o'clock on the morning of the 27th, Ben Zoof walked deliberately into his master's apartment, and, in reply to a question as to what he wanted, announced with the utmost composure that a ship was in sight.

"A ship!" exclaimed Servadac, starting to his feet. "A ship! Ben Zoof, you donkey! you speak as unconcernedly as though you were telling me that my dinner was ready."

"Are we not philosophers, captain?" said the orderly.

But the captain was out of hearing.

CHAPTER IX.

INQUIRIES UNSATISFIED

Fast as his legs could carry him, Servadac had made his way to the top of the cliff. It was quite true that a vessel was in sight, hardly more than six miles from the shore; but owing to the increase in the earth's convexity, and the consequent limitation of the range of vision, the rigging of the topmasts alone was visible above the water. This was enough, however, to indicate that the ship was a schooner—an impression that was confirmed when, two hours later, she came entirely in sight.

"The *Dobryna!*" exclaimed Servadac, keeping his eye unmoved at his telescope.

"Impossible, sir!" rejoined Ben Zoof; "there are no signs of smoke."

"The *Dobryna!*" repeated the captain, positively. "She is under sail; but she is Count Timascheff's yacht."

He was right. If the count were on board, a strange fatality was bringing him to the presence of his rival. But no longer now could Servadac regard him in the light of an adversary; circumstances had changed, and all animosity was absorbed in the eagerness with which he hailed the prospect of obtaining some information about the recent startling and inexplicable events. During the twenty-seven days that she had been absent, the *Dobryna*, he conjectured, would have explored the Mediterranean, would very probably have visited Spain, France, or Italy, and accordingly would convey to Gourbi Island some intelligence from one or other of those countries. He reckoned, therefore, not only upon ascertaining the extent of the late catastrophe, but upon learning its cause. Count Timascheff was, no doubt, magnanimously coming to the rescue of himself and his orderly.

The wind being adverse, the *Dobryna* did not make very rapid progress; but as the weather, in spite of a few clouds, remained calm, and the sea was quite smooth, she was enabled to hold a steady course. It seemed unaccountable that she should not use her engine, as who-

ever was on board, would be naturally impatient to reconnoiter the new
island, which must just have come within their view. The probability
that suggested itself was that the schooner's fuel was exhausted.

Servadac took it for granted that the *Dobryna* was endeavoring to
put in. It occurred to him, however, that the count, on discovering an
island where he had expected to find the mainland of Africa, would not
unlikely be at a loss for a place of anchorage. The yacht was evidently
making her way in the direction of the former mouth of the Shelif, and
the captain was struck with the idea that he would do well to investigate whether there was any suitable mooring towards which he might
signal her. Zephyr and Galette were soon saddled, and in twenty minutes had carried their riders to the western extremity of the island,
where they both dismounted and began to explore the coast.

They were not long in ascertaining that on the farther side of the
point there was a small well-sheltered creek of sufficient depth to accommodate a vessel of moderate tonnage. A narrow channel formed a
passage through the ridge of rocks that protected it from the open sea,
and which, even in the roughest weather, would ensure the calmness
of its waters.

Whilst examining the rocky shore, the captain observed, to his
great surprise, long and well-defined rows of seaweed, which undoubtedly betokened that there had been a very considerable ebb and flow
of the waters—a thing unknown in the Mediterranean, where there
is scarcely any perceptible tide. What, however, seemed most remarkable, was the manifest evidence that ever since the highest flood
(which was caused, in all probability, by the proximity of the body of
which the huge disc had been so conspicuous on the night of the 31st
of December) the phenomenon had been gradually lessening, and in
fact was now reduced to the normal limits which had characterized it
before the convulsion.

Without doing more than note the circumstance, Servadac turned
his entire attention to the *Dobryna*, which, now little more than a mile
from shore, could not fail to see and understand his signals. Slightly
changing her course, she first struck her mainsail, and, in order to facilitate the movements of her helmsman, soon carried nothing but her
two topsails, brigantine and jib. After rounding the peak, she steered
direct for the channel to which Servadac by his gestures was pointing
her, and was not long in entering the creek. As soon as the anchor,

imbedded in the sandy bottom, had made good its hold, a boat was lowered. In a few minutes more Count Timascheff had landed on the island. Captain Servadac hastened towards him.

"First of all, count," he exclaimed impetuously, "before we speak one other word, tell me what has happened."

"Before we speak one other word, tell me what has happened."

The count, whose imperturbable composure presented a singular contrast to the French officer's enthusiastic vivacity, made a stiff bow, and in his Russian accent replied: "First of all, permit me to express my surprise at seeing you here. I left you on a continent, and here I have the honor of finding you on an island."

"I assure you, count, I have never left the place."

"I am quite aware of it. Captain Servadac, and I now beg to offer you my sincere apologies for failing to keep my appointment with you."

"Never mind, now," interposed the captain; "we will talk of that by-and-by. First, tell me what has happened."

"The very question I was about to put to you, Captain Servadac."

"Do you mean to say you know nothing of the cause, and can tell me nothing of the extent, of the catastrophe which has transformed this part of Africa into an island?"

"Nothing more than you know yourself."

"But surely, Count Timascheff, you can inform me whether upon the northern shore of the Mediterranean—"

"Are you certain that this is the Mediterranean?" asked the count significantly, and added, "I have discovered no sign of land."

The captain stared in silent bewilderment. For some moments he seemed perfectly stupefied; then, recovering himself, he began to overwhelm the count with a torrent of questions. Had he noticed, ever since the 1st of January, that the sun had risen in the west? Had he noticed that the days had been only six hours long, and that the weight of the atmosphere was so much diminished? Had he observed that the moon had quite disappeared, and that the earth had been in imminent hazard of running foul of the planet Venus? Was he aware, in short, that the entire motions of the terrestrial sphere had undergone a complete modification? To all these inquiries, the count responded in the affirmative. He was acquainted with everything that had transpired; but, to Servadac's increasing astonishment, he could throw no light upon the cause of any of the phenomena.

"On the night of the 31st of December," he said, "I was proceeding by sea to our appointed place of meeting, when my yacht was suddenly caught on the crest of an enormous wave, and carried to a height which it is beyond my power to estimate. Some mysterious force seemed to have brought about a convulsion of the elements. Our engine was damaged, nay disabled, and we drifted entirely at the mercy of the terrible hurricane that raged during the succeeding days. That the *Dobryna* escaped at all is little less than a miracle, and I can only attribute her safety to the fact that she occupied the center of the vast cyclone, and consequently did not experience much change of position."

He paused, and added: "Your island is the first land we have seen."

"Then let us put out to sea at once and ascertain the extent of the disaster," cried the captain, eagerly. "You will take me on board, count, will you not?"

A house with a dome on the top.

"My yacht is at your service, sir, even should you require to make a tour round the world."

"A tour round the Mediterranean will suffice for the present, I think," said the captain, smiling.

The count shook his head.

"I am not sure," said he, "but what the tour of the Mediterranean will prove to be the tour of the world."

Servadac made no reply, but for a time remained silent and absorbed in thought.

After the silence was broken, they consulted as to what course was best to pursue; and the plan they proposed was, in the first place, to discover how much of the African coast still remained, and to carry on the tidings of their own experiences to Algiers; or, in the event of the southern shore having actually disappeared, they would make their way northwards and put themselves in communication with the population on the river banks of Europe.

Before starting, it was indispensable that the engine of the *Dobryna* should be repaired: to sail under canvas only would in contrary winds and rough seas be both tedious and difficult. The stock of coal on board was adequate for two months' consumption; but as it would at the expiration of that time be exhausted, it was obviously the part of prudence to employ it in reaching a port where fuel could be replenished.

The damage sustained by the engine proved to be not very serious; and in three days after her arrival the *Dobryna* was again ready to put to sea.

Servadac employed the interval in making the count acquainted with all he knew about his small domain. They made an entire circuit of the island, and both agreed that it must be beyond the limits of that circumscribed territory that they must seek an explanation of what had so strangely transpired.

It was on the last day of January that the repairs of the schooner were completed. A slight diminution in the excessively high temperature which had prevailed for the last few weeks, was the only apparent change in the general order of things; but whether this was to be attributed to any alteration in the earth's orbit was a question which would still require several days to decide. The weather remained fine, and although a few clouds had accumulated, and might have caused a trifling fall of the barometer, they were not sufficiently threatening to delay the departure of the *Dobryna*.

Doubts now arose, and some discussion followed, whether or not it was desirable for Ben Zoof to accompany his master. There were various reasons why he should be left behind, not the least important being that the schooner had no accommodation for horses, and the orderly would have found it hard to part with Zephyr, and much more with his own favorite Galette; besides, it was advisable that there should be some one left to receive any strangers that might possibly arrive, as well as to keep an eye upon the herds of cattle which, in the dubious prospect before them, might prove to be the sole resource of the survivors of the catastrophe. Altogether, taking into consideration that the brave fellow would incur no personal risk by remaining upon the island, the captain was induced with much reluctance to forego the attendance of his servant, hoping very shortly to return and to restore him to his country, when he had ascertained the reason of the mysteries in which they were enveloped.

On the 31st, then, Ben Zoof was "invested with governor's powers," and took an affecting leave of his master, begging him, if chance should carry him near Montmartre, to ascertain whether the beloved "mountain" had been left unmoved.

Farewells over, the *Dobryna* was carefully steered through the creek, and was soon upon the open sea.

CHAPTER X.

A SEARCH FOR ALGERIA

The *Dobryna*, a strong craft of 200 tons burden, had been built in the famous shipbuilding yards in the Isle of Wight. Her sea going qualities were excellent, and would have amply sufficed for a circumnavigation of the globe. Count Timascheff was himself no sailor, but had the greatest confidence in leaving the command of his yacht in the hands of Lieutenant Procope, a man of about thirty years of age, and an excellent seaman. Born on the count's estates, the son of a serf who had been emancipated long before the famous edict of the Emperor Alexander, Procope was sincerely attached, by a tie of gratitude as well as of duty and affection, to his patron's service. After an apprenticeship on a merchant ship he had entered the imperial navy, and had already reached the rank of lieutenant when the count appointed him to the charge of his own private yacht, in which he was accustomed to spend by far the greater part of his time, throughout the winter generally cruising in the Mediterranean, whilst in the summer he visited more northern waters.

The ship could not have been in better hands. The lieutenant was well informed in many matters outside the pale of his profession, and his attainments were alike creditable to himself and to the liberal friend who had given him his education. He had an excellent crew, consisting of Tiglew the engineer, four sailors named Niegoch, Tolstoy, Etkef, and Panofka, and Mochel the cook. These men, without exception, were all sons of the count's tenants, and so tenaciously, even out at sea, did they cling to their old traditions, that it mattered little to them what physical disorganization ensued, so long as they felt they were sharing the experiences of their lord and master. The late astounding events, however, had rendered Procope manifestly uneasy, and not the less so from his consciousness that the count secretly partook of his own anxiety.

Lieutenant Procope

Steam up and canvas spread, the schooner started eastwards. With a favorable wind she would certainly have made eleven knots an hour had not the high waves somewhat impeded her progress. Although only a moderate breeze was blowing, the sea was rough, a circumstance to be accounted for only by the diminution in the force of the earth's attraction rendering the liquid particles so buoyant, that by the mere effect of oscillation they were carried to a height that was quite unprecedented. M. Arago has fixed twenty-five or twenty-six feet as the maximum elevation ever attained by the highest waves, and his astonishment would have been very great to see them rising fifty or even sixty feet. Nor did these waves in the usual way partially unfurl themselves and rebound against the sides of the vessel; they might rather be described as long undulations carrying the schooner (its weight diminished from the same cause as that of the water) alternately to such heights and depths, that if Captain Servadac had been subject to seasickness he must have found himself in sorry plight. As the pitching, however, was the result of a long uniform swell, the yacht did not labor much harder than she would against the ordinary short strong waves of the Mediterranean; the main inconvenience that was experienced was the diminution in her proper rate of speed.

For a few miles she followed the line hitherto presumably occupied by the coast of Algeria; but no land appeared to the south. The changed positions of the planets rendered them of no avail for purposes of nautical observation, nor could Lieutenant Procope calculate his latitude and longitude by the altitude of the sun, as his reckonings would be useless when applied to charts that had been constructed for the old order of things; but nevertheless, by means of the log, which gave him the rate of progress, and by the compass which indicated the direction in which they were sailing, he was able to form an estimate of his position that was sufficiently free from error for his immediate need.

Happily the recent phenomena had no effect upon the compass; the magnetic needle, which in these regions had pointed about 22 degrees from the north pole, had never deviated in the least—a proof that, although east and west had apparently changed places, north and south continued to retain their normal position as cardinal points. The log and the compass, therefore, were able to be called upon to do the work of the sextant, which had become utterly useless.

On the first morning of the cruise Lieutenant Procope, who, like most Russians, spoke French fluently, was explaining these peculiarities to Captain Servadac; the count was present, and the conversation perpetually recurred, as naturally it would, to the phenomena which remained so inexplicable to them all.

"It is very evident," said the lieutenant, "that ever since the 1st of January the earth has been moving in a new orbit, and from some unknown cause has drawn nearer to the sun."

"No doubt about that," said Servadac; "and I suppose that, having crossed the orbit of Venus, we have a good chance of running into the orbit of Mercury."

"And finish up by a collision with the sun!" added the count.

"There is no fear of that, sir. The earth has undoubtedly entered upon a new orbit, but she is not incurring any probable risk of being precipitated onto the sun."

"Can you satisfy us of that?" asked the count.

"Can you satisfy us of that?" asked the count.

"I can, sir. I can give you a proof which I think you will own is conclusive. If, as you suppose, the earth is being drawn on so as to be precipitated against the sun, the great center of attraction of our system, it could only be because the centrifugal and centripetal forces that cause the planets to rotate in their several orbits had been entirely suspended: in that case, indeed, the earth would rush onwards towards the sun, and in sixty-four days and a half the catastrophe you dread would inevitably happen."

"And what demonstration do you offer," asked Servadac eagerly, "that it will not happen?"

"Simply this, captain: that since the earth entered her new orbit half the sixty-four days has already elapsed, and yet it is only just recently that she has crossed the orbit of Venus, hardly one-third of the distance to be traversed to reach the sun."

The lieutenant paused to allow time for reflection, and added: "Moreover, I have every reason to believe that we are not so near the sun as we have been. The temperature has been gradually diminishing; the heat upon Gourbi Island is not greater now than we might ordinarily expect to find in Algeria. At the same time, we have the problem still unsolved that the Mediterranean has evidently been transported to the equatorial zone."

Both the count and the captain expressed themselves reassured by his representations, and observed that they must now do all in their power to discover what had become of the vast continent of Africa, of which, they were hitherto failing so completely to find a vestige.

Twenty-four hours after leaving the island, the *Dobryna* had passed over the sites where Tenes, Cherchil, Koleah, and Sidi-Feruch once had been, but of these towns not one appeared within range of the telescope. Ocean reigned supreme. Lieutenant Procope was absolutely certain that he had not mistaken his direction; the compass showed that the wind had never shifted from the west, and this, with the rate of speed as estimated by the log, combined to assure him that at this date, the 2d of February, the schooner was in lat. 36 degrees 49 min N. and long. 3 degrees 25 min E., the very spot which ought to have been occupied by the Algerian capital. But Algiers, like all the other coast-towns, had apparently been absorbed into the bowels of the earth.

Captain Servadac, with clenched teeth and knitted brow, stood sternly, almost fiercely, regarding the boundless waste of water. His pulse beat fast as he recalled the friends and comrades with whom he had spent the last few years in that vanished city. All the images of his past life floated upon his memory; his thoughts sped away to his native France, only to return again to wonder whether the depths of ocean would reveal any traces of the Algerian metropolis.

Captain Servadac, with clenched teeth and knitted brow, stood sternly, almost
fiercely, regarding the boundless waste of water.

"Is it not impossible," he murmured aloud, "that any city should
disappear so completely? Would not the loftiest eminences of the city
at least be visible? Surely some portion of the Casbah must still rise
above the waves? The imperial fort, too, was built upon an elevation of
750 feet; it is incredible that it should be so totally submerged. Unless
some vestiges of these are found, I shall begin to suspect that the whole
of Africa has been swallowed in some vast abyss."

Another circumstance was most remarkable. Not a material object
of any kind was to be noticed floating on the surface of the water; not
one branch of a tree had been seen drifting by, nor one spar belonging to one of the numerous vessels that a month previously had been
moored in the magnificent bay which stretched twelve miles across
from Cape Matafuz to Point Pexade. Perhaps the depths might disclose what the surface failed to reveal, and Count Timascheff, anxious
that Servadac should have every facility afforded him for solving his
doubts, called for the sounding-line. Forthwith, the lead was greased
and lowered. To the surprise of all, and especially of Lieutenant Procope, the line indicated a bottom at a nearly uniform depth of from
four to five fathoms; and although the sounding was persevered with
continuously for more than two hours over a considerable area, the dif-
ferences of level were insignificant, not corresponding in any degree
to what would be expected over the site of a city that had been terraced
like the seats of an amphitheater. Astounding as it seemed, what alternative was left but to suppose that the Algerian capital had been
completely leveled by the flood?

The sea-bottom was composed of neither rock, mud, sand, nor
shells; the sounding-lead brought up nothing but a kind of metallic
dust, which glittered with a strange iridescence, and the nature of
which it was impossible to determine, as it was totally unlike what
had ever been known to be raised from the bed of the Mediterranean.

"You must see, lieutenant, I should think, that we are not so near
the coast of Algeria as you imagined."

The lieutenant shook his head. After pondering awhile, he said: "If
we were farther away I should expect to find a depth of two or three
hundred fathoms instead of five fathoms. Five fathoms! I confess I am
puzzled."

For the next thirty-six hours, until the 4th of February, the sea
was examined and explored with the most unflagging perseverance.
Its depth remained invariable, still four, or at most five, fathoms; and
although its bottom was assiduously dredged, it was only to prove it
barren of marine production of any type.

The yacht made its way to lat. 36 degrees, and by reference to the
charts it was tolerably certain that she was cruising over the site of
the Sahel, the ridge that had separated the rich plain of the Mitidja
from the sea, and of which the highest peak, Mount Boujereah, had

reached an altitude of 1,200 feet; but even this peak, which might have been expected to emerge like an islet above the surface of the sea, was nowhere to be traced. Nothing was to be done but to put about, and return in disappointment towards the north.

Thus the *Dobryna* regained the waters of the Mediterranean without discovering a trace of the missing province of Algeria.

CHAPTER XI.

AN ISLAND TOMB

No longer, then, could there be any doubt as to the annihilation of a considerable portion of the colony. Not merely had there been a submersion of the land, but the impression was more and more confirmed that the very bowels of the earth must have yawned and closed again upon a large territory. Of the rocky substratum of the province it became more evident than ever that not a trace remained, and a new soil of unknown formation had certainly taken the place of the old sandy sea-bottom. As it altogether transcended the powers of those on board to elucidate the origin of this catastrophe, it was felt to be incumbent on them at least to ascertain its extent.

After a long and somewhat wavering discussion, it was at length decided that the schooner should take advantage of the favorable wind and weather, and proceed at first towards the east, thus following the outline of what had formerly represented the coast of Africa, until that coast had been lost in boundless sea.

Not a vestige of it all remained; from Cape Matafuz to Tunis it had all gone, as though it had never been. The maritime town of Dellis, built like Algiers, amphitheater-wise, had totally disappeared; the highest points were quite invisible; not a trace on the horizon was left of the Jurjura chain, the topmost point of which was known to have an altitude of more than 7,000 feet.

Unsparing of her fuel, the *Dobryna* made her way at full steam towards Cape Blanc. Neither Cape Negro nor Cape Serrat was to be seen. The town of Bizerta, once charming in its oriental beauty, had vanished utterly; its marabouts, or temple-tombs, shaded by magnificent palms that fringed the gulf, which by reason of its narrow mouth had the semblance of a lake, all had disappeared, giving place to a vast waste of sea, the transparent waves of which, as still demonstrated by the sounding-line, had ever the same uniform and arid bottom.

In the course of the day the schooner rounded the point where, five weeks previously, Cape Blanc had been so conspicuous an object, and she was now stemming the waters of what once had been the Bay of Tunis. But bay there was none, and the town from which it had derived its name, with the Arsenal, the Goletta, and the two peaks of Bou-Kournein, had all vanished from the view. Cape Bon, too, the most northern promontory of Africa and the point of the continent nearest to the island of Sicily, had been included in the general devastation.

Before the occurrence of the recent prodigy, the bottom of the Mediterranean just at this point had formed a sudden ridge across the Straits of Libya. The sides of the ridge had shelved to so great an extent that, while the depth of water on the summit had been little more than eleven fathoms, that on either hand of the elevation was little short of a hundred fathoms. A formation such as this plainly indicated that at some remote epoch Cape Bon had been connected with Cape Furina, the extremity of Sicily, in the same manner as Ceuta has doubtless been connected with Gibraltar.

Lieutenant Procope was too well acquainted with the Mediterranean to be unaware of this peculiarity, and would not lose the opportunity of ascertaining whether the submarine ridge still existed, or whether the sea-bottom between Sicily and Africa had undergone any modification.

Both Timascheff and Servadac were much interested in watching the operations. At a sign from the lieutenant, a sailor who was stationed at the foot of the fore-shrouds dropped the sounding-lead into the water, and in reply to Procope's inquiries, reported—"Five fathoms and a flat bottom."

The next aim was to determine the amount of depression on either side of the ridge, and for this purpose the *Dobryna* was shifted for a distance of half a mile both to the right and left, and the soundings taken at each station. "Five fathoms and a flat bottom," was the unvaried announcement after each operation. Not only, therefore, was it evident that the submerged chain between Cape Bon and Cape Furina no longer existed, but it was equally clear that the convulsion had caused a general leveling of the sea-bottom, and that the soil, degenerated, as it has been said, into a metallic dust of unrecognized composition, bore no trace of the sponges, sea-anemones, star-fish, sea-nettles, hydrophytes, and shells with which the submarine rocks of the Mediterranean had hitherto been prodigally clothed.

The *Dobryna* now put about and resumed her explorations in a southerly direction. It remained, however, as remarkable as ever how completely throughout the voyage the sea continued to be deserted; all expectations of hailing a vessel bearing news from Europe were entirely falsified, so that more and more each member of the crew began to be conscious of his isolation, and to believe that the schooner, like a second Noah's ark, carried the sole survivors of a calamity that had overwhelmed the earth.

On the 9th of February the *Dobryna* passed over the site of the city of Dido, the ancient Byrsa—a Carthage, however, which was now more completely destroyed than ever Punic Carthage had been destroyed by Scipio Africanus or Roman Carthage by Hassan the Saracen.

In the evening, as the sun was sinking below the eastern horizon, Captain Servadac was lounging moodily against the taffrail. From the heaven above, where stars kept peeping fitfully from behind the moving clouds, his eye wandered mechanically to the waters below, where the long waves were rising and falling with the evening breeze.

All at once, his attention was arrested by a luminous speck straight ahead on the southern horizon. At first, imagining that he was the victim of some spectral illusion, he observed it with silent attention; but when, after some minutes, he became convinced that what he saw was actually a distant light, he appealed to one of the sailors, by whom his impression was fully corroborated. The intelligence was immediately imparted to Count Timascheff and the lieutenant.

"Is it land, do you suppose?" inquired Servadac, eagerly.

"I should be more inclined to think it is a light on board some ship," replied the count.

"Whatever it is, in another hour we shall know all about it," said Servadac.

"No, captain," interposed Lieutenant Procope; "we shall know nothing until to-morrow."

"What! not bear down upon it at once?" asked the count in surprise.

"No, sir; I should much rather lay to and wait till daylight. If we are really near land, I should be afraid to approach it in the dark."

The count expressed his approval of the lieutenant's caution, and thereupon all sail was shortened so as to keep the *Dobryna* from making any considerable progress all through the hours of night. Few as those hours were, they seemed to those on board as if their end would never come. Fearful lest the faint glimmer should at any moment cease to be visible, Hector Servadac did not quit his post upon the deck; but the light continued unchanged. It shone with about the same degree of luster as a star of the second magnitude, and from the fact of its remaining stationary, Procope became more and more convinced that it was on land and did not belong to a passing vessel.

They made their way into the enclosure, and found an open door.

At sunrise every telescope was pointed with keenest interest towards the center of attraction. The light, of course, had ceased to be visible, but in the direction where it had been seen, and at a distance of about ten miles, there was the distinct outline of a solitary island

of very small extent; rather, as the count observed, it had the appearance of being the projecting summit of a mountain all but submerged.
Whatever it was, it was agreed that its true character must be ascertained, not only to gratify their own curiosity, but for the benefit of all
future navigators. The schooner accordingly was steered directly towards it, and in less than an hour had cast anchor within a few cables'
lengths of the shore.

The little island proved to be nothing more than an arid rock rising
abruptly about forty feet above the water. It had no outlying reefs, a
circumstance that seemed to suggest the probability that in the recent
convulsion it had sunk gradually, until it had reached its present position of equilibrium.

Without removing his eye from his telescope, Servadac exclaimed:
"There is a habitation on the place; I can see an erection of some kind
quite distinctly. Who can tell whether we shall not come across a human being?"

Lieutenant Procope looked doubtful. The island had all the appearance of being deserted, nor did a cannon-shot fired from the schooner
have the effect of bringing any resident to the shore. Nevertheless, it
was undeniable that there was a stone building situated on the top of
the rock, and that this building had much the character of an Arabian
mosque.

The boat was lowered and manned by the four sailors; Servadac,
Timascheff and Procope were quickly rowed ashore, and lost no time
in commencing their ascent of the steep acclivity. Upon reaching the
summit, they found their progress arrested by a kind of wall, or rampart of singular construction, its materials consisting mainly of vases,
fragments of columns, carved bas-reliefs, statues, and portions of broken stelae, all piled promiscuously together without any pretense to
artistic arrangement. They made their way into the enclosure, and
finding an open door, they passed through and soon came to a second
door, also open, which admitted them to the interior of the mosque,
consisting of a single chamber, the walls of which were ornamented in
the Arabian style by sculptures of indifferent execution. In the center
was a tomb of the very simplest kind, and above the tomb was suspended a large silver lamp with a capacious reservoir of oil, in which
floated a long lighted wick, the flame of which was evidently the light
that had attracted Servadac's attention on the previous night.

"Must there not have been a custodian of the shrine?" they mutually asked; but if such there had ever been, he must, they concluded, either have fled or have perished on that eventful night. Not a soul was there in charge, and the sole living occupants were a flock of wild cormorants which, startled at the entrance of the intruders, rose on wing, and took a rapid flight towards the south.

"The tomb of St. Louis!" he exclaimed.

An old French prayer-book was lying on the corner of the tomb; the volume was open, and the page exposed to view was that which contained the office for the celebration of the 25th of August. A sudden revelation dashed across Servadac's mind. The solemn isolation of the island tomb, the open breviary, the ritual of the ancient anniversary, all combined to apprise him of the sanctity of the spot upon which he stood.

"The tomb of St. Louis!" he exclaimed, and his companions involuntarily followed his example, and made a reverential obeisance to the venerated monument.

It was, in truth, the very spot on which tradition asserts that the canonized monarch came to die, a spot to which for six centuries and more his countrymen had paid the homage of a pious regard. The lamp that had been kindled at the memorial shrine of a saint was now in all probability the only beacon that threw a light across the waters of the Mediterranean, and even this ere long must itself expire.

There was nothing more to explore. The three together quitted the mosque, and descended the rock to the shore, whence their boat re-conveyed them to the schooner, which was soon again on her southward voyage; and it was not long before the tomb of St. Louis, the only spot that had survived the mysterious shock, was lost to view.

CHAPTER XII.

AT THE MERCY OF THE WINDS

As the affrighted cormorants had winged their flight towards the south, there sprang up a sanguine hope on board the schooner that land might be discovered in that direction. Thither, accordingly, it was determined to proceed, and in a few hours after quitting the island of the tomb, the *Dobryna* was traversing the shallow waters that now covered the peninsula of Dakhul, which had separated the Bay of Tunis from the Gulf of Hammamet. For two days she continued an undeviating course, and after a futile search for the coast of Tunis, reached the latitude of 34 degrees.

Here, on the 11th of February, there suddenly arose the cry of "Land!" and in the extreme horizon, right ahead, where land had never been before, it was true enough that a shore was distinctly to be seen. What could it be? It could not be the coast of Tripoli; for not only would that low-lying shore be quite invisible at such a distance, but it was certain, moreover, that it lay two degrees at least still further south. It was soon observed that this newly discovered land was of very irregular elevation, that it extended due east and west across the horizon, thus dividing the gulf into two separate sections and completely concealing the island of Jerba, which must lie behind. Its position was duly traced on the *Dobryna*'s chart.

"How strange," exclaimed Hector Servadac, "that after sailing all this time over sea where we expected to find land, we have at last come upon land where we thought to find sea!"

"Strange, indeed," replied Lieutenant Procope; "and what appears to me almost as remarkable is that we have never once caught sight either of one of the Maltese tartans or one of the Levantine xebecs that traffic so regularly on the Mediterranean."

"Eastwards or westwards," asked the count—"which shall be our course? All farther progress to the south is checked."

"Westwards, by all means," replied Servadac quickly. "I am longing to know whether anything of Algeria is left beyond the Shelif; besides, as we pass Gourbi Island we might take Ben Zoof on board, and then make away for Gibraltar, where we should be sure to learn something, at least, of European news."

With his usual air of stately courtesy, Count Timascheff begged the captain to consider the yacht at his own disposal, and desired him to give the lieutenant instructions accordingly.

Lieutenant Procope, however, hesitated, and after revolving matters for a few moments in his mind, pointed out that as the wind was blowing directly from the west, and seemed likely to increase, if they went to the west in the teeth of the weather, the schooner would be reduced to the use of her engine only, and would have much difficulty in making any headway; on the other hand, by taking an eastward course, not only would they have the advantage of the wind, but, under steam and canvas, might hope in a few days to be off the coast of Egypt, and from Alexandria or some other port they would have the same opportunity of getting tidings from Europe as they would at Gibraltar.

Intensely anxious as he was to revisit the province of Oran, and eager, too, to satisfy himself of the welfare of his faithful Ben Zoof, Servadac could not but own the reasonableness of the lieutenant's objections, and yielded to the proposal that the eastward course should be adopted. The wind gave signs only too threatening of the breeze rising to a gale; but, fortunately, the waves did not culminate in breakers, but rather in a long swell which ran in the same direction as the vessel.

During the last fortnight the high temperature had been gradually diminishing, until it now reached an average of 20 degrees Cent. (or 68 degrees Fahr.), and sometimes descended as low as 15 degrees. That this diminution was to be attributed to the change in the earth's orbit was a question that admitted of little doubt. After approaching so near to the sun as to cross the orbit of Venus, the earth must now have receded so far from the sun that its normal distance of ninety-one millions of miles was greatly increased, and the probability was great that it was approximating to the orbit of Mars, that planet which in its physical constitution most nearly resembles our own. Nor was this supposition suggested merely by the lowering of the temperature; it was strongly corroborated by the reduction of the apparent diameter of the sun's disc to the precise dimensions which it would assume to an observer actually stationed on the surface of Mars. The necessary inference that seemed to follow from these phenomena was that the earth had been projected into a new orbit, which had the form of a very elongated ellipse.

The *Dobryna* dashed in between its Perpendicular Walls.

Very slight, however, in comparison was the regard which these astronomical wonders attracted on board the *Dobryna*. All interest there was too much absorbed in terrestrial matters, and in ascertaining what changes had taken place in the configuration of the earth itself, to permit much attention to be paid to its erratic movements through space.

The schooner kept bravely on her way, but well out to sea, at a distance of two miles from land. There was good need of this precaution, for so precipitous was the shore that a vessel driven upon it must inevitably have gone to pieces; it did not offer a single harbor of refuge, but, smooth and perpendicular as the walls of a fortress, it rose to a height of two hundred, and occasionally of three hundred feet. The waves dashed violently against its base. Upon the general substratum rested a massive conglomerate, the crystallizations of which rose like a forest of gigantic pyramids and obelisks.

But what struck the explorers more than anything was the appearance of singular newness that pervaded the whole of the region. It all seemed so recent in its formation that the atmosphere had had no opportunity of producing its wonted effect in softening the hardness of its lines, in rounding the sharpness of its angles, or in modifying the color of its surface; its outline was clearly marked against the sky, and its substance, smooth and polished as though fresh from a founder's mold, glittered with the metallic brilliancy that is characteristic of pyrites. It seemed impossible to come to any other conclusion but that the land before them, continent or island, had been upheaved by subterranean forces above the surface of the sea, and that it was mainly composed of the same metallic element as had characterized the dust so frequently uplifted from the bottom.

The extreme nakedness of the entire tract was likewise very extraordinary. Elsewhere, in various quarters of the globe, there may be sterile rocks, but there are none so adamant as to be altogether unfurrowed by the filaments engendered in the moist residuum of the condensed vapor; elsewhere there may be barren steeps, but none so rigid as not to afford some hold to vegetation, however low and elementary may be its type; but here all was bare, and blank, and desolate—not a symptom of vitality was visible.

Such being the condition of the adjacent land, it could hardly be a matter of surprise that all the sea-birds, the albatross, the gull, the sea-mew, sought continual refuge on the schooner; day and night they perched fearlessly upon the yards, the report of a gun failing to dislodge them, and when food of any sort was thrown upon the deck, they would dart down and fight with eager voracity for the prize. Their extreme avidity was recognized as a proof that any land where they could obtain a sustenance must be far remote.

All the sea-birds, the albatross, the gull, the sea-mew, sought
continual refuge on the schooner;

Onwards thus for several days the *Dobryna* followed the contour
of the inhospitable coast, of which the features would occasionally
change, sometimes for two or three miles assuming the form of a simple arris, sharply defined as though cut by a chisel, when suddenly
the prismatic lamellae soaring in rugged confusion would again recur;
but all along there was the same absence of beach or tract of sand to
mark its base, neither were there any of those shoals of rock that are
ordinarily found in shallow water. At rare intervals there were some
narrow fissures, but not a creek available for a ship to enter to replenish its supply of water; and the wide roadsteads were unprotected and
exposed to well-nigh every point of the compass.

But after sailing two hundred and forty miles, the progress of the *Dobryna* was suddenly arrested. Lieutenant Procope, who had sedulously inserted the outline of the newly revealed shore upon the maps, announced that it had ceased to run east and west, and had taken a turn due north, thus forming a barrier to their continuing their previous direction. It was, of course, impossible to conjecture how far this barrier extended; it coincided pretty nearly with the fourteenth meridian of east longitude; and if it reached, as probably it did, beyond Sicily to Italy, it was certain that the vast basin of the Mediterranean, which had washed the shores alike of Europe, Asia, and Africa, must have been reduced to about half its original area.

It was resolved to proceed upon the same plan as heretofore, following the boundary of the land at a safe distance. Accordingly, the head of the *Dobryna* was pointed north, making straight, as it was presumed, for the south of Europe. A hundred miles, or somewhat over, in that direction, and it was to be anticipated she would come in sight of Malta, if only that ancient island, the heritage in succession of Phoenicians, Carthaginians, Sicilians, Romans, Vandals, Greeks, Arabians, and the knights of Rhodes, should still be undestroyed.

But Malta, too, was gone; and when, upon the 14th, the sounding-line was dropped upon its site, it was only with the same result so oftentimes obtained before.

"The devastation is not limited to Africa," observed the count.

"Assuredly not," assented the lieutenant; adding, "and I confess I am almost in despair whether we shall ever ascertain its limits. To what quarter of Europe, if Europe still exists, do you propose that I should now direct your course?"

"To Sicily, Italy, France!" ejaculated Servadac, eagerly,— "anywhere where we can learn the truth of what has befallen us."

"How if we are the sole survivors?" said the count, gravely.

Hector Servadac was silent; his own secret presentiment so thoroughly coincided with the doubts expressed by the count, that he refrained from saying another word.

The coast, without deviation, still tended towards the north. No alternative, therefore, remained than to take a westerly course and to attempt to reach the northern shores of the Mediterranean. On the 16th the *Dobryna* essayed to start upon her altered way, but it seemed as if the elements had conspired to obstruct her progress. A furious tempest arose; the wind beat dead in the direction of the coast, and the danger incurred by a vessel of a tonnage so light was necessarily very great.

Lieutenant Procope was extremely uneasy. He took in all sail, struck his topmasts, and resolved to rely entirely on his engine. But the peril seemed only to increase. Enormous waves caught the schooner and carried her up to their crests, whence again she was plunged deep into the abysses that they left. The screw failed to keep its hold upon the water, but continually revolved with useless speed in the vacant air; and thus, although the steam was forced on to the extremest limit consistent with safety, the vessel held her way with the utmost difficulty, and recoiled before the hurricane.

Still, not a single resort for refuge did the inaccessible shore present. Again and again the lieutenant asked himself what would become of him and his comrades, even if they should survive the peril of shipwreck, and gain a footing upon the cliff. What resources could they expect to find upon that scene of desolation? What hope could they entertain that any portion of the old continent still existed beyond that dreary barrier?

It was a trying time, but throughout it all the crew behaved with the greatest courage and composure; confident in the skill of their commander, and in the stability of their ship, they performed their duties with steadiness and unquestioning obedience.

But neither skill, nor courage, nor obedience could avail; all was in vain. Despite the strain put upon her engine, the schooner, bare of canvas (for not even the smallest stay-sail could have withstood the violence of the storm), was drifting with terrific speed towards the menacing precipices, which were only a. few short miles to leeward. Fully alive to the hopelessness of their situation, the crew were all on deck.

"All over with us, sir!" said Procope to the count. "I have done everything that man could do; but our case is desperate. Nothing short of a miracle can save us now. Within an hour we must go to pieces upon yonder rocks."

"Let us, then, commend ourselves to the providence of Him to Whom nothing is impossible," replied the count, in a calm, clear voice that could be distinctly heard by all; and as he spoke, he reverently uncovered, an example in which he was followed by all the rest.

The destruction of the vessel seeming thus inevitable, Lieutenant Procope took the best measures he could to insure a few days' supply of food for any who might escape ashore. He ordered several cases of provisions and kegs of water to be brought on deck, and saw that they were securely lashed to some empty barrels, to make them float after the ship had gone down.

Less and less grew the distance from the shore, but no creek, no inlet, could be discerned in the towering wall of cliff, which seemed about to topple over and involve them in annihilation. Except a change of wind or, as Procope observed, a supernatural rifting of the rock, nothing could bring deliverance now. But the wind did not veer, and in a few minutes more the schooner was hardly three cables' distance from the fatal land. All were aware that their last moment had arrived. Servadac and the count grasped each other's hands for a long farewell; and, tossed by the tremendous waves, the schooner was on the very point of being hurled upon the cliff, when a ringing shout was heard. "Quick, boys, quick! Hoist the jib, and right the tiller!"

Sudden and startling as the unexpected orders were, they were executed as if by magic.

The lieutenant, who had shouted from the bow, rushed astern and took the helm, and before anyone had time to speculate upon the object of his maneuvers, he shouted again, "Look out! sharp! watch the sheets!"

An involuntary cry broke forth from all on board. But it was no cry of terror. Right ahead was a narrow opening in the solid rock; it was hardly forty feet wide. Whether it was a passage or no, it mattered little; it was at least a refuge; and, driven by wind and wave, the *Dobryna*, under the dexterous guidance of the lieutenant, dashed in between its perpendicular walls.

Had she not immured herself in a perpetual prison?

CHAPTER XIII.

A ROYAL SALUTE

"Then I take your bishop, major," said Colonel Murphy, as he made a move that he had taken since the previous evening to consider.

"I was afraid you would," replied Major Oliphant, looking intently at the chess-board.

Such was the way in which a long silence was broken on the morning of the 17th of February by the old calendar.

Another day elapsed before another move was made. It was a protracted game; it had, in fact, already lasted some months—the players being so deliberate, and so fearful of taking a step without the most mature consideration, that even now they were only making the twentieth move.

Both of them, moreover, were rigid disciples of the renowned Philidor, who pronounces that to play the pawns well is "the soul of chess"; and, accordingly, not one pawn had been sacrificed without a most vigorous defense.

The men who were thus beguiling their leisure were two officers in the British army—Colonel Heneage Finch Murphy and Major Sir John Temple Oliphant. Remarkably similar in personal appearance, they were hardly less so in personal character. Both of them were about forty years of age; both of them were tall and fair, with bushy whiskers and mustaches; both of them were phlegmatic in temperament, and both much addicted to the wearing of their uniforms. They were proud of their nationality, and exhibited a manifest dislike, verging upon contempt, of everything foreign. Probably they would have felt no surprise if they had been told that Anglo-Saxons were fashioned out of some specific clay, the properties of which surpassed the investigation of chemical analysis. Without any intentional disparagement they might, in a certain way, be compared to two scarecrows which, though perfectly harmless in themselves, inspire some measure of respect, and are excellently adapted to protect the territory intrusted to their guardianship.

English-like, the two officers had made themselves thoroughly at home in the station abroad in which it had been their lot to be quartered. The faculty of colonization seems to be indigenous to the native character; once let an Englishman plant his national standard on the surface of the moon, and it would not be long before a colony was established round it.

The officers had a servant, named Kirke, and a company of ten soldiers of the line. This party of thirteen men were apparently the sole survivors of an overwhelming catastrophe, which on the 1st of January had transformed an enormous rock, garrisoned with well-nigh two thousand troops, into an insignificant island far out to sea. But although the transformation had been so marvelous, it cannot be said that either Colonel Murphy or Major Oliphant had made much demonstration of astonishment.

"This is all very peculiar, Sir John," observed the colonel.

"Yes, colonel; very peculiar," replied the major.

"England will be sure to send for us," said one officer.

"No doubt she will," answered the other.

Accordingly, they came to the mutual resolution that they would "stick to their post."

To say the truth, it would have been a difficult matter for the gallant officers to do otherwise; they had but one small boat; therefore, it was well that they made a virtue of necessity, and resigned themselves to patient expectation of the British ship which, in due time, would bring relief.

They had no fear of starvation. Their island was mined with subterranean stores, more than ample for thirteen men—nay, for thirteen Englishmen—for the next five years at least. Preserved meat, ale, brandy—all were in abundance; consequently, as the men expressed it, they were in this respect "all right."

Of course, the physical changes that had taken place had attracted the notice both of officers and men. But the reversed position of east and west, the diminution of the force of gravity, the altered rotation of the earth, and her projection upon a new orbit, were all things that gave them little concern and no uneasiness; and when the colonel and the major had replaced the pieces on the board which had been disturbed by the convulsion, any surprise they might have felt at the chess-men losing some portion of their weight was quite forgotten in the satisfaction of seeing them retain their equilibrium.

"Say on, then," said Colonel Murphy. "What is it about your pay?"

One phenomenon, however, did not fail to make its due impression upon the men; this was the diminution in the length of day and night. Three days after the catastrophe, Corporal Pim, on behalf of himself and his comrades, solicited a formal interview with the officers. The request having been granted, Pim, with the nine soldiers, all punctiliously wearing the regimental tunic of scarlet and trousers of invisible green, presented themselves at the door of the colonel's room, where he

and his brother-officer were continuing their game. Raising his hand
respectfully to his cap, which he wore poised jauntily over his right
ear, and scarcely held on by the strap below his under lip, the corporal
waited permission to speak.

After a lingering survey of the chess-board, the colonel slowly lifted his eyes, and said with official dignity, "Well, men, what is it?"

"First of all, sir," replied the corporal, "we want to speak to you
about our pay, and then we wish to have a word with the major about
our rations."

"Say on, then," said Colonel Murphy. "What is it about your pay?"

"Just this, sir; as the days are only half as long as they were, we
should like to know whether our pay is to be diminished in proportion."

The colonel was taken somewhat aback, and did not reply immediately, though by some significant nods towards the major, he indicated
that he thought the question very reasonable. After a few moments'
reflection, he replied, "It must, I think, be allowed that your pay was
calculated from sunrise to sunrise; there was no specification of what
the interval should be. Your pay will continue as before. England can
afford it."

A buzz of approval burst involuntarily from all the men, but military discipline and the respect due to their officers kept them in check
from any boisterous demonstration of their satisfaction.

"And now, corporal, what is your business with me?" asked Major
Oliphant.

"We want to know whether, as the days are only six hours long, we
are to have but two meals instead of four?"

The officers looked at each other, and by their glances agreed that
the corporal was a man of sound common sense.

"Eccentricities of nature," said the major, "cannot interfere with
military regulations. It is true that there will be but an interval of an
hour and a half between them, but the rule stands good—four meals
a day. England is too rich to grudge her soldiers any of her soldiers'
due. Yes; four meals a day."

"Hurrah!" shouted the soldiers, unable this time to keep their
delight within the bounds of military decorum; and, turning to the
right-about, they marched away, leaving the officers to renew the all-
absorbing game.

However confident everyone upon the island might profess to be that succor would be sent them from their native land—for Britain never abandons any of her sons—it could not be disguised that that succor was somewhat tardy in making its appearance. Many and various were the conjectures to account for the delay. Perhaps England was engrossed with domestic matters, or perhaps she was absorbed in diplomatic difficulties; or perchance, more likely than all, Northern Europe had received no tidings of the convulsion that had shattered the south. The whole party throve remarkably well upon the liberal provisions of the commissariat department, and if the officers failed to show the same tendency to *embonpoint* which was fast becoming characteristic of the men, it was only because they deemed it due to their rank to curtail any indulgences which might compromise the fit of their uniform.

On the whole, time passed indifferently well. An Englishman rarely suffers from *ennui*, and then only in his own country, when required to conform to what he calls "the humbug of society"; and the two officers, with their similar tastes, ideas, and dispositions, got on together admirably. It is not to be questioned that they were deeply affected by a sense of regret for their lost comrades, and astounded beyond measure at finding themselves the sole survivors of a garrison of 1,895 men, but with true British pluck and self-control, they had done nothing more than draw up a report that 1,882 names were missing from the muster-roll.

The island itself, the sole surviving fragment of an enormous pile of rock that had reared itself some 1,600 feet above the sea, was not, strictly speaking, the only land that was visible; for about twelve miles to the south there was another island, apparently the very counterpart of what was now occupied by the Englishmen. It was only natural that this should awaken some interest even in the most imperturbable minds, and there was no doubt that the two officers, during one of the rare intervals when they were not absorbed in their game, had decided that it would be desirable at least to ascertain whether the island was deserted, or whether it might not be occupied by some others, like themselves, survivors from the general catastrophe. Certain it is that one morning, when the weather was bright and calm, they had embarked alone in the little boat, and been absent for seven or eight hours. Not even to Corporal Pim did they communicate the object of

their excursion, nor say one syllable as to its result, and it could only
be inferred from their manner that they were quite satisfied with what
they had seen; and very shortly afterwards Major Oliphant was observed to draw up a lengthy document, which was no sooner finished
than it was formally signed and sealed with the seal of the 33rd Regiment. It was directed:

To the First Lord of the Admiralty,

London,

and kept in readiness for transmission by the first ship that should
hail in sight. But time elapsed, and here was the 18th of February
without an opportunity having been afforded for any communication
with the British Government.

At breakfast that morning, the colonel observed to the major that
he was under the most decided impression that the 18th of February
was a royal anniversary; and he went on to say that, although he had
received no definite instructions on the subject, he did not think that
the peculiar circumstances under which they found themselves should
prevent them from giving the day its due military honors.

The major quite concurred; and it was mutually agreed that the
occasion must be honored by a bumper of port, and by a royal salute.
Corporal Pim must be sent for. The corporal soon made his appearance, smacking his lips, having, by a ready intuition, found a pretext
for a double morning ration of spirits.

"The 18th of February, you know, Pim," said the colonel; "we must
have a salute of twenty-one guns."

"Very good," replied Pim, a man of few words.

"And take care that your fellows don't get their arms and legs
blown off," added the officer.

"Very good, sir," said the corporal; and he made his salute and
withdrew.

Of all the bombs, howitzers, and various species of artillery with
which the fortress had been crowded, one solitary piece remained.
This was a cumbrous muzzle-loader of 9-inch caliber, and, in default
of the smaller ordnance generally employed for the purpose, had to be
brought into requisition for the royal salute.

A sufficient number of charges having been provided, the corporal
brought his men to the reduct, whence the gun's mouth projected over

a sloping embrasure. The two officers, in cocked hats and full staff uniform, attended to take charge of the proceedings. The gun was maneuvered in strict accordance with the rules of "The Artilleryman's Manual," and the firing commenced.

The corporal was most careful between each discharge to see that every vestige of fire was extinguished.

Not unmindful of the warning he had received, the corporal was most careful between each discharge to see that every vestige of fire was extinguished, so as to prevent an untimely explosion while the men were reloading; and accidents, such as so frequently mar public rejoicings, were all happily avoided.

Much to the chagrin of both Colonel Murphy and Major Oliphant, the effect of the salute fell altogether short of their anticipations. The weight of the atmosphere was so reduced that there was comparatively little resistance to the explosive force of the gases, liberated at the cannon's mouth, and there was consequently none of the reverberation, like rolling thunder, that ordinarily follows the discharge of heavy artillery.

Twenty times had the gun been fired, and it was on the point of being loaded for the last time, when the colonel laid his hand upon the arm of the man who had the ramrod. "Stop!" he said; "we will have a ball this time. Let us put the range of the piece to the test."

"A good idea!" replied the major. "Corporal, you hear the orders."

In quick time an artillery-wagon was on the spot, and the men lifted out a full-sized shot, weighing 200 lbs., which, under ordinary circumstances, the cannon would carry about four miles. It was proposed, by means of telescopes, to note the place where the ball first touched the water, and thus to obtain an approximation sufficiently accurate as to the true range.

Having been duly charged with powder and ball, the gun was raised to an angle of something under 45 degrees, so as to allow proper development to the curve that the projectile would make, and, at a signal from the major, the light was applied to the priming.

"Heavens!" "By all that's good!" exclaimed both officers in one breath, as, standing open-mouthed, they hardly knew whether they were to believe the evidence of their own senses. "Is it possible?"

The diminution of the force of attraction at the earth's surface was so considerable that the ball had sped beyond the horizon.

"Incredible!" ejaculated the colonel.

"Incredible!" echoed the major.

"Six miles at least!" observed the one.

"Ay, more than that!" replied the other.

Awhile, they gazed at the sea and at each other in mute amazement. But in the midst of their perplexity, what sound was that which startled them? Was it mere fancy? Was it the reverberation of the cannon still booming in their ears? Or was it not truly the report of another and a distant gun in answer to their own? Attentively and eagerly they listened. Twice, thrice did the sound repeat itself. It was quite distinct. There could be no mistake.

"I told you so," cried the colonel, triumphantly. "I knew our country would not forsake us; it is an English ship, no doubt."

In half an hour two masts were visible above the horizon. "See! Was I not right? Our country was sure to send to our relief. Here is the ship."

"Yes," replied the major; "she responded to our gun."

"It is to be hoped," muttered the corporal, "that our ball has done her no damage."

Before long the hull was full in sight. A long trail of smoke betokened her to be a steamer; and very soon, by the aid of the glass, it could be ascertained that she was a schooner-yacht, and making straight for the island. A flag at her mast-head fluttered in the breeze, and towards this the two officers, with the keenest attention, respectively adjusted their focus.

Simultaneously the two telescopes were lowered. The colonel and the major stared at each other in blank astonishment. "Russian!" they gasped.

And true it was that the flag that floated at the head of yonder mast was the blue cross of Russia.

CHAPTER XIV.

SENSITIVE NATIONALITY

WHEN the schooner had approached the island, the Englishmen were able to make out the name "*Dobryna*" painted on the aft-board. A sinuous irregularity of the coast had formed a kind of cove, which, though hardly spacious enough for a few fishing-smacks, would afford the yacht a temporary anchorage, so long as the wind did not blow violently from either west or south. Into this cove the *Dobryna* was duly signaled, and as soon as she was safely moored, she lowered her four-oar, and Count Timascheff and Captain Servadac made their way at once to land.

Colonel Heneage Finch Murphy and Major Sir John Temple Oliphant stood, grave and prim, formally awaiting the arrival of their visitors. Captain Servadac, with the uncontrolled vivacity natural to a Frenchman, was the first to speak.

"A joyful sight, gentlemen!" he exclaimed. "It will give us unbounded pleasure to shake hands again with some of our fellow-creatures. You, no doubt, have escaped the same disaster as ourselves."

But the English officers, neither by word nor gesture, made the slightest acknowledgment of this familiar greeting.

"What news can you give us of France, England, or Russia?" continued Servadac, perfectly unconscious of the stolid rigidity with which his advances were received. "We are anxious to hear anything you can tell us. Have you had communications with Europe? Have you—"

"To whom have we the honor of speaking?" at last interposed Colonel Murphy, in the coldest and most measured tone, and drawing himself up to his full height.

"Ah! how stupid! I forgot," said Servadac, with the slightest possible shrug of the shoulders; "we have not been introduced."

Then, with a wave of his hand towards his companion, who meanwhile had exhibited a reserve hardly less than that of the British officers, he said:

"Allow me to introduce you to Count Wassili Timascheff."

"Allow me to introduce you to Count Wassili Timascheff."

"Major Sir John Temple Oliphant," replied the colonel.

The Russian and the Englishman mutually exchanged the stiffest of bows.

"I have the pleasure of introducing Captain Servadac," said the count in his turn.

"And this is Colonel Heneage Finch Murphy," was the major's grave rejoinder.

More bows were interchanged and the ceremony brought to its due conclusion. It need hardly be said that the conversation had been carried on in French, a language which is generally known both by Russians and Englishmen—a circumstance that is probably in some measure to be accounted for by the refusal of Frenchmen to learn either Russian or English.

The formal preliminaries of etiquette being thus complete, there was no longer any obstacle to a freer intercourse. The colonel, signing to his guests to follow, led the way to the apartment occupied jointly by himself and the major, which, although only a kind of casemate hollowed in the rock, nevertheless wore a general air of comfort. Major Oliphant accompanied them, and all four having taken their seats, the conversation was commenced.

Irritated and disgusted at all the cold formalities, Hector Servadac resolved to leave all the talking to the count; and he, quite aware that the Englishmen would adhere to the fiction that they could be supposed to know nothing that had transpired previous to the introduction felt himself obliged to recapitulate matters from the very beginning.

"You must be aware, gentlemen," began the count, "that a most singular catastrophe occurred on the 1st of January last. Its cause, its limits we have utterly failed to discover, but from the appearance of the island on which we find you here, you have evidently experienced its devastating consequences."

The Englishmen, in silence, bowed assent.

"Captain Servadac, who accompanies me," continued the count, "has been most severely tried by the disaster. Engaged as he was in an important mission as a staff-officer in Algeria—"

"A French colony, I believe," interposed Major Oliphant, half shutting his eyes with an expression of supreme indifference.

Servadac was on the point of making some cutting retort, but Count Timascheff, without allowing the interruption to be noticed, calmly continued his narrative:

"It was near the mouth of the Shelif that a portion of Africa, on that eventful night, was transformed into an island which alone survived; the rest of the vast continent disappeared as completely as if it had never been."

The announcement seemed by no means startling to the phlegmatic colonel.

"Indeed!" was all he said.

"And where were you?" asked Major Oliphant.

"I was out at sea, cruising in my yacht; hard by; and I look upon it as a miracle, and nothing less, that I and my crew escaped with our lives."

"I congratulate you on your luck," replied the major.

The count resumed: "It was about a month after the great disruption that I was sailing—my engine having sustained some damage in the shock—along the Algerian coast, and had the pleasure of meeting with my previous acquaintance, Captain Servadac, who was resident upon the island with his orderly, Ben Zoof."

"Ben who?" inquired the major.

"Zoof! Ben Zoof!" ejaculated Servadac, who could scarcely shout loud enough to relieve his pent-up feelings.

Ignoring this ebullition of the captain's spleen, the count went on to say: "Captain Servadac was naturally most anxious to get what news he could. Accordingly, he left his servant on the island in charge of his horses, and came on board the *Dobryna* with me. We were quite at a loss to know where we should steer, but decided to direct our course to what previously had been the east, in order that we might, if possible, discover the colony of Algeria; but of Algeria not a trace remained."

The colonel curled his lip, insinuating only too plainly that to him it was by no means surprising that a French colony should be wanting in the element of stability. Servadac observed the supercilious look, and half rose to his feet, but, smothering his resentment, took his seat again without speaking.

"The devastation, gentlemen," said the count, who persistently refused to recognize the Frenchman's irritation, "everywhere was terrible and complete. Not only was Algeria lost, but there was no trace of Tunis, except one solitary rock, which was crowned by an ancient tomb of one of the kings of France—"

"Louis the Ninth, I presume," observed the colonel.

"Saint Louis," blurted out Servadac, savagely.

Colonel Murphy slightly smiled.

Proof against all interruption, Count Timascheff, as if he had not heard it, went on without pausing. He related how the schooner had pushed her way onwards to the south, and had reached the Gulf of Cabes; and how she had ascertained for certain that the Sahara Sea had no longer an existence.

The smile of disdain again crossed the colonel's face; he could not conceal his opinion that such a destiny for the work of a Frenchman could be no matter of surprise.

"Our next discovery," continued the count, "was that a new coast had been upheaved right along in front of the coast of Tripoli, the geological formation of which was altogether strange, and which extended to the north as far as the proper place of Malta."

"And Malta," cried Servadac, unable to control himself any longer; "Malta—town, forts, soldiers, governor, and all—has vanished just like Algeria."

For a moment a cloud rested upon the colonel's brow, only to give place to an expression of decided incredulity.

"The statement seems highly incredible," he said.

"Incredible?" repeated Servadac. "Why is it that you doubt my word?"

The captain's rising wrath did not prevent the colonel from replying coolly, "Because Malta belongs to England."

"I can't help that," answered Servadac, sharply; "it has gone just as utterly as if it had belonged to China."

Colonel Murphy turned deliberately away from Servadac, and appealed to the count: "Do you not think you may have made some error, count, in reckoning the bearings of your yacht?"

"No, colonel, I am quite certain of my reckonings; and not only can I testify that Malta has disappeared, but I can affirm that a large section of the Mediterranean has been closed in by a new continent. After the most anxious investigation, we could discover only one narrow opening in all the coast, and it is by following that little channel that we have made our way hither. England, I fear, has suffered grievously by the late catastrophe. Not only has Malta been entirely lost, but of the Ionian Islands that were under England's protection, there seems to be but little left."

"Ay, you may depend upon it," said Servadac, breaking in upon the conversation petulantly, "your grand resident lord high commissioner has not much to congratulate himself about in the condition of Corfu."

The Englishmen were mystified.

"Corfu, did you say?" asked Major Oliphant.

"Yes, Corfu; I said Corfu," replied Servadac, with a sort of malicious triumph.

The officers were speechless with astonishment.

"Corfu, did you say?" asked Major Oliphant.

The silence of bewilderment was broken at length by Count Timascheff making inquiry whether nothing had been heard from England, either by telegraph or by any passing ship.

"No," said the colonel; "not a ship has passed; and the cable is broken."

"But do not the Italian telegraphs assist you?" continued the count.

"Italian! I do not comprehend you. You must mean the Spanish, surely."

"How?" demanded Timascheff.

"Confound it!" cried the impatient Servadac. "What matters whether it be Spanish or Italian? Tell us, have you had no communication at all from Europe?—no news of any sort from London?"

"Hitherto, none whatever," replied the colonel; adding with a stately emphasis, "but we shall be sure to have tidings from England before long."

"Whether England is still in existence or not, I suppose," said Servadac, in a tone of irony.

The Englishmen started simultaneously to their feet.

"England in existence?" the colonel cried. "England! Ten times more probable that France—"

"France!" shouted Servadac in a passion. "France is not an island that can be submerged; France is an integral portion of a solid continent. France, at least, is safe."

A scene appeared inevitable, and Count Timascheff's efforts to conciliate the excited parties were of small avail.

"You are at home here," said Servadac, with as much calmness as he could command; "it will be advisable, I think, for this discussion to be carried on in the open air." And hurriedly he left the room. Followed immediately by the others, he led the way to a level piece of ground, which he considered he might fairly claim as neutral territory.

"Now, gentlemen," he began haughtily, "permit me to represent that, in spite of any loss France may have sustained in the fate of Algeria, France is ready to answer any provocation that affects her honor. Here I am the representative of my country, and here, on neutral ground—"

"Neutral ground?" objected Colonel Murphy; "I beg your pardon. This, Captain Servadac, is English territory. Do you not see the English flag?" and, as he spoke, he pointed with national pride to the British standard floating over the top of the island.

"Pshaw!" cried Servadac, with a contemptuous sneer; "that flag, you know, has been hoisted but a few short weeks."

"That flag has floated where it is for ages," asserted the colonel.

"An imposture!" shouted Servadac, as he stamped with rage.

Recovering his composure in a degree, he continued: "Can you suppose that I am not aware that this island on which we find you is what remains of the Ionian representative republic, over which you English exercise the right of protection, but have no claim of government?"

"This, Captain Servadac, is English territory. Do you not see the English flag?"

The colonel and the major looked at each other in amazement.

Although Count Timascheff secretly sympathized with Servadac, he had carefully refrained from taking part in the dispute; but he was on the point of interfering, when the colonel, in a greatly subdued tone, begged to be allowed to speak.

"I begin to apprehend," he said, "that you must be la-boring un-der some strange mistake. There is no room for questioning that the territory here is England's—England's by right of conquest; ceded to England by the Treaty of Utrecht. Three times, indeed—in 1727, 1779, and 1792—France and Spain have disputed our title, but always to no purpose. You are, I assure you, at the present moment, as much on English soil as if you were in London, in the middle of Trafalgar Square."

It was now the turn of the captain and the count to look surprised. "Are we not, then, in Corfu?" they asked.

"You are at Gibraltar," replied the colonel.

Gibraltar! The word fell like a thunderclap upon their ears. Gibral-tar! the western extremity of the Mediterranean! Why, had they not been sailing persistently to the east? Could they be wrong in imagin-ing that they had reached the Ionian Islands? What new mystery was this?

Count Timascheff was about to proceed with a more rigorous in-vestigation, when the attention of all was arrested by a loud outcry. Turning round, they saw that the crew of the *Dobryna* was in hot dis-pute with the English soldiers. A general altercation had arisen from a disagreement between the sailor Panofka and Corporal Pim. It had transpired that the cannon-ball fired in experiment from the island had not only damaged one of the spars of the schooner, but had broken Panofka's pipe, and, moreover, had just grazed his nose, which, for a Russian's, was unusually long. The discussion over this mishap led to mutual recriminations, till the sailors had almost come to blows with the garrison.

Servadac was just in the mood to take Panofka's part, which drew from Major Oliphant the remark that England could not be held re-sponsible for any accidental injury done by her cannon, and if the Russian's long nose came in the way of the ball, the Russian must submit to the mischance.

This was too much for Count Timascheff, and having poured out a torrent of angry invective against the English officers, he ordered his crew to embark immediately.

"We shall meet again," said Servadac, as they pushed off from shore.

"Whenever you please," was the cool reply.

The geographical mystery haunted the minds of both the count and the captain, and they felt they could never rest till they had ascertained what had become of their respective countries. They were glad to be on board again, that they might résumé their voyage of investigation, and in two hours were out of sight of the sole remaining fragment of Gibraltar.

CHAPTER XV.

LIEUTENANT PROCOPE had been left on board in charge of the *Dobryna*, and on resuming the voyage it was a task of some difficulty to make him understand the fact that had just come to light. Some hours were spent in discussion and in attempting to penetrate the mysteries of the situation.

There were certain things of which they were perfectly certain. They could be under no misapprehension as to the distance they had positively sailed from Gourbi Island towards the east before their further progress was arrested by the unknown shore; as nearly as possible that was fifteen degrees; the length of the narrow strait by which they had made their way across that land to regain the open sea was about three miles and a half; thence onward to the island, which they had been assured, on evidence that they could not disbelieve, to be upon the site of Gibraltar, was four degrees; while from Gibraltar to Gourbi Island was seven degrees or but little more. What was it altogether? Was it not less than thirty degrees? In that latitude, the degree of longitude represents eight and forty miles. What, then, did it all amount to? Indubitably, to less than 1,400 miles. So brief a voyage would bring the *Dobryna* once again to her starting-point, or, in other words, would enable her to complete the circumnavigation of the globe. How changed the condition of things! Previously, to sail from Malta to Gibraltar by an eastward course would have involved the passage of the Suez Canal, the Red Sea, the Indian Ocean, the Pacific, the Atlantic; but what had happened now? Why, Gibraltar had been reached as if it had been just at Corfu, and some three hundred and thirty degrees of the earth's circuit had vanished utterly.

After allowing for a certain margin of miscalculation, the main fact remained undeniable; and the necessary inference that Lieutenant Procope drew from the round of the earth being completed in 1,400 miles, was that the earth's diameter had been reduced by about fifteen sixteenths of its length.

"If that be so," observed the count, "it accounts for some of the strange phenomena we witness. If our world has become so insignificant a spheroid, not only has its gravity diminished, but its rotary speed has been accelerated; and this affords an adequate explanation of our days and nights being thus curtailed. But how about the new orbit in which we are moving?"

He paused and pondered, and then looked at Procope as though awaiting from him some further elucidation of the difficulty. The lieutenant hesitated. When, in a few moments, he began to speak, Servadac smiled intelligently, anticipating the answer he was about to hear.

"My conjecture is," said Procope, "that a fragment of considerable magnitude has been detached from the earth; that it has carried with it an envelope of the earth's atmosphere, and that it is now traveling through the solar system in an orbit that does not correspond at all with the proper orbit of the earth."

The hypothesis was plausible; but what a multitude of bewildering speculations it entailed! If, in truth, a certain mass had been broken off from the terrestrial sphere, whither would it wend its way? What would be the measure of the eccentricity of its path? What would be its period round the sun? Might it not, like a comet, be carried away into the vast infinity of space? or, on the other hand, might it not be attracted to the great central source of light and heat, and be absorbed in it? Did its orbit correspond with the orbit of the ecliptic? and was there no chance of its ever uniting again with the globe, from which it had been torn off by so sudden and violent a disruption?

A thoughtful silence fell upon them all, which Servadac was the first to break. "Lieutenant," he said, "your explanation is ingenious, and accounts for many appearances; but it seems to me that in one point it fails."

"How so?" replied Procope. "To my mind the theory meets all objections."

"I think not," Servadac answered. "In one point, at least, it appears to me to break down completely."

"What is that?" asked the lieutenant.

"Stop a moment," said the captain. "Let us see that we understand each other right. Unless I mistake you, your hypothesis is that a frag-

ment of the earth, comprising the Mediterranean and its shores from
Gibraltar to Malta, has been developed into a new asteroid, which is
started on an independent orbit in the solar regions. Is not that your
meaning?"

"Precisely so," the lieutenant acquiesced.

"Well, then," continued Servadac, "it seems to me to be at fault in
this respect: it fails, and fails completely, to account for the geological
character of the land that we have found now encompassing this sea.
Why, if the new land is a fragment of the old—why does it not retain
its old formation? What has become of the granite and the calcareous
deposits? How is it that these should all be changed into a mineral
concrete with which we have no acquaintance?"

No doubt, it was a serious objection; for, however likely it might
be that a mass of the earth on being detached would be eccentric in
its movements, there was no probable reason to be alleged why the
material of its substance should undergo so complete a change. There
was nothing to account for the fertile shores, rich in vegetation, being
transformed into rocks arid and barren beyond precedent.

The lieutenant felt the difficulty, and owned himself unprepared
to give at once an adequate solution; nevertheless, he declined to renounce his theory. He asserted that the arguments in favor of it carried conviction to his mind, and that he entertained no doubt but that,
in the course of time, all apparently antagonistic circumstances would
be explained so as to become consistent with the view he took. He was
careful, however, to make it understood that with respect to the original cause of the disruption he had no theory to offer; and although he
knew what expansion might be the result of subterranean forces, he
did not venture to say that he considered it sufficient to produce so
tremendous an effect. The origin of the catastrophe was a problem still
to be solved.

"Ah! well," said Servadac, "I don't know that it matters much
where our new little planet comes from, or what it is made of, if only
it carries France along with it."

"And Russia," added the count.

"And Russia, of course," said Servadac, with a polite bow.

There was, however, not much room for this sanguine expectation, for if a new asteroid had thus been brought into existence, it
must be a sphere of extremely limited dimensions, and there could be

little chance that it embraced more than the merest fraction of either France or Russia. As to England, the total cessation of all telegraphic communication between her shores and Gibraltar was a virtual proof that England was beyond its compass.

And what was the true measurement of the new little world? At Gourbi Island the days and nights were of equal length, and this seemed to indicate that it was situated on the equator; hence the distance by which the two poles stood apart would be half what had been reckoned would be the distance completed by the *Dobryna* in her circuit. That distance had been already estimated to be something under 1,400 miles, so that the Arctic Pole of their recently fashioned world must be about 350 miles to the north, and the Antarctic about 350 miles to the south of the island. Compare these calculations with the map, and it is at once apparent that the northernmost limit barely touched the coast of Provence, while the southernmost reached to about lat. 20 degrees N., and fell in the heart of the desert. The practical test of these conclusions would be made by future investigation, but meanwhile the fact appeared very much to strengthen the presumption that, if Lieutenant Procope had not arrived at the whole truth, he had made a considerable advance towards it.

The weather, ever since the storm that had driven the *Dobryna* into the creek, had been magnificent. The wind continued favorable, and now under both steam and canvas, she made a rapid progress towards the north, a direction in which she was free to go in consequence of the total disappearance of the Spanish coast, from Gibraltar right away to Alicante. Malaga, Almeria, Cape Gata, Carthagena. Cape Palos—all were gone. The sea was rolling over the southern extent of the peninsula, so that the yacht advanced to the latitude of Seville before it sighted any land at all, and then, not shores such as the shores of Andalusia, but a bluff and precipitous cliff, in its geological features resembling exactly the stern and barren rock that she had coasted beyond the site of Malta. Here the sea made a decided indentation on the coast; it ran up in an acute-angled triangle till its apex coincided with the very spot upon which Madrid had stood. But as hitherto the sea had encroached upon the land, the land in its turn now encroached upon the sea; for a frowning headland stood out far into the basin of the Mediterranean, and formed a promontory stretching out beyond the proper places of the Balearic Isles. Curiosity was all alive. There was

the intensest interest awakened to determine whether no vestige could
be traced of Majorca, Minorca, or any of the group, and it was during
a deviation from the direct course for the purpose of a more thorough
scrutiny, that one of the sailors raised a thrill of general excitement by
shouting, "A bottle in the sea!"

The count, the captain, the lieutenant, everybody hurried to the forecastle.

Here, then, at length was a communication from the outer world.
Surely now they would find a document which would throw some
light upon all the mysteries that had happened? Had not the day now
dawned that should set their speculations all at rest?

It was the morning of the 21st of February. The count, the captain, the lieutenant, everybody hurried to the forecastle; the schooner was dexterously put about, and all was eager impatience until the supposed bottle was hauled on deck.

There was no maker's name to be deciphered.

It was not, however, a bottle; it proved to be a round leather telescope-case, about a foot long, and the first thing to do before investigating its contents was to make a careful examination of its exterior. The lid was fastened on by wax, and so securely that it would take a long immersion before any water could penetrate; there was no maker's name to be deciphered; but impressed very plainly with a seal on the wax were the two initials "P. R."

When the scrutiny of the outside was finished, the wax was removed and the cover opened, and the lieutenant drew out a slip of ruled paper, evidently torn from a common note-book. The paper had an inscription written in four lines, which were remarkable for the profusion of notes of admiration and interrogation with which they were interspersed:

"Gallia???
Ab sole, au 15 fev. 59,000,000 l.!
Chemin parcouru de janv. a fev. 82,000,000 l.!!
Va bene! All right!! Parfait!!!"

There was a general sigh of disappointment. They turned the paper over and over, and handed it from one to another. "What does it all mean?" exclaimed the count.

"Something mysterious here!" said Servadac. "But yet," he continued, after a pause, "one thing is tolerably certain: on the 15th, six days ago, someone was alive to write it."

"Yes; I presume there is no reason to doubt the accuracy of the date," assented the count.

To this strange conglomeration of French, English, Italian, and Latin, there was no signature attached; nor was there anything to give a clue as to the locality in which it had been committed to the waves. A telescope-case would probably be the property of some one on board a ship; and the figures obviously referred to the astronomical wonders that had been experienced.

To these general observations Captain Servadac objected that he thought it unlikely that any one on board a ship would use a telescope-case for this purpose, but would be sure to use a bottle as being more secure; and, accordingly, he should rather be inclined to believe that the message had been set afloat by some *savant* left alone, perchance, upon some isolated coast.

"But, however interesting it might be," observed the count, "to know the author of the lines, to us it is of far greater moment to ascertain their meaning."

And taking up the paper again, he said, "Perhaps we might analyze it word by word, and from its detached parts gather some clue to its sense as a whole."

"What can be the meaning of all that cluster of interrogations after Gallia?" asked Servadac.

Lieutenant Procope, who had hitherto not spoken, now broke his silence by saying, "I beg, gentlemen, to submit my opinion that this document goes very far to confirm my hypothesis that a fragment of the earth has been precipitated into space."

Captain Servadac hesitated, and then replied, "Even if it does, I do not see how it accounts in the least for the geological character of the new asteroid."

"But will you allow me for one minute to take my supposition for granted?" said Procope. "If a new little planet has been formed, as I imagine, by disintegration from the old, I should conjecture that Gallia is the name assigned to it by the writer of this paper. The very notes of interrogation are significant that he was in doubt what he should write."

"You would presume that he was a Frenchman?" asked the count.

"I should think so," replied the lieutenant.

"Not much doubt about that," said Servadac; "it is all in French, except a few scattered words of English, Latin, and Italian, inserted to attract attention. He could not tell into whose hands the message would fall first."

"Well, then," said Count Timascheff, "we seem to have found a name for the new world we occupy."

"But what I was going especially to observe," continued the lieutenant, "is that the distance, 59,000,000 leagues, represents precisely the distance we ourselves were from the sun on the 15th. It was on that day we crossed the orbit of Mars."

"Yes, true," assented the others.

"And the next line," said the lieutenant, after reading it aloud, "apparently registers the distance traversed by Gallia, the new little planet, in her own orbit. Her speed, of course, we know by Kepler's laws, would vary according to her distance from the sun, and if she were—as I conjecture from the temperature at that date—on the 15th of January at her perihelion, she would be traveling twice as fast as the earth, which moves at the rate of between 50,000 and 60,000 miles an hour."

"You think, then," said Servadac, with a smile, "you have determined the perihelion of our orbit; but how about the aphelion? Can you form a judgment as to what distance we are likely to be carried?"

"You are asking too much," remonstrated the count.

"I confess," said the lieutenant, "that just at present I am not able to clear away the uncertainty of the future; but I feel confident that by careful observation at various points we shall arrive at conclusions which not only will determine our path, but perhaps may clear up the mystery about our geological structure."

"Allow me to ask," said Count Timascheff, "whether such a new asteroid would not be subject to ordinary mechanical laws, and whether, once started, it would not have an orbit that must be immutable?"

"Decidedly it would, so long as it was undisturbed by the attraction of some considerable body; but we must recollect that, compared to the great planets, Gallia must be almost infinitesimally small, and so might be attracted by a force that is irresistible."

"Altogether, then," said Servadac, "we seem to have settled it to our entire satisfaction that we must be the population of a young little world called Gallia. Perhaps some day we may have the honor of being registered among the minor planets."

"No chance of that," quickly rejoined Lieutenant Procope. "Those minor planets all are known to rotate in a narrow zone between the orbits of Mars and Jupiter; in their perihelia they cannot approximate the sun as we have done; we shall not be classed with them."

"Our lack of instruments," said the count, "is much to be deplored; it baffles our investigations in every way."

"Ah, never mind! Keep up your courage, count!" said Servadac, cheerily.

And Lieutenant Procope renewed his assurances that he entertained good hopes that every perplexity would soon be solved.

"I suppose," remarked the count, "that we cannot attribute much importance to the last line:

'Va bene! All right!! Parfait!!!'"

The captain answered, "At least, it shows that whoever wrote it had no murmuring or complaint to make, but was quite content with the new order of things."

CHAPTER XVI.

THE RESIDUUM OF A CONTINENT

ALMOST unconsciously, the voyagers in the *Dobryna* fell into the habit of using Gallia as the name of the new world in which they became aware they must be making an extraordinary excursion through the realms of space. Nothing, however, was allowed to divert them from their ostensible object of making a survey of the coast of the Mediterranean, and accordingly they persevered in following that singular boundary which had revealed itself to their extreme astonishment.

Having rounded the great promontory that had barred her farther progress to the north, the schooner skirted its upper edge. A few more leagues and they ought to be abreast of the shores of France. Yes, of France.

But who shall describe the feelings of Hector Servadac when, instead of the charming outline of his native land, he beheld nothing but a solid boundary of savage rock? Who shall paint the look of consternation with which he gazed upon the stony rampart—rising perpendicularly for a thousand feet—that had replaced the shores of the smiling south? Who shall reveal the burning anxiety with which he throbbed to see beyond that cruel wall?

But there seemed no hope. Onwards and onwards the yacht made her way, and still no sign of France. It might have been supposed that Servadac's previous experiences would have prepared him for the discovery that the catastrophe which had overwhelmed other sites had brought destruction to his own country as well. But he had failed to realize how it might extend to France; and when now he was obliged with his own eyes to witness the waves of ocean rolling over what once had been the lovely shores of Provence, he was well-nigh frantic with desperation.

"Am I to believe that Gourbi Island, that little shred of Algeria, constitutes all that is left of our glorious France? No, no; it cannot be. Not yet have we reached the pole of our new world. There is—there must be—something more behind that frowning rock. Oh, that for a moment we could scale its towering height and look beyond! By Heaven, I adjure you, let us disembark, and mount the summit and explore! France lies beyond."

Disembarkation, however, was an utter impossibility. There was no semblance of a creek in which the *Dobryna* could find an anchorage. There was no outlying ridge on which a footing could be gained. The precipice was perpendicular as a wall, its topmost height crowned with the same conglomerate of crystallized lamellae that had all along been so pronounced a feature.

With her steam at high pressure, the yacht made rapid progress towards the east. The weather remained perfectly fine, the temperature became gradually cooler, so that there was little prospect of vapors accumulating in the atmosphere; and nothing more than a few cirri, almost transparent, veiled here and there the clear azure of the sky. Throughout the day the pale rays of the sun, apparently lessened in its magnitude, cast only faint and somewhat uncertain shadows; but at night the stars shone with surpassing brilliancy. Of the planets, some, it was observed, seemed to be fading away in remote distance. This was the case with Mars, Venus, and that unknown orb which was moving in the orbit of the minor planets; but Jupiter, on the other hand, had assumed splendid proportions; Saturn was superb in its luster, and Uranus, which hitherto had been imperceptible without a telescope was pointed out by Lieutenant Procope, plainly visible to the naked eye. The inference was irresistible that Gallia was receding from the sun, and traveling far away across the planetary regions.

On the 24th of February, after following the sinuous course of what before the date of the convulsion had been the coast line of the department of Var, and after a fruitless search for Hyeres, the peninsula of St. Tropez, the Lerius Islands, and the gulfs of Cannes and Jouar, the *Dobryna* arrived upon the site of the Cape of Antibes.

Here, quite unexpectedly, the explorers made the discovery that the massive wall of cliff had been rent from the top to the bottom by a narrow rift, like the dry bed of a mountain torrent, and at the base of the opening, level with the sea, was a little strand upon which there was just space enough for their boat to be hauled up.

"Joy! joy!" shouted Servadac, half beside himself with ecstasy; "we can land at last!"

Count Timascheff and the lieutenant were scarcely less impatient than the captain, and little needed his urgent and repeated solicitations: "Come on! Quick! Come on! no time to lose!"

Thin layers of snow were glittering upon the surface of the fractured rocks.

It was half-past seven in the morning, when they set their foot upon this untried land. The bit of strand was only a few square yards in area, quite a narrow strip. Upon it might have been recognized some fragments of that agglutination of yellow limestone which is characteristic of the coast of Provence. But the whole party was far too eager to wait and examine these remnants of the ancient shore; they hurried on to scale the heights.

The narrow ravine was not only perfectly dry, but manifestly had never been the bed of any mountain torrent. The rocks that rested at the bottom—just as those which formed its sides—were of the same lamellous formation as the entire coast, and had not hitherto been subject to the disaggregation which the lapse of time never fails to work. A skilled geologist would probably have been able to assign them their proper scientific classification, but neither Servadac, Timascheff, nor the lieutenant could pretend to any acquaintance with their specific character.

Although, however, the bottom of the chasm had never as yet been the channel of a stream, indications were not wanting that at some future time it would be the natural outlet of accumulated waters; for already, in many places, thin layers of snow were glittering upon the surface of the fractured rocks, and the higher the elevation that was gained, the more these layers were found to increase in area and in depth.

"Here is a trace of fresh water, the first that Gallia has exhibited," said the count to his companions, as they toiled up the precipitous path.

"And probably," replied the lieutenant, "as we ascend we shall find not only snow but ice. We must suppose this Gallia of ours to be a sphere, and if it is so, we must now be very close to her Arctic regions; it is true that her axis is not so much inclined as to prolong day and night as at the poles of the earth, but the rays of the sun must reach us here only very obliquely, and the cold, in all likelihood, will be intense."

"So cold, do you think," asked Servadac, "that animal life must be extinct?"

"I do not say that, captain," answered the lieutenant; "for, however far our little world may be removed from the sun, I do not see why its temperature should fall below what prevails in those outlying regions beyond our system where sky and air are not." "And what temperature may that be?" inquired the captain with a shudder.

"Fourier estimates that even in those vast unfathomable tracts, the temperature never descends lower than 60 degrees," said Procope.

"Sixty! Sixty degrees below zero!" cried the count. "Why, there's not a Russian could endure it!"

"I beg your pardon, count. It is placed on record that the English *have* survived it, or something quite approximate, upon their Arctic expeditions. When Captain Parry was on Melville Island, he knew the thermometer to fall to 56 degrees," said Procope.

As the explorers advanced, they seemed glad to pause from time to time, that they might recover their breath; for the air, becoming more and more rarefied, made respiration somewhat difficult and the ascent fatiguing. Before they had reached an altitude of 600 feet they noticed a sensible diminution of the temperature; but neither cold nor fatigue deterred them, and they were resolved to persevere. Fortunately, the deep striae or furrows in the surface of the rocks that made the bottom of the ravine in some degree facilitated their progress, but it was not until they had been toiling up for two hours more that they succeeded in reaching the summit of the cliff.

Eagerly and anxiously did they look around. To the south there was nothing but the sea they had traversed; to the north, nothing but one drear, inhospitable stretch.

Servadac could not suppress a cry of dismay. Where was his beloved France? Had he gained this arduous height only to behold the rocks carpeted with ice and snow, and reaching interminably to the far-off horizon? His heart sank within him.

The whole region appeared to consist of nothing but the same strange, uniform mineral conglomerate, crystallized into regular hexagonal prisms. But whatever was its geological character, it was only too evident that it had entirely replaced the former soil, so that not a vestige of the old continent of Europe could be discerned. The lovely scenery of Provence, with the grace of its rich and undulating landscape; its gardens of citrons and oranges rising tier upon tier from the deep red soil—all, all had vanished. Of the vegetable kingdom, there was not a single representative; the most meager of Arctic plants, the most insignificant of lichens, could obtain no hold upon that stony waste. Nor did the animal world assert the feeblest sway. The mineral kingdom reigned supreme.

Captain Servadac's deep dejection was in strange contrast to his general hilarity. Silent and tearful, he stood upon an ice-bound rock, straining his eyes across the boundless vista of the mysterious territory. "It cannot be!" he exclaimed. "We must somehow have mistaken our bearings. True, we have encountered this barrier; but France is there beyond! Yes, France is *there!* Come, count, come! By all that's pitiful, I entreat you, come and explore the farthest verge of the ice-bound track!"

It proved to be a fragment of dis-colored marble.

He pushed onwards along the rugged surface of the rock, but had
not proceeded far before he came to a sudden pause. His foot had come
in contact with something hard beneath the snow, and, stooping down,
he picked up a little block of stony substance, which the first glance
revealed to be of a geological character altogether alien to the universal rocks around. It proved to be a fragment of dis-colored marble,
on which several letters were inscribed, of which the only part at all
decipherable was the syllable "Vil."

"Vil—Villa!" he cried out, in his excitement dropping the marble,
which was broken into atoms by the fall.

What else could this fragment be but the sole surviving remnant of some sumptuous mansion that once had stood on this unrivaled site? Was it not the residue of some edifice that had crowned the luxuriant headland of Antibes, overlooking Nice, and commanding the gorgeous panorama that embraced the Maritime Alps and reached beyond Monaco and Mentone to the Italian height of Bordighera? And did it not give in its sad and too convincing testimony that Antibes itself had been involved in the great destruction? Servadac gazed upon the shattered marble, pensive and disheartened.

Count Timascheff laid his hand kindly on the captain's shoulder, and said, "My friend, do you not remember the motto of the old Hope family?"

He shook his head mournfully.

"*Orbe fracto, spes illoesa,*" continued the count—"Though the world be shattered, hope is unimpaired."

Servadac smiled faintly, and replied that he felt rather compelled to take up the despairing cry of Dante,

"All hope abandon, ye who enter here."

"Nay, not so," answered the count; "for the present at least, let our maxim be *Nil desperandum!*"

CHAPTER XVII.

A SECOND ENIGMA

UPON re-embarking, the bewildered explorers began to discuss the question whether it would not now be desirable to make their way back to Gourbi Island, which was apparently the only spot in their new world from which they could hope to derive their future sustenance. Captain Servadac tried to console himself with the reflection that Gourbi Island was, after all, a fragment of a French colony, and as such almost like a bit of his dear France; and the plan of returning thither was on the point of being adopted, when Lieutenant Procope remarked that they ought to remember that they had not hitherto made an entire circuit of the new shores of the sea on which they were sailing.

"We have," he said, "neither investigated the northern shore from the site of Cape Antibes to the strait that brought us to Gibraltar, nor have we followed the southern shore that stretches from the strait to the Gulf of Cabes. It is the old coast, and not the new, that we have been tracing; as yet, we cannot say positively that there is no outlet to the south; as yet, we cannot assert that no oasis of the African desert has escaped the catastrophe. Perhaps, even here in the north, we may find that Italy and Sicily and the larger islands of the Mediterranean may still maintain their existence."

"I entirely concur with you," said Count Timascheff. "I quite think we ought to make our survey of the confines of this new basin as complete as possible before we withdraw."

Servadac, although he acknowledged the justness of these observations, could not help pleading that the explorations might be deferred until after a visit had been paid to Gourbi Island.

"Depend upon it, captain, you are mistaken," replied the lieutenant; "the right thing to do is to use the *Dobryna* while she is available."

"Available! What do you mean?" asked the count, somewhat taken by surprise.

"I mean," said Procope, "that the farther this Gallia of ours recedes from the sun, the lower the temperature will fall. It is likely enough, I think, that before long the sea will be frozen over, and navigation will be impossible. Already you have learned something of the difficulties of traversing a field of ice, and I am sure, therefore, you will acquiesce in my wish to continue our explorations while the water is still open."

The heavens were illuminated by a superb shower of falling stars,

"No doubt you are right, lieutenant," said the count. "We will continue our search while we can for some remaining fragment of Europe. Who shall tell whether we may not meet with some more survivors from the catastrophe, to whom it might be in our power to afford assistance, before we go into our winter quarters?"

Generous and altogether unselfish as this sentiment really was, it was obviously to the general interest that they should become acquainted, and if possible establish friendly relations, with any human inhabitant who might be sharing their own strange destiny in being rolled away upon a new planet into the infinitude of space. All difference of race, all distinction of nationality, must be merged into the one thought that, few as they were, they were the sole surviving representatives of a world which it seemed exceedingly improbable that they would ever see again; and common sense dictated that they were bound to direct all their energies to insure that their asteroid should at least have a united and sympathizing population.

It was on the 25th of February that the yacht left the little creek in which she had taken refuge, and setting off at full steam eastwards, she continued her way along the northern shore. A brisk breeze tended to increase the keenness of the temperature, the thermometer being, on an average, about two degrees below zero. Salt water freezes only at a lower temperature than fresh; the course of the *Dobryna* was therefore unimpeded by ice, but it could not be concealed that there was the greatest necessity to maintain the utmost possible speed.

The nights continued lovely; the chilled condition of the atmosphere prevented the formation of clouds; the constellations gleamed forth with unsullied luster; and, much as Lieutenant Procope, from nautical considerations, might regret the absence of the moon, he could not do otherwise than own that the magnificent nights of Gallia were such as must awaken the enthusiasm of an astronomer. And, as if to compensate for the loss of the moonlight, the heavens were illuminated by a superb shower of falling stars, far exceeding, both in number and in brilliancy, the phenomena which are commonly distinguished as the August and November meteors; in fact, Gallia was passing through that meteoric ring which is known to lie exterior to the earth's orbit, but almost concentric with it. The rocky coast, its metallic surface reflecting the glow of the dazzling luminaries, appeared literally stippled with light, whilst the sea, as though spattered with burning hailstones, shone with a phosphorescence that was perfectly splendid. So great, however, was the speed at which Gallia was receding from the sun, that this meteoric storm lasted scarcely more than four and twenty hours.

Next day the direct progress of the *Dobryna* was arrested by a long projection of land, which obliged her to turn southwards, until she reached what formerly would have been the southern extremity of Corsica. Of this, however, there was now no trace; the Strait of Bonifacio had been replaced by a vast expanse of water, which had at first all the appearance of being utterly desert; but on the following morning the explorers unexpectedly sighted a little island, which, unless it should prove, as was only too likely, to be of recent origin they concluded, from its situation, must be a portion of the northernmost territory of Sardinia.

The *Dobryna* approached the land as nearly as was prudent, the boat was lowered, and in a few minutes the count and Servadac had landed upon the islet, which was a mere plot of meadow land, not much more than two acres in extent, dotted here and there with a few myrtle-bushes and lentisks, interspersed with some ancient olives. Having ascertained, as they imagined, that the spot was devoid of living creature, they were on the point of returning to their boat, when their attention was arrested by a faint bleating, and immediately afterwards a solitary she-goat came bounding towards the shore. The creature had dark, almost black hair, and small curved horns, and was a specimen of that domestic breed which, with considerable justice, has gained for itself the title of "the poor man's cow." So far from being alarmed at the presence of strangers, the goat ran nimbly towards them, and then, by its movements and plaintive cries, seemed to be enticing them to follow it.

"Come," said Servadac; "let us see where it will lead us; it is more than probable it is not alone."

The count agreed; and the animal, as if comprehending what was said, trotted on gently for about a hundred paces, and stopped in front of a kind of cave or burrow that was half concealed by a grove of lentisks. Here a little girl, seven or eight years of age, with rich brown hair and lustrous dark eyes, beautiful as one of Murillo's angels, was peeping shyly through the branches. Apparently discovering nothing in the aspect of the strangers to excite her apprehensions, the child suddenly gained confidence, darted forwards with outstretched hands, and in a voice, soft and melodious as the language which she spoke, said in Italian:

"I like you; you will not hurt me, will you?"

Nina and her goat Marzy.

"Hurt you, my child?" answered Servadac. "No, indeed; we will be your friends; we will take care of you."

And after a few moments' scrutiny of the pretty maiden, he added:

"Tell us your name, little one."

"Nina!" was the child's reply.

"Well, then, Nina, can you tell us where we are?"

"At Madalena, I think," said the little girl; "at least, I know I was there when that dreadful shock came and altered everything."

The count knew that Madalena was close to Caprera, to the north of Sardinia, which had entirely disappeared in the disaster. By dint of a series of questions, he gained from the child a very intelligent account of her experiences. She told him that she had no parents, and had been employed in taking care of a flock of goats belonging to one of the land-owners, when one day, all of a sudden, everything around her, except this little piece of land, had been swallowed up, and that she and Marzy, her pet goat, had been left quite alone. She went on to say that at first she had been very frightened; but when she found that the earth did not shake any more, she had thanked the great God, and had soon made herself very happy living with Marzy. She had enough food, she said, and had been waiting for a boat to fetch her, and now a boat had come and she was quite ready to go away; only they must let her goat go with her: they would both like so much to get back to the old farm.

"Here, at least, is one nice little inhabitant of Gallia," said Captain Servadac, as he caressed the child and conducted her to the boat.

Half an hour later, both Nina and Marzy were safely quartered on board the yacht. It is needless to say that they received the heartiest of welcomes. The Russian sailors, ever superstitious, seemed almost to regard the coming of the child as the appearance of an angel; and, in-credible as it may seem, more than one of them wondered whether she had wings, and amongst themselves they commonly referred to her as "the little Madonna."

Soon out of sight of Madalena, the *Dobryna* for some hours held a southeasterly course along the shore, which here was fifty leagues in advance of the former coast-line of Italy, demonstrating that a new continent must have been formed, substituted as it were for the old peninsula, of which not a vestige could be identified. At a lati-tude corresponding with the latitude of Rome, the sea took the form of a deep gulf, extending back far beyond the site of the Eternal City; the coast making a wide sweep round to the former position of Calabria, and jutting far beyond the outline of "the boot," which Italy resembles. But the beacon of Messina was not to be discerned; no trace, indeed, survived of any portion of Sicily; the very peak of Etna, 11,000 feet as it had reared itself above the level of the sea, had vanished utterly.

Another sixty leagues to the south, and the *Dobryna* sighted the entrance of the strait which had afforded her so providential a refuge from the tempest, and had conducted her to the fragmentary relic of Gibraltar. Hence to the Gulf of Cabes had been already explored, and as it was universally allowed that it was unnecessary to renew the search in that direction, the lieutenant started off in a transverse course, towards a point hitherto uninvestigated. That point was reached on the 3rd of March, and thence the coast was continuously followed, as it led through what had been Tunis, across the province of Constantine, away to the oasis of Ziban; where, taking a sharp turn, it first reached a latitude of 32°, and then returned again, thus forming a sort of irregular gulf, enclosed by the same unvarying border of mineral concrete. This colossal boundary then stretched away for nearly 150 leagues over the Sahara desert, and, extending to the south of Gourbi Island, occupied what, if Morocco had still existed, would have been its natural frontier.

Adapting her course to these deviations of the coastline, the *Dobryna* was steering northwards, and had barely reached the limit of the bay, when the attention of all on board was arrested by the phenomenon of a volcano, at least 3,000 feet high, its crater crowned with smoke, which occasionally was streaked by tongues of flame.

"A burning mountain!" they exclaimed.

"Gallia, then, has some internal heat," said Servadac.

"And why not, captain?" rejoined the lieutenant. "If our asteroid has carried with it a portion of the old earth's atmosphere, why should it not likewise retain something of its central fire?"

"Ah, well!" said the captain, shrugging his shoulders, "I dare say there is caloric enough in our little world to supply the wants of its population."

Count Timascheff interrupted the silence that followed this conversation by saying, "And now, gentlemen, as our course has brought us on our way once more towards Gibraltar, what do you say to our renewing our acquaintance with the Englishmen? They will be interested in the result of our voyage."

"For my part," said Servadac, "I have no desire that way. They know where to find Gourbi Island; they can betake themselves thither just when they please. They have plenty of provisions. If the water freezes, 120 leagues is no very great distance. The reception they gave us was not so cordial that we need put ourselves out of the way to repeat our visit."

"What you say is too true," replied the count. "I hope we shall show them better manners when they condescend to visit us."

"Ay," said Servadac, "we must remember that we are all one people now; no longer Russian, French, or English. Nationality is extinct."

"I am sadly afraid, however," continued the count, "that an Englishman will be an Englishman ever."

"Yes," said the captain, "that is always their failing."

And thus all further thought of making their way again to the little garrison of Gibraltar was abandoned.

But even if their spirit of courtesy had disposed them to renew their acquaintance with the British officers, there were two circumstances that just then would have rendered such a proposal very unadvisable. In the first place, Lieutenant Procope was convinced that it could not be much longer now before the sea would be entirely frozen; and, besides this, the consumption of their coal, through the speed they had maintained, had been so great that there was only too much reason to fear that fuel would fail them. Anyhow, the strictest economy was necessary, and it was accordingly resolved that the voyage should not be much prolonged. Beyond the volcanic peak, moreover, the waters seemed to expand into a boundless ocean, and it might be a thing full of risk to be frozen up while the yacht was so inadequately provisioned. Taking all these things into account, it was agreed that further investigations should be deferred to a more favorable season, and that, without delay, the *Dobryna* should return to Gourbi Island.

This decision was especially welcome to Hector Servadac, who, throughout the whole of the last five weeks, had been agitated by much anxious thought on account of the faithful servant he had left behind.

The transit from the volcano to the island was not long, and was marked by only one noticeable incident. This was the finding of a second mysterious document, in character precisely similar to what they had found before. The writer of it was evidently engaged upon a calculation, probably continued from day to day, as to the motions of the planet Gallia upon its orbit, and committing the results of his reckonings to the waves as the channel of communication.

Instead of being enclosed in a telescope-case, it was this time secured in a preserved-meat tin, hermetically sealed, and stamped with the same initials on the wax that fastened it. The greatest care was used in opening it, and it was found to contain the following message:

"Gallia (?)
Ab sole, au 1 mars, dist. 78,000,000 l.!
Chemin parcouru de fev. à mars: 59,000,000 l.!
Va bene! All right! Nil desperandum!
"Enchanté!"

"Another enigma!" exclaimed Servadac; "and still no intelligible signature, and no address. No clearing up of the mystery!"

"I have no doubt, in my own mind," said the count, "that it is one of a series. It seems to me probable that they are being sent broadcast upon the sea."

"I wonder where the hare-brained *savant* that writes them can be living?" observed Servadac.

"Very likely he may have met with the fate of Æsop's abstracted astronomer, who found himself at the bottom of a well."

"Ay; but where *is* that well?" demanded the captain.

This was a question which the count was incapable of settling; and they could only speculate afresh as to whether the author of the riddles was dwelling upon some solitary island, or, like themselves, was navigating the waters of the new Mediterranean. But they could detect nothing to guide them to a definite decision.

After thoughtfully regarding the document for some time. Lieutenant Procope proceeded to observe that he believed the paper might be considered as genuine, and accordingly, taking its statements as reliable, he deduced two important conclusions: first, that whereas, in the month of January, the distance traveled by the planet (hypothetically called Gallia) had been recorded as 82,000,000 leagues, the distance traveled in February was only 59,000,000 leagues—a difference of 23,000,000 leagues in one month; secondly, that the distance of the planet from the sun, which on the 15th of February had been 59,000,000 leagues, was on the 1st of March 78,000,000 leagues—an increase of 19,000,000 leagues in a fortnight. Thus, in proportion as Gallia receded from the sun, so did the rate of speed diminish by which she traveled along her orbit; facts to be observed in perfect conformity with the known laws of celestial mechanism.

"And your inference?" asked the count.

"My inference," replied the lieutenant, "is a confirmation of my surmise that we are following an orbit decidedly elliptical, although we have not yet the material to determine its eccentricity."

"As the writer adheres to the appellation of Gallia, do you not think," asked the count, "that we might call these new waters the Gallian Sea?"

"There can be no reason to the contrary, count," replied the lieutenant; "and as such I will insert it upon my new chart."

"Our friend," said Servadac, "seems to be more and more gratified with the condition of things; not only has he adopted our motto, '*Nil desperandum!*' but see how enthusiastically he has wound up with his '*Enchante!*'"

The conversation dropped.

A few hours later the man on watch announced that Gourbi Island was in sight.

CHAPTER XVIII.

THE *Dobryna* was now back again at the island. Her cruise had lasted from the 31st of January to the 5th of March, a period of thirty-five days (for it was leap year), corresponding to seventy days as accomplished by the new little world.

Many a time during his absence Hector Servadac had wondered how his present vicissitudes would end, and he had felt some misgivings as to whether he should ever again set foot upon the island, and see his faithful orderly, so that it was not without emotion that he had approached the coast of the sole remaining fragment of Algerian soil. But his apprehensions were groundless; Gourbi Island was just as he had left it, with nothing unusual in its aspect, except that a very peculiar cloud was hovering over it, at an altitude of little more than a hundred feet. As the yacht approached the shore, this cloud appeared to rise and fall as if acted upon by some invisible agency, and the captain, after watching it carefully, perceived that it was not an accumulation of vapors at all, but a dense mass of birds packed as closely together as a swarm of herrings, and uttering deafening and discordant cries, amidst which from time to time the noise of the report of a gun could be plainly distinguished.

The *Dobryna* signalized her arrival by firing her cannon, and dropped anchor in the little port of the Shelif. Almost within a minute Ben Zoof was seen running, gun in hand, towards the shore; he cleared the last ridge of rocks at a single bound, and then suddenly halted. For a few seconds he stood motionless, his eyes fixed, as if obeying the instructions of a drill sergeant, on a point some fifteen yards distant, his whole attitude indicating submission and respect; but the sight of the captain, who was landing, was too much for his equanimity, and darting forward, he seized his master's hand and covered it with kisses. Instead, however, of uttering any expressions of welcome or rejoicing at the captain's return, Ben Zoof broke out into the most vehement ejaculations.

"Thieves, captain! beastly thieves! Bedouins! pirates! devils!"

"Why, Ben Zoof, what's the matter?" said Servadac soothingly.

"They are thieves! downright, desperate thieves! those infernal birds! That's what's the matter. It is a good thing you have come. Here have I for a whole month been spending my powder and shot upon them, and the more I kill them, the worse they get; and yet, if I were to leave them alone, we should not have a grain of corn upon the island."

It was soon evident that the orderly had only too much cause for alarm. The crops had ripened rapidly during the excessive heat of January, when the orbit of Gallia was being traversed at its perihelion, and were now exposed to the depredations of many thousands of birds; and although a goodly number of stacks attested the industry of Ben Zoof during the time of the *Dobryna*'s voyage, it was only too apparent that the portion of the harvest that remained ungathered was liable to the most imminent risk of being utterly devoured. It was, perhaps, only natural that this clustered mass of birds, as representing the whole of the feathered tribe upon the surface of Gallia, should resort to Gourbi Island, of which the meadows seemed to be the only spot from which they could get sustenance at all; but as this sustenance would be obtained at the expense, and probably to the serious detriment, of the human population, it was absolutely necessary that every possible resistance should be made to the devastation that was threatened.

Once satisfied that Servadac and his friends would cooperate with him in the raid upon "the thieves," Ben Zoof became calm and content, and began to make various inquiries. "And what has become," he said, "of all our old comrades in Africa?"

"As far as I can tell you," answered the captain, "they are all in Africa still; only Africa isn't by any means where we expected to find it."

"And France? Montmartre?" continued Ben Zoof eagerly. Here was the cry of the poor fellow's heart.

As briefly as he could, Servadac endeavored to explain the true condition of things; he tried to communicate the fact that Paris, France, Europe, nay, the whole world was more than eighty millions of leagues away from Gourbi Island; as gently and cautiously as he could he expressed his fear that they might never see Europe, France, Paris, Montmartre again.

"No, no, sir!" protested Ben Zoof emphatically; "that is all non-sense. It is altogether out of the question to suppose that we are not to see Montmartre again." And the orderly shook his head resolutely, with the air of a man determined, in spite of argument, to adhere to his own opinion.

"Very good, my brave fellow," replied Servadac, "hope on, hope while you may. The message has come to us over the sea, 'Never despair'; but one thing, nevertheless, is certain; we must forthwith commence arrangements for making this island our permanent home."

Captain Servadac now led the way to the gourbi, which, by his servant's exertions, had been entirely rebuilt; and here he did the honors of his modest establishment to his two guests, the count and the lieutenant, and gave a welcome, too, to little Nina, who had accompanied them on shore, and between whom and Ben Zoof the most friendly relations had already been established.

The adjacent building continued in good preservation, and Captain Servadac's satisfaction was very great in finding the two horses, Zephyr and Galette, comfortably housed there and in good condition.

After the enjoyment of some refreshment, the party proceeded to a general consultation as to what steps must be taken for their future welfare. The most pressing matter that came before them was the consideration of the means to be adopted to enable the inhabitants of Gallia to survive the terrible cold, which, in their ignorance of the true eccentricity of their orbit, might, for aught they knew, last for an almost indefinite period. Fuel was far from abundant; of coal there was none; trees and shrubs were few in number, and to cut them down in prospect of the cold seemed a very questionable policy; but there was no doubt some expedient must be devised to prevent disaster, and that without delay.

The victualing of the little colony offered no immediate difficulty. Water was abundant, and the cisterns could hardly fail to be replenished by the numerous streams that meandered along the plains; moreover, the Gallian Sea would ere long be frozen over, and the melted ice (water in its congealed state being divested of every particle of salt) would afford a supply of drink that could not be exhausted. The crops that were now ready for the harvest, and the flocks and herds scattered over the island, would form an ample reserve. There was little doubt that throughout the winter the soil would remain unproductive, and no fresh fodder for domestic animals could then be obtained; it would therefore be necessary, if the exact duration of Gallia's year should ever be calculated, to proportion the number of animals to be reserved to the real length of the winter.

The next thing requisite was to arrive at a true estimate of the number of the population. Without including the thirteen Englishmen at Gibraltar, about whom he was not particularly disposed to give himself much concern at present, Servadac put down the names of the eight Russians, the two Frenchman, and the little Italian girl, eleven in all, as the entire list of the inhabitants of Gourbi Island.

"Oh, pardon me," interposed Ben Zoof, "you are mistaking the state of the case altogether. You will be surprised to learn that the total of people on the island is double that. It is twenty-two."

"Twenty-two!" exclaimed the captain; "twenty-two people on this island? What do you mean?"

"The opportunity has not occurred," answered Ben Zoof, "for me to tell you before, but I have had company."

"Explain yourself, Ben Zoof," said Servadac. "What company have you had?"

"You could not suppose," replied the orderly, "that my own unassisted hands could have accomplished all that harvest work that you see has been done."

"I confess," said Lieutenant Procope, "we do not seem to have noticed that."

"Well, then," said Ben Zoof, "if you will be good enough to come with me for about a mile, I shall be able to show you my companions. But we must take our guns."

"Why take our guns?" asked Servadac. "I hope we are not going to fight."

"No, not with men," said Ben Zoof; "but it does not answer to throw a chance away for giving battle to those thieves of birds."

Leaving little Nina and her goat in the gourbi, Servadac, Count Timascheff, and the lieutenant, greatly mystified, took up their guns and followed the orderly. All along their way they made unsparing slaughter of the birds that hovered over and around them. Nearly every species of the feathered tribe seemed to have its representative in that living cloud. There were wild ducks in thousands; snipe, larks, rooks, and swallows; a countless variety of sea-birds—widgeons, gulls, and seamews; beside a quantity of game—quails, partridges, and woodcocks. The sportsmen did their best; every shot told; and the depredators fell by dozens on either hand.

They made unsparing slaughter of the birds that hovered over and around them

Instead of following the northern shore of the island, Ben Zoof cut obliquely across the plain. Making their progress with the unwonted rapidity which was attributable to their specific lightness, Servadac and his companions soon found themselves near a grove of sycamores and eucalyptus massed in picturesque confusion at the base of a little hill. Here they halted.

"Ah! the vagabonds! the rascals! the thieves!" suddenly exclaimed Ben Zoof, stamping his foot with rage.

"How now? Are your friends the birds at their pranks again?" asked the captain.

"No, I don't mean the birds: I mean those lazy beggars that are shirking their work. Look here; look there!" And as Ben Zoof spoke, he pointed to some scythes, and sickles, and other implements of husbandry that had been left upon the ground.

"What is it you mean?" asked Servadac, getting somewhat impatient.

"Hush, hush! listen!" was all Ben Zoof's reply; and he raised his finger as if in warning.

Listening attentively, Servadac and his associates could distinctly recognize a human voice, accompanied by the notes of a guitar and by the measured click of castanets.

"Spaniards!" said Servadac.

"No mistake about that, sir," replied Ben Zoof; "a Spaniard would rattle his castanets at the cannon's mouth."

"But what is the meaning of it all?" asked the captain, more puzzled than before.

"Hark!" said Ben Zoof; "it is the old man's turn."

And then a voice, at once gruff and harsh, was heard vociferating, "My money! my money! when will you pay me my money? Pay me what you owe me, you miserable majos."

Meanwhile the song continued:

"*Tu sandunga y cigarro,*
Y una cana de Jerez,
Mi jamelgo y un trabuco,
Que mas gloria puede haver?"

Servadac's knowledge of Gascon enabled him partially to comprehend the rollicking tenor of the Spanish patriotic air, but his attention was again arrested by the voice of the old man growling savagely, "Pay me you shall; yes, by the God of Abraham, you shall pay me."

"A Jew!" exclaimed Servadac.

"Ay, sir, a German Jew," said Ben Zoof.

The party was on the point of entering the thicket, when a singular spectacle made them pause. A group of Spaniards had just begun dancing their national fandango, and the extraordinary lightness

which had become the physical property of every object in the new
planet made the dancers bound to a height of thirty feet or more into
the air, considerably above the tops of the trees. What followed was
irresistibly comic. Four sturdy majos had dragged along with them
an old man incapable of resistance, and compelled him, *nolens volens*,
to join in the dance; and as they all kept appearing and disappearing
above the bank of foliage, their grotesque attitudes, combined with the
pitiable countenance of their helpless victim, could not do otherwise
than recall most forcibly the story of Sancho Panza tossed in a blanket
by the merry drapers of Segovia.

He rushed with an effort towards Servadac.

Servadac, the count, Procope, and Ben Zoof now proceeded to make their way through the thicket until they came to a little glade, where two men were stretched idly on the grass, one of them playing the guitar, and the other a pair of castanets; both were exploding with laughter, as they urged the performers to greater and yet greater exertions in the dance. At the sight of strangers they paused in their music, and simultaneously the dancers, with their victim, alighted gently on the sward.

Isaac Hakkabut

Breathless and half exhausted as was the Jew, he rushed with an effort towards Servadac, and exclaimed in French, marked by a strong

Teutonic accent, "Oh, my lord governor, help me, help! These rascals defraud me of my rights; they rob me; but, in the name of the God of Israel, I ask you to see justice done!"

The captain glanced inquiringly towards Ben Zoof, and the orderly, by a significant nod, made his master understand that he was to play the part that was implied by the title. He took the cue, and promptly ordered the Jew to hold his tongue at once. The man bowed his head in servile submission, and folded his hands upon his breast.

Servadac surveyed him leisurely. He was a man of about fifty, but from his appearance might well have been taken for at least ten years older. Small and skinny, with eyes bright and cunning, a hooked nose, a short yellow beard, unkempt hair, huge feet, and long bony hands, he presented all the typical characteristics of the German Jew, the heartless, wily usurer, the hardened miser and skinflint. As iron is attracted by the magnet, so was this Shylock attracted by the sight of gold, nor would he have hesitated to draw the life-blood of his creditors, if by such means he could secure his claims.

His name was Isaac Hakkabut, and he was a native of Cologne. Nearly the whole of his time, however, he informed Captain Servadac, had been spent upon the sea, his real business being that of a merchant trading at all the ports of the Mediterranean. A tartan, a small vessel of two hundred tons burden, conveyed his entire stock of merchandise, and, to say the truth, was a sort of floating emporium, conveying nearly every possible article of commerce, from a lucifer match to the radiant fabrics of Frankfort and Epinal. Without wife or children, and having no settled home, Isaac Hakkabut lived almost entirely on board the *Hansa*, as he had named his tartan; and engaging a mate, with a crew of three men, as being adequate to work so light a craft, he cruised along the coasts of Algeria, Tunis, Egypt, Turkey, and Greece, visiting, moreover, most of the harbors of the Levant. Careful to be always well supplied with the products in most general demand—coffee, sugar, rice, tobacco, cotton stuffs, and gunpowder—and being at all times ready to barter, and prepared to deal in secondhand wares, he had contrived to amass considerable wealth.

On the eventful night of the 1st of January the *Hansa* had been at Ceuta, the point on the coast of Morocco exactly opposite Gibraltar. The mate and three sailors had all gone on shore, and, in common with many of their fellow-creatures, had entirely disappeared; but the most projecting rock of Ceuta had been undisturbed by the general catastrophe, and half a score of Spaniards, who had happened to be upon it, had escaped with their lives. They were all Andalusian majos, agricultural laborers, and naturally as careless and apathetic as men of their class usually are, but they could not help being very considerably embarrassed when they discovered that they were left in solitude upon a detached and isolated rock. They took what mutual counsel they could, but became only more and more perplexed. One of them was named Negrete, and he, as having traveled somewhat more than the rest, was tacitly recognized as a sort of leader; but although he was by far the most enlightened of them all, he was quite incapable of forming the least conception of the nature of what had occurred. The one thing upon which they could not fail to be conscious was that they had no prospect of obtaining provisions, and consequently their first business was to devise a scheme for getting away from their present abode. The *Hansa* was lying off shore. The Spaniards would not have had the slightest hesitation in summarily taking possession of her, but their utter ignorance of seamanship made them reluctantly come to the conclusion that the more prudent policy was to make terms with the owner.

And now came a singular part of the story. Negrete and his companions had meanwhile received a visit from two English officers from Gibraltar. What passed between them the Jew did not know; he only knew that, immediately after the conclusion of the interview, Negrete came to him and ordered him to set sail at once for the nearest point of Morocco. The Jew, afraid to disobey, but with his eye ever upon the main chance, stipulated that at the end of their voyage the Spaniards should pay for their passage—terms to which, as they would to any other, they did not demur, knowing that they had not the slightest intention of giving him a single real.

The *Hansa* had weighed anchor on the 3rd of February. The wind blew from the west, and consequently the working of the tartan was easy enough. The unpracticed sailors had only to hoist their sails and, though they were quite unconscious of the fact, the breeze carried them to the only spot upon the little world they occupied which could afford them a refuge.

Thus it fell out that one morning Ben Zoof, from his lookout on Gourbi Island, saw a ship, not the *Dobryna*, appear upon the horizon, and make quietly down towards what had formerly been the right bank of the Shelif.

Such was Ben Zoof's version of what had occurred, as he had gathered it from the new-comers. He wound up his recital by remarking that the cargo of the *Hansa* would be of immense service to them; he expected, indeed, that Isaac Hakkabut would be difficult to manage, but considered there could be no harm in appropriating the goods for the common welfare, since there could be no opportunity now for selling them.

Ben Zoof added, "And as to the difficulties between the Jew and his passengers, I told him that the governor general was absent on a tour of inspection, and that he would see everything equitably settled."

Smiling at his orderly's tactics, Servadac turned to Hakkabut, and told him that he would take care that his claims should be duly investigated and all proper demands should be paid. The man appeared satisfied, and, for the time at least, desisted from his complaints and importunities.

When the Jew had retired, Count Timascheff asked, "But how in the world can you ever make those fellows pay anything?"

"They have lots of money," said Ben Zoof.

"Not likely," replied the count; "when did you ever know Spaniards like them to have lots of money?"

"But I have seen it myself," said Ben Zoof; "and it is English money."

"English money!" echoed Servadac; and his mind again reverted to the excursion made by the colonel and the major from Gibraltar, about which they had been so reticent. "We must inquire more about this," he said.

Then, addressing Count Timascheff, he added, "Altogether, I think the countries of Europe are fairly represented by the population of Gallia."

"True, captain," answered the count; "we have only a fragment of a world, but it contains natives of France, Russia, Italy, Spain, and England. Even Germany may be said to have a representative in the person of this miserable Jew."

"And even in him," said Servadac, "perhaps we shall not find so indifferent a representative as we at present imagine."

CHAPTER XIX.

GALLIA'S GOVERNOR GENERAL

THE Spaniards who had arrived on board the *Hansa* consisted of nine men and a lad of twelve years of age, named Pablo. They all received Captain Servadac, whom Ben Zoof introduced as the governor general, with due respect, and returned quickly to their separate tasks. The captain and his friends, followed at some distance by the eager Jew, soon left the glade and directed their steps towards the coast where the *Hansa* was moored.

As they went they discussed their situation. As far as they had ascertained, except Gourbi Island, the sole surviving fragments of the Old World were four small islands: the bit of Gibraltar occupied by the Englishmen; Ceuta, which had just been left by the Spaniards; Madalena, where they had picked up the little Italian girl; and the site of the tomb of Saint Louis on the coast of Tunis. Around these there was stretched out the full extent of the Gallian Sea, which apparently comprised about one-half of the Mediterranean, the whole being encompassed by a barrier like a framework of precipitous cliffs, of an origin and a substance alike unknown.

Of all these spots only two were known to be inhabited: Gibraltar, where the thirteen Englishmen were amply provisioned for some years to come, and their own Gourbi Island. Here there was a population of twenty-two, who would all have to subsist upon the natural products of the soil. It was indeed not to be forgotten that, perchance, upon some remote and undiscovered isle there might be the solitary writer of the mysterious papers which they had found, and if so, that would raise the census of their new asteroid to an aggregate of thirty-six.

Even upon the supposition that at some future date the whole population should be compelled to unite and find a residence upon Gourbi Island, there did not appear any reason to question but that eight hundred acres of rich soil, under good management, would yield them all an ample sustenance. The only critical matter was how long the cold season would last; every hope depended upon the land again becoming productive; at present, it seemed impossible to determine, even if Gallia's orbit were really elliptic, when she would reach her aphelion, and it was consequently necessary that the Gallians for the time being should reckon on nothing beyond their actual and present resources.

These resources were, first, the provisions of the *Dobryna*, consisting of preserved meat, sugar, wine, brandy, and other stores sufficient for about two months; secondly, the valuable cargo of the *Hansa*, which, sooner or later, the owner, whether he would or not, must be compelled to surrender for the common benefit; and lastly, the produce of the island, animal and vegetable, which with proper economy might be made to last for a considerable period.

In the course of the conversation, Count Timascheff took an opportunity of saying that, as Captain Servadac had already been presented to the Spaniards as governor of the island, he thought it advisable that he should really assume that position.

"Every body of men," he observed, "must have a head, and you, as a Frenchman, should, I think, take the command of this fragment of a French colony. My men, I can answer for it, are quite prepared to recognize you as their superior officer."

"Most unhesitatingly," replied Servadac, "I accept the post with all its responsibilities. We understand each other so well that I feel sure we shall try and work together for the common good; and even if it be our fate never again to behold our fellow creatures, I have no misgivings but that we shall be able to cope with whatever difficulties may be before us."

As he spoke, he held out his hand. The count took it, at the same time making a slight bow. It was the first time since their meeting that the two men had shaken hands; on the other hand, not a single word about their former rivalry had ever escaped their lips; perhaps that was all forgotten now.

The silence of a few moments was broken by Servadac saying, "Do you not think we ought to explain our situation to the Spaniards?"

"No, no, your Excellency," burst in Ben Zoof, emphatically; "the fellows are chicken-hearted enough already; only tell them what has happened, and in sheer despondency they will not do another stroke of work."

"Besides," said Lieutenant Procope, who took very much the same view as the orderly, "they are so miserably ignorant they would be sure to misunderstand you."

"Understand or misunderstand," replied Servadac, "I do not think it matters. They would not care. They are all fatalists. Only give them a guitar and their castanets, and they will soon forget all care and anxiety. For my own part, I must adhere to my belief that it will be advisable to tell them everything. Have you any opinion to offer, count?"

"My own opinion, captain, coincides entirely with yours. I have followed the plan of explaining all I could to my men on board the *Dobryna*, and no inconvenience has arisen."

"Well, then, so let it be," said the captain; adding, "It is not likely that these Spaniards are so ignorant as not to have noticed the change in the length of the days; neither can they be unaware of the physical changes that have transpired. They shall certainly be told that we are being carried away into unknown regions of space, and that this island is nearly all that remains of the Old World."

"Ha! ha!" laughed Ben Zoof, aloud; "it will be fine sport to watch the old Jew's face, when he is made to comprehend that he is flying away millions and millions of leagues from all his debtors."

Isaac Hakkabut was about fifty yards behind, and was consequently unable to overhear the conversation. He went shambling along, half whimpering and not unfrequently invoking the God of Israel; but every now and then a cunning light gleamed from his eyes, and his lips became compressed with a grim significance.

None of the recent phenomena had escaped his notice, and more than once he had attempted to entice Ben Zoof into conversation upon the subject; but the orderly made no secret of his antipathy to him, and generally replied to his advances either by satire or by banter. He told him that he had everything to gain under the new system of nights and days, for, instead of living the Jew's ordinary life of a century, he would reach to the age of two centuries; and he congratulated him upon the circumstance of things having become so light, because it would prevent him feeling the burden of his years. At another time he would declare that, to an old usurer like him, it could not matter in the least what had become of the moon, as he could not possibly have advanced any money upon her. And when Isaac, undaunted by his jeers, persevered in besetting him with questions, he tried to silence him by saying, "Only wait till the governor general comes; he is a shrewd fellow, and will tell you all about it."

"But will he protect my property?" poor Isaac would ask tremulously.

The *Hansa* had anchored in an exposed bay.

"To be sure he will! He would confiscate it all rather than that you should be robbed of it."

With this Job's comfort the Jew had been obliged to content himself as best he could, and to await the promised arrival of the governor.

When Servadac and his companions reached the shore, they found that the *Hansa* had anchored in an exposed bay, protected but barely by a few projecting rocks, and in such a position that a gale rising from the west would inevitably drive her on to the land, where she must be dashed in pieces. It would be the height of folly to leave her in her present moorings; without loss of time she must be brought round to the mouth of the Shelif, in immediate proximity to the Russian yacht.

The consciousness that his tartan was the subject of discussion made the Jew give way to such vehement ejaculations of anxiety, that Servadac turned round and peremptorily ordered him to desist from his clamor. Leaving the old man under the surveillance of the count and Ben Zoof, the captain and the lieutenant stepped into a small boat and were soon alongside the floating emporium.

A very short inspection sufficed to make them aware that both the tartan and her cargo were in a perfect state of preservation. In the hold were sugar-loaves by hundreds, chests of tea, bags of coffee, hogsheads of tobacco, pipes of wine, casks of brandy, barrels of dried herrings, bales of cotton, clothing of every kind, shoes of all sizes, caps of various shape, tools, household utensils, china and earthenware, reams of paper, bottles of ink, boxes of lucifer matches, blocks of salt, bags of pepper and spices, a stock of huge Dutch cheeses, and a collection of almanacs and miscellaneous literature. At a rough guess the value could not be much under pounds 5,000 sterling. A new cargo had been taken in only a few days before the catastrophe, and it had been Isaac Hakkabut's intention to cruise from Ceuta to Tripoli, calling wherever he had reason to believe there was likely to be a market for any of his commodities.

"A fine haul, lieutenant," said the captain.

"Yes, indeed," said the lieutenant; "but what if the owner refuses to part with it?"

"No fear; no fear," replied the captain. "As soon as ever the old rascal finds that there are no more Arabs or Algerians for him to fleece, he will be ready enough to transact a little business with us. We will pay him by bills of acceptance on some of his old friends in the Old World."

"But why should he want any payment?" inquired the lieutenant. "Under the circumstances, he must know that you have a right to make a requisition of his goods."

"No, no," quickly rejoined Servadac; "we will not do that. Just because the fellow is a German we shall not be justified in treating him
in German fashion. We will transact our business in a business way.
Only let him once realize that he is on a new globe, with no prospect
of getting back to the old one, and he will be ready enough to come to
terms with us."

"Perhaps you are right," replied the lieutenant; "I hope you are.
But anyhow, it will not do to leave the tartan here; not only would she
be in danger in the event of a storm, but it is very questionable whether
she could resist the pressure of the ice, if the water were to freeze."

"Quite true, Procope; and accordingly I give you the commission
to see that your crew bring her round to the Shelif as soon as may be."

"To-morrow morning it shall be done," answered the lieutenant,
promptly.

Upon returning to the shore, it was arranged that the whole of the
little colony should forthwith assemble at the gourbi. The Spaniards
were summoned and Isaac, although he could only with reluctance take
his wistful gaze from his tartan, obeyed the governor's orders to follow.

An hour later and the entire population of twenty-two had met
in the chamber adjoining the gourbi. Young Pablo made his first acquaintance with little Nina, and the child seemed highly delighted to
find a companion so nearly of her own age. Leaving the children to
entertain each other, Captain Servadac began his address.

Before entering upon further explanation, he said that he counted
upon the cordial co-operation of them all for the common welfare.

Negrete interrupted him by declaring that no promises or pledges
could be given until he and his countrymen knew how soon they could
be sent back to Spain.

"To Spain, do you say?" asked Servadac.

"To Spain!" echoed Isaac Hakkabut, with a hideous yell. "Do they
expect to go back to Spain till they have paid their debts? Your Excellency, they owe me twenty reals apiece for their passage here; they owe
me two hundred reals. Are they to be allowed...?"

"Silence, Mordecai, you fool!" shouted Ben Zoof, who was accustomed to call the Jew by any Hebrew name that came uppermost to
his memory. "Silence!"

Servadac was disposed to appease the old man's anxiety by promising to see that justice was ultimately done; but, in a fever of frantic

excitement, he went on to implore that he might have the loan of a few sailors to carry his ship to Algiers.

Captain Servadac began his address.

"I will pay you honestly; I will pay you *well*," he cried; but his ingrained propensity for making a good bargain prompted him to add, "provided you do not overcharge me."

Ben Zoof was about again to interpose some angry exclamation; but Servadac checked him, and continued in Spanish: "Listen to me, my friends. Something very strange has happened. A most wonderful event has cut us off from Spain, from France, from Italy, from every country of Europe. In fact, we have left the Old World entirely. Of the whole earth, nothing remains except this island on which you are now taking refuge. The old globe is far, far away. Our present abode is but an insignificant fragment that is left. I dare not tell you that there is any chance of your ever again seeing your country or your homes."

He paused. The Spaniards evidently had no conception of his meaning.

Negrete begged him to tell them all again. He repeated all that he had said, and by introducing some illustrations from familiar things, he succeeded to a certain extent in conveying some faint idea of the convulsion that had happened. The event was precisely what he had foretold. The communication was received by all alike with the most supreme indifference.

Hakkabut did not say a word. He had listened with manifest attention, his lips twitching now and then as if suppressing a smile. Servadac turned to him, and asked whether he was still disposed to put out to sea and make for Algiers.

The Jew gave a broad grin, which, however, he was careful to conceal from the Spaniards. "Your Excellency jests," he said in French; and turning to Count Timascheff, he added in Russian: "The governor has made up a wonderful tale."

The count turned his back in disgust, while the Jew sidled up to little Nina and muttered in Italian. "A lot of lies, pretty one; a lot of lies!"

"Confound the knave!" exclaimed Ben Zoof; "he gabbles every tongue under the sun!"

"Yes," said Servadac; "but whether he speaks French, Russian, Spanish, German, or Italian, he is neither more nor less than a Jew."

CHAPTER XX.

A LIGHT ON THE HORIZON

On the following day, without giving himself any further concern about the Jew's incredulity, the captain gave orders for the *Hansa* to be shifted round to the harbor of the Shelif. Hakkabut raised no objection, not only because he was aware that the move insured the immediate safety of his tartan, but because he was secretly entertaining the hope that he might entice away two or three of the *Dobryna's* crew and make his escape to Algiers or some other port.

Operations now commenced for preparing proper winter quarters. Spaniards and Russians alike joined heartily in the work, the diminution of atmospheric pressure and of the force of attraction contributing such an increase to their muscular force as materially facilitated all their labors.

The first business was to accommodate the building adjacent to the gourbi to the wants of the little colony. Here for the present the Spaniards were lodged, the Russians retaining their berths upon the yacht, while the Jew was permitted to pass his nights upon the *Hansa*. This arrangement, however, could be only temporary. The time could not be far distant when ships' sides and ordinary walls would fail to give an adequate protection from the severity of the cold that must be expected; the stock of fuel was too limited to keep up a permanent supply of heat in their present quarters, and consequently they must be driven to seek some other refuge, the internal temperature of which would at least be bearable.

The plan that seemed to commend itself most to their consideration was, that they should dig out for themselves some subterraneous pits similar to "silos," such as are used as receptacles for grain. They presumed that when the surface of Gallia should be covered by a thick layer of ice, which is a bad conductor of heat, a sufficient amount of warmth for animal vitality might still be retained in excavations of this kind.

After a long consultation they failed to devise any better expedient, and were forced to resign themselves to this species of troglodyte existence.

Spaniards and Russians alike joined heartily in the work

In one respect they congratulated themselves that they should be better off than many of the whalers in the polar seas, for as it is impossible to get below the surface of a frozen ocean, these adventurers have to seek refuge in huts of wood and snow erected on their ships, which at best can give but slight protection from extreme cold; but here, with a solid subsoil, the Gallians might hope to dig down a hundred feet or so and secure for themselves a shelter that would enable them to brave the hardest severity of climate.

The order, then, was at once given. The work was commenced. A stock of shovels, mattocks, and pick-axes was brought from the gourbi, and with Ben Zoof as overseer, both Spanish majos and Russian sailors set to work with a will.

It was not long, however, before a discovery, more unexpected than agreeable, suddenly arrested their labors. The spot chosen for the excavation was a little to the right of the gourbi, on a slight elevation of the soil. For the first day everything went on prosperously enough; but at a depth of eight feet below the surface, the navvies came in contact with a hard surface, upon which all their tools failed to make the slightest impression. Servadac and the count were at once apprised of the fact, and had little difficulty in recognizing the substance that had revealed itself as the very same which composed the shores as well as the subsoil of the Gallian sea. It evidently formed the universal substructure of the new asteroid. Means for hollowing it failed them utterly. Harder and more resisting than granite, it could not be blasted by ordinary powder; dynamite alone could suffice to rend it.

The disappointment was very great. Unless some means of protection were speedily devised, death seemed to be staring them in the face. Were the figures in the mysterious documents correct? If so, Gallia must now be a hundred millions of leagues from the sun, nearly three times the distance of the earth at the remotest section of her orbit. The intensity of the solar light and heat, too, was very seriously diminishing, although Gourbi Island (being on the equator of an orb which had its axes always perpendicular to the plane in which it revolved) enjoyed a position that gave it a permanent summer. But no advantage of this kind could compensate for the remoteness of the sun. The temperature fell steadily; already, to the discomfiture of the little Italian girl, nurtured in sunshine, ice was beginning to form in the crevices of the rocks, and manifestly the time was impending when the sea itself would freeze.

Some shelter must be found before the temperature should fall to 60 degrees below zero. Otherwise death was inevitable. Hitherto, for the last few days, the thermometer had been registering an average of about 6 degrees below zero, and it had become matter of experience that the stove, although replenished with all the wood that was available, was altogether inadequate to effect any sensible mitigation of the severity of the cold. Nor could any amount of fuel be enough. It was certain that ere long the very mercury and spirit in the thermometers would be congealed. Some other resort must assuredly be soon found, or they must perish. That was clear.

The idea of betaking themselves to the *Dobryna* and *Hansa* could not for a moment be seriously entertained; not only did the structure of the vessels make them utterly insufficient to give substantial shelter, but they were totally unfitted to be trusted as to their stability when exposed to the enormous pressure of the accumulated ice.

Neither Servadac, nor the count, nor Lieutenant Procope were men to be easily disheartened, but it could not be concealed that they felt themselves in circumstances by which they were equally harassed and perplexed. The sole expedient that their united counsel could suggest was to obtain a refuge below ground, and *that* was denied them by the strange and impenetrable substratum of the soil; yet hour by hour the sun's disc was lessening in its dimensions, and although at midday some faint radiance and glow were to be distinguished, during the night the painfulness of the cold was becoming almost intolerable.

Mounted upon Zephyr and Galette, the captain and the count scoured the island in search of some available retreat. Scarcely a yard of ground was left unexplored, the horses clearing every obstacle as if they were, like Pegasus, furnished with wings. But all in vain. Soundings were made again and again, but invariably with the same result; the rock, hard as adamant, never failed to reveal itself within a few feet of the surface of the ground.

The excavation of any silo being thus manifestly hopeless, there seemed nothing to be done except to try and render the buildings alongside the gourbi impervious to frost. To contribute to the supply of fuel, orders were given to collect every scrap of wood, dry or green, that the island produced; and this involved the necessity of felling the numerous trees that were scattered over the plain. But toil as they might at the accumulation of firewood, Captain Servadac and his companions could not resist the conviction that the consumption of a very short period would exhaust the total stock. And what would happen then?

Studious if possible to conceal his real misgivings, and anxious that the rest of the party should be affected as little as might be by his own uneasiness, Servadac would wander alone about the island, racking his brain for an idea that would point the way out of the serious difficulty. But still all in vain.

The horses clearing every obstacle as if they were, like Pegasus, furnished with wings.

One day he suddenly came upon Ben Zoof, and asked him whether he had no plan to propose. The orderly shook his head, but after a few moments' pondering, said: "Ah! master, if only we were at Montmartre, we would get shelter in the charming stone-quarries."

"Idiot!" replied the captain, angrily, "if we were at Montmartre, you don't suppose that we should need to live in stone-quarries?"

But the means of preservation which human ingenuity had failed to secure were at hand from the felicitous provision of Nature herself. It was on the 10th of March that the captain and Lieutenant Procope started off once more to investigate the northwest corner of the island; on their way their conversation naturally was engrossed by the subject of the dire necessities which only too manifestly were awaiting them. A discussion more than usually animated arose between them, for the two men were not altogether of the same mind as to the measures that ought to be adopted in order to open the fairest chance of avoiding a fatal climax to their exposure; the captain persisted that an entirely new abode must be sought, while the lieutenant was equally bent upon devising a method of some sort by which their present quarters might be rendered sufficiently warm. All at once, in the very heat of his argument, Procope paused; he passed his hand across his eyes, as if to dispel a mist, and stood, with a fixed gaze centered on a point towards the south. "What is that?" he said, with a kind of hesitation. "No, I am not mistaken," he added; "it is a light on the horizon."

"A light!" exclaimed Servadac; "show me where."

"Look there!" answered the lieutenant, and he kept pointing steadily in its direction, until Servadac also distinctly saw the bright speck in the distance.

It increased in clearness in the gathering shades of evening. "Can it be a ship?" asked the captain.

"If so, it must be in flames; otherwise we should not be able to see it so far off," replied Procope.

"It does not move," said Servadac; "and unless I am greatly deceived, I can hear a kind of reverberation in the air."

For some seconds the two men stood straining eyes and ears in rapt attention. Suddenly an idea struck Servadac's mind. "The volcano!" he cried; "may it not be the volcano that we saw, whilst we were on board the *Dobryna?*"

The lieutenant agreed that it was very probable.

"Heaven be praised!" ejaculated the captain, and he went on in the tones of a keen excitement: "Nature has provided us with our winter quarters; the stream of burning lava that is flowing there is the gift of a bounteous Providence; it will provide us all the warmth we need. No time to lose! To-morrow, my dear Procope, to-morrow we will explore it all; no doubt the life, the heat we want is reserved for us in the heart and bowels of our own Gallia!"

Whilst the captain was indulging in his expressions of enthusiasm, Procope was endeavoring to collect his thoughts. Distinctly he remembered the long promontory which had barred the *Dobryna's* progress while coasting the southern confines of the sea, and which had obliged her to ascend northwards as far as the former latitude of Oran; he remembered also that at the extremity of the promontory there was a rocky headland crowned with smoke; and now he was convinced that he was right in identifying the position, and in believing that the smoke had given place to an eruption of flame.

"No, I am not mistaken," he added; "it is a light on the horizon."

When Servadac gave him a chance of speaking, he said, "The more I consider it, captain, the more I am satisfied that your conjecture is correct. Beyond a doubt, what we see is the volcano, and to-morrow we will not fail to visit it."

On returning to the gourbi, they communicated their discovery to Count Timascheff only, deeming any further publication of it to be premature. The count at once placed his yacht at their disposal, and expressed his intention of accompanying them.

"The yacht, I think," said Procope, "had better remain where she is; the weather is beautifully calm, and the steam-launch will answer our purpose better; at any rate, it will convey us much closer to shore than the schooner."

The count replied that the lieutenant was by all means to use his own discretion, and they all retired for the night.

Like many other modern pleasure-yachts, the *Dobryna*, in addition to her four-oar, was fitted with a fast-going little steam-launch, its screw being propelled, on the Oriolle system, by means of a boiler, small but very effective. Early next morning, this handy little craft was sufficiently freighted with coal (of which there was still about ten tons on board the *Dobryna*), and manned by nobody except the captain, the count, and the lieutenant, left the harbor of the Shelif, much to the bewilderment of Ben Zoof, who had not yet been admitted into the secret. The orderly, however, consoled himself with the reflection that he had been temporarily invested with the full powers of governor general, an office of which he was not a little proud.

The eighteen miles between the island and the headland were made in something less than three hours. The volcanic eruption was manifestly very considerable, the entire summit of the promontory being enveloped in flames. To produce so large a combustion either the oxygen of Gallia's atmosphere had been brought into contact with the explosive gases contained beneath her soil, or perhaps, still more probable, the volcano, like those in the moon, was fed by an internal supply of oxygen of her own.

It took more than half an hour to settle on a suitable landing-place. At length, a small semi-circular creek was discovered among the rocks, which appeared advantageous, because, if circumstances should so require, it would form a safe anchorage for both the *Dobryna* and the *Hansa*.

The launch securely moored, the passengers landed on the side of the promontory opposite to that on which a torrent of burning lava was descending to the sea. With much satisfaction they experienced, as they approached the mountain, a sensible difference in the temperature, and their spirits could not do otherwise than rise at the prospect of having their hopes confirmed, that a deliverance from the threatened calamity had so opportunely been found. On they went, up the steep acclivity, scrambling over its rugged projections, scaling the irregularities of its gigantic strata, bounding from point to point with the agility of chamois, but never alighting on anything except on the accumulation of the same hexagonal prisms with which they had now become so familiar.

Their exertions were happily rewarded. Behind a huge pyramidal rock they found a hole in the mountain-side, like the mouth of a great tunnel. Climbing up to this orifice, which was more than sixty feet above the level of the sea, they ascertained that it opened into a long dark gallery. They entered and groped their way cautiously along the sides. A continuous rumbling, that increased as they advanced, made them aware that they must be approaching the central funnel of the volcano; their only fear was lest some insuperable wall of rock should suddenly bar their further progress.

Servadac was some distance ahead.

"Come on!" he cried cheerily, his voice ringing through the darkness, "come on! Our fire is lighted! no stint of fuel! Nature provides that! Let us make haste and warm ourselves!"

Inspired by his confidence, the count and the lieutenant advanced bravely along the unseen and winding path. The temperature was now at least fifteen degrees above zero, and the walls of the gallery were beginning to feel quite warm to the touch, an indication, not to be overlooked, that the substance of which the rock was composed was metallic in its nature, and capable of conducting heat.

"Follow me!" shouted Servadac again; "we shall soon find a regular stove!"

Onwards they made their way, until at last a sharp turn brought them into a sudden flood of light. The tunnel had opened into a vast cavern, and the gloom was exchanged for an illumination that was perfectly dazzling. Although the temperature was high, it was not in any way intolerable.

One glance was sufficient to satisfy the explorers that the grateful light and heat of this huge excavation were to be attributed to a torrent of lava that was rolling downwards to the sea, completely subtending the aperture of the cave. Not inaptly might the scene be compared

to the celebrated Grotto of the Winds at the rear of the central fall
of Niagara, only with the exception that here, instead of a curtain of
rushing water, it was a curtain of roaring flame that hung before the
cavern's mouth.

The gloom was exchanged for an illumination that was perfectly dazzling.

"Heaven be praised!" cried Servadac, with glad emotion; "here is
all that we hoped for, and more besides!"

CHAPTER XXI.

WINTER QUARTERS

THE habitation that had now revealed itself, well lighted and thoroughly warm, was indeed marvelous. Not only would it afford ample accommodation for Hector Servadac and "his subjects," as Ben Zoof delighted to call them, but it would provide shelter for the two horses, and for a considerable number of domestic animals.

This enormous cavern was neither more or less than the common junction of nearly twenty tunnels (similar to that which had been traversed by the explorers), forming ramifications in the solid rock, and the pores, as it were, by which the internal heat exuded from the heart of the mountain. Here, as long as the volcano retained its activity, every living creature on the new asteroid might brave the most rigorous of climates; and as Count Timascheff justly remarked, since it was the only burning mountain they had sighted, it was most probably the sole outlet for Gallia's subterranean fires, and consequently the eruption might continue unchanged for ages to come.

But not a day, not an hour, was to be lost now. The steam-launch returned to Gourbi Island, and preparations were forthwith taken in hand for conveying man and beast, corn and fodder, across to the volcanic headland. Loud and hearty were the acclamations of the little colony, especially of the Spaniards, and great was the relief of Nina, when Servadac announced to them the discovery of their future domicile; and with requickened energies they labored hard at packing, anxious to reach their genial winter quarters without delay.

For three successive days the *Dobryna*, laden to her very gunwale, made a transit to and fro. Ben Zoof was left upon the island to superintend the stowage of the freight, whilst Servadac found abundant occupation in overlooking its disposal within the recesses of the mountain. First of all, the large store of corn and fodder, the produce of the recent harvest, was landed and deposited in one of the vaults; then, on the 15th, about fifty head of live cattle—bullocks, cows, sheep, and pigs—were conveyed to their rocky stalls. These were saved for the sake of preserving the several breeds, the bulk of the island cattle being slaughtered, as the extreme severity of the climate insured all meat remaining fresh for almost an indefinite period. The winter which they were expecting would probably be of unprecedented length; it was quite likely that it would exceed the six months' duration by which many arctic explorers have been tried; but the population of Gallia had no anxiety in the matter of provisions—their stock was far more than adequate; while as for drink, as long as they were satisfied with pure water, a frozen sea would afford them an inexhaustible reservoir.

The need for haste in forwarding their preparations became more and more manifest; the sea threatened to be un-navigable very soon, as ice was already forming which the noonday sun was unable to melt. And if haste were necessary, so also were care, ingenuity, and forethought. It was indispensable that the space at their command should be properly utilized, and yet that the several portions of the store should all be readily accessible.

On further investigation an unexpected number of galleries was discovered, so that, in fact, the interior of the mountain was like a vast bee-hive perforated with innumerable cells; and in compliment to the little Italian it was unanimously voted by the colony that their new home should be called "Nina's Hive."

The first care of Captain Servadac was to ascertain how he could make the best possible use of the heat which nature had provided for them so opportunely and with so lavish a hand. By opening fresh vents in the solid rock (which by the action of the heat was here capable of fissure) the stream of burning lava was diverted into several new channels, where it could be available for daily use; and thus Mochel, the *Dobryna's* cook, was furnished with an admirable kitchen, provided with a permanent stove, where he was duly installed with all his culinary apparatus.

"What a saving of expense it would be," exclaimed Ben Zoof, "if every household could be furnished with its own private volcano!"

The large cavern at the general junction of the galleries was fitted up as a drawing-room, and arranged with all the best furniture both of the gourbi and of the cabin of the *Dobryna*. Hither was also brought the schooner's library, containing a good variety of French and Russian books; lamps were suspended over the different tables; and the walls of the apartment were tapestried with the sails and adorned with the flags belonging to the yacht. The curtain of fire extending over the opening of the cavern provided it, as already stated, with light and heat.

The torrent of lava fell into a small rock-bound basin that had no apparent communication with the sea, and was evidently the aperture of a deep abyss, of which the waters, heated by the descent of the eruptive matter, would no doubt retain their liquid condition long after the Gallian Sea had become a sheet of ice.

A small excavation to the left of the common hall was allotted for the special use of Servadac and the count; another on the right was appropriated to the lieutenant and Ben Zoof; whilst a third recess, immediately at the back, made a convenient little chamber for Nina. The Spaniards and the Russian sailors took up their sleeping-quarters in the adjacent galleries, and found the temperature quite comfortable.

Such were the internal arrangements of Nina's Hive, the refuge where the little colony were full of hope that they would be able to brave the rigors of the stern winter-time that lay before them—a winter-time during which Gallia might possibly be projected even to the orbit of Jupiter, where the temperature would not exceed one twenty-fifth of the normal winter temperature of the earth.

The only discontented spirit was Isaac Hakkabut. Throughout all the preparations which roused even the Spaniards to activity, the Jew, still incredulous and deaf to every representation of the true state of things, insisted upon remaining in the creek at Gourbi Island; nothing could induce him to leave his tartan, where, like a miser, he would keep guard over his precious cargo, ever grumbling and growling, but with his weather-eye open in the hope of catching sight of some passing sail. It must be owned that the whole party were far from sorry to be relieved of his presence; his uncomely figure and repulsive countenance was a perpetual bugbear. He had given out in plain terms that he did not intend to part with any of his property, except for current money, and Servadac, equally resolute, had strictly forbidden any purchases to be made, hoping to wear out the rascal's obstinacy.

Hakkabut persistently refused to credit the real situation; he could not absolutely deny that some portions of the terrestrial globe had

undergone a certain degree of modification, but nothing could bring
him to believe that he was not, sooner or later, to résumé his old line
of business in the Mediterranean. With his wonted distrust of all with
whom he came in contact, he regarded every argument that was urged
upon him only as evidence of a plot that had been devised to deprive
him of his goods. Repudiating, as he did utterly, the hypothesis that
a fragment had become detached from the earth, he scanned the horizon for hours together with an old telescope, the case of which had
been patched up till it looked like a rusty stove-pipe, hoping to descry
the passing trader with which he might effect some bartering upon
advantageous terms.

At first he professed to regard the proposed removal into winter-
quarters as an attempt to impose upon his credulity; but the frequent
voyages made by the *Dobryna* to the south, and the repeated consign-
ments of corn and cattle, soon served to make him aware that Captain
Servadac and his companions were really contemplating a departure
from Gourbi Island.

The movement set him thinking. What, he began to ask himself—
what if all that was told him was true? What if this sea was no longer
the Mediterranean? What if he should never again behold his German fatherland? What if his marts for business were gone for ever? A
vague idea of ruin began to take possession of his mind: he must yield
to necessity; he must do the best he could. As the result of his cogitations, he occasionally left his tartan and made a visit to the shore. At
length he endeavored to mingle with the busy group, who were hurrying on their preparations; but his advances were only met by jeers and
scorn, and, ridiculed by all the rest, he was fain to turn his attention to
Ben Zoof, to whom he offered a few pinches of tobacco.

"No, old Zebulon," said Ben Zoof, steadily refusing the gift, "it is
against orders to take anything from you. Keep your cargo to yourself; eat and drink it all if you can; we are not to touch it."

Finding the subordinates incorruptible, Isaac determined to go to
the fountain-head. He addressed himself to Servadac, and begged him
to tell him the whole truth, piteously adding that surely it was unwor-
thy of a French officer to deceive a poor old man like himself.

"Tell you the truth, man!" cried Servadac. "Confound it, I have told
you the truth twenty times. Once for all, I tell you now, you have left
yourself barely time enough to make your escape to yonder mountain."

"God and Mahomet have mercy on me!" muttered the Jew, whose creed frequently assumed a very ambiguous character.

"I will tell you what," continued the captain—"you shall have a few men to work the *Hansa* across, if you like."

"But I want to go to Algiers," whimpered Hakkabut.

"How often am I to tell you that Algiers is no longer in existence? Only say yes or no—are you coming with us into winter-quarters?"

"God of Israel! what is to become of all my property?"

"But, mind you," continued the captain, not heeding the interruption, "if you do not choose voluntarily to come with us, I shall have the *Hansa*, by my orders, removed to a place of safety. I am not going to let your cursed obstinacy incur the risk of losing your cargo altogether."

"Merciful Heaven! I shall be ruined!" moaned Isaac, in despair.

"You are going the right way to ruin yourself, and it would serve you right to leave you to your own devices. But be off! I have no more to say."

And, turning contemptuously on his heel, Servadac left the old man vociferating bitterly, and with uplifted hands protesting vehemently against the rapacity of the Gentiles.

By the 20th all preliminary arrangements were complete, and everything ready for a final departure from the island. The thermometer stood on an average at 8 degrees below zero, and the water in the cistern was completely frozen. It was determined, therefore, for the colony to embark on the following day, and take up their residence in Nina's Hive.

A final consultation was held about the *Hansa*. Lieutenant Procope pronounced his decided conviction that it would be impossible for the tartan to resist the pressure of the ice in the harbor of the Shelif, and that there would be far more safety in the proximity of the volcano. It was agreed on all hands that the vessel must be shifted; and accordingly orders were given, four Russian sailors were sent on board, and only a few minutes elapsed after the *Dobryna* had weighed anchor, before the great lateen sail of the tartan was unfurled, and the "shop-ship," as Ben Zoof delighted to call it, was also on her way to the southward.

Long and loud were the lamentations of the Jew. He kept exclaiming that he had given no orders, that he was being moved against his will, that he had asked for no assistance, and needed none; but it required no very keen discrimination to observe that all along there was a lurking gleam of satisfaction in his little gray eyes, and when, a few hours later, he found himself securely anchored, and his property in a place of safety, he quite chuckled with glee.

"God of Israel!" he said in an undertone, "they have made no charge; the idiots have piloted me here for nothing."

For nothing! His whole nature exulted in the consciousness that he was enjoying a service that had been rendered gratuitously.

Destitute of human inhabitants, Gourbi Island was now left to the tenancy of such birds and beasts as had escaped the recent promiscuous slaughter. Birds, indeed, that had migrated in search of warmer shores, had returned, proving that this fragment of the French colony was the only shred of land that could yield them any sustenance; but their life must necessarily be short. It was utterly impossible that they could survive the cold that would soon ensue.

The colony took possession of their new abode with but few formalities. Everyone, however, approved of all the internal arrangements of Nina's Hive, and were profuse in their expressions of satisfaction at finding themselves located in such comfortable quarters. The only malcontent was Hakkabut; he had no share in the general enthusiasm, refused even to enter or inspect any of the galleries, and insisted on remaining on board his tartan.

"He is afraid," said Ben Zoof, "that he will have to pay for his lodgings. But wait a bit; we shall see how he stands the cold out there; the frost, no doubt, will drive the old fox out of his hole."

Towards evening the pots were set boiling, and a bountiful supper, to which all were invited, was spread in the central hall. The stores of the *Dobryna* contained some excellent wine, some of which was broached to do honor to the occasion. The health of the governor general was drunk, as well as the toast "Success to his council," to which Ben Zoof was called upon to return thanks. The entertainment passed off merrily. The Spaniards were in the best of spirits; one of them played the guitar, another the castanets, and the rest joined in a ringing chorus. Ben Zoof contributed the famous Zouave refrain, well known throughout the French army, but rarely performed in finer style than by this *virtuoso:*

> "Misti goth dar dar tire lyre!
> Flic! floc! flac! lirette, lira!
> Far la rira,

Tour tala rire,
Tour la Ribaud,
Ricandeau,
Sans repos, repit, repit, repos, ris pot, ripette!
Si vous attrapez mon refrain,
Fameux vous etes."

Ben Zoof contributed the famous Zouave refrain, well known throughout the French army.

The concert was succeeded by a ball, unquestionably the first that had ever taken place in Gallia. The Russian sailors exhibited some of their national dances, which gained considerable applause, even although they followed upon the marvelous fandangos of the Spaniards.

Ben Zoof, in his turn, danced a *pas seul* (often performed in the Elysee Montmartre) with an elegance and vigor that earned many compliments from Negrete.

It was nine o'clock before the festivities came to an end, and by that time the company, heated by the high temperature of the hall, and by their own exertions, felt the want of a little fresh air. Accordingly the greater portion of the party, escorted by Ben Zoof, made their way into one of the adjacent galleries that led to the shore. Servadac, with the count and lieutenant, did not follow immediately; but shortly afterwards they proceeded to join them, when on their way they were startled by loud cries from those in advance.

Their first impression was that they were cries of distress, and they were greatly relieved to find that they were shouts of delight, which the dryness and purity of the atmosphere caused to re-echo like a volley of musketry.

Reaching the mouth of the gallery, they found the entire group pointing with eager interest to the sky.

"Well, Ben Zoof," asked the captain, "what's the matter now?"

"Oh, your Excellency," ejaculated the orderly, "look there! look there! The moon! the moon's come back!"

And, sure enough, what was apparently the moon was rising above the mists of evening.

CHAPTER XXII.

A FROZEN OCEAN

THE moon! She had disappeared for weeks; was she now returning? Had she been faithless to the earth? and had she now approached to be a satellite of the new-born world?

"Impossible!" said Lieutenant Procope; "the earth is millions and millions of leagues away, and it is not probable that the moon has ceased to revolve about her."

"Why not?" remonstrated Servadac. "It would not be more strange than the other phenomena which we have lately witnessed. Why should not the moon have fallen within the limits of Gallia's attraction, and become her satellite?"

"Upon that supposition," put in the count, "I should think that it would be altogether unlikely that three months would elapse without our seeing her."

"Quite incredible!" continued Procope. "And there is another thing which totally disproves the captain's hypothesis; the magnitude of Gallia is far too insignificant for her power of attraction to carry off the moon."

"But," persisted Servadac, "why should not the same convulsion that tore us away from the earth have torn away the moon as well? After wandering about as she would for a while in the solar regions, I do not see why she should not have attached herself to us."

The lieutenant repeated his conviction that it was not likely.

"But why not?" again asked Servadac impetuously.

"Because, I tell you, the mass of Gallia is so inferior to that of the moon, that Gallia would become the moon's satellite; the moon could not possibly become hers."

"Assuming, however," continued Servadac, "such to be the case—"

"I am afraid," said the lieutenant, interrupting him, "that I cannot assume anything of the sort even for a moment."

Servadac smiled good-humoredly.

"I confess you seem to have the best of the argument, and if Gallia had become a satellite of the moon, it would not have taken three months to catch sight of her. I suppose you are right."

While this discussion had been going on, the satellite, or whatever it might be, had been rising steadily above the horizon, and had reached a position favorable for observation. Telescopes were brought, and it was very soon ascertained, beyond a question, that the new luminary was not the well-known Phoebe of terrestrial nights; it had no feature in common with the moon. Although it was apparently much nearer to Gallia than the moon to the earth, its superficies was hardly one-tenth as large, and so feebly did it reflect the light of the remote sun, that it scarcely emitted radiance enough to extinguish the dim luster of stars of the eighth magnitude. Like the sun, it had risen in the west, and was now at its full. To mistake its identity with the moon was absolutely impossible; not even Servadac could discover a trace of the seas, chasms, craters, and mountains which have been so minutely delineated in lunar charts, and it could not be denied that any transient hope that had been excited as to their once again being about to enjoy the peaceful smiles of "the queen of night" must all be resigned.

Count Timascheff finally suggested, though somewhat doubtfully, the question of the probability that Gallia, in her course across the zone of the minor planets, had carried off one of them; but whether it was one of the 169 asteroids already included in the astronomical catalogues, or one previously unknown, he did not presume to determine. The idea to a certain extent was plausible, inasmuch as it has been ascertained that several of the telescopic planets are of such small dimensions that a good walker might make a circuit of them in four and twenty hours; consequently Gallia, being of superior volume, might be supposed capable of exercising a power of attraction upon any of these miniature microcosms.

The first night in Nina's Hive passed without special incident; and next morning a regular scheme of life was definitely laid down. "My lord governor," as Ben Zoof until he was peremptorily forbidden delighted to call Servadac, had a wholesome dread of idleness and its consequences, and insisted upon each member of the party undertaking some special duty to fulfill. There was plenty to do. The domestic animals required a great deal of attention; a supply of food had to be

secured and preserved; fishing had to be carried on while the condition
of the sea would allow it; and in several places the galleries had to be
further excavated to render them more available for use. Occupation,
then, need never be wanting, and the daily round of labor could go on
in orderly routine.

A perfect concord ruled the little colony. The Russians and Spaniards
amalgamated well, and both did their best to pick up various scraps of
French, which was considered the official language of the place. Servadac himself undertook the tuition of Pablo and Nina, Ben Zoof being their companion in play-hours, when he entertained them with en-
chanting stories in the best Parisian French, about "a lovely city at the
foot of a mountain," where he always promised one day to take them.

The end of March came, but the cold was not intense to such a
degree as to confine any of the party to the interior of their resort;
several excursions were made along the shore, and for a radius of three
or four miles the adjacent district was carefully explored. Investigation, however, always ended in the same result; turn their course in
whatever direction they would, they found that the country retained
everywhere its desert character, rocky, barren, and without a trace
of vegetation. Here and there a slight layer of snow, or a thin coating of ice arising from atmospheric condensation indicated the existence of superficial moisture, but it would require a period indefinitely
long, exceeding human reckoning, before that moisture could collect
into a stream and roll downwards over the stony strata to the sea. It
seemed at present out of their power to determine whether the land
upon which they were so happily settled was an island or a continent,
and till the cold was abated they feared to undertake any lengthened
expedition to ascertain the actual extent of the strange concrete of
metallic crystallization.

By ascending one day to the summit of the volcano, Captain Servadac and the count succeeded in getting a general idea of the aspect
of the country. The mountain itself was an enormous block rising sym-
metrically to a height of nearly 3,000 feet above the level of the sea,
in the form of a truncated cone, of which the topmost section was
crowned by a wreath of smoke issuing continuously from the mouth of
a narrow crater.

Under the old condition of terrestrial things, the ascent of this
steep acclivity would have been attended with much fatigue, but as

the effect of the altered condition of the law of gravity, the travelers
performed perpetual prodigies in the way of agility, and in little over
an hour reached the edge of the crater, without more sense of exertion
than if they had traversed a couple of miles on level ground. Gallia had
its drawbacks, but it had some compensating advantages.

Telescopes in hand, the explorers from the summit scanned the
surrounding view.

Telescopes in hand, the explorers from the summit scanned the
surrounding view. Their anticipations had already realized what they
saw. Just as they expected, on the north, east, and west lay the Gallian Sea, smooth and motionless as a sheet of glass, the cold having,

as it were, congealed the atmosphere so that there was not a breath of
wind. Towards the south there seemed no limit to the land, and the
volcano formed the apex of a triangle, of which the base was beyond
the reach of vision. Viewed even from this height, whence distance
would do much to soften the general asperity, the surface nevertheless seemed to be bristling with its myriads of hexagonal lamellae,
and to present difficulties which, to an ordinary pedestrian, would be
insurmountable.

"Oh for some wings, or else a balloon!" cried Servadac, as he gazed
around him; and then, looking down to the rock upon which they
were standing, he added, "We seem to have been transplanted to a soil
strange enough in its chemical character to bewilder the *savants* at a
museum."

"And do you observe, captain," asked the count, "how the convexity of our little world curtails our view? See, how circumscribed is the
horizon!"

Servadac replied that he had noticed the same circumstance from
the top of the cliffs of Gourbi Island.

"Yes," said the count; "it becomes more and more obvious that ours
is a very tiny world, and that Gourbi Island is the sole productive
spot upon its surface. We have had a short summer, and who knows
whether we are not entering upon a winter that may last for years,
perhaps for centuries?"

"But we must not mind, count," said Servadac, smiling. "We have
agreed, you know, that, come what may, we are to be philosophers."

"Ay, true, my friend," rejoined the count; "we must be philosophers
and something more; we must be grateful to the good Protector who
has hitherto befriended us, and we must trust His mercy to the end."

For a few moments they both stood in silence, and contemplated
land and sea; then, having given a last glance over the dreary panorama, they prepared to wend their way down the mountain. Before,
however, they commenced their descent, they resolved to make a closer examination of the crater. They were particularly struck by what
seemed to them almost the mysterious calmness with which the eruption was effected. There was none of the wild disorder and deafening
tumult that usually accompany the discharge of volcanic matter, but
the heated lava, rising with a uniform gentleness, quietly overran the
limits of the crater, like the flow of water from the bosom of a peace-

ful lake. Instead of a boiler exposed to the action of an angry fire,
the crater rather resembled a brimming basin, of which the contents
were noiselessly escaping. Nor were there any igneous stones or red-
hot cinders mingled with the smoke that crowned the summit; a circumstance that quite accorded with the absence of the pumice-stones,
obsidians, and other minerals of volcanic origin with which the base of
a burning mountain is generally strewn.

Nina balanced the piece of ice two or three times in her hand, and threw it
forward with all her strength.

Captain Servadac was of opinion that this peculiarity augured
favorably for the continuance of the eruption. Extreme violence in

physical, as well as in moral nature, is never of long duration. The most terrible storms, like the most violent fits of passion, are not lasting; but here the calm flow of the liquid fire appeared to be supplied from a source that was inexhaustible, in the same way as the waters of Niagara, gliding on steadily to their final plunge, would defy all effort to arrest their course.

Before the evening of this day closed in, a most important change was effected in the condition of the Gallian Sea by the intervention of human agency. Notwithstanding the increasing cold, the sea, unruffled as it was by a breath of wind, still retained its liquid state. It is an established fact that water, under this condition of absolute stillness, will remain uncongealed at a temperature several degrees below zero, whilst experiment, at the same time, shows that a very slight shock will often be sufficient to convert it into solid ice. It had occurred to Servadac that if some communication could be opened with Gourbi Island, there would be a fine scope for hunting expeditions. Having this ultimate object in view, he assembled his little colony upon a projecting rock at the extremity of the promontory, and having called Nina and Pablo out to him in front, he said: "Now, Nina, do you think you could throw something into the sea?"

"I think I could," replied the child, "but I am sure that Pablo would throw it a great deal further than I can."

"Never mind, you shall try first."

Putting a fragment of ice into Nina's hand, he addressed himself to Pablo:

"Look out, Pablo; you shall see what a nice little fairy Nina is! Throw, Nina, throw, as hard as you can."

Nina balanced the piece of ice two or three times in her hand, and threw it forward with all her strength.

A sudden thrill seemed to vibrate across the motionless waters to the distant horizon, and the Gallian Sea had become a solid sheet of ice!

CHAPTER XXIII.

A CARRIER-PIGEON

WHEN, three hours after sunset, on the 23d of March, the Gallian moon rose upon the western horizon, it was observed that she had entered upon her last quarter. She had taken only four days to pass from syzygy to quadrature, and it was consequently evident that she would be visible for little more than a week at a time, and that her lunation would be accomplished within sixteen days. The lunar months, like the solar days, had been diminished by one-half. Three days later the moon was in conjunction with the sun, and was consequently lost to view; Ben Zoof, as the first observer of the satellite, was extremely interested in its movements, and wondered whether it would ever reappear.

On the 26th, under an atmosphere perfectly clear and dry, the thermometer fell to 12 degrees F. below zero. Of the present distance of Gallia from the sun, and the number of leagues she had traversed since the receipt of the last mysterious document, there were no means of judging; the extent of diminution in the apparent disc of the sun did not afford sufficient basis even for an approximate calculation; and Captain Servadac was perpetually regretting that they could receive no further tidings from the anonymous correspondent, whom he persisted in regarding as a fellow-countryman.

The solidity of the ice was perfect; the utter stillness of the air at the time when the final congelation of the waters had taken place had resulted in the formation of a surface that for smoothness would rival a skating-rink; without a crack or flaw it extended far beyond the range of vision.

The contrast to the ordinary aspect of polar seas was very remarkable. There, the ice-fields are an agglomeration of hummocks and icebergs, massed in wild confusion, often towering higher than the masts of the largest whalers, and from the instability of their foundations liable to an instantaneous loss of equilibrium; a breath of wind, a slight modification of the temperature, not unfrequently serving to bring about a series of changes outrivaling the most elaborate transformation scenes of a pantomime. Here, on the contrary, the vast white plain was level as the desert of Sahara or the Russian steppes; the waters of the Gallian Sea were imprisoned beneath the solid sheet, which became continually stouter in the increasing cold.

Captain Servadac, an adept in athletics, almost outvied his instructor.

Accustomed to the uneven crystallizations of their own frozen seas, the Russians could not be otherwise than delighted with the polished surface that afforded them such excellent opportunity for enjoying their favorite pastime of skating. A supply of skates, found hidden away amongst the *Dobryna's* stores, was speedily brought into use. The Russians undertook the instruction of the Spaniards, and at the end of a few days, during which the temperature was only endurable through the absence of wind, there was not a Gallian who could not skate tolerably well, while many of them could describe figures involving the most complicated curves. Nina and Pablo earned loud applause by their rapid proficiency; Captain Servadac, an adept in athletics, almost outvied his instructor, the count; and Ben Zoof, who had upon some rare occasions skated upon the Lake of Montmartre (in his eyes, of course, a sea), performed prodigies in the art.

This exercise was not only healthful in itself, but it was acknowledged that, in case of necessity, it might become a very useful means of locomotion. As Captain Servadac remarked, it was almost a substitute for railways, and as if to illustrate this proposition, Lieutenant Procope, perhaps the greatest expert in the party, accomplished the twenty miles to Gourbi Island and back in considerably less than four hours.

The temperature, meanwhile, continued to decrease, and the average reading of the thermometer was about 16 degrees F. below zero; the light also diminished in proportion, and all objects appeared to be enveloped in a half-defined shadow, as though the sun were undergoing a perpetual eclipse. It was not surprising that the effect of this continuously overhanging gloom should be to induce a frequent depression of spirits amongst the majority of the little population, exiles as they were from their mother earth, and not unlikely, as it seemed, to be swept far away into the regions of another planetary sphere. Probably Count Timascheff, Captain Servadac, and Lieutenant Procope were the only members of the community who could bring any scientific judgment to bear upon the uncertainty that was before them, but a general sense of the strangeness of their situation could not fail at times to weigh heavily upon the minds of all. Under these circumstances it was very necessary to counteract the tendency to despond by continual diversion; and the recreation of skating thus opportunely provided, seemed just the thing to arouse the flagging spirits, and to restore a wholesome excitement.

With dogged obstinacy, Isaac Hakkabut refused to take any share either in the labors or the amusements of the colony. In spite of the cold, he had not been seen since the day of his arrival from Gourbi

Island. Captain Servadac had strictly forbidden any communication with him; and the smoke that rose from the cabin chimney of the *Hansa* was the sole indication of the proprietor being still on board. There was nothing to prevent him, if he chose, from partaking gratuitously of the volcanic light and heat which were being enjoyed by all besides; but rather than abandon his close and personal oversight of his precious cargo, he preferred to sacrifice his own slender stock of fuel.

Both the schooner and the tartan had been carefully moored in the way that seemed to promise best for withstanding the rigor of the winter. After seeing the vessels made secure in the frozen creek. Lieutenant Procope, following the example of many Arctic explorers, had the precaution to have the ice beveled away from the keels, so that there should be no risk of the ships' sides being crushed by the increasing pressure; he hoped that they would follow any rise in the level of the ice-field, and when the thaw should come, that they would easily regain their proper water-line.

On his last visit to Gourbi Island, the lieutenant had ascertained that north, east, and west, far as the eye could reach, the Gallian Sea had become one uniform sheet of ice. One spot alone refused to freeze; this was the pool immediately below the central cavern, the receptacle for the stream of burning lava. It was entirely enclosed by rocks, and if ever a few icicles were formed there by the action of the cold, they were very soon melted by the fiery shower. Hissing and spluttering as the hot lava came in contact with it, the water was in a continual state of ebullition, and the fish that abounded in its depths defied the angler's craft; they were, as Ben Zoof remarked, "too much boiled to bite."

At the beginning of April the weather changed. The sky became overcast, but there was no rise in the temperature. Unlike the polar winters of the earth, which ordinarily are affected by atmospheric influence, and liable to slight intermissions of their severity at various shiftings of the wind, Gallia's winter was caused by her immense distance from the source of all light and heat, and the cold was consequently destined to go on steadily increasing until it reached the limit ascertained by Fourier to be the normal temperature of the realms of space.

With the over-clouding of the heavens there arose a violent tempest; but although the wind raged with an almost inconceivable fury, it was unaccompanied by either snow or rain. Its effect upon the burning curtain that covered the aperture of the central hall was very remarkable. So far from there being any likelihood of the fire being extinguished by the vehemence of the current of air, the hurricane seemed rather to act as a ventilator, which fanned the flame into greater activity, and the utmost care was necessary to avoid being burnt by the fragments of lava that were drifted into the interior of the grotto. More than once the curtain itself was rifted entirely asunder, but only to close up again immediately after allowing a momentary draught of cold air to penetrate the hall in a way that was refreshing and rather advantageous than otherwise.

On the 4th of April, after an absence of about four days, the new satellite, to Ben Zoof's great satisfaction, made its reappearance in a crescent form, a circumstance that seemed to justify the anticipation that henceforward it would continue to make a periodic revolution every fortnight.

The crust of ice and snow was far too stout for the beaks of the strongest birds to penetrate, and accordingly large swarms had left the island, and, following the human population, had taken refuge on the volcanic promontory; not that there the barren shore had anything in the way of nourishment to offer them, but their instinct impelled them to haunt now the very habitations which formerly they would have shunned. Scraps of food were thrown to them from the galleries; these were speedily devoured, but were altogether inadequate in quantity to meet the demand. At length, emboldened by hunger, several hundred birds ventured through the tunnel, and took up their quarters actually in Nina's Hive. Congregating in the large hall, the half-famished creatures did not hesitate to snatch bread, meat, or food of any description from the hands of the residents as they sat at table, and soon became such an intolerable nuisance that it formed one of the daily diversions to hunt them down; but although they were vigorously attacked by stones and sticks, and even occasionally by shot, it was with some difficulty that their number could be sensibly reduced.

By a systematic course of warfare the bulk of the birds were all expelled, with the exception of about a hundred, which began to build in the crevices of the rocks. These were left in quiet possession of their quarters, as not only was it deemed advisable to perpetuate the various breeds, but it was found that these birds acted as a kind of police, never failing either to chase away or to kill any others of their species who infringed upon what they appeared to regard as their own special privilege in intruding within the limits of their domain.

On the 15th loud cries were suddenly heard issuing from the mouth of the principal gallery.

"Help, help! I shall be killed!"

Pablo in a moment recognized the voice as Nina's. Outrunning even Ben Zoof he hurried to the assistance of his little playmate, and discovered that she was being attacked by half a dozen great sea-gulls, and only after receiving some severe blows from their beaks could he succeed by means of a stout cudgel in driving them away.

She was being attacked by half a dozen great sea-gulls.

"Tell me, Nina, what is this?" he asked as soon as the tumult had subsided.

The child pointed to a bird which she was caressing tenderly in her bosom.

"A pigeon!" exclaimed Ben Zoof, who had reached the scene of commotion, adding:

"A carrier-pigeon! And by all the saints of Montmartre, there is a little bag attached to its neck!"

He took the bird, and rushing into the hall placed it in Servadac's hands.

"Another message, no doubt," cried the captain, "from our unknown friend. Let us hope that this time he has given us his name and address."

All crowded round, eager to hear the news. In the struggle with the gulls the bag had been partially torn open, but still contained the following dispatch:

"Gallia!
Chemin parcouru du 1er Mars au 1ᵉʳ Avril: 39,000,000 l.!
Distance du soleil: 110,000,000 l.!
Capte Nerina en passant.
Vivres vont manquer et..."

The rest of the document had been so damaged by the beaks of the gulls that it was illegible. Servadac was wild with vexation. He felt more and more convinced that the writer was a Frenchman, and that the last line indicated that he was in distress from scarcity of food. The very thought of a fellow-countryman in peril of starvation drove him well-nigh to distraction, and it was in vain that search was made everywhere near the scene of conflict in hopes of finding the missing scrap that might bear a signature or address.

Suddenly little Nina, who had again taken possession of the pigeon, and was hugging it to her breast, said:

"Look here, Ben Zoof!"

And as she spoke she pointed to the left wing of the bird. The wing bore the faint impress of a postage-stamp, and the one word:

"FORMENTERA."

CHAPTER XXIV.

A SLEDGE-RIDE

FORMENTERA was at once recognized by Servadac and the count as the name of one of the smallest of the Balearic Islands. It was more than probable that the unknown writer had thence sent out the mysterious documents, and from the message just come to hand by the carrier-pigeon, it appeared all but certain that at the beginning of April, a fortnight back, he had still been there. In one important particular the present communication differed from those that had preceded it: it was written entirely in French, and exhibited none of the ecstatic exclamations in other languages that had been remarkable in the two former papers. The concluding line, with its intimation of failing provisions, amounted almost to an appeal for help. Captain Servadac briefly drew attention to these points, and concluded by saying, "My friends, we must, without delay, hasten to the assistance of this unfortunate man."

"For my part," said the count, "I am quite ready to accompany you; it is not unlikely that he is not alone in his distress."

Lieutenant Procope expressed much surprise. "We must have passed close to Formentera," he said, "when we explored the site of the Balearic Isles; this fragment must be very small; it must be smaller than the remaining splinter of Gibraltar or Ceuta; otherwise, surely it would never have escaped our observation."

"However small it may be," replied Servadac, "we must find it. How far off do you suppose it is?"

"It must be a hundred and twenty leagues away," said the lieutenant, thoughtfully; "and I do not quite understand how you would propose to get there."

"Why, on skates of course; no difficulty in that, I should imagine," answered Servadac, and he appealed to the count for confirmation of his opinion.

The count assented, but Procope looked doubtful.

"Your enterprise is generous," he said, "and I should be most unwilling to throw any unnecessary obstacle in the way of its execution; but, pardon me, if I submit to you a few considerations which to my mind are very important. First of all, the thermometer is already down to 22 degrees below zero, and the keen wind from the south is making the temperature absolutely unendurable; in the second place, supposing you travel at the rate of twenty leagues a day, you would be exposed for at least six consecutive days; and thirdly, your expedition will be of small avail unless you convey provisions not only for yourselves, but for those whom you hope to relieve."

"We can carry our own provisions on our backs in knapsacks," interposed Servadac, quickly, unwilling to recognize any difficulty in the way.

"Granted that you can," answered the lieutenant, quietly; "but where, on this level ice-field, will you find shelter in your periods of rest? You must perish with cold; you will not have the chance of digging out ice-huts like the Esquimaux."

"As to rest," said Servadac, "we shall take none; we shall keep on our way continuously; by traveling day and night without intermission, we shall not be more than three days in reaching Formentera."

"Believe me," persisted the lieutenant, calmly, "your enthusiasm is carrying you too far; the feat you propose is impossible; but even conceding the possibility of your success in reaching your destination, what service do you imagine that you, half-starved and half-frozen yourself, could render to those who are already perishing by want and exposure? you would only bring them away to die."

The obvious and dispassionate reasoning of the lieutenant could not fail to impress the minds of those who listened to him; the impracticability of the journey became more and more apparent; unprotected on that drear expanse, any traveler must assuredly succumb to the snow-drifts that were continually being whirled across it. But Hector Servadac, animated by the generous desire of rescuing a suffering fellow-creature, could scarcely be brought within the bounds of common sense. Against his better judgment he was still bent upon the expedition, and Ben Zoof declared himself ready to accompany his master in the event of Count Timascheff hesitating to encounter the peril which the undertaking involved. But the count entirely repudiated all idea of shrinking from what, quite as much as the captain, he regarded as a sacred duty, and turning to Lieutenant Procope, told him that unless some better plan could be devised, he was prepared to start off at once and make the attempt to skate across to Formentera. The lieutenant, who was lost in thought, made no immediate reply.

"I wish we had a sledge," said Ben Zoof.

"I dare say that a sledge of some sort could be contrived," said the count; "but then we should have no dogs or reindeers to draw it."

"Why not rough-shoe the two horses?"

"They would never be able to endure the cold," objected the count.

"Never mind," said Servadac, "let us get our sledge and put them to the test. Something must be done!"

"I think," said Lieutenant Procope, breaking his thoughtful silence, "that I can tell you of a sledge already provided for your hand, and I can suggest a motive power surer and swifter than horses."

"What do you mean?" was the eager inquiry.

"I mean the *Dobryna*'s yawl," answered the lieutenant; "and I have no doubt that the wind would carry her rapidly along the ice."

The idea seemed admirable. Lieutenant Procope was well aware to what marvelous perfection the Americans had brought their sail-sledges, and had heard how in the vast prairies of the United States they had been known to outvie the speed of an express train, occasionally attaining a rate of more than a hundred miles an hour. The wind was still blowing hard from the south, and assuming that the yawl could be propelled with a velocity of about fifteen or at least twelve leagues an hour, he reckoned that it was quite possible to reach Formentera within twelve hours, that is to say, in a single day between the intervals of sunrise and sunrise.

The yawl was about twelve feet long, and capable of holding five or six people. The addition of a couple of iron runners would be all that was requisite to convert it into an excellent sledge, which, if a sail were hoisted, might be deemed certain to make a rapid progress over the smooth surface of the ice. For the protection of the passengers it was proposed to erect a kind of wooden roof lined with strong cloth; beneath this could be packed a supply of provisions, some warm furs, some cordials, and a portable stove to be heated by spirits of wine.

For the outward journey the wind was as favorable as could be desired; but it was to be apprehended that, unless the direction of the wind should change, the return would be a matter of some difficulty; a system of tacking might be carried out to a certain degree, but it was not likely that the yawl would answer her helm in any way corresponding to what would occur in the open sea. Captain Servadac, however, would not listen to any representation of probable difficulties; the future, he said, must provide for itself.

The engineer and several of the sailors set vigorously to work, and before the close of the day the yawl was furnished with a pair of stout iron runners, curved upwards in front, and fitted with a metal scull designed to assist in maintaining the directness of her course; the roof was put on, and beneath it were stored the provisions, the wraps, and the cooking utensils.

A strong desire was expressed by Lieutenant Procope that he should be allowed to accompany Captain Servadac instead of Count Timascheff. It was unadvisable for all three of them to go, as, in case of there being several persons to be rescued, the space at their command would be quite inadequate. The lieutenant urged that he was the most experienced seaman, and as such was best qualified to take command of the sledge and the management of the sails; and as it was not to be expected that Servadac would resign his intention of going in person to relieve his fellow-countryman, Procope submitted his own wishes to the count. The count was himself very anxious to have his share in the philanthropic enterprise, and demurred considerably to the proposal; he yielded, however, after a time, to Servadac's representations that in the event of the expedition proving disastrous, the little colony would need his services alike as governor and protector, and overcoming his reluctance to be left out of the perilous adventure, was prevailed upon to remain behind for the general good of the community at Nina's Hive.

At sunrise on the following morning, the 16th of April, Captain Servadac and the lieutenant took their places in the yawl. The thermometer was more than 20 degrees below zero, and it was with deep emotion that their companions beheld them thus embarking upon the vast white plain. Ben Zoof's heart was too full for words; Count Timascheff could not forbear pressing his two brave friends to his bosom; the Spaniards and the Russian sailors crowded round for a farewell shake of the hand, and little Nina, her great eyes flooded with tears, held up her face for a parting kiss. The sad scene was not permitted to be long.

The sail was quickly hoisted, and the sledge, just as if it had expanded a huge white wing, was in a little while carried far away beyond the horizon.

Count Timascheff could not forbear pressing his two brave friends
to his bosom;

Light and unimpeded, the yawl scudded on with incredible speed. Two sails, a brigantine and a jib, were arranged to catch the wind to the greatest advantage, and the travelers estimated that their progress would be little under the rate of twelve leagues an hour. The motion of their novel vehicle was singularly gentle, the oscillation being less than that of an ordinary railway-carriage, while the diminished force of gravity contributed to the swiftness. Except that the clouds of ice-dust raised by the metal runners were an evidence that they had not actually left the level surface of the ice, the captain and lieutenant might again and again have imagined that they were being conveyed through the air in a balloon.

Lieutenant Procope, with his head all muffled up for fear of frost-bite, took an occasional peep through an aperture that had been intentionally left in the roof, and by the help of a compass, maintained a proper and straight course for Formentera. Nothing could be more dejected than the aspect of that frozen sea; not a single living creature relieved the solitude; both the travelers, Procope from a scientific point of view, Servadac from an aesthetic, were alike impressed by the solemnity of the scene, and where the lengthened shadow of the sail cast upon the ice by the oblique rays of the setting sun had disappeared, and day had given place to night, the two men, drawn together as by an involuntary impulse, mutually held each other's hands in silence.

There had been a new moon on the previous evening; but, in the absence of moonlight, the constellations shone with remarkable brilliancy. The new pole-star close upon the horizon was resplendent, and even had Lieutenant Procope been destitute of a compass, he would have had no difficulty in holding his course by the guidance of that alone. However great was the distance that separated Gallia from the sun, it was after all manifestly insignificant in comparison with the remoteness of the nearest of the fixed stars.

Observing that Servadac was completely absorbed in his own thoughts, Lieutenant Procope had leisure to contemplate some of the present perplexing problems, and to ponder over the true astronomical position. The last of the three mysterious documents had represented that Gallia, in conformity with Kepler's second law, had traveled along her orbit during the month of March twenty millions of leagues less than she had done in the previous month; yet, in the same time, her distance from the sun had nevertheless been increased by thirty-two millions of leagues. She was now, therefore, in the center of the zone of telescopic planets that revolve between the orbits of Mars and Jupiter, and had captured for herself a satellite which, according to the document, was Nerina, one of the asteroids most recently identified. If thus, then, it was within the power of the unknown writer to estimate with such apparent certainty Gallia's exact position, was it not likely that his mathematical calculations would enable him to arrive at some definite conclusion as to the date at which she would begin again to approach the sun? Nay, was it not to be expected that he had already estimated, with sufficient approximation to truth, what was to be the true length of the Gallian year?

So intently had they each separately been following their own train of thought, that daylight reappeared almost before the travelers were aware of it. On consulting their instruments, they found that they must have traveled close upon a hundred leagues since they started, and they resolved to slacken their speed. The sails were accordingly taken in a little, and in spite of the intensity of the cold, the explorers ventured out of their shelter, in order that they might reconnoiter the plain, which was apparently as boundless as ever. It was completely desert; not so much as a single point of rock relieved the bare uniformity of its surface.

"Are we not considerably to the west of Formentera?" asked Servadac, after examining the chart.

"Most likely," replied Procope. "I have taken the same course as I should have done at sea, and I have kept some distance to windward of the island; we can bear straight down upon it whenever we like."

"Bear down then, now; and as quickly as you can."

The yawl was at once put with her head to the northeast and Captain Servadac, in defiance of the icy blast, remained standing at the bow, his gaze fixed on the horizon.

All at once his eye brightened.

"Look! look!" he exclaimed, pointing to a faint outline that broke the monotony of the circle that divided the plain from the sky.

In an instant the lieutenant had seized his telescope.

"I see what you mean," said he; "it is a pylone that has been used for some geodesic survey."

The next moment the sail was filled, and the yawl was bearing down upon the object with inconceivable swiftness, both Captain Servadac and the lieutenant too excited to utter a word. Mile after mile the distance rapidly grew less, and as they drew nearer the pylone they could see that it was erected on a low mass of rocks that was the sole interruption to the dull level of the field of ice. No wreath of smoke rose above the little island; it was manifestly impossible, they conceived, that any human being could there have survived the cold;

the sad presentiment forced itself upon their minds that it was a mere cairn to which they had been hurrying.

"Look! look!" cried the Captain.

Ten minutes later, and they were so near the rock that the lieutenant took in his sail, convinced that the impetus already attained would be sufficient to carry him to the land. Servadac's heart bounded as he caught sight of a fragment of blue canvas fluttering in the wind from the top of the pylone: it was all that now remained of the French national standard. At the foot of the pylone stood a miserable shed, its shutters tightly closed. No other habitation was to be seen; the entire island was less than a quarter of a mile in circumference; and the conclusion was irresistible that it was the sole surviving remnant of Formentera, once a member of the Balearic Archipelago.

To leap on shore, to clamber over the slippery stones, and to reach the cabin was but the work of a few moments. The worm-eaten door was bolted on the inside. Servadac began to knock with all his might. No answer. Neither shouting nor knocking could draw forth a reply.

"Let us force it open, Procope!" he said.

"No; he is alive!" he said.

The two men put their shoulders to the door, which soon yielded to their vigorous efforts, and they found themselves inside the shed, and in almost total darkness. By opening a shutter they admitted what daylight they could. At first sight the wretched place seemed to be deserted; the little grate contained the ashes of a fire long since extinguished; all looked black and desolate. Another instant's investigation, however, revealed a bed in the extreme corner, and extended on the bed a human form.

"Dead!" sighed Servadac; "dead of cold and hunger!"

Lieutenant Procope bent down and anxiously contemplated the body.

"No; he is alive!" he said, and drawing a small flask from his pocket he poured a few drops of brandy between the lips of the senseless man.

There was a faint sigh, followed by a feeble voice, which uttered the one word, "Gallia?"

"Yes, yes! Gallia!" echoed Servadac, eagerly.

"My comet, my comet!" said the voice, so low as to be almost inaudible, and the unfortunate man relapsed again into unconsciousness.

"Where have I seen this man?" thought Servadac to himself; "his face is strangely familiar to me."

But it was no time for deliberation. Not a moment was to be lost in getting the unconscious astronomer away from his desolate quarters. He was soon conveyed to the yawl; his books, his scanty wardrobe, his papers, his instruments, and the blackboard which had served for his calculations, were quickly collected; the wind, by a fortuitous Providence, had shifted into a favorable quarter; they set their sail with all speed, and ere long were on their journey back from Formentera.

Thirty-six hours later, the brave travelers were greeted by the acclamations of their fellow-colonists, who had been most anxiously awaiting their reappearance, and the still senseless *savant*, who had neither opened his eyes nor spoken a word throughout the journey, was safely deposited in the warmth and security of the great hall of Nina's Hive.

END OF FIRST BOOK

BOOK II.

CHAPTER I.

THE ASTRONOMER

BY the return of the expedition, conveying its contribution from Formentera, the known population of Gallia was raised to a total of thirty-six.

On learning the details of his friends' discoveries, Count Timascheff did not hesitate in believing that the exhausted individual who was lying before him was the author alike of the two unsigned documents picked up at sea, and of the third statement so recently brought to hand by the carrier-pigeon. Manifestly, he had arrived at some knowledge of Gallia's movements: he had estimated her distance from the sun; he had calculated the diminution of her tangential speed; but there was nothing to show that he had arrived at the conclusions which were of the most paramount interest to them all. Had he ascertained the true character of her orbit? had he established any data from which it would be possible to reckon what time must elapse before she would again approach the earth?

The only intelligible words which the astronomer had uttered had been, "My comet!"

To what could the exclamation refer? Was it to be conjectured that a fragment of the earth had been chipped off by the collision of a comet? and if so, was it implied that the name of the comet itself was Gallia, and were they mistaken in supposing that such was the name given by the *savant* to the little world that had been so suddenly launched into space? Again and again they discussed these questions; but no satisfactory answer could be found. The only man who was able to throw any light upon the subject was lying amongst them in an unconscious and half-dying condition.

Apart from motives of humanity, motives of self-interest made it a matter of the deepest concern to restore animation to that senseless form. Ben Zoof, after making the encouraging remark that *savants*

have as many lives as a cat, proceeded, with Negrete's assistance, to
give the body such a vigorous rubbing as would have threatened serious injury to any ordinary mortal, whilst they administered cordials
and restoratives from the *Dobryna's* medical stores powerful enough,
one might think, to rouse the very dead.

Palmyrin Rosette

Meanwhile the captain was racking his brain in his exertions to
recall what were the circumstances of his previous acquaintance with
the Frenchman upon whose features he was gazing; he only grew
more and more convinced that he had once been familiar with them.
Perhaps it was not altogether surprising that he had almost forgotten

him; he had never seen him since the days of his youth, that time of life which, with a certain show of justice, has been termed the age of ingratitude; for, in point of fact, the astronomer was none other than Professor Palmyrin Rosette, Servadac's old science-master at the Lycee Charlemagne.

After completing his year of elementary studies, Hector Servadac had entered the school at Saint Cyr, and from that time he and his former tutor had never met, so that naturally they would well-nigh pass from each other's recollection. One thing, however, on the other hand, might conduce to a mutual and permanent impression on their memories; during the year at the Lycee, young Servadac, never of a very studious turn of mind, had contrived, as the ringleader of a set of like caliber as himself, to lead the poor professor a life of perpetual torment. On the discovery of each delinquency he would fume and rage in a manner that was a source of unbounded delight to his audience.

Two years after Servadac left the Lycee, Professor Rosette had thrown up all educational employment in order that he might devote himself entirely to the study of astronomy. He endeavored to obtain a post at the Observatory, but his ungenial character was so well known in scientific circles that he failed in his application; however, having some small private means, he determined on his own account to carry on his researches without any official salary. He had really considerable genius for the science that he had adopted; besides discovering three of the latest of the telescopic planets, he had worked out the elements of the three hundred and twenty-fifth comet in the catalogue; but his chief delight was to criticize the publications of other astronomers, and he was never better pleased than when he detected a flaw in their reckonings.

When Ben Zoof and Negrete had extricated their patient from the envelope of furs in which he had been wrapped by Servadac and the lieutenant, they found themselves face to face with a shrivelled little man, about five feet two inches high, with a round bald head, smooth and shiny as an ostrich's egg, no beard unless the unshorn growth of a week could be so described, and a long hooked nose that supported a huge pair of spectacles such as with many near-sighted people seems to have become a part of their individuality. His nervous system was remarkably developed, and his body might not inaptly be compared to one of the Rhumkorff's bobbins of which the thread, several hundred

yards in length, is permeated throughout by electric fluid. But whatever he was, his life, if possible, must be preserved. When he had been
partially divested of his clothing, his heart was found to be still beat-
ing, though very feebly. Asserting that while there was life there was
hope, Ben Zoof recommenced his friction with more vigor than ever.

When the rubbing had been continued without a moment's intermission for the best part of half an hour, the astronomer heaved a
faint sigh, which ere long was followed by another and another. He
half opened his eyes, closed them again, then opened them completely,
but without exhibiting any consciousness whatever of his situation.
A few words seemed to escape his lips, but they were quite unintel-
ligible. Presently he raised his right hand to his forehead as though
instinctively feeling for something that was missing; then, all of a
sudden, his features became contracted, his face flushed with apparent
irritation, and he exclaimed fretfully, "My spectacles!—where are my
spectacles?"

In order to facilitate his operations, Ben Zoof had removed the
spectacles in spite of the tenacity with which they seemed to adhere to
the temples of his patient; but he now rapidly brought them back and
readjusted them as best he could to what seemed to be their natural position on the aquiline nose. The professor heaved a long sigh of relief,
and once more closed his eyes.

Before long the astronomer roused himself a little more, and glanced
inquiringly about him, but soon relapsed into his comatose condition.
When next he opened his eyes, Captain Servadac happened to be bend-
ing down closely over him, examining his features with curious scrutiny. The old man darted an angry look at him through the spectacles,
and said sharply, "Servadac, five hundred lines to-morrow!"

It was an echo of days of old. The words were few, but they were
enough to recall the identity which Servadac was trying to make out.

"Is it possible?" he exclaimed. "Here is my old tutor, Mr. Rosette,
in very flesh and blood."

"Can't say much for the flesh," muttered Ben Zoof.

The old man had again fallen back into a torpid slumber. Ben Zoof
continued, "His sleep is getting more composed. Let him alone; he will
come round yet. Haven't I heard of men more dried up than he is, being brought all the way from Egypt in cases covered with pictures?"

"You idiot!—those were mummies; they had been dead for ages."

Ben Zoof did not answer a word. He went on preparing a warm bed, into which he managed to remove his patient, who soon fell into a calm and natural sleep.

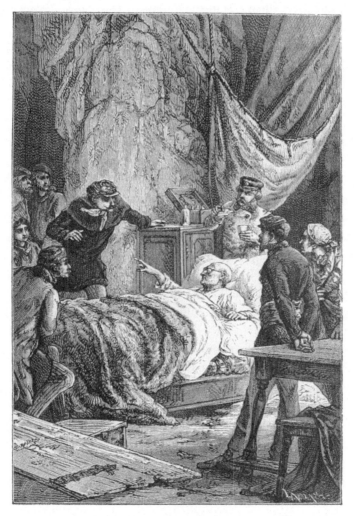

"Servadac, five hundred lines to-morrow!"

Too impatient to await the awakening of the astronomer and to hear what representations he had to make, Servadac, the count, and the lieutenant, constituting themselves what might be designated "the Academy of Sciences" of the colony, spent the whole of the remainder of the day in starting and discussing the wildest conjectures about their situation. The hypothesis, to which they had now accustomed themselves for so long, that a new asteroid had been formed by a fracture of the earth's surface, seemed to fall to the ground when they found that Professor Palmyrin Rosette had associated the name of Gallia, not with their present home, but with what he called "my comet"; and that theory being abandoned, they were driven to make the most improbable speculations to replace it.

Alluding to Rosette, Servadac took care to inform his companions that, although the professor was always eccentric, and at times very irascible, yet he was really exceedingly good-hearted; his bark was worse than his bite; and if suffered to take their course without observation, his outbreaks of ill-temper seldom lasted long.

"We will certainly do our best to get on with him," said the count. "He is no doubt the author of the papers, and we must hope that he will be able to give us some valuable information."

"Beyond a question the documents have originated with him," assented the lieutenant. "Gallia was the word written at the top of every one of them, and Gallia was the first word uttered by him in our hearing."

The astronomer slept on. Meanwhile, the three together had no hesitation in examining his papers, and scrutinizing the figures on his extemporized blackboard. The handwriting corresponded with that of the papers already received; the blackboard was covered with algebraical symbols traced in chalk, which they were careful not to obliterate; and the papers, which consisted for the most part of detached scraps, presented a perfect wilderness of geometrical figures, conic sections of every variety being repeated in countless profusion.

Lieutenant Procope pointed out that these curves evidently had reference to the orbits of comets, which are variously parabolic, hyperbolic, or elliptic. If either of the first two, the comet, after once appearing within the range of terrestrial vision, would vanish forever in the outlying regions of space; if the last, it would be sure, sooner or later, after some periodic interval, to return.

From the *prima facie* appearance of his papers, then, it seemed probable that the astronomer, during his sojourn at Formentera, had been devoting himself to the study of cometary orbits; and as calculations of this kind are ordinarily based upon the assumption that the orbit is a parabola, it was not unlikely that he had been endeavoring to trace the path of some particular comet.

"I wonder whether these calculations were made before or after the 1st of January; it makes all the difference," said Lieutenant Procope.

"We must bide our time and hear," replied the count.

Servadac paced restlessly up and down. "I would give a month of my life," he cried, impetuously, "for every hour that the old fellow goes sleeping on."

"You might be making a bad bargain," said Procope, smiling. "Perhaps after all the comet has had nothing to do with the convulsion that we have experienced."

"Nonsense!" exclaimed the captain; "I know better than that, and so do you. Is it not as clear as daylight that the earth and this comet have been in collision, and the result has been that our little world has been split off and sent flying far into space?"

Count Timascheff and the lieutenant looked at each other in silence. "I do not deny your theory," said Procope after a while. "If it be correct, I suppose we must conclude that the enormous disc we observed on the night of the catastrophe was the comet itself; and the velocity with which it was traveling must have been so great that it was hardly arrested at all by the attraction of the earth."

"Plausible enough," answered Count Timascheff; "and it is to this comet that our scientific friend here has given the name of Gallia."

It still remained a puzzle to them all why the astronomer should apparently be interested in the comet so much more than in the new little world in which their strange lot was cast.

"Can you explain this?" asked the count.

"There is no accounting for the freaks of philosophers, you know," said Servadac; "and have I not told you that this philosopher in particular is one of the most eccentric beings in creation?"

"Besides," added the lieutenant, "it is exceedingly likely that his observations had been going on for some considerable period before the convulsion happened."

Thus, the general conclusion arrived at by the Gallian Academy of Science was this: That on the night of the 31st of December, a comet, crossing the ecliptic, had come into collision with the earth, and that the violence of the shock had separated a huge fragment from the globe, which fragment from that date had been traversing the remote inter-planetary regions.

Palmyrin Rosette would doubtless confirm their solution of the phenomenon.

CHAPTER II.

A REVELATION

To the general population of the colony the arrival of the stranger was a matter of small interest. The Spaniards were naturally too indolent to be affected in any way by an incident that concerned themselves so remotely; while the Russians felt themselves simply reliant on their master, and as long as they were with him were careless as to where or how they spent their days. Everything went on with them in an accustomed routine; and they lay down night after night, and awoke to their avocations morning after morning, just as if nothing extraordinary had occurred.

All night long Ben Zoof would not leave the professor's bedside. He had constituted himself sick nurse, and considered his reputation at stake if he failed to set his patient on his feet again. He watched every movement, listened to every breath, and never failed to administer the strongest cordials upon the slightest pretext. Even in his sleep Rosette's irritable nature revealed itself. Ever and again, sometimes in a tone of uneasiness, and sometimes with the expression of positive anger, the name of Gallia escaped his lips, as though he were dreaming that his claim to the discovery of the comet was being contested or denied; but although his attendant was on the alert to gather all he could, he was able to catch nothing in the incoherent sentences that served to throw any real light upon the problem that they were all eager to solve.

When the sun reappeared on the western horizon the professor was still sound asleep; and Ben Zoof, who was especially anxious that the repose which promised to be so beneficial should not be disturbed, felt considerable annoyance at hearing a loud knocking, evidently of some blunt heavy instrument against a door that had been placed at the entrance of the gallery, more for the purpose of retaining internal warmth than for guarding against intrusion from without.

"Confound it!" said Ben Zoof. "I must put a stop to this;" and he made his way towards the door.

"Who's there?" he cried, in no very amiable tone.

"I." replied the quavering voice.

"Who are you?"

"Who's there?" he cried, in no very amiable tone.

"Isaac Hakkabut. Let me in; do, please, let me in."

"Oh, it is you, old Ashtaroth, is it? What do you want? Can't you get anybody to buy your stuffs?"

"Nobody will pay me a proper price."

"Well, old Shimei, you won't find a customer here. You had better be off."

"No; but do, please—do, please, let me in," supplicated the Jew. "I want to speak to his Excellency, the governor."

"The governor is in bed, and asleep."

"I can wait until he awakes."

"Then wait where you are."

And with this inhospitable rejoinder the orderly was about to return to his place at the side of his patient, when Servadac, who had been roused by the sound of voices, called out, "What's the matter, Ben Zoof?"

"Oh, nothing, sir; only that hound of a Hakkabut says he wants to speak to you."

"Let him in, then."

Ben Zoof hesitated.

"Let him in, I say," repeated the captain, peremptorily.

However reluctantly, Ben Zoof obeyed. The door was unfastened, and Isaac Hakkabut, enveloped in an old overcoat, shuffled into the gallery. In a few moments Servadac approached, and the Jew began to overwhelm him with the most obsequious epithets. Without vouchsafing any reply, the captain beckoned to the old man to follow him, and leading the way to the central hall, stopped, and turning so as to look him steadily in the face, said, "Now is your opportunity. Tell me what you want."

"Oh, my lord, my lord," whined Isaac, "you must have some news to tell me."

"News? What do you mean?"

"From my little tartan yonder, I saw the yawl go out from the rock here on a journey, and I saw it come back, and it brought a stranger; and I thought—I thought—I thought—"

"Well, you thought—what did you think?"

"Why, that perhaps the stranger had come from the northern shores of the Mediterranean, and that I might ask him—"

He paused again, and gave a glance at the captain.

"Ask him what? Speak out, man?"

"Ask him if he brings any tidings of Europe," Hakkabut blurted out at last.

"Ask him if he brings any tidings of Europe."

Servadac shrugged his shoulders in contempt and turned away. Here was a man who had been resident three months in Gallia, a living witness of all the abnormal phenomena that had occurred, and yet refusing to believe that his hope of making good bargains with European traders was at an end. Surely nothing, thought the captain, will convince the old rascal now; and he moved off in disgust. The orderly, however, who had listened with much amusement, was by no means disinclined for the conversation to be continued. "Are you satisfied, old Ezekiel?" he asked.

"Isn't it so? Am I not right? Didn't a stranger arrive here last night?" inquired the Jew.

"Yes, quite true."

"Where from?"

"From the Balearic Isles."

"The Balearic Isles?" echoed Isaac.

"Yes."

"Fine quarters for trade! Hardly twenty leagues from Spain! He must have brought news from Europe!"

"Well, old Manasseh, what if he has?"

"I should like to see him."

"Can't be."

The Jew sidled close up to Ben Zoof, and laying his hand on his arm, said in a low and insinuating tone, "I am poor, you know; but I would give you a few reals if you would let me talk to this stranger."

But as if he thought he was making too liberal an offer, he added, "Only it must be at once."

"He is too tired; he is worn out; he is fast asleep," answered Ben Zoof.

"But I would pay you to wake him."

The captain had overheard the tenor of the conversation, and interposed sternly, "Hakkabut! if you make the least attempt to disturb our visitor, I shall have you turned outside that door immediately."

"No offense, my lord, I hope," stammered out the Jew. "I only meant—"

"Silence!" shouted Servadac. The old man hung his head, abashed.

"I will tell you what," said Servadac after a brief interval; "I will give you leave to hear what this stranger has to tell as soon as he is able to tell us anything; at present we have not heard a word from his lips."

The Jew looked perplexed.

"Yes," said Servadac; "when we hear his story, you shall hear it too."

"And I hope it will be to your liking, old Ezekiel!" added Ben Zoof in a voice of irony.

They had none of them long to wait, for within a few minutes Rosette's peevish voice was heard calling, "Joseph! Joseph!"

The professor did not open his eyes, and appeared to be slumbering on, but very shortly afterwards called out again, "Joseph! Confound the fellow! where is he?" It was evident that he was half dreaming about a former servant now far away on the ancient globe. "Where's my blackboard, Joseph?"

"Quite safe, sir," answered Ben Zoof, quickly.

Rosette unclosed his eyes and fixed them full upon the orderly's face. "Are you Joseph?" he asked.

"At your service, sir," replied Ben Zoof with imperturbable gravity.

"Then get me my coffee, and be quick about it."

Ben Zoof left to go into the kitchen, and Servadac approached the professor in order to assist him in rising to a sitting posture.

"Do you recognize your quondam pupil, professor?" he asked.

"Ah, yes, yes; you are Servadac," replied Rosette. "It is twelve years or more since I saw you; I hope you have improved."

"Quite a reformed character, sir, I assure you," said Servadac, smiling.

"Well, that's as it should be; that's right," said the astronomer with fussy importance. "But let me have my coffee," he added impatiently; "I cannot collect my thoughts without my coffee."

Fortunately, Ben Zoof appeared with a great cup, hot and strong. After draining it with much apparent relish, the professor got out of bed, walked into the common hall, round which he glanced with a pre-occupied air, and proceeded to seat himself in an armchair, the most comfortable which the cabin of the *Dobryna* had supplied. Then, in a voice full of satisfaction, and that involuntarily recalled the exclamations of delight that had wound up the two first of the mysterious documents that had been received, he burst out, "Well, gentlemen, what do you think of Gallia?"

There was no time for anyone to make a reply before Isaac Hakkabut had darted forward.

"By the God—"

"Who is that?" asked the startled professor; and he frowned, and made a gesture of repugnance.

Regardless of the efforts that were made to silence him, the Jew continued, "By the God of Abraham, I beseech you, give me some tidings of Europe!"

"Europe?" shouted the professor, springing from his seat as if he were electrified; "what does the man want with Europe?"

"I want to get there!" screeched the Jew; and in spite of every exertion to get him away, he clung most tenaciously to the professor's chair, and again and again implored for news of Europe.

Rosette made no immediate reply. After a moment or two's reflection, he turned to Servadac and asked him whether it was not the middle of April.

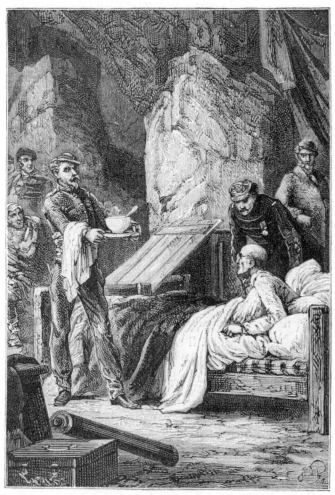

Fortunately, Ben Zoof appeared with a great cup, hot and strong.

"It is the twentieth," answered the captain.

"Then to-day," said the astronomer, speaking with the greatest deliberation—"to-day we are just three millions of leagues away from Europe."

The Jew was utterly crestfallen.

"You seem here," continued the professor, "to be very ignorant of the state of things."

"You are on my comet, on Gallia itself!"

"How far we are ignorant," rejoined Servadac, "I cannot tell. But I will tell you all that we do know, and all that we have surmised." And as briefly as he could, he related all that had happened since the memorable night of the thirty-first of December; how they had experienced the shock; how the *Dobryna* had made her voyage; how they had discovered nothing except the fragments of the old continent at Tunis, Sardinia, Gibraltar, and now at Formentera; how at intervals

the three anonymous documents had been received; and, finally, how
the settlement at Gourbi Island had been abandoned for their present
quarters at Nina's Hive.

The astronomer had hardly patience to hear him to the end. "And
what do you say is your surmise as to your present position?" he asked.

"Our supposition," the captain replied, "is this. We imagine that
we are on a considerable fragment of the terrestrial globe that has been
detached by collision with a planet to which you appear to have given
the name of Gallia."

"Better than that!" cried Rosette, starting to his feet with
excitement.

"How? Why? What do you mean?" cried the voices of the listeners.

"You are correct to a certain degree," continued the professor. "It
is quite true that at 47' 35.6" after two o'clock on the morning of the
first of January there was a collision; my comet grazed the earth; and
the bits of the earth which you have named were carried clean away."

They were all fairly bewildered.

"Where, then," cried Servadac eagerly, "where are we?"

"You are on my comet, on Gallia itself!"

And the professor gazed around him with a perfect air of triumph.

CHAPTER III.

COMETS, OLD AND NEW.

As if moved by some unconscious presentiment of his future destiny, Professor Palmyrin Rosette had always evidenced a strong predilection for the study of comets. He had based his opinions on the best authorities, and was never more in his element than when he was expatiating on his favorite theme as he presided at some astronomical conference.

"Comets, gentlemen," he would say, "are nebulous bodies which occasionally appear in the heavens, consisting ordinarily of a bright central light called the nucleus and in the more conspicuous cases accompanied by a long trail of light called the *tail*. Owing to the great eccentricity of their orbits, they are visible to the earth during only a portion of their course."

The professor never failed to point out the two characteristics by which they were to be distinguished from other heavenly bodies:

"Although these comets, gentlemen, may be deficient either with respect to the luminous tail or to the nebulous coma, the progressive motion with which they are endued prevents them from ever being mistaken for fixed stars, while the extreme length of the ellipses which they describe makes it impossible to confound them with planets,"

During the long years of the astronomer's application to his fascinating study, he had composed an elaborate treatise, exhibiting the results of all his investigations, and when, after the sudden convulsion, he found himself actually upon the surface of one of the very bodies the properties of which had engrossed so much of his interest, it was necessarily a disappointment to feel that, alone upon Formentera, he had no audience to whom he could address himself.

The treatise which Rosette had compiled had been arranged under four distinct heads:

1. The number of comets.
2. Periodic and non-periodic comets.
3. The probability of collision between a comet and the earth.
4. The consequences of such a collision.

First: with respect to the number of comets, the professor had recorded that, according to Arago, who grounded his estimate on the number that revolve between Mercury and the sun, there are at least 17,000,000 of these luminous bodies in our solar system; whilst Lambert asserts that within the orbit of Saturn, that is, within a radius of 872,135,000 miles, there are no less then 500,000,000. According to Kepler, two hundred years previously, the number of comets can only be compared to the fishes in the sea, and in following out his simile he declares that an angler throwing out his line from the surface of the sun could not fail to touch several of them; and now in recent times a computation has been made that their aggregate reaches a total of 74,000,000,000 distinct comets. The truth seems to be that their number really sets all calculation at defiance; so erratic, moreover, are their movements, that they sometimes pass from system to system, and whilst some, entirely escaping the influence of the sun, vanish, to find a new centre of attraction, others never before observed make their appearance upon the terrestrial horizon.

Even the comets which belong exclusively to our own system are by no means exempt from strange irregularities; the orbits of several, ceasing to be ellipses, have become parabolas or hyperbolas; and the planets, Jupiter in particular, have been observed to exercise a large disturbing action upon their paths.

Secondly: under the head of periodic and non-periodic comets, Professor Rosette had stated that as many as 500 or 600 comets have been made objects of careful astronomical investigation; those being called "periodic" of which the return at fixed intervals has been established as a certainty; those, on the other hand, being classed as "non-periodic" which recede to such immeasurable distances from the sun that it cannot be determined whether they will return or not.

Of the periodic comets there are not more than *forty* of which the times of their revolution have been ascertained with exact precision; but of these there are ten, generally known as the "short-period comets," the movements of which have been established with the nicest accuracy.

The short-period comets are respectively called by the names of their discoverers, and are commonly distinguished as Halley's comet, Enckes, Gambart's or Biela's, Faye's, Brörsen's, D'Arrest's, Tattle's, Winnecke's, De Vico's, and Tempel's.

Subjoined is a brief account of each of these in detail.

Halley's comet is that which has been the longest known. It is supposed to be identical with the one which was observed in the years 134 and 52 B.C., and afterwards in the years 400, 855, 930, 1006, 1230, 1305, 1380, 1456, 1531, 1607, 1682, 1759, and 1835 A.D. It revolves from east to west, in a direction contrary to the planets. The intervals between its consecutive appearances vary from 75 to 76 years, according as its course is less or more disturbed by the attraction of Jupiter and Saturn, which sometimes influence its course to such an extent as to make a difference of 200 days in the period of its arrival. The last appearance of this comet was in 1835, when Sir John Herschel, at the Cape of Good Hope, a more favorable station for observation than any in the northern hemisphere, was able to watch it until the end of March 1836, after which its distance from the earth rendered it invisible. At its aphelion it is 3,200,000,000 miles from the sun, that is to say, it is beyond the orbit of Neptune, but at its perihelion it is less than 57,000,000 miles from the sun, and consequently is nearer than the planet Venus.

Little did the professor dream, at the time when he drew up his treatise, that his own Gallia would transport him to a still closer proximity to the great luminary.

Encke's comet has the shortest period of any, its revolution being accomplished in about 1205 days, or less than three years and a half. Unlike Halley's, it moves as the planets, from west to east. It was observed on the 26th of November, 1818, and a calculation of its elements proved it to be identical with the comet of 1805. According to prediction, it was seen again in 1822, and since that time has never failed in making its appearance at regular intervals. Its orbit lies within that of Jupiter, and it never recedes more than 387,000,000 miles from the sun, its perihelion distance being only 32,000,000 miles, or less than that of Mercury.

One important observation that has been made with regard to Encke's comet, places it beyond doubt that the axis major of its elliptical orbit is gradually diminishing, and consequently its average distance from the sun is growing continuously less and less, so that the probability arises that unless it is previously volatilized by the solar heat, it may be ultimately absorbed in the sun itself.

Gambart's comet (otherwise known as Biela's) was noticed in 1772, 1789, 1795, and 1805; but it was not until the 28th of February, 1826, that its elements were satisfactorily determined. Its motion is direct, and its period of revolution 2410 days, or about seven years. At perihelion it passes 82,000,000 miles from the sun, rather nearer than the earth; at aphelion it is beyond the orbit of Jupiter.

A singular phenomenon with regard to Biela's comet was first observed in the year 1846: it appeared like a double star, in two distinct fragments, doubtless sundered by the action of some internal force; these fragments travelled together at an interval of about 160,000 miles apart, but at the next appearance in 1852 this interval was found to be largely increased.

Faye's comet was discovered by him for the first time on the 22nd of November, 1843. The elements of its orbit were calculated, and it was predicted that it would return again in 1851, after a period of 2718 days, or in about seven years and a half. The prediction was realized; the comet was visible at the time announced, and has subsequently appeared at similar intervals. Its motion is direct At perihelion it is 192,000,000 miles from the sun, never approaching so near as Mars; at aphelion it is distant 603,000,000 miles, so that it recedes, like Biela's comet, beyond the pathway of Jupiter.

Brörsen's comet was discovered on the 26th of February, 1846. Its movement is from west to east; it accomplishes its revolution in about 2042 days; its perihelion distance is 64,000,000 miles, its aphelion 537,000,000 miles.

Of the other short-period comets, D'Arrest's, which in 1862 passed within 30,000,000 miles of the planet Jupiter, completes its revolution in rather more than six years and a half; Tuttle's revolves in thirteen years and eight months; Winnecke's and Temple's in about five years and a half; whilst that of De Vico, after being computed to revolve in a period of rather more than five years, seems to have wandered away altogether into space.

Then follows a short enumeration of some of the "long-period" comets.

The comet of 1556, commonly called the comet of Charles-Quint, was expected again in 1860, but did not re-appear.

The comet of 1680 furnished the data for Newton's cometary theories, and, according to Whiston, was the cause of the deluge, on account of its close approximation to the earth. Its revolution takes about 575 years, so that it was visible in 1106 and 531, as well as in 43 B.C. and probably in 619 B.C. At its perihelion it passes so near the sun that it receives 28,000 times more heat than the earth, that is, it is 2000 times hotter than molten iron.

The comet of 1744 was by far the most brilliant of the eighteenth century; it was seen on the 1st of March in full daylight, and had six tails, spread out like a fan across a large space in the heavens.

The great comet of 1811, which has caused the year of its appearance to be familiarly recognized as "the comet-year," had a nucleus 2637 miles in diameter; its head was 1,270,000 miles in diameter, and its tail 100,000,000 miles in length.

The comet of 1843, observed by Cassini, has been supposed to be identical with that of 1668, 1494, and 1317, but astronomers are not agreed upon the period of its revolution. At its perihelion it passes nearer to the sun than any other comet recorded in history, travelling at a rate of more than 40,000 miles a second. The heat that it thus receives is equal to that which 47,000 suns would communicate to the earth, and to such a degree does this prodigious temperature increase its density, that at its last appearance its tail was visible in broad daylight.

Donati's comet, which in 1858 shone with such brilliancy amongst the northern constellations, has a mass that has been estimated at .07 of that of the earth.

The comet of 1862 was adorned with luminous tufts or aigrettes, and resembled some fantastic mollusk.

The list is completed by the comet of 1868, the revolution of which occupies a period of no less than 2800 centuries, so that it may practically be considered as having vanished in infinite space.

Thirdly: the next section of the professor's dissertation was devoted to the probability of a collision between any one of these numerous comets and the earth.

As represented in plane diagrams, the orbits of planetary and cometary bodies appear continually to be intersecting one another; but in free space of three dimensions this is by no means necessarily the case; the planes of the orbits being inclined at various angles to the ecliptic, which is the plane of the terrestrial orbit. Nevertheless, out of the large number of comets, is it impossible that one of them should come in contact with the earth?

In conducting this investigation, it had to be recollected that as the earth never leaves the plane of the ecliptic, three conditions must be fulfilled in order to bring about the result of impact: first, the comet must meet the earth in the ecliptic; secondly, the earth and the comet must arrive at the point of intersection of their orbits at the same moment; and thirdly, the distance between the centres of the bodies themselves must be less than the sum of their radii. The problem, therefore, resolved itself into an inquiry whether these three conditions could occur simultaneously.

Laplace did not reject the possibility of such an encounter, and in his "Exposition du Système du Monde" has at some length detailed the consequences. Arago, when asked his opinion on the subject, replied that by calculation there were 280,000,000 chances to 1 against a collision. The illustrious astronomer, however, based his estimate upon two conditions that are only fulfilled with the greatest uncertainty; in the first place, that at perihelion the comet should be nearer the sun than the earth is; and in the next, that the diameter of the comet should be equal to one-fourth of that of the earth. On the other hand, he only reckoned for the earth coming in contact with the actual nucleus, whilst if the whole extent of the nebulosity were to be taken into account, the chances of collision would be increased tenfold.

In enunciating his problem, Arago adds:

"If we take it for granted that the result of a comet running foul of the earth would be the total annihilation of the human race, then the risk of death which each individual incurs from the probability of such a catastrophe is just what would be his chance of drawing, at the first draw, the only white ball out of an urn containing 280,000,000 colored ones." So remote appear the chances of collision.

All astronomers, moreover, concur in distinctly denying that any such collision has ever happened Arago asserts that if it had happened, the consequences would have been an immediate alteration in the earth s axis of rotation, and a general disturbance of terrestrial latitudes; but he alleges no evidence in proof of his assertion. He speaks, however, much more to the purpose when he declares that "the theory held by some, that the depression of the Caspian Sea 300 feet below the level of the ocean is to be attributed to the shock of a comet, is utterly untenable."

But the matter under consideration was not whether collision had ever occurred, but whether it ever could occur.

Now in 1832, at the re-appearance of Gambart's comet, the world was thrown Into some alarm because it was announced as the result of astronomical calculations, that at the time of the passage of the comet through its descending node on the 29th of October, the earth would be travelling precisely in the same region. Contact seemed not only probable but inevitable, if Olbers' observation was correct, that the radius of the comet was five times as large as that of the earth. Happily, however, the earth did not arrive at that point of the ecliptic until the 30th of November, by which time the comet was more than 50,000,000 miles away. But supposing that the earth had reached that place of intersection of the two orbits a month sooner, or the comet a month later, it is hard to say what could have obviated the likelihood of collision. At the very least, some singular perturbations must have ensued. In 1805 Indeed, this identical comet had passed within 6,000,000 miles of the earth, ten times closer than in 1832, but as its proximity was unknown, the fact did not excite any panic.

Again in 1843 there seemed reasonable ground for fear that the atmosphere of the earth would be vitiated by passing through the nebulous tail of a comet 150,000,000 miles in length.

Altogether, therefore, from the entire evidence, it appeared a necessary inference that collision between the earth and a comet was by no means impossible.

Fourthly, then, Professor Rosette had to discuss the remaining question to bring his treatise to a close; as to the probable consequences of such a collision.

These consequences would manifestly vary according as the comet had or had not a nucleus. As some fruits have no kernel, so some comets have no nucleus, and such is the tenuity of their substance, that stars of the tenth magnitude have been seen through them without any sensible diminution of light. It is a property that must make their external form very susceptible of change, and tends in a degree to make them difficult of recognition. The same transparency characterises the tail, the development of which is apparently due entirely to the evaporation of the coma under the action of solar heat; in proof of which it is notified that no tail, either single or multiple, has ever been found attached to a comet until that comet has arrived within 80,000,000 miles of the sun; whilst it has been observed that some comets, presumably composed of denser structure, have emitted no tail at all.

In the case of the earth coming into contact with a comet destitute of a nucleus, there would be no violent collision; strictly speaking, there would be no shock at all. The astronomer Faye asserts that a cannon ball would find more resistance in a cobweb than in the nebulous parts of a comet; and for the nebulous matter to be injurious, it must either be incandescent, in which case it would scorch up the surface of the earth, or it must be impregnated with noxious elements, in which case it might be fatally destructive to life. This latter contingency, how- ever, is unlikely to arise; for, according to Babinet, the earth's atmo- sphere possesses sufficient density of its own to resist the penetration of any cometary vapors, of which the tenuity is so slight, that Newton has calculated that if a comet, without a nucleus, 1,000,000,000 miles in radius, were reduced to the density of the air at the earth's surface, it might all be contained in a thimble less than an inch in diameter.

Concluding thus that from comets purely nebulous there was a minimum of danger to be apprehended, the professor proceeded to inquire what would be the result of concussion if the comet consisted of a solid nucleus.

First of all, however, rises the preliminary question whether in any case the nucleus of a comet is really solid, There can be no doubt that if a comet can attain a degree of concentration sufficient to pass out of its gaseous condition, it will, if interposed between the earth and a star, make an occultation of that star. No sound reliance is to be placed on testimony such as that of Anaxagoras, who, living in the time of Xerxes, about the year 480 B.C., recorded that the sun was eclipsed by a comet; nor on that of Dion, who maintains that a similar eclipse occurred a few days before the death of Augustus, which could not be occasioned by the moon, then in direct opposition. Modern science has, with more than sufficient justice, entirely repudiated the accuracy of these statements; but the indisputable testimony of recent observation all goes to establish the certainty of the existence of comets with a solid nucleus. The comets of 1774 and of 1828 are known to have caused the occultation of stars of the eighth magnitude; it is admitted on all hands that the comets of 1402, 1532, and 1744 were solid masses; whilst, as for the comet of 1843, the fact is patent to the world that the body could be seen close to the sun, in broad daylight, by the naked eye.

Not only, therefore, do they exist, but in some cases these solid nuclei have been actually measured. Their diameters vary considerably in length; that of Gambart's comet being only 30 or 40 miles, that of the comet of 1845 being 8800 miles, considerably longer than the diameter of the earth, so that in the event of a collision between the two bodies, the preponderance would have been on the side of the comet. The nebulous surroundings have also, in a variety of instances, been measured, and found to vary from 200,000 to 1,000,000 miles in diameter.

Upon the whole, modern investigation bears out the general statement of M. Arago that there are three kind? of comets; that is to say, comets without any nucleus; comets with a transparent nucleus; and comets with a nucleus both solid and opaque.

It had to be borne in mind that without any actual shock by collision, the mere proximity of a comet to the earth might entail some very singular phenomena. Not that from a comet of inferior mass any serious consequences could be expected, for the comet of 1770, which approached within 1,600,000 miles of the earth, did not affect the length of the terrestrial year a single second, although the action of the earth retarded the period of the comet's revolution by three whole days. But if the mass of the two bodies were equal, and if the comet passed within 150,000 miles of the earth, the result would be that the terrestrial year would be prolonged by sixteen hours and five minutes, and the obliquity of the ecliptic altered by two degrees, to say nothing of the chance that the comet might capture the moon in its passage.

What, finally, would happen in the event of the one body actually impinging on the other? The consequences, manifestly, would be far more considerable. Either the comet, in grazing the earth's surface, would leave behind it a fragment detached from itself, or it would carry off with itself a fragment detached from the earth. If, instead of being oblique, the impact should be direct, there would at least be a rupture of continents, even if the globe were not shivered into pieces.

In any case, the tangential velocity of the earth must receive a sudden check or a sudden impulse; trees, houses, living creatures, would be precipitated backwards or forwards with increased momentum; the seas, dashed from their natural basins, would overwhelm all that lay in the path of their projection; the central forces of the globe, still in their normal state of fusion, would be propelled to the surface; the terrestrial axis would undergo a change in its direction, so that a new equator would be established, and as the conditions of equilibrium would be disturbed, there might be nothing properly to counter-balance the attraction of the sun, the consequence of which, by the law of gravity, would be that the earth, drawn perpetually on in a straight line, in the space of sixty-four days and a half would be absorbed into the elements of the great central luminary of the system.

One speculation there was which to the last remained doubtful; whether, according to Tyndall's theory that heat is only a form of motion, the velocity of the earth would not, under the sudden elevation of the temperature, mechanically transform itself into heat so intense, that through its action, the earth itself, in the course of a few seconds, would be completely volatilized.

Such were the deductions of Palmyrin Rosette's treatise, which he brought to a conclusion by a repetition of the philosopher's comforting assurance, that the chances were as 280,000,000 to 1 against the occurrence of any collision.

How little could the professor, as he tabulated his scientific notes, anticipate his experiences in the future, with regard to his own Gallia!

How little could he foresee, that at some future *séance*, he would be in the position to say:

"You see, gentlemen, that we have drawn the one white ball from the urn!"

CHAPTER IV.

THE PROFESSOR'S EXPERIENCES

"YES, my comet!" repeated the professor, and from time to time he knitted his brows, and looked around him with a defiant air, as though he could not get rid of the impression that someone was laying an unwarranted claim to its proprietorship, or that the individuals before him were intruders upon his own proper domain.

But for a considerable while, Servadac, the count, and the lieutenant remained silent and sunk in thought. Here then, at last, was the unriddling of the enigma they had been so long endeavoring to solve; both the hypotheses they had formed in succession had now to give way before the announcement of the real truth. The first supposition, that the rotatory axis of the earth had been subject to some accidental modification, and the conjecture that replaced it, namely, that a certain portion of the terrestrial sphere had been splintered off and carried into space, had both now to yield to the representation that the earth had been grazed by an unknown comet, which had caught up some scattered fragments from its surface, and was bearing them far away into sidereal regions. Unfolded lay the past and the present before them; but this only served to awaken a keener interest about the future. Could the professor throw any light upon that? they longed to inquire, but did not yet venture to ask him.

Meanwhile Rosette assumed a pompous professional air, and appeared to be waiting for the entire party to be ceremoniously introduced to him. Nothing unwilling to humor the vanity of the eccentric little man, Servadac proceeded to go through the expected formalities.

"Allow me to present to you my excellent friend, the Count Timascheff," he said.

"You are very welcome," said Rosette, bowing to the count with a smile of condescension.

"Although I am not precisely a voluntary resident on your comet, Mr. Professor, I beg to acknowledge your courteous reception," gravely responded Timascheff.

Servadac could not quite conceal his amusement at the count's irony, but continued, "This is Lieutenant Procope, the officer in command of the *Dobryna*."

The professor bowed again in frigid dignity.

"His yacht has conveyed us right round Gallia," added the captain.

"Round Gallia?" eagerly exclaimed the professor.

"Yes, entirely round it," answered Servadac, and without allowing time for reply, proceeded, "And this is my orderly, Ben Zoof."

"Aide-de-camp to his Excellency the Governor of Gallia," interposed Ben Zoof himself, anxious to maintain his master's honor as well as his own.

Rosette scarcely bent his head.

The rest of the population of the Hive were all presented in succession: the Russian sailors, the Spaniards, young Pablo, and little Nina, on whom the professor, evidently no lover of children, glared fiercely through his formidable spectacles. Isaac Hakkabut, after his introduction, begged to be allowed to ask one question.

"How soon may we hope to get back?" he inquired.

"Get back!" rejoined Rosette, sharply; "who talks of getting back? We have hardly started yet."

Seeing that the professor was inclined to get angry, Captain Servadac adroitly gave a new turn to the conversation by asking him whether he would gratify them by relating his own recent experiences. The astronomer seemed pleased with the proposal, and at once commenced a verbose and somewhat circumlocutory address, of which the following summary presents the main features.

The French Government, being desirous of verifying the measurement already made of the arc of the meridian of Paris, appointed a scientific commission for that purpose. From that commission the name of Palmyrin Rosette was omitted, apparently for no other reason than his personal unpopularity. Furious at the slight, the professor resolved to set to work independently on his own account, and declaring that there were inaccuracies in the previous geodesic operations, he determined to re-examine the results of the last triangulation which had united Formentera to the Spanish coast by a triangle, one of the sides of which measured over a hundred miles, the very operation which had already been so successfully accomplished by Arago and Biot.

Accordingly, leaving Paris for the Balearic Isles, he placed his observatory on the highest point of Formentera, and accompanied as he was only by his servant, Joseph, led the life of a recluse. He secured the services of a former assistant, and dispatched him to a high peak on the coast of Spain, where he had to superintend a reverberator, which, with the aid of a glass, could be seen from Formentera. A few books and instruments, and two months' victuals, was all the baggage he took with him, except an excellent astronomical telescope, which was, indeed, almost part and parcel of himself, and with which he assiduously scanned the heavens, in the sanguine anticipation of making some discovery which would immortalize his name.

The task he had undertaken demanded the utmost patience. Night after night, in order to fix the apex of his triangle, he had to linger on the watch for the assistant's signal-light, but he did not forget that his predecessors, Arago and Biot, had had to wait sixty-one days for a similar purpose. What retarded the work was the dense fog which, it has been already mentioned, at that time enveloped not only that part of Europe, but almost the entire world.

Never failing to turn to the best advantage the few intervals when the mist lifted a little, the astronomer would at the same time cast an inquiring glance at the firmament, as he was greatly interested in the revision of the chart of the heavens, in the region contiguous to the constellation Gemini.

To the naked eye this constellation consists of only six stars, but through a telescope ten inches in diameter, as many as six thousand are visible. Rosette, however, did not possess a reflector of this magnitude, and was obliged to content himself with the good but comparatively small instrument he had.

On one of these occasions, whilst carefully gauging the recesses of Gemini, he espied a bright speck which was unregistered in the chart, and which at first he took for a small star that had escaped being entered in the catalogue. But the observation of a few separate nights soon made it manifest that the star was rapidly changing its position with regard to the adjacent stars, and the astronomer's heart began to leap at the thought that the renown of the discovery of a new planet would be associated with his name.

Redoubling his attention, he soon satisfied himself that what he saw was not a planet; the rapidity of its displacement rather forced him to the conjecture that it must be a comet, and this opinion was soon strengthened by the appearance of a coma, and subsequently confirmed, as the body approached the sun, by the development of a tail.

He followed the object.

A comet! The discovery was fatal to all further progress in the triangulation. However conscientiously the assistant on the Spanish coast might look to the kindling of the beacon, Rosette had no glances to spare for that direction; he had no eyes except for the one object of his notice, no thoughts apart from that one quarter of the firmament.

A comet! No time must be lost in calculating its elements.

Now, in order to calculate the elements of a comet, it is always deemed the safest mode of procedure to assume the orbit to be a parabola. Ordinarily, comets are conspicuous at their perihelia, as being their shortest distances from the sun, which is the focus of their orbit, and inasmuch as a parabola is but an ellipse with its axis indefinitely produced, for some short portion of its pathway the orbit may be indifferently considered either one or the other; but in this particular case the professor was right in adopting the supposition of its being parabolic.

Just as in a circle, it is necessary to know three points to determine the circumference; so in ascertaining the elements of a comet, three different positions must be observed before what astronomers call its "ephemeris" can be established.

But Professor Rosette did not content himself with three positions; taking advantage of every rift in the fog he made ten, twenty, thirty observations both in right ascension and in declination, and succeeded in working out with the most minute accuracy the five elements of the comet which was evidently advancing with astounding rapidity towards the earth.

These elements were:

1. The inclination of the plane of the cometary orbit to the plane of the ecliptic, an angle which is generally considerable, but in this case the planes were proved to coincide.

2. The position of the ascending node, or the point where the comet crossed the terrestrial orbit.

These two elements being obtained, the position in space of the comet's orbit was determined.

3. The direction of the axis major of the orbit, which was found by calculating the longitude of the comet's perihelion.

4. The perihelion distance from the sun, which settled the precise form of the parabola.

5. The motion of the comet, as being retrograde, or, unlike the planets, from east to west.

Rosette thus found himself able to calculate the date at which the comet would reach its perihelion, and, overjoyed at his discovery, without thinking of calling it Palmyra or Rosette, after his own name, he resolved that it should be known as Gallia.

His next business was to draw up a formal report. Not only did he at once recognize that a collision with the earth was possible, but he soon foresaw that it was inevitable, and that it must happen on the night of the 31st of December; moreover, as the bodies were moving in opposite directions, the shock could hardly fail to be violent.

To say that he was elated at the prospect was far below the truth; his delight amounted almost to delirium. Anyone else would have hurried from the solitude of Formentera in sheer fright; but, without communicating a word of his startling discovery, he remained resolutely at his post. From occasional newspapers which he had received, he had learnt that fogs, dense as ever, continued to envelop both hemispheres, so that he was assured that the existence of the comet was utterly unknown elsewhere; and the ignorance of the world as to the peril that threatened it averted the panic that would have followed the publication of the facts, and left the philosopher of Formentera in sole possession of the great secret. He clung to his post with the greater persistency, because his calculations had led him to the conclusion that the comet would strike the earth somewhere to the south of Algeria, and as it had a solid nucleus, he felt sure that, as he expressed it, the effect would be "unique," and he was anxious to be in the vicinity.

The shock came, and with it the results already recorded. Palmyrin Rosette was suddenly separated from his servant Joseph, and when, after a long period of unconsciousness, he came to himself, he found that he was the solitary occupant of the only fragment that survived of the Balearic Archipelago.

Such was the substance of the narrative which the professor gave with sundry repetitions and digressions; while he was giving it, he frequently paused and frowned as if irritated in a way that seemed by no means justified by the patient and good-humored demeanor of his audience.

"But now, gentlemen," added the professor, "I must tell you something more. Important changes have resulted from the collision; the cardinal points have been displaced; gravity has been diminished: not that I ever supposed for a minute, as you did, that I was still upon the earth. No! the earth, attended by her moon, continued to rotate along her proper orbit. But we, gentlemen, have nothing to complain of; our destiny might have been far worse; we might all have been crushed to death, or the comet might have remained in adhesion to the earth; and in neither of these cases should we have had the satisfaction of making this marvelous excursion through untraversed solar regions. No, gentlemen, I repeat it, we have nothing to regret."

The solitary occupant of the only fragment that survived of the
Balearic Archipelago.

And as the professor spoke, he seemed to kindle with the emotion of such supreme contentment that no one had the heart to gainsay his assertion. Ben Zoof alone ventured an unlucky remark to the effect that if the comet had happened to strike against Montmartre, instead of a bit of Africa, it would have met with some resistance.

"Pshaw!" said Rosette, disdainfully. "A mole-hill like Montmartre would have been ground to powder in a moment."

"Mole-hill!" exclaimed Ben Zoof, stung to the quick. "I can tell you
it would have caught up your bit of a comet and worn it like a feather
in a cap."

The professor looked angry, and Servadac having imposed silence
upon his orderly, explained the worthy soldier's sensitiveness on all
that concerned Montmartre. Always obedient to his master, Ben Zoof
held his tongue; but he felt that he could never forgive the slight that
had been cast upon his beloved home.

It was now all-important to learn whether the astronomer had
been able to continue his observations, and whether he had learned
sufficient of Gallia's path through space to make him competent to
determine, at least approximately, the period of its revolution round
the sun. With as much tact and caution as he could, Lieutenant Procope endeavored to intimate the general desire for some information
on this point.

"Before the shock, sir," answered the professor, "I had conclusively
demonstrated the path of the comet; but, in consequence of the modi-
fications which that shock has entailed upon my comet's orbit, I have
been compelled entirely to recommence my calculations."

The lieutenant looked disappointed.

"Although the orbit of the earth was unaltered," continued the professor, "the result of the collision was the projection of the comet into
a new orbit altogether."

"And may I ask," said Procope, deferentially, "whether you have
got the elements of the fresh orbit?"

"Yes."

"Then perhaps you know—"

"I know this, sir, that at 47 minutes 35.6 seconds after two o'clock
on the morning of the 1st of January last, Gallia, in passing its ascending node, came in contact with the earth; that on the 10th of January it crossed the orbit of Venus; that it reached its perihelion on the
15th; that it re-crossed the orbit of Venus; that on the 1st of February
it passed its descending node; on the 13th crossed the orbit of Mars;
entered the zone of the telescopic planets on the 10th of March, and,
attracting Nerina, carried it off as a satellite."

Servadac interposed:

"We are already acquainted with well-nigh all these extraordinary
facts; many of them, moreover, we have learned from documents which

we have picked up, and which, although unsigned, we cannot entertain a doubt have originated with you."

Professor Rosette drew himself up proudly and said: "Of course,
they originated with me. I sent them off by hundreds. From whom
else could they come?"

"From no one but yourself, certainly," rejoined the count, with
grave politeness.

The brilliant comet.

Hitherto the conversation had thrown no light upon the future
movements of Gallia, and Rosette was disposed apparently to evade, or
at least to postpone, the subject. When, therefore, Lieutenant Procope

was about to press his inquiries in a more categorical form, Servadac, thinking it advisable not prematurely to press the little *savant* too far, interrupted him by asking the professor how he accounted for the earth having suffered so little from such a formidable concussion.

"I account for it in this way," answered Rosette: "the earth was traveling at the rate of 28,000 leagues an hour, and Gallia at the rate of 57,000 leagues an hour, therefore the result was the same as though a train rushing along at a speed of about 86,000 leagues an hour had suddenly encountered some obstacle. The nucleus of the comet, being excessively hard, has done exactly what a ball would do fired with that velocity close to a pane of glass. It has crossed the earth without cracking it."

"It is possible you may be right," said Servadac, thoughtfully.

"Right! of course I am right!" replied the snappish professor. Soon, however, recovering his equanimity, he continued: "It is fortunate that the earth was only touched obliquely; if the comet had impinged perpendicularly, it must have plowed its way deep below the surface, and the disasters it might have caused are beyond reckoning. Perhaps," he added, with a smile, "even Montmartre might not have survived the calamity."

"Sir!" shouted Ben Zoof, quite unable to bear the unprovoked attack.

"Quiet, Ben Zoof!" said Servadac sternly.

Fortunately for the sake of peace, Isaac Hakkabut, who at length was beginning to realize something of the true condition of things, came forward at this moment, and in a voice trembling with eagerness, implored the professor to tell him when they would all be back again upon the earth.

"Are you in a great hurry?" asked the professor coolly.

The Jew was about to speak again, when Captain Servadac interposed: "Allow me to say that, in somewhat more scientific terms, I was about to ask you the same question. Did I not understand you to say that, as the consequence of the collision, the character of the comet's orbit has been changed?"

"You did, sir."

"Did you imply that the orbit has ceased to be a parabola?"

"Just so."

"Is it then an hyperbola? and are we to be carried on far and away into remote distance, and never, never to return?"

"I did not say an hyperbola."

"And is it not?"

"It is not."

"Then it must be an ellipse?"

"Yes."

"And does its plane coincide with the plane of the earth?"

"Yes."

"Then it must be a periodic comet?"

"It is."

Servadac involuntarily raised a ringing shout of joy that echoed again along the gallery.

"Yes," continued the professor, "Gallia is a periodic comet, and allowing for the perturbations to which it is liable from the attraction of Mars and Jupiter and Saturn, it will return to the earth again in two years precisely."

"You mean that in two years after the first shock, Gallia will meet the earth at the same point as they met before?" said Lieutenant Procope.

"I am afraid so," said Rosette.

"Why afraid?"

"Because we are doing exceedingly well as we are." The professor stamped his foot upon the ground, by way of emphasis, and added, "If I had my will, Gallia should never return to the earth again!"

CHAPTER V.

A REVISED CALENDAR

ALL previous hypotheses, then, were now forgotten in the presence of the one great fact that Gallia was a comet and gravitating through remote solar regions. Captain Servadac became aware that the huge disc that had been looming through the clouds after the shock was the form of the retreating earth, to the proximity of which the one high tide they had experienced was also to be attributed.

As to the fulfillment of the professor's prediction of an ultimate return to the terrestrial sphere, that was a point on which it must be owned that the captain, after the first flush of his excitement was over, was not without many misgivings.

The next day or two were spent in providing for the accommodation of the new comer. Fortunately his desires were very moderate; he seemed to live among the stars, and as long as he was well provided with coffee, he cared little for luxuries, and paid little or no regard to the ingenuity with which all the internal arrangements of Nina's Hive had been devised. Anxious to show all proper respect to his former tutor, Servadac proposed to leave the most comfortable apartment of the place at his disposal; but the professor resolutely declined to occupy it, saying that what he required was a small chamber, no matter how small, provided that it was elevated and secluded, which he could use as an observatory and where he might prosecute his studies without disturbance. A general search was instituted, and before long they were lucky enough to find, about a hundred feet above the central grotto, a small recess or reduct hollowed, as it were, in the mountain side, which would exactly answer their purpose. It contained room enough for a bed, a table, an arm-chair, a chest of drawers, and, what was of still more consequence, for the indispensable telescope. One small stream of lava, an off-shoot of the great torrent, sufficed to warm the apartment enough.

In these retired quarters the astronomer took up his abode. It was on all hands acknowledged to be advisable to let him go on entirely in his own way. His meals were taken to him at stated intervals; he slept but little; carried on his calculations by day, his observations by night, and very rarely made his appearance amongst the rest of the little community.

In these retired quarters the astronomer took up his abode.

The cold now became very intense, the thermometer registering 30 degrees F. below zero. The mercury, however, never exhibited any of those fluctuations that are ever and again to be observed in variable climates, but continued slowly and steadily to fall, and in all probability would continue to do so until it reached the normal temperature of the regions of outlying space.

This steady sinking of the mercury was accompanied by a complete stillness of the atmosphere; the very air seemed to be congealed; no particle of it stirred; from zenith to horizon there was never a cloud; neither were there any of the damp mists or dry fogs which so often extend over the polar regions of the earth; the sky was always clear; the sun shone by day and the stars by night without causing any perceptible difference in the temperature.

These peculiar conditions rendered the cold endurable even in the open air. The cause of so many of the diseases that prove fatal to Arctic explorers resides in the cutting winds, unwholesome fogs, or terrible snow drifts, which, by drying up, relaxing, or otherwise affecting the lungs, make them incapable of fulfilling their proper functions. But during periods of calm weather, when the air has been absolutely still, many polar navigators, well-clothed and properly fed, have been known to withstand a temperature when the thermometer has fallen to 60 degrees below zero. It was the experience of Parry upon Melville Island, of Kane beyond latitude 81 degrees north, and of Hall and the crew of the *Polaris*, that, however intense the cold, in the absence of the wind they could always brave its rigor.

Notwithstanding, then, the extreme lowness of the temperature, the little population found that they were able to move about in the open air with perfect immunity. The governor general made it his special care to see that his people were all well fed and warmly clad. Food was both wholesome and abundant, and besides the furs brought from the *Dobryna's* stores, fresh skins could very easily be procured and made up into wearing apparel. A daily course of out-door exercise was enforced upon everyone; not even Pablo and Nina were exempted from the general rule; the two children, muffled up in furs, looking like little Esquimeaux, skated along together, Pablo ever at his companion's side, ready to give her a helping hand whenever she was weary with her exertions.

After his interview with the newly arrived astronomer, Isaac Hakkabut slunk back again to his tartan. A change had come over his ideas; he could no longer resist the conviction that he was indeed millions and millions of miles away from the earth, where he had carried on so varied and remunerative a traffic. It might be imagined that this realization of his true position would have led him to a better mind, and that, in some degree at least, he would have been induced to regard the few fellow-creatures with whom his lot had been so strangely cast, otherwise than as mere instruments to be turned to his own personal and pecuniary advantage; but no—the desire of gain was too thoroughly ingrained into his hard nature ever to be eradicated, and secure in his knowledge that he was under the protection of a French officer, who, except under the most urgent necessity, would not permit him to be molested in retaining his property, he determined to wait for some emergency to arise which should enable him to use his present situation for his own profit.

On the one hand, the Jew took it into account that although the chances of returning to the earth might be remote, yet from what he had heard from the professor he could not believe that they were improbable; on the other, he knew that a considerable sum of money, in English and Russian coinage, was in the possession of various members of the little colony, and this, although valueless now, would be worth as much as ever if the proper condition of things should be restored; accordingly, he set his heart on getting all the monetary wealth of Gallia into his possession, and to do this he must sell his goods. But he would not sell them yet; there might come a time when for many articles the supply would not be equal to the demand; that would be the time for him; by waiting he reckoned he should be able to transact some lucrative business.

Such in his solitude were old Isaac's cogitations, whilst the universal population of Nina's Hive were congratulating themselves upon being rid of his odious presence.

As already stated in the message brought by the carrier pigeon, the distance traveled by Gallia in April was 39,000,000 leagues, and at the end of the month she was 110,000,000 leagues from the sun. A diagram representing the elliptical orbit of the planet, accompanied by an ephemeris made out in minute detail, had been drawn out by the professor. The curve was divided into twenty-four sections of unequal length, representing respectively the distance described in the twenty-four months of the Gallian year, the twelve former divisions, according to Kepler's law, gradually diminishing in length as they approached the point denoting the aphelion and increasing as they neared the perihelion.

It was on the 12th of May that Rosette exhibited this result of his labors to Servadac, the count, and the lieutenant, who visited his apartment and naturally examined the drawing with the keenest interest. Gallia's path, extending beyond the orbit of Jupiter, lay clearly defined before their eyes, the progress along the orbit and the solar distances being inserted for each month separately. Nothing could look plainer, and if the professor's calculations were correct (a point upon which they dared not, if they would, express the semblance of a doubt), Gallia would accomplish her revolution in precisely two years, and would meet the earth, which would in the same period of time have completed two annual revolutions, in the very same spot as before. What would be the consequences of a second collision they scarcely ventured to think.

Without lifting his eye from the diagram, which he was still carefully scrutinizing, Servadac said, "I see that during the month of May, Gallia will only travel 30,400,000 leagues, and that this will leave her about 140,000,000 leagues distant from the sun."

"Just so," replied the professor.

"Then we have already passed the zone of the telescopic planets, have we not?" asked the count.

"Can you not use your eyes?" said the professor, testily. "If you will look you will see the zone marked clearly enough upon the map."

Without noticing the interruption, Servadac continued his own remarks, "The comet then, I see, is to reach its aphelion on the 15th of January, exactly a twelvemonth after passing its perihelion."

"A twelvemonth! Not a Gallian twelvemonth?" exclaimed Rosette.

Servadac looked bewildered. Lieutenant Procope could not suppress a smile.

"What are you laughing at?" demanded the professor, turning round upon him angrily.

"Nothing, sir; only it amuses me to see how you want to revise the terrestrial calendar."

"I want to be logical, that's all."

"By all manner of means, my dear professor, let us be logical."

"Well, then, listen to me," resumed the professor, stiffly. "I presume you are taking it for granted that the Gallian year—by which I mean the time in which Gallia makes one revolution round the sun—is equal in length to two terrestrial years."

They signified their assent.

"And that year, like every other year, ought to be divided into twelve months."

A new shining point.

"Yes, certainly, if you wish it," said the captain, acquiescing.

"If I wish it!" exclaimed Rosette. "Nothing of the sort! Of course a year must have twelve months!"

"Of course," said the captain.

"And how many days will make a month?" asked the professor.

"I suppose sixty or sixty-two, as the case may be. The days now are only half as long as they used to be," answered the captain.

"Servadac, don't be thoughtless!" cried Rosette, with all the petulant impatience of the old pedagogue. "If the days are only half as long as they were, sixty of them cannot make up a twelfth part of Gallia's year—cannot be a month."

"I suppose not," replied the confused captain.

"Do you not see, then," continued the astronomer, "that if a Gallian month is twice as long as a terrestrial month, and a Gallian day is only half as long as a terrestrial day, there must be a hundred and twenty days in every month?"

"No doubt you are right, professor," said Count Timascheff; "but do you not think that the use of a new calendar such as this would practically be very troublesome?"

"Not at all! not at all! I do not intend to use any other," was the professor's bluff reply.

After pondering for a few moments, the captain spoke again. "According, then, to this new calendar, it isn't the middle of May at all; it must now be some time in March."

"Yes," said the professor, "to-day is the 26th of March. It is the 266th day of the Gallian year. It corresponds with the 133d day of the terrestrial year. You are quite correct, it is the 26th of March."

"Strange!" muttered Servadac.

"And a month, a terrestrial month, thirty old days, sixty new days hence, it will be the 86th of March."

"Ha, ha!" roared the captain; "this is logic with a vengeance!"

The old professor had an undefined consciousness that his former pupil was laughing at him; and as it was growing late, he made an excuse that he had no more leisure. The visitors accordingly quitted the observatory.

It must be owned that the revised calendar was left to the professor's sole use, and the colony was fairly puzzled whenever he referred to such unheard-of dates as the 47th of April or the 118th of May.

According to the old calendar, June had now arrived; [illustration omitted] [page intentionally blank] and by the professor's tables Gallia during the month would have advanced 27,500,000 leagues farther along its orbit, and would have attained a distance of 155,000,000 leagues from the sun. The thermometer continued to fall; the atmosphere remained clear as heretofore. The population performed their daily avocations with systematic routine; and almost the only thing that

broke the monotony of existence was an occasional visit from the blus-
tering, nervous, little professor, when some sudden fancy induced him
to throw aside his astronomical studies for a time, and pay a visit to the
common hall. His arrival there was generally hailed as the precursor of
a little season of excitement. Somehow or other the conversation would
eventually work its way round to the topic of a future collision between
the comet and the earth; and in the same degree as this was a matter of
sanguine anticipation to Captain Servadac and his friends, it was a matter of aversion to the astronomical enthusiast, who had no desire to quit
his present quarters in a sphere which, being of his own discovery, he
could hardly have cared for more if it had been of his own creation. The
interview would often terminate in a scene of considerable animation.

On the 27th of June (old calendar) the professor burst like a cannon-
ball into the central hall, where they were all assembled, and without
a word of salutation or of preface, accosted the lieutenant in the way in
which in earlier days he had been accustomed to speak to an idle school-
boy, "Now, lieutenant! no evasions! no shufflings! Tell me, have you or
have you not circumnavigated Gallia?"

The lieutenant drew himself up stiffly. "Evasions! shufflings! I am
not accustomed, sir—" he began in a tone evidencing no little resentment; but catching a hint from the count he subdued his voice, and
simply said, "We have."

"And may I ask," continued the professor, quite unaware of his previous discourtesy, "whether, when you made your voyage, you took any
account of distances?"

"As approximately as I could," replied the lieutenant; "I did what
I could by log and compass. I was unable to take the altitude of sun or
star."

"At what result did you arrive? What is the measurement of our
equator?"

"I estimate the total circumference of the equator to be about 1,400
miles."

"Ah!" said the professor, more than half speaking to himself, "a
circumference of 1,400 miles would give a diameter of about 450 miles.
That would be approximately about one-sixteenth of the diameter of the
earth."

Raising his voice, he continued, "Gentlemen, in order to complete
my account of my comet Gallia, I require to know its area, its mass, its
volume, its density, its specific gravity."

"Since we know the diameter," remarked the lieutenant, "there can be no difficulty in finding its surface and its volume."

"And did I say there was any difficulty?" asked the professor, fiercely. "I have been able to reckon that ever since I was born."

"Cock-a-doodle-doo!" cried Ben Zoof, delighted at any opportunity of paying off his old grudge.

The professor looked at him, but did not vouchsafe a word. Addressing the captain, he said, "Now, Servadac, take your paper and a pen, and find me the surface of Gallia."

With more submission than when he was a school-boy, the captain sat down and endeavored to recall the proper formula.

"The surface of a sphere? Multiply circumference by diameter."

"Right!" cried Rosette; "but it ought to be done by this time."

"Circumference, 1,400; diameter, 450; area of surface, 630,000," read the captain.

"True," replied Rosette, "630,000 square miles; just 292 times less than that of the earth."

"Pretty little comet! nice little comet!" muttered Ben Zoof.

The astronomer bit his lip, snorted, and cast at him a withering look, but did not take any further notice.

"Now, Captain Servadac," said the professor, "take your pen again, and find me the volume of Gallia."

The captain hesitated.

"Quick, quick!" cried the professor, impatiently; "surely you have not forgotten how to find the volume of a sphere!"

"A moment's breathing time, please."

"Breathing time, indeed! A mathematician should not want breathing time! Come, multiply the surface by the third of the radius. Don't you recollect?"

Captain Servadac applied himself to his task while the by-standers waited, with some difficulty suppressing their inclination to laugh. There was a short silence, at the end of which Servadac announced that the volume of the comet was 47,880,000 cubic miles.

"Just about 5,000 times less than the earth," observed the lieutenant.

"Nice little comet! pretty little comet!" said Ben Zoof.

The professor scowled at him, and was manifestly annoyed at having the insignificant dimensions of his comet pointed out in so disparaging a manner. Lieutenant Procope further remarked that from the earth he supposed it to be about as conspicuous as a star of the seventh magnitude, and would require a good telescope to see it.

"Ha, ha!" laughed the orderly, aloud; "charming little comet! so pretty; and so modest!"

A mathematician should not want breathing time!

"You rascal!" roared the professor, and clenched his hand in passion, as if about to strike him. Ben Zoof laughed the more, and was on the point of repeating his satirical comments, when a stern order from the captain made him hold his tongue. The truth was that the professor was just as sensitive about his comet as the orderly was about

Montmartre, and if the contention between the two had been allowed
to go on unchecked, it is impossible to say what serious quarrel might
not have arisen.

When Professor Rosette's equanimity had been restored, he said,
"Thus, then, gentlemen, the diameter, the surface, the volume of my
comet are settled; but there is more to be done. I shall not be satisfied
until, by actual measurement, I have determined its mass, its density,
and the force of gravity at its surface."

"A laborious problem," remarked Count Timascheff.

"Laborious or not, it has to be accomplished. I am resolved to find
out what my comet weighs."

"Would it not be of some assistance, if we knew of what substance
it is composed?" asked the lieutenant.

"That is of no moment at all," replied the professor; "the problem
is independent of it."

"Then we await your orders," was the captain's reply.

"You must understand, however," said Rosette, "that there are
various preliminary calculations to be made; you will have to wait till
they are finished."

"As long as you please," said the count.

"No hurry at all," observed the captain, who was not in the least
impatient to continue his mathematical exercises.

"Then, gentlemen," said the astronomer, "with your leave we will
for this purpose make an appointment a few weeks hence. What do
you say to the 62d of April?"

Without noticing the general smile which the novel date provoked,
the astronomer left the hall, and retired to his observatory.

CHAPTER VI.

WANTED: A STEELYARD

UNDER the still diminishing influence of the sun's attraction, but without let or hindrance, Gallia continued its interplanetary course, accompanied by Nerina, its captured satellite, which performed its fortnightly revolutions with unvarying regularity.

Meanwhile, the question beyond all others important was ever recurring to the minds of Servadac and his two companions: were the astronomer's calculations correct, and was there a sound foundation for his prediction that the comet would again touch the earth? But whatever might be their doubts or anxieties, they were fain to keep all their misgivings to themselves; the professor was of a temper far too cross-grained for them to venture to ask him to revise or re-examine the results of his observations.

The rest of the community by no means shared in their uneasiness. Negrete and his fellow-countrymen yielded to their destiny with philosophical indifference. Happier and better provided for than they had ever been in their lives, it did not give them a passing thought, far less cause any serious concern, whether they were still circling round the sun, or whether they were being carried right away within the limits of another system. Utterly careless of the future, the majos, light-hearted as ever, carolled out their favorite songs, just as if they had never quitted the shores of their native land.

Happiest of all were Pablo and Nina. Racing through the galleries of the Hive, clambering over the rocks upon the shore, one day skating far away across the frozen ocean, the next fishing in the lake that was kept liquid by the heat of the lava-torrent, the two children led a life of perpetual enjoyment. Nor was their recreation allowed to interfere with their studies. Captain Servadac, who in common with the count really liked them both, conceived that the responsibilities of a parent in some degree had devolved upon him, and took great care in superin-

tending their daily lessons, which he succeeded in making hardly less
pleasant than their sports.

Indulged and loved by all, it was little wonder that young Pablo had
no longing for the scorching plains of Andalusia, or that little Nina
had lost all wish to return with her pet goat to the barren rocks of
Sardinia. They had now a home in which they had nothing to desire.

"Have you no father nor mother?" asked Pablo, one day.

"No," she answered.

"No more have I," said the boy, "I used to run along by the side of
the diligences when I was in Spain."

"I used to look after goats at Madalena," said Nina; "but it is much
nicer here—I am so happy here. I have you for a brother, and everybody is so kind. I am afraid they will spoil us, Pablo," she added,
smiling.

"Oh, no, Nina; you are too good to be spoiled, and when I am with
you, you make me good too," said Pablo, gravely.

July had now arrived. During the month Gallia's advance along its
orbit would be reduced to 22,000,000 leagues, the distance from the sun
at the end being 172,000,000 leagues, about four and a half times as
great as the average distance of the earth from the sun. It was traveling
now at about the same speed as the earth, which traverses the ecliptic at
a rate of 21,000,000 leagues a month, or 28,800 leagues an hour.

In due time the 62d April, according to the revised Gallian calendar,
dawned; and in punctual fulfillment of the professor's appointment, a
note was delivered to Servadac to say that he was ready, and hoped that
day to commence operations for calculating the mass and density of his
comet, as well as the force of gravity at its surface.

A point of far greater interest to Captain Servadac and his friends
would have been to ascertain the nature of the substance of which the
comet was composed, but they felt pledged to render the professor any
aid they could in the researches upon which he had set his heart. Without delay, therefore, they assembled in the central hall, where they were
soon joined by Rosette, who seemed to be in fairly good temper.

"Gentlemen," he began, "I propose to-day to endeavor to complete
our observations of the elements of my comet. Three matters of investigation are before us. First, the measure of gravity at its surface;
this attractive force we know, by the increase of our own muscular
force, must of course be considerably less than that at the surface of

the earth. Secondly, its mass, that is, the quality of its matter. And thirdly, its density or quantity of matter in a unit of its volume. We will proceed, gentlemen, if you please, to weigh Gallia."

Ben Zoof, who had just entered the hall, caught the professor's last sentence, and without saying a word, went out again and was absent for some minutes. When he returned, he said, "If you want to weigh this comet of yours, I suppose you want a pair of scales; but I have been to look, and I cannot find a pair anywhere. And what's more," he added mischievously, "you won't get them anywhere."

The professor communicated his work.

A frown came over the professor's countenance. Servadac saw it, and gave his orderly a sign that he should desist entirely from his bantering.

"I require, gentlemen," resumed Rosette, "first of all to know by how much the weight of a kilogram here differs from its weight upon the earth; the attraction, as we have said, being less, the weight will proportionately be less also."

"Then an ordinary pair of scales, being under the influence of attraction, I suppose, would not answer your purpose," submitted the lieutenant.

"And the very kilogram weight you used would have become lighter," put in the count, deferentially.

"Pray, gentlemen, do not interrupt me," said the professor, authoritatively, as if *ex cathedra*. "I need no instruction on these points."

Procope and Timascheff demurely bowed their heads.

The professor resumed. "Upon a steelyard, or spring-balance, dependent upon mere tension or flexibility, the attraction will have no influence. If I suspend a weight equivalent to the weight of a kilogram, the index will register the proper weight on the surface of Gallia. Thus I shall arrive at the difference I want: the difference between the earth's attraction and the comet's. Will you, therefore, have the goodness to provide me at once with a steelyard and a tested kilogram?"

The audience looked at one another, and then at Ben Zoof, who was thoroughly acquainted with all their resources. "We have neither one nor the other," said the orderly.

The professor stamped with vexation.

"I believe old Hakkabut has a steelyard on board his tartan," said Ben Zoof, presently.

"Then why didn't you say so before, you idiot?" roared the excitable little man.

Anxious to pacify him, Servadac assured him that every exertion should be made to procure the instrument, and directed Ben Zoof to go to the Jew and borrow it.

"No, stop a moment," he said, as Ben Zoof was moving away on his, errand; "perhaps I had better go with you myself; the old Jew may make a difficulty about lending us any of his property."

"Why should we not all go?" asked the count; "we should see what kind of a life the misanthrope leads on board the *Hansa*."

The proposal met with general approbation. Before they started, Professor Rosette requested that one of the men might be ordered to cut him a cubic decimeter out of the solid substance of Gallia. "My engineer is the man for that," said the count; "he will do it well for you if you will give him the precise measurement."

They descended from the high rocks.

"What! you don't mean," exclaimed the professor, again going off into a passion, "that you haven't a proper measure of length?"

Ben Zoof was sent off to ransack the stores for the article in question, but no measure was forthcoming. "Most likely we shall find one on the tartan," said the orderly.

"Then let us lose no time in trying," answered the professor, as he hustled with hasty strides into the gallery.

The rest of the party followed, and were soon in the open air upon the rocks that overhung the shore. They descended to the level of the frozen water and made their way towards the little creek where the *Dobryna* and the *Hansa* lay firmly imprisoned in their icy bonds.

The temperature was low beyond previous experience; but well muffled up in fur, they all endured it without much actual suffering. Their breath issued in vapor, which was at once congealed into little crystals upon their whiskers, beards, eyebrows, and eyelashes, until their faces, covered with countless snow-white prickles, were truly ludicrous. The little professor, most comical of all, resembled nothing so much as the cub of an Arctic bear.

It was eight o'clock in the morning. The sun was rapidly approaching the zenith; but its disc, from the extreme remoteness, was proportionately dwarfed; its beams being all but destitute of their proper warmth and radiance. The volcano to its very summit and the surrounding rocks were still covered with the unsullied mantle of snow that had fallen while the atmosphere was still to some extent charged with vapor; but on the north side the snow had given place to the cascade of fiery lava, which, making its way down the sloping rocks as far as the vaulted opening of the central cavern, fell thence perpendicularly into the sea. Above the cavern, 130 feet up the mountain, was a dark hole, above which the stream of lava made a bifurcation in its course. From this hole projected the case of an astronomer's telescope; it was the opening of Palmyrin Rosette's observatory.

Sea and land seemed blended into one dreary whiteness, to which the pale blue sky offered scarcely any contrast. The shore was indented with the marks of many footsteps left by the colonists either on their way to collect ice for drinking purposes, or as the result of their skating expeditions; the edges of the skates had cut out a labyrinth of curves complicated as the figures traced by aquatic insects upon the surface of a pool.

Across the quarter of a mile of level ground that lay between the mountain and the creek, a series of footprints, frozen hard into the snow, marked the course taken by Isaac Hakkabut on his last return from Nina's Hive.

On approaching the creek, Lieutenant Procope drew his companions' attention to the elevation of the *Dobryna's* and *Hansa's* waterline, both vessels being now some fifteen feet above the level of the sea.

"What a strange phenomenon!" exclaimed the captain.

"It makes me very uneasy," rejoined the lieutenant; "in shallow places like this, as the crust of ice thickens, it forces everything upwards with irresistible force."

"But surely this process of congelation must have a limit!" said the count.

"But who can say what that limit will be? Remember that we have not yet reached our maximum of cold," replied Procope.

"Indeed, I hope not!" exclaimed the professor; "where would be the use of our traveling 200,000,000 leagues from the sun, if we are only to experience the same temperature as we should find at the poles of the earth?"

"Fortunately for us, however, professor," said the lieutenant, with a smile, "the temperature of the remotest space never descends beyond 70 degrees below zero."

"And as long as there is no wind," added Servadac, "we may pass comfortably through the winter, without a single attack of catarrh."

Lieutenant Procope proceeded to impart to the count his anxiety about the situation of his yacht. He pointed out that by the constant superposition of new deposits of ice, the vessel would be elevated to a great height, and consequently in the event of a thaw, it must be exposed to a calamity similar to those which in polar seas cause destruction to so many whalers.

There was no time now for concerting measures offhand to prevent the disaster, for the other members of the party had already reached the spot where the *Hansa* lay bound in her icy trammels. A flight of steps, recently hewn by Hakkabut himself, gave access for the present to the gangway, but it was evident that some different contrivance would have to be resorted to when the tartan should be elevated perhaps to a hundred feet.

A thin curl of blue smoke issued from the copper funnel that projected above the mass of snow which had accumulated upon the deck of the *Hansa*. The owner was sparing of his fuel, and it was only the non-conducting layer of ice enveloping the tartan that rendered the internal temperature endurable.

"Hi! old Nebuchadnezzar, where are you?" shouted Ben Zoof, at the full strength of his lungs.

At the sound of his voice, the cabin door opened, and the Jew's head and shoulders protruded onto the deck.

CHAPTER VII.

MONEY AT A PREMIUM

"Who's there? I have nothing here for anyone. Go away!" Such was the inhospitable greeting with which Isaac Hakkabut received his visitors.

"Hakkabut! do you take us for thieves?" asked Servadac, in tones of stern displeasure.

"Oh, your Excellency, my lord, I did not know that it was you," whined the Jew, but without emerging any farther from his cabin.

"Now, old Hakkabut, come out of your shell! Come and show the governor proper respect, when he gives you the honor of his company," cried Ben Zoof, who by this time had clambered onto the deck.

After considerable hesitation, but still keeping his hold upon the cabin-door, the Jew made up his mind to step outside. "What do you want?" he inquired, timorously.

"I want a word with you," said Servadac, "but I do not want to stand talking out here in the cold."

Followed by the rest of the party, he proceeded to mount the steps. The Jew trembled from head to foot. "But I cannot let you into my cabin. I am a poor man; I have nothing to give you," he moaned piteously.

"Here he is!" laughed Ben Zoof, contemptuously; "he is beginning his chapter of lamentations over again. But standing out here will never do. Out of the way, old Hakkabut, I say! out of the way!" and, without more ado, he thrust the astonished Jew on one side and opened the door of the cabin.

Servadac, however, declined to enter until he had taken the pains to explain to the owner of the tartan that he had no intention of laying violent hands upon his property, and that if the time should ever come that his cargo was in requisition for the common use, he should receive a proper price for his goods, the same as he would in Europe.

"Europe, indeed!" muttered the Jew maliciously between his teeth. "European prices will not do for me. I must have Gallian prices—and of my own fixing, too!"

So large a portion of the vessel had been appropriated to the cargo that the space reserved for the cabin was of most meager dimensions. In one corner of the compartment stood a small iron stove, in which smoldered a bare handful of coals; in another was a trestle-board which served as a bed; two or three stools and a rickety deal table, together with a few cooking utensils, completed a stock of furniture which was worthy of its proprietor.

On entering the cabin, Ben Zoof's first proceeding was to throw on the fire a liberal supply of coals, utterly regardless of the groans of poor Isaac, who would almost as soon have parted with his own bones as submit to such reckless expenditure of his fuel. The perishing temperature of the cabin, however, was sufficient justification for the orderly's conduct, and by a little skillful manipulation he soon succeeded in getting up a tolerable fire.

The visitors having taken what seats they could, Hakkabut closed the door, and, like a prisoner awaiting his sentence, stood with folded hands, expecting the captain to speak.

"Listen," said Servadac; "we have come to ask a favor."

Imagining that at least half his property was to be confiscated, the Jew began to break out into his usual formula about being a poor man and having nothing to spare; but Servadac, without heeding his complainings, went on: "We are not going to ruin you, you know."

Hakkabut looked keenly into the captain's face.

"We have only come to know whether you can lend us a steelyard."

So far from showing any symptom of relief, the old miser exclaimed, with a stare of astonishment, as if he had been asked for some thousand francs: "A steelyard?"

"Yes!" echoed the professor, impatiently; "a steelyard."

"Have you not one?" asked Servadac.

"To be sure he has!" said Ben Zoof.

Old Isaac stammered and stuttered, but at last confessed that perhaps there might be one amongst the stores.

"Then, surely, you will not object to lend it to us?" said the captain.

"Only for one day," added the professor.

The Jew stammered again, and began to object. "It is a very delicate instrument, your Excellency. The cold, you know, the cold may do injury to the spring; and perhaps you are going to use it to weigh something very heavy."

"Why, old Ephraim, do you suppose we are going to weigh a mountain with it?" said Ben Zoof.

"Better than that!" cried out the professor, triumphantly; "we are going to weigh Gallia with it; my comet."

"Merciful Heaven!" shrieked Isaac, feigning consternation at the bare suggestion.

Servadac knew well enough that the Jew was holding out only for a good bargain, and assured him that the steelyard was required for no other purpose than to weigh a kilogram, which (considering how much lighter everything had become) could not possibly put the slightest strain upon the instrument.

The Jew still spluttered, and moaned, and hesitated.

"Well, then," said Servadac, "if you do not like to lend us your steelyard, do you object to sell it to us?"

Isaac fairly shrieked aloud. "God of Israel!" he ejaculated, "sell my steelyard? Would you deprive me of one of the most indispensable of my means of livelihood? How should I weigh my merchandise without my steelyard—my solitary steelyard, so delicate and so correct?"

The orderly wondered how his master could refrain from strangling the old miser upon the spot; but Servadac, rather amused than otherwise, determined to try another form of persuasion. "Come, Hakkabut, I see that you are not disposed either to lend or to sell your steelyard. What do you say to letting us hire it?"

The Jew's eyes twinkled with a satisfaction that he was unable to conceal. "But what security would you give? The instrument is very valuable;" and he looked more cunning than ever.

"What is it worth? If it is worth twenty francs, I will leave a deposit of a hundred. Will that satisfy you?"

He shook his head doubtfully. "It is very little; indeed, it is too little, your Excellency. Consider, it is the only steelyard in all this new world of ours; it is worth more, much more. If I take your deposit it must be in gold—all gold. But how much do you agree to give me for the hire—the hire, one day?"

"You shall have twenty francs," said Servadac.

"Oh, it is dirt cheap; but never mind, for one day, you shall have it. Deposit in gold money a hundred francs, and twenty francs for the hire." The old man folded his hands in meek resignation.

"The fellow knows how to make a good bargain," said Servadac, as Isaac, after casting a distrustful look around, went out of the cabin.

"Detestable old wretch!" replied the count, full of disgust.

Hardly a minute elapsed before the Jew was back again, carrying his precious steelyard with ostentatious care. It was of an ordinary kind. A spring balance, fitted with a hook, held the article to be weighed; a pointer, revolving on a disc, indicated the weight of the article. Professor Rosette was manifestly right in asserting that such a machine would register results quite independently of any change in the force of attraction. On the earth it would have registered a kilogram as a kilogram; here it recorded a different value altogether, as the result of the altered force of gravity.

Gold coinage to the worth of one hundred and twenty francs was handed over to the Jew, who clutched at the money with unmistakable eagerness. The steelyard was committed to the keeping of Ben Zoof, and the visitors prepared to quit the *Hansa*.

All at once it occurred to the professor that the steelyard would be absolutely useless to him, unless he had the means for ascertaining the precise measurement of the unit of the soil of Gallia which he proposed to weigh. "Something more you must lend me," he said, addressing the Jew. "I must have a measure, and I must have a kilogram."

"I have neither of them," answered Isaac. "I have neither. I am sorry; I am very sorry." And this time the old Jew spoke the truth. He would have been really glad to do another stroke or two of business upon terms as advantageous as the transaction he had just concluded.

Palmyrin Rosette scratched his head in perplexity, glaring round upon his companions as if they were personally responsible for his annoyance. He muttered something about finding a way out of his difficulty, and hastily mounted the cabin-ladder. The rest followed, but they had hardly reached the deck when the chink of money was heard in the room below. Hakkabut was locking away the gold in one of the drawers.

Back again, down the ladder, scrambled the little professor, and before the Jew was aware of his presence he had seized him by the tail of his slouchy overcoat. "Some of your money! I must have money!" he said.

"Money!" gasped Hakkabut; "I have no money." He was pale with fright, and hardly knew what he was saying.

"Falsehood!" roared Rosette. "Do you think I cannot see?" And peering down into the drawer which the Jew was vainly trying to close, he cried, "Heaps of money! French money! Five-franc pieces! the very thing I want! I must have them!"

The captain and his friends, who had returned to the cabin looked on with mingled amusement and bewilderment.

"Heaps of money! French money! Five-franc pieces! the very thing I want! I must have them!"

"They are mine!" shrieked Hakkabut.

"I will have them!" shouted the professor.

"You shall kill me first!" bellowed the Jew.

"No, but I must!" persisted the professor again.

It was manifestly time for Servadac to interfere. "My dear professor," he said, smiling, "allow me to settle this little matter for you."

"Ah! your Excellency," moaned the agitated Jew, "protect me! I am but a poor man—"

"None of that, Hakkabut. Hold your tongue." And, turning to Rosette, the captain said, "If, sir, I understand right, you require some silver five-franc pieces for your operation?"

"Forty," said Rosette, surlily.

"Two hundred francs!" whined Hakkabut.

"Silence!" cried the captain.

"I must have more than that," the professor continued. "I want ten two-franc pieces, and twenty half-francs."

"Let me see," said Servadac, "how much is that in all? Two hundred and thirty francs, is it not?"

"I dare say it is," answered the professor.

"Count, may I ask you," continued Servadac, "to be security to the Jew for this loan to the professor?"

"Loan!" cried the Jew, "do you mean only a loan?"

"Silence!" again shouted the captain.

Count Timascheff, expressing his regret that his purse contained only paper money, begged to place it at Captain Servadac's disposal.

"No paper, no paper!" exclaimed Isaac. "Paper has no currency in Gallia."

"About as much as silver," coolly retorted the count.

"I am a poor man," began the Jew.

"Now, Hakkabut, stop these miserable lamentations of yours, once for all. Hand us over two hundred and thirty francs in silver money, or we will proceed to help ourselves."

Isaac began to yell with all his might: "Thieves! thieves!"

In a moment Ben Zoof's hand was clasped tightly over his mouth. "Stop that howling, Belshazzar!"

"Let him alone, Ben Zoof. He will soon come to his senses," said Servadac, quietly.

When the old Jew had again recovered himself, the captain addressed him. "Now, tell us, what interest do you expect?"

Nothing could overcome the Jew's anxiety to make another good bargain. He began: "Money is scarce, very scarce, you know—"

"No more of this!" shouted Servadac. "What interest, I say, what interest do you ask?"

Faltering and undecided still, the Jew went on. "Very scarce, you know. Ten francs a day, I think, would not be unreasonable, considering—"

The count had no patience to allow him to finish what he was about to say. He flung down notes to the value of several rubles. With a greediness that could not be concealed, Hakkabut grasped them all. Paper, indeed, they were; but the cunning Israelite knew that they would in any case be security far beyond the value of his cash. He was making some eighteen hundred per cent. interest, and accordingly chuckled within himself at his unexpected stroke of business.

The professor pocketed his French coins with a satisfaction far more demonstrative. "Gentlemen," he said, "with these franc pieces I obtain the means of determining accurately both a meter and a kilogram."

CHAPTER VIII.

A QUARTER of an hour later, the visitors to the *Hansa* had reassembled in the common hall of Nina's Hive.

"Now, gentlemen, we can proceed," said the professor. "May I request that this table may be cleared?"

Ben Zoof removed the various articles that were lying on the table, and the coins which had just been borrowed from the Jew were placed upon it in three piles, according to their value.

The professor commenced. "Since none of you gentlemen, at the time of the shock, took the precaution to save either a meter measure or a kilogram weight from the earth, and since both these articles are necessary for the calculation on which we are engaged, I have been obliged to devise means of my own to replace them."

This exordium delivered, he paused and seemed to watch its effect upon his audience, who, however, were too well acquainted with the professor's temper to make any attempt to exonerate themselves from the rebuke of carelessness, and submitted silently to the implied reproach.

"I have taken pains," he continued, "to satisfy myself that these coins are in proper condition for my purpose. I find them unworn and unchipped; indeed, they are almost new. They have been hoarded instead of circulated; accordingly, they are fit to be utilized for my purpose of obtaining the precise length of a terrestrial meter."

Ben Zoof looked on in perplexity, regarding the lecturer with much the same curiosity as he would have watched the performances of a traveling mountebank at a fair in Montmartre; but Servadac and his two friends had already divined the professor's meaning. They knew that French coinage is all decimal, the franc being the standard of which the other coins, whether gold, silver, or copper, are multiples or measures; they knew, too, that the caliber or diameter of each piece of money is rigorously determined by law, and that the diameters of the silver coins representing five francs, two francs, and fifty centimes measure thirty-seven, twenty-seven, and eighteen millimeters respectively; and they accordingly guessed that Professor Rosette had conceived the plan of placing such a number of these coins in juxtaposition that the length of their united diameters should measure exactly the thousand millimeters that make up the terrestrial meter.

"Here we have the measure of a meter exactly."

The measurement thus obtained was by means of a pair of compasses divided accurately into ten equal portions, or decimeters, each of course 3.93 inches long. A lath was then cut of this exact length and given to the engineer of the *Dobryna*, who was directed to cut out of the solid rock the cubic decimeter required by the professor.

The next business was to obtain the precise weight of a kilogram. This was by no means a difficult matter. Not only the diameters, but also the weights, of the French coins are rigidly determined by law, and as the silver five-franc pieces always weigh exactly twenty-five grams, the united weight of forty of these coins is known to amount to one kilogram.

"Oh!" cried Ben Zoof; "to be able to do all this I see you must be rich as well as learned."

With a good-natured laugh at the orderly's remark, the meeting adjourned for a few hours. By the appointed time the engineer had finished his task, and with all due care had prepared a cubic decimeter of the material of the comet.

"Now, gentlemen," said Professor Rosette, "we are in a position to complete our calculation; we can now arrive at Gallia's attraction, density, and mass."

Everyone gave him his complete attention.

"Before I proceed," he resumed, "I must recall to your minds Newton's general law, 'that the attraction of two bodies is directly proportional to the product of their masses, and inversely proportional to the square of their distances.'"

"Yes," said Servadac; "we remember that."

"Well, then," continued the professor, "keep it in mind for a few minutes now. Look here! In this bag are forty five-franc pieces—altogether they weigh exactly a kilogram; by which I mean that if we were on the earth, and I were to hang the bag on the hook of the steel-yard, the indicator on the dial would register one kilogram. This is clear enough, I suppose?"

As he spoke the professor designedly kept his eyes fixed upon Ben Zoof. He was avowedly following the example of Arago, who was accustomed always in lecturing to watch the countenance of the least intelligent of his audience, and when he felt that he had made his meaning clear to him, he concluded that he must have succeeded with all the rest. In this case, however, it was technical ignorance, rather than any lack of intelligence, that justified the selection of the orderly for this special attention.

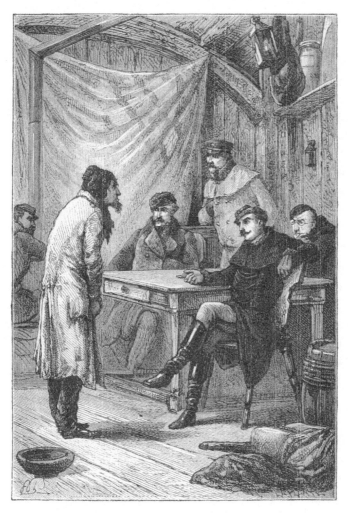

"Master Isaac." said the captain.

Satisfied with his scrutiny of Ben Zoof's face, the professor went
on. "And now, gentlemen, we have to see what these coins weigh here
upon Gallia."

He suspended the money bag to the hook; the needle oscillated, and
stopped. "Read it off!" he said.

The weight registered was one hundred and thirty-three grams.

"There, gentlemen, one hundred and thirty-three grams! Less than
one-seventh of a kilogram! You see, consequently, that the force of
gravity here on Gallia is not one-seventh of what it is upon the earth!"

"Interesting!" cried Servadac, "most interesting! But let us go on and compute the mass."

"No, captain, the density first," said Rosette.

"Certainly," said the lieutenant; "for, as we already know the volume, we can determine the mass as soon as we have ascertained the density."

The professor took up the cube of rock. "You know what this is," he went on to say. "You know, gentlemen, that this block is a cube hewn from the substance of which everywhere, all throughout your voyage of circumnavigation, you found Gallia to be composed—a substance to which your geological attainments did not suffice to assign a name."

"Our curiosity will be gratified," said Servadac, "if you will enlighten our ignorance."

But Rosette did not take the slightest notice of the interruption.

"A substance it is which no doubt constitutes the sole material of the comet, extending from its surface to its innermost depths. The probability is that it would be so; your experience confirms that probability: you have found no trace of any other substance. Of this rock here is a solid decimeter; let us get at its weight, and we shall have the key which will unlock the problem of the whole weight of Gallia. We have demonstrated that the force of attraction here is only one-seventh of what it is upon the earth, and shall consequently have to multiply the apparent weight of our cube by seven, in order to ascertain its proper weight. Do you understand me, goggle-eyes?"

This was addressed to Ben Zoof, who was staring hard at him. "No!" said Ben Zoof.

"I thought not; it is of no use waiting for your puzzle-brains to make it out. I must talk to those who can understand."

The professor took the cube, and, on attaching it to the hook of the steelyard, found that its apparent weight was one kilogram and four hundred and thirty grams.

"Here it is, gentlemen; one kilogram, four hundred and thirty grams. Multiply that by seven; the product is, as nearly as possible, ten kilograms. What, therefore, is our conclusion? Why, that the density of Gallia is just about double the density of the earth, which we know is only five kilograms to a cubic decimeter. Had it not been for this greater density, the attraction of Gallia would only have been one-fifteenth instead of one-seventh of the terrestrial attraction."

The professor could not refrain from exhibiting his gratification that, however inferior in volume, in density, at least, his comet had the advantage over the earth.

Nothing further now remained than to apply the investigations thus finished to the determining of the mass or weight. This was a matter of little labor.

"Let me see," said the captain; "what is the force of gravity upon the various planets?"

"You can't mean, Servadac, that you have forgotten that? But you always were a disappointing pupil."

The captain could not help himself: he was forced to confess that his memory had failed him.

"Well, then," said the professor, "I must remind you. Taking the attraction on the earth as 1, that on Mercury is 1.15, on Venus it is 0.92, on Mars 0.5, and on Jupiter 2.45; on the moon the attraction is 0.16, whilst on the surface of the sun a terrestrial kilogram would weigh 28 kilograms."

"Therefore, if a man upon the surface of the sun were to fall down, he would have considerable difficulty in getting up again. A cannon ball, too, would only fly a few yards," said Lieutenant Procope.

"A jolly battle-field for cowards!" exclaimed Ben Zoof.

"Not so jolly, Ben Zoof, as you fancy," said his master; "the cowards would be too heavy to run away."

Ben Zoof ventured the remark that, as the smallness of Gallia secured to its inhabitants such an increase of strength and agility, he was almost sorry that it had not been a little smaller still.

"Though it could not anyhow have been very much smaller," he added, looking slyly at the professor.

"Idiot!" exclaimed Rosette. "Your head is too light already; a puff of wind would blow it away."

"I must take care of my head, then, and hold it on," replied the irrepressible orderly.

Unable to get the last word, the professor was about to retire, when Servadac detained him.

"Permit me to ask you one more question," he said. "Can you tell me what is the nature of the soil of Gallia?"

"Yes, I can answer that. And in this matter I do not think your impertinent orderly will venture to put Montmartre into the comparison.

This soil is of a substance not unknown upon the earth." And speaking very slowly, the professor said: "It contains 70 per cent. of tellurium, and 30 per cent. of gold."

Servadac uttered an exclamation of surprise.

"And the sum of the specific gravities of these two substances is 10, precisely the number that represents Gallia's density."

"A comet of gold!" ejaculated the captain.

He suspended the money bag to the hook; the needle oscillated, and stopped.

"Yes; a realization of what the illustrious Maupertuis has already deemed probable," replied the astronomer.

"If Gallia, then, should ever become attached to the earth, might it not bring about an important revolution in all monetary affairs?" inquired the count.

"No doubt about it!" said Rosette, with manifest satisfaction. "It would supply the world with about 246,000 trillions of francs."

"A comet of gold!" ejaculated the captain.

"It would make gold about as cheap as dirt, I suppose," said Servadac.

The last observation, however, was entirely lost upon the professor, who had left the hall with an air almost majestic, and was already on his way to the observatory.

"And what, I wonder, is the use of all these big figures?" said Ben Zoof to his master, when next day they were alone together.

"That's just the charm of them, my good fellow," was the captain's cool reply, "that they are of no use whatever."

CHAPTER IX.

EXCEPT as to the time the comet would take to revolve round the sun, it must be confessed that all the professor's calculations had comparatively little interest for anyone but himself, and he was consequently left very much to pursue his studies in solitude.

The following day was the 1st of August, or, according to Rosette, the 63rd of April. In the course of this month Gallia would travel 16,500,000 leagues, attaining at the end a distance of 197,000,000 leagues from the sun. This would leave 81,000,000 leagues more to be traversed before reaching the aphelion of the 15th of January, after which it would begin once more to approach the sun.

But meanwhile, a marvelous world, never before so close within the range of human vision, was revealing itself. No wonder that Palmyrin Rosette cared so little to quit his observatory; for throughout those calm, clear Gallian nights, when the book of the firmament lay open before him, he could revel in a spectacle which no previous astronomer had ever been permitted to enjoy.

The glorious orb that was becoming so conspicuous an object was none other than the planet Jupiter, the largest of all the bodies existing within the influence of solar attraction. During the seven months that had elapsed since its collision with the earth, the comet had been continuously approaching the planet, until the distance between them was scarcely more than 61,000,000 leagues, and this would go on diminishing until the 15th of October.

Under these circumstances, was it perfectly certain that no danger could accrue? Was not Gallia, when its pathway led it into such close proximity to this enormous planet, running a risk of being attracted within its influence? Might not that influence be altogether disastrous? The professor, it is true, in his estimate of the duration of his comet's revolution, had represented that he had made all proper allowances for any perturbations that would be caused either by Jupiter, by Saturn, or by Mars; but what if there were any errors in his calculations? what if there should be any elements of disturbance on which he had not reckoned?

Beautiful nights.

Speculations of this kind became more and more frequent, and Lieutenant Procope pointed out that the danger incurred might be of a fourfold character: first, that the comet, being irresistibly attracted, might be drawn on to the very surface of the planet, and there annihilated; secondly, that as the result of being brought under that attraction, it might be transformed into a satellite, or even a sub-satellite, of that mighty world; thirdly, that it might be diverted into a new orbit, which would never be coincident with the ecliptic; or, lastly, its course might be so retarded that it would only reach the ecliptic too late to permit any junction with the earth. The occurrence of any one of these contingencies would be fatal to their hopes of reunion with the globe, from which they had been so strangely severed.

To Rosette, who, without family ties which he had never found leisure or inclination to contract, had no shadow of desire to return to the earth, it would be only the first of these probabilities that could give him any concern. Total annihilation might not accord with his views, but he would be quite content for Gallia to miss its mark with regard to the earth, indifferent whether it revolved as a new satellite around Jupiter, or whether it wended its course through the untraversed regions of the milky way. The rest of the community, however, by no means sympathized with the professor's sentiments, and the following month was a period of considerable doubt and anxiety.

On the 1st of September the distance between Gallia and Jupiter was precisely the same as the mean distance between the earth and the sun; on the 16th, the distance was further reduced to 26,000,000 leagues. The planet began to assume enormous dimensions, and it almost seemed as if the comet had already been deflected from its elliptical orbit, and was rushing on in a straight line towards the overwhelming luminary.

The more they contemplated the character of this gigantic planet, the more they became impressed with the likelihood of a serious perturbation in their own course. The diameter of Jupiter is 85,390 miles, nearly eleven times as great as that of the earth; his volume is 1,387 times, and his mass 300 times greater; and although the mean density is only about a quarter of that of the earth, and only a third of that of water (whence it has been supposed that the superficies of Jupiter is liquid), yet his other proportions were large enough to warrant the apprehension that important disturbances might result from his proximity.

"I forget my astronomy, lieutenant," said Servadac. "Tell me all you can about this formidable neighbor."

The lieutenant having refreshed his memory by reference to Flammarion's *Recits de l'Infini*, of which he had a Russian translation, and some other books, proceeded to recapitulate that Jupiter accomplishes his revolution round the sun in 4,332 days 14 hours and 2 minutes;

that he travels at the rate of 467 miles a minute along an orbit measuring 2,976 millions of miles; and that his rotation on his axis occupies only 9 hours and 55 minutes.

"His days, then, are shorter than ours?" interrupted the captain.

"Considerably," answered the lieutenant, who went on to describe how the displacement of a point at the equator of Jupiter was twenty-seven times as rapid as on the earth, causing the polar compression to be about 2,378 miles; how the axis, being nearly perpendicular, caused the days and nights to be nearly of the same length, and the seasons to be invariable; and how the amount of light and heat received by the planet is only a twenty-fifth part of that received by the earth, the average distance from the sun being 475,693,000 miles.

"And how about these satellites? Sometimes, I suppose, Jupiter has the benefit of four moons all shining at once?" asked Servadac.

Of the satellites, Lieutenant Procope went on to say that one is rather smaller than our own moon; that another moves round its primary at an interval about equal to the moon's distance from ourselves; but that they all revolve in considerably less time: the first takes only 1 day 18 hours 27 minutes; the second takes 3 days 13 hours 14 minutes; the third, 7 days 3 hours 42 minutes; whilst the largest of all takes but 16 days 16 hours 32 minutes. The most remote revolves round the planet at a distance of 1,192,820 miles.

"They have been enlisted into the service of science," said Procope. "It is by their movements that the velocity of light has been calculated; and they have been made available for the determination of terrestrial longitudes."

"It must be a wonderful sight," said the captain.

"Yes," answered Procope. "I often think Jupiter is like a prodigious clock with four hands."

"I only hope that we are not destined to make a fifth hand," answered Servadac.

Such was the style of the conversation that was day by day reiterated during the whole month of suspense. Whatever topic might be started, it seemed soon to settle down upon the huge orb that was looming upon them with such threatening aspect.

"The more remote that these planets are from the sun," said Procope, "the more venerable and advanced in formation are they found to be. Neptune, situated 2,746,271,000 miles from the sun, issued from the solar nebulosity, thousands of millions of centuries back. Uranus, revolving 1,753,851,000 miles from the center of the planetary system, is of an age amounting to many hundred millions of centuries. Jupiter, the colossal planet, gravitating at a distance of 475,693,000 miles, may be reckoned as 70,000,000 centuries old. Mars has existed for 1,000,000,000 years at a distance of 139,212,000 miles. The earth, 91,430,000 miles from the sun, quitted his burning bosom 100,000,000 years ago. Venus, revolving now 66,131,000 miles away, may be assigned the age of 50,000,000 years at least; and Mercury, nearest of all, and youngest of all, has been revolving at a distance of 35,393,000 miles for the space of 10,000,000 years—the same time as the moon has been evolved from the earth."

Servadac listened attentively. He was at a loss what to say; and the only reply he made to the recital of this novel theory was to the effect that, if it were true, he would prefer being captured by Mercury than by Jupiter, for Mercury, being so much the younger, would probably prove the less imperative and self-willed master.

It was on the 1st of September that the comet had crossed the orbit of Jupiter, and on the 1st of October the two bodies were calculated to be at their minimum separation. No direct shock, however, could be apprehended; the demonstration was sufficiently complete that the orbit of Gallia did not coincide with that of the planet, the orbit of Jupiter being inclined at an angle of 1 degrees 19 mins to the orbit of the earth, with which that of Gallia was, no doubt, coincident.

As the month of September verged towards its close, Jupiter began to wear an aspect that must have excited the admiration of the most ignorant or the most indifferent observer. Its salient points were illumined with novel and radiant tints, and the solar rays, reflected from its disc, glowed with a mingled softness and intensity upon Gallia, so that Nerina had to pale her beauty.

Who could wonder that Rosette, enthusiast as he was, should be irremovable from his observatory? Who could expect otherwise than that, with the prospect before him of viewing the giant among planets, ten times nearer than any mortal eye had ever done, he should have begrudged every moment that distracted his attention?

Meanwhile, as Jupiter grew large, the sun grew small.

From its increased remoteness the diameter of the sun's disc was diminished to 5 degrees 46 mins.

They were visible to the naked eye.

And what an increased interest began to be associated with the satellites! They were visible to the naked eye! Was it not a new record in the annals of science?

Although it is acknowledged that they are not ordinarily visible on earth without the aid of a somewhat powerful telescope, it has been asserted that a favored few, endued with extraordinary powers of vision, have been able to identify them with an unassisted eye; but here, at least, in Nina's Hive were many rivals, for everyone could so far distinguish them one from the other as to describe them by their colors. The first was of a dull white shade; the second was blue; the third was white and brilliant; the fourth was orange, at times approaching to a red. It was further observed that Jupiter itself was almost void of scintillation.

Rosette, in his absorbing interest for the glowing glories of the planet, seemed to be beguiled into comparative forgetfulness of the charms of his comet; but no astronomical enthusiasm of the professor could quite allay the general apprehension that some serious collision might be impending.

Time passed on. There was nothing to justify apprehension. The question was continually being asked, "What does the professor really think?"

"Our friend the professor," said Servadac, "is not likely to tell us very much; but we may feel pretty certain of one thing: he wouldn't keep us long in the dark, if he thought we were not going back to the earth again. The greatest satisfaction he could have would be to inform us that we had parted from the earth for ever."

"I trust from my very soul," said the count, "that his prognostications are correct."

"The more I see of him, and the more I listen to him," replied Servadac, "the more I become convinced that his calculations are based on a solid foundation, and will prove correct to the minutest particular."

Ben Zoof here interrupted the conversation. "I have something on my mind," he said.

"Something on your mind? Out with it!" said the captain.

"That telescope!" said the orderly; "it strikes me that that telescope which the old professor keeps pointed up at yonder big sun is bringing it down straight upon us."

The captain laughed heartily.

"Laugh, captain, if you like; but I feel disposed to break the old telescope into atoms."

"Ben Zoof," said Servadac, his laughter exchanged for a look of stern displeasure, "touch that telescope, and you shall swing for it!"

The orderly looked astonished.

"I am governor here," said Servadac.

Ben Zoof knew what his master meant, and to him his master's wish was law.

The interval between the comet and Jupiter was, by the 1st of October, reduced to 43,000,000 miles. The belts all parallel to Jupiter's equator were very distinct in their markings. Those immediately north and south of the equator were of a dusky hue; those toward the poles were alternately dark and light; the intervening spaces of the planet's superficies, between edge and edge, being intensely bright. The belts themselves were occasionally broken by spots, which the records of astronomy describe as varying both in form and in extent.

The physiology of belts and spots alike was beyond the astronomer's power to ascertain; and even if he should be destined once again to take his place in an astronomical congress on the earth, he would be just as incapable as ever of determining whether or no they owed their existence to the external accumulation of vapor, or to some internal agency. It would not be Professor Rosette's lot to enlighten his brother *savants* to any great degree as to the mysteries that are associated with this, which must ever rank as one of the most magnificent amongst the heavenly orbs.

As the comet approached the critical point of its career it cannot be denied that there was an unacknowledged consciousness of alarm. Mutually reserved, though ever courteous, the count and the captain were secretly drawn together by the prospect of a common danger; and as their return to the earth appeared to them to become more and more dubious, they abandoned their views of narrow isolation, and tried to embrace the wider philosophy that acknowledges the credibility of a habitable universe.

But no philosophy could be proof against the common instincts of their humanity; their hearts, their hopes, were set upon their natural home; no speculation, no science, no experience, could induce them to give up their fond and sanguine anticipation that once again they were to come in contact with the earth.

"Only let us escape Jupiter," said Lieutenant Procope, repeatedly, "and we are free from anxiety."

"But would not Saturn lie ahead?" asked Servadac and the count in one breath.

"No!" said Procope; "the orbit of Saturn is remote, and does not come athwart our path. Jupiter is our sole hindrance. Of Jupiter we must say, as William Tell said, 'Once through the ominous pass and all is well.'"

The 15th of October came, the date of the nearest approximation of the comet to the planet. They were only 31,000,000 miles apart. What would now transpire? Would Gallia be diverted from its proper way? or would it hold the course that the astronomer had predicted?

Early next morning the captain ventured to take the count and the lieutenant up to the observatory. The professor was in the worst of tempers.

That was enough. It was enough, without a word, to indicate the course which events had taken. The comet was pursuing an unaltered way.

The astronomer, correct in his prognostications, ought to have been the most proud and contented of philosophers; his pride and contentment were both overshadowed by the certainty that the career of his comet was destined to be so transient, and that it must inevitably once again come into collision with the earth.

CHAPTER X

MARKET PRICES IN GALLIA

"ALL right!" said Servadac, convinced by the professor's ill humor that the danger was past; "no doubt we are in for a two years' excursion, but fifteen months more will take us back to the earth!"

"And we shall see Montmartre again!" exclaimed Ben Zoof, in excited tones that betrayed his delight in the anticipation.

To use a nautical expression, they had safely "rounded the point," and they had to be congratulated on their successful navigation; for if, under the influence of Jupiter's attraction, the comet had been retarded for a single hour, in that hour the earth would have already traveled 2,300,000 miles from the point where contact would ensue, and many centuries would elapse before such a coincidence would possibly again occur.

On the 1st of November Gallia and Jupiter were 40,000,000 miles apart. It was little more than ten weeks to the 15th of January, when the comet would begin to re-approach the sun. Though light and heat were now reduced to a twenty-fifth part of their terrestrial intensity, so that a perpetual twilight seemed to have settled over Gallia, yet the population felt cheered even by the little that was left, and buoyed up by the hope that they should ultimately regain their proper position with regard to the great luminary, of which the temperature has been estimated as not less than 5,000,000 degrees.

Of the anxiety endured during the last two months Isaac Hakkabut had known nothing. Since the day he had done his lucky stroke of business he had never left the tartan; and after Ben Zoof, on the following day, had returned the steelyard and the borrowed cash, receiving back the paper roubles deposited, all communication between the Jew and Nina's Hive had ceased. In the course of the few minutes' conversation which Ben Zoof had held with him, he had mentioned that he knew that the whole soil of Gallia was made of gold; but the old man, guessing that the orderly was only laughing at him as usual, paid no attention to the remark, and only meditated upon the means he could devise to get every bit of the money in the new world into his own possession. No one grieved over the life of solitude which Hakkabut persisted in leading. Ben Zoof giggled heartily, as he repeatedly observed "it was astonishing how they reconciled themselves to his absence."

The Lieutenant reading.

The time came, however, when various circumstances prompted him to think he must renew his intercourse with the inhabitants of the Hive. Some of his goods were beginning to spoil, and he felt the necessity of turning them into money, if he would not be a loser; he hoped, moreover, that the scarcity of his commodities would secure very high prices.

It happened, just about this same time, that Ben Zoof had been calling his master's attention to the fact that some of their most necessary provisions would soon be running short, and that their stock of coffee, sugar, and tobacco would want replenishing. Servadac's mind, of course, turned to the cargo on board the *Hansa*, and he resolved, according to his promise, to apply to the Jew and become a purchaser. Mutual interest and necessity thus conspired to draw Hakkabut and the captain together.

Often and often had Isaac gloated in his solitude over the prospect of first selling a portion of his merchandise for all the gold and silver in the colony. His recent usurious transaction had whetted his appetite. He would next part with some more of his cargo for all the paper money they could give him; but still he should have goods left, and they would want these. Yes, they should have these, too, for promissory notes. Notes would hold good when they got back again to the earth; bills from his Excellency the governor would be good bills; anyhow there would be the sheriff. By the God of Israel! he would get good prices, and he would get fine interest!

Although he did not know it, he was proposing to follow the practice of the Gauls of old, who advanced money on bills for payment in a future life. Hakkabut's "future life," however, was not many months in advance of the present.

Still Hakkabut hesitated to make the first advance, and it was accordingly with much satisfaction that he hailed Captain Servadac's appearance on board the *Hansa*.

"Hakkabut," said the captain, plunging without further preface into business, "we want some coffee, some tobacco, and other things. I have come to-day to order them, to settle the price, and to-morrow Ben Zoof shall fetch the goods away."

"Merciful, heavens!" the Jew began to whine; but Servadac cut him short.

"None of that miserable howling! Business! I am come to buy your goods. I shall pay for them."

"Ah yes, your Excellency," whispered the Jew, his voice trembling like a street beggar. "Don't impose on me. I am poor; I am nearly ruined already."

"Cease your wretched whining!" cried Servadac. "I have told you once, I shall pay for all I buy."

"Ready money?" asked Hakkabut.

"Yes, ready money. What makes you ask?" said the captain, curious to hear what the Jew would say.

"Surely you can trust the banks of England, France, and Russia."

"Well, you see—you see, your Excellency," stammered out the Jew, "to give credit to one wouldn't do, unless I gave credit to another. You are solvent—I mean honorable, and his lordship the count is honorable; but maybe—maybe—"

"Well?" said Servadac, waiting, but inclined to kick the old rascal out of his sight.

"I shouldn't like to give credit," he repeated.

"I have not asked you for credit. I have told you, you shall have ready money."

"Very good, your Excellency. But how will you pay me?"

"Pay you? Why, we shall pay you in gold and silver and copper, while our money lasts, and when that is gone we shall pay you in bank notes."

"Oh, no paper, no paper!" groaned out the Jew, relapsing into his accustomed whine.

"Nonsense, man!" cried Servadac.

"No paper!" reiterated Hakkabut.

"Why not? Surely you can trust the banks of England, France, and Russia."

"Ah no! I must have gold. Nothing so safe as gold."

"Well then," said the captain, not wanting to lose his temper, "you shall have it your own way; we have plenty of gold for the present. We will leave the bank notes for by and by." The Jew's countenance brightened, and Servadac, repeating that he should come again the next day, was about to quit the vessel.

"One moment, your Excellency," said Hakkabut, sidling up with a hypocritical smile; "I suppose I am to fix my own prices."

"You will, of course, charge ordinary prices—proper market prices; European prices, I mean."

"Merciful heavens!" shrieked the old man, "you rob me of my rights; you defraud me of my privilege. The monopoly of the market belongs to me. It is the custom; it is my right; it is my privilege to fix my own prices."

Servadac made him understand that he had no intention of swerving from his decision.

"Merciful heavens!" again howled the Jew, "it is sheer ruin. The time of monopoly is the time for profit; it is the time for speculation."

"The very thing, Hakkabut, that I am anxious to prevent. Just stop now, and think a minute. You seem to forget *my* rights; you are forgetting that, if I please, I can confiscate all your cargo for the common use. You ought to think yourself lucky in getting any price at all. Be contented with European prices; you will get no more. I am not going to waste my breath on you. I will come again to-morrow;" and, without allowing Hakkabut time to renew his lamentations, Servadac went away.

All the rest of the day the Jew was muttering bitter curses against the thieves of Gentiles in general, and the governor of Gallia in particular, who were robbing him of his just profits, by binding him down to a maximum price for his goods, just as if it were a time of revolution in the state. But he would be even with them yet; he would have it all out of them: he would make European prices pay, after all. He had a plan—he knew how; and he chuckled to himself, and grinned maliciously.

True to his word, the captain next morning arrived at the tartan. He was accompanied by Ben Zoof and two Russian sailors. "Good-morning, old Eleazar; we have come to do our little bit of friendly business with you, you know," was Ben Zoof's greeting.

"What do you want to-day?" asked the Jew.

"To-day we want coffee, and we want sugar, and we want tobacco. We must have ten kilograms of each. Take care they are all good; all first rate. I am commissariat officer, and I am responsible."

"I thought you were the governor's aide-de-camp," said Hakkabut.

"So I am, on state occasions; but to-day, I tell you. I am superintendent of the commissariat department. Now, look sharp!"

Hakkabut hereupon descended into the hold of the tartan, and soon returned, carrying ten packets of tobacco, each weighing one kilogram, and securely fastened by strips of paper, labeled with the French government stamp.

"Ten kilograms of tobacco at twelve francs a kilogram: a hundred and twenty francs," said the Jew.

Ben Zoof was on the point of laying down the money, when Servadac stopped him.

"Let us just see whether the weight is correct."

Hakkabut pointed out that the weight was duly registered on every packet, and that the packets had never been unfastened. The captain, however, had his own special object in view, and would not be diverted. The Jew fetched his steelyard, and a packet of the tobacco was suspended to it.

"Merciful heavens!" screamed Isaac.

The index registered only 133 grams!

"You see, Hakkabut, I was right. I was perfectly justified in having your goods put to the test," said Servadac, quite seriously.

"But—but, your Excellency—" stammered out the bewildered man.

"You will, of course, make up the deficiency," the captain continued, not noticing the interruption.

"Oh, my lord, let me say—" began Isaac again.

"Come, come, old Caiaphas, do you hear? You are to make up the deficiency," exclaimed Ben Zoof.

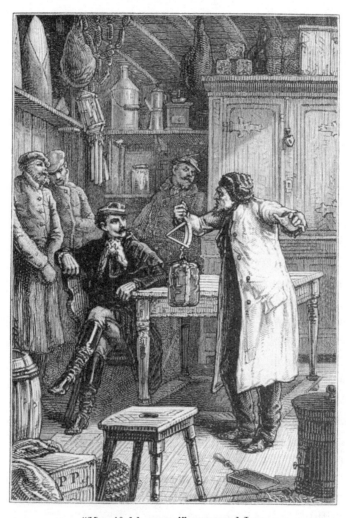

"Merciful heavens!" screamed Isaac.

"Ah, yes, yes; but—"

The unfortunate Israelite tried hard to speak, but his agitation prevented him. He understood well enough the cause of the phenomenon, but he was overpowered by the conviction that the "cursed Gentiles" wanted to cheat him. He deeply regretted that he had not a pair of common scales on board.

"Come, I say, old Jedediah, you are a long while making up what's short," said Ben Zoof, while the Jew was still stammering on.

As soon as he recovered his power of articulation, Isaac began to pour out a medley of lamentations and petitions for mercy. The captain was inexorable. "Very sorry, you know, Hakkabut. It is not my fault that the packet is short weight; but I cannot pay for a kilogram except I have a kilogram."

Hakkabut pleaded for some consideration.

"A bargain is a bargain," said Servadac. "You must complete your contract."

And, moaning and groaning, the miserable man was driven to make up the full weight as registered by his own steelyard. He had to repeat the process with the sugar and coffee: for every kilogram he had to weigh seven. Ben Zoof and the Russians jeered him most unmercifully.

"I say, old Mordecai, wouldn't you rather give your goods away, than sell them at this rate? I would."

"I say, old Pilate, a monopoly isn't always a good thing, is it?"

"I say, old Sepharvaim, what a flourishing trade you're driving!"

Meanwhile seventy kilograms of each of the articles required were weighed, and the Jew for each seventy had to take the price of ten.

All along Captain Servadac had been acting only in jest. Aware that old Isaac was an utter hypocrite, he had no compunction in turning a business transaction with him into an occasion for a bit of fun. But the joke at an end, he took care that the Jew was properly paid all his legitimate due.

CHAPTER XI.

FAR INTO SPACE

A MONTH passed away. Gallia continued its course, bearing its little population onwards, so far removed from the ordinary influence of human passions that it might almost be said that its sole ostensible vice was represented by the greed and avarice of the miserable Jew.

After all, they were but making a voyage—a strange, yet a transient, excursion through solar regions hitherto untraversed; but if the professor's calculations were correct—and why should they be doubted?—their little vessel was destined, after a two years' absence, once more to return "to port." The landing, indeed, might be a matter of difficulty; but with the good prospect before them of once again standing on terrestrial shores, they had nothing to do at present except to make themselves as comfortable as they could in their present quarters.

Thus confident in their anticipations, neither the captain, the count, nor the lieutenant felt under any serious obligation to make any extensive provisions for the future; they saw no necessity for expending the strength of the people, during the short summer that would intervene upon the long severity of winter, in the cultivation or the preservation of their agricultural resources. Nevertheless, they often found themselves talking over the measures they would have been driven to adopt, if they had found themselves permanently attached to their present home.

Even after the turning-point in their career, they knew that at least nine months would have to elapse before the sea would be open to navigation; but at the very first arrival of summer they would be bound to arrange for the *Dobryna* and the *Hansa* to retransport themselves and all their animals to the shores of Gourbi Island, where they would have to commence their agricultural labors to secure the crops that must form their winter store. During four months or thereabouts, they would lead the lives of farmers and of sportsmen; but no sooner would their haymaking and their corn harvest have been accomplished, than they would be compelled again, like a swarm of bees, to retire to their semi-troglodyte existence in the cells of Nina's Hive.

Now and then the captain and his friends found themselves speculating whether, in the event of their having to spend another winter upon Gallia, some means could not be devised by which the dreariness of a second residence in the recesses of the volcano might be escaped. Would not another exploring expedition possibly result in the discovery of a vein of coal or other combustible matter, which could be turned to account in warming some erection which they might hope to put up? A prolonged existence in their underground quarters was felt to be monotonous and depressing, and although it might be all very well for a man like Professor Rosette, absorbed in astronomical studies, it was ill suited to the temperaments of any of themselves for any longer period than was absolutely indispensable.

One contingency there was, almost too terrible to be taken into account. Was it not to be expected that the time might come when the internal fires of Gallia would lose their activity, and the stream of lava would consequently cease to flow? Why should Gallia be exempt from the destiny that seemed to await every other heavenly body? Why should it not roll onwards, like the moon, a dark cold mass in space?

In the event of such a cessation of the volcanic eruption, whilst the comet was still at so great a distance from the sun, they would indeed be at a loss to find a substitute for what alone had served to render life endurable at a temperature of 60 degrees below zero. Happily, however, there was at present no symptom of the subsidence of the lava's stream; the volcano continued its regular and unchanging discharge, and Servadac, ever sanguine, declared that it was useless to give themselves any anxiety upon the matter.

On the 15th of December, Gallia was 276,000,000 leagues from the sun, and, as it was approximately to the extremity of its axis major, would travel only some 11,000,000 or 12,000,000 leagues during the month. Another world was now becoming a conspicuous object in the heavens, and Palmyrin Rosette, after rejoicing in an approach nearer to Jupiter than any other mortal man had ever attained, was now to be privileged to enjoy a similar opportunity of contemplating the planet Saturn. Not that the circumstances were altogether so favorable. Scarcely 31,000,000 miles had separated Gallia from Jupiter; the minimum distance of Saturn would not be less than 415,000,000 miles; but even this distance, although too great to affect the comet's progress more than had been duly reckoned on, was considerably shorter than what had ever separated Saturn from the earth.

Saturn and its satellites.

To get any information about the planet from Rosette appeared quite impossible. Although equally by night and by day he never seemed to quit his telescope, he did not evince the slightest inclination to impart the result of his observations. It was only from the few astronomical works that happened to be included in the *Dobryna's* library

that any details could be gathered, but these were sufficient to give a
large amount of interesting information.

Ben Zoof, when he was made aware that the earth would be invisible to the naked eye from the surface of Saturn, declared that he then,
for his part, did not care to learn any more about such a planet; to
him it was indispensable that the earth should remain in sight, and
it was his great consolation that hitherto his native sphere had never
vanished from his gaze.

At this date Saturn was revolving at a distance of 420,000,000
miles from Gallia, and consequently 874,440,000 miles from the sun,
receiving only a hundredth part of the light and heat which that luminary bestows upon the earth. On consulting their books of reference,
the colonists found that Saturn completes his revolution round the sun
in a period of 29 years and 167 days, traveling at the rate of more than
21,000 miles an hour along an orbit measuring 5,490 millions of miles
in length. His circumference is about 220,000 miles; his superficies,
144,000 millions of square miles; his volume, 143,846 millions of cubic miles. Saturn is 735 times larger than the earth, consequently he
is smaller than Jupiter; in mass he is only 90 times greater than the
earth, which gives him a density less than that of water. He revolves
on his axis in 10 hours 29 minutes, causing his own year to consist of
86,630 days; and his seasons, on account of the great inclination of his
axis to the plane of his orbit, are each of the length of seven terrestrial
years.

Although the light received from the sun is comparatively feeble,
the nights upon Saturn must be splendid. Eight satellites—Mimas,
Enceladus, Tethys, Dione, Rhea, Titan, Hyperion, and Japetus—accompany the planet; Mimas, the nearest to its primary, rotating on its
axis in 22 1/2 hours, and revolving at a distance of only 120,800 miles,
whilst Japetus, the most remote, occupies 79 days in its rotation, and
revolves at a distance of 2,314,000 miles.

Another most important contribution to the magnificence of the
nights upon Saturn is the triple ring with which, as a brilliant setting,
the planet is encompassed. To an observer at the equator, this ring,
which has been estimated by Sir William Herschel as scarcely 100
miles in thickness, must have the appearance of a narrow band of light
passing through the zenith 12,000 miles above his head. As the observer, however, increases his latitude either north or south, the band

will gradually widen out into three detached and concentric rings, of which the innermost, dark though transparent, is 9,625 miles in breadth; the intermediate one, which is brighter than the planet itself, being 17,605 miles broad; and the outer, of a dusky hue, being 8,660 miles broad.

Sometimes they would appear as an illuminated arch.

Such, they read, is the general outline of this strange appendage, which revolves in its own plane in 10 hours 32 minutes. Of what matter it is composed, and how it resists disintegration, is still an unsettled question; but it might almost seem that the Designer of the universe, in permitting its existence, had been willing to impart to His intelligent creatures the manner in which celestial bodies are evolved, and that this remarkable ring-system is a remnant of the nebula from which Saturn was himself developed, and which, from some unknown cause, has become solidified. If at any time it should disperse, it would either fall into fragments upon the surface of Saturn, or the fragments, mutually coalescing, would form additional satellites to circle round the planet in its path.

To any observer stationed on the planet, between the extremes of lat. 45 degrees on either side of the equator, these wonderful rings would present various strange phenomena. Sometimes they would appear as an illuminated arch, with the shadow of Saturn passing over it like the hour-hand over a dial; at other times they would be like a semi-aureole of light. Very often, too, for periods of several years, daily eclipses of the sun must occur through the interposition of this triple ring.

Truly, with the constant rising and setting of the satellites, some with bright discs at their full, others like silver crescents, in quadrature, as well as by the encircling rings, the aspect of the heavens from the surface of Saturn must be as impressive as it is gorgeous.

Unable, indeed, the Gallians were to realize all the marvels of this strange world. After all, they were practically a thousand times further off than the great astronomers have been able to approach by means of their giant telescopes. But they did not complain; their little comet, they knew, was far safer where it was; far better out of the reach of an attraction which, by affecting their path, might have annihilated their best hopes.

The distances of several of the brightest of the fixed stars have been estimated. Amongst others, Vega in the constellation Lyra is 100 millions of millions of miles away; Sirius in Canis Major, 123 millions of millions; the Pole-star, 282 millions of millions; and Capella, 340 millions of millions of miles, a figure represented by no less than fifteen digits.

The hard numerical statement of these enormous figures, however, fails altogether in any adequate way to convey a due impression of the magnitude of these distances. Astronomers, in their ingenuity, have endeavored to use some other basis, and have found "the velocity of light" to be convenient for their purpose. They have made their representations something in this way:

"Suppose," they say, "an observer endowed with an infinite length of vision: suppose him stationed on the surface of Capella; looking thence towards the earth, he would be a spectator of events that had happened seventy years previously; transport him to a star ten times distant, and he will be reviewing the terrestrial sphere of 720 years back; carry him away further still, to a star so remote that it requires something less than nineteen centuries for light to reach it, and he would be a witness of the birth and death of Christ; convey him further again, and he shall be looking upon the dread desolation of the Deluge; take him away further yet (for space is infinite), and he shall be a spectator of the Creation of the spheres. History is thus stereotyped in space; nothing once accomplished can ever be effaced."

Who can altogether be astonished that Palmyrin Rosette, with his burning thirst for astronomical research, should have been conscious of a longing for yet wider travel through the sidereal universe? With his comet now under the influence of one star, now of another, what various systems might he not have explored! what undreamed-of marvels might not have revealed themselves before his gaze! The stars, fixed and immovable in name, are all of them in motion, and Gallia might have followed them in their un-tracked way.

But Gallia had a narrow destiny. She was not to be allowed to wander away into the range of attraction of another center; nor to mingle with the star clusters, some of which have been entirely, others partially resolved; nor was she to lose herself amongst the 5,000 nebulae which have resisted hitherto the grasp of the most powerful reflectors. No; Gallia was neither to pass beyond the limits of the solar system, nor to travel out of sight of the terrestrial sphere. Her orbit was circumscribed to little over 1,500 millions of miles; and, in comparison with the infinite space beyond, this was a mere nothing.

CHAPTER XII.

A FÊTE DAY

THE temperature continued to decrease; the mercurial thermometer, which freezes at 42 degrees below zero, was no longer of service, and the spirit thermometer of the *Dobryna* had been brought into use. This now registered 53 degrees below freezing-point.

In the creek, where the two vessels had been moored for the winter, the elevation of the ice, in anticipation of which Lieutenant Procope had taken the precautionary measure of beveling, was going on slowly but irresistibly, and the tartan was upheaved fifty feet above the level of the Gallian Sea, while the schooner, as being lighter, had been raised to a still greater altitude.

So irresistible was this gradual process of elevation, so utterly defying all human power to arrest, that the lieutenant began to feel very anxious as to the safety of his yacht. With the exception of the engine and the masts, everything had been cleared out and conveyed to shore, but in the event of a thaw it appeared that nothing short of a miracle could prevent the hull from being dashed to pieces, and then all means of leaving the promontory would be gone. The *Hansa*, of course, would share a similar fate; in fact, it had already heeled over to such an extent as to render it quite dangerous for its obstinate owner, who, at the peril of his life, resolved that he would stay where he could watch over his all-precious cargo, though continually invoking curses on the ill-fate of which he deemed himself the victim.

There was, however, a stronger will than Isaac Hakkabut's. Although no one of all the community cared at all for the safety of the Jew, they cared very much for the security of his cargo, and when Servadac found that nothing would induce the old man to abandon his present quarters voluntarily, he very soon adopted measures of coercion that were far more effectual than any representations of personal danger.

"Stop where you like, Hakkabut," said the captain to him; "but understand that I consider it my duty to make sure that your cargo is taken care of. I am going to have it carried across to land, at once."

Neither groans, nor tears, nor protestations on the part of the Jew, were of the slightest avail. Forthwith, on the 20th of December, the removal of the goods commenced.

Ben Zoof and the Russian cook had quite surpassed themselves.

Both Spaniards and Russians were all occupied for several days in the work of unloading the tartan. Well muffled up as they were in furs, they were able to endure the cold with impunity, making it their special care to avoid actual contact with any article made of metal, which, in the low state of the temperature, would inevitably have taken all the skin off their hands, as much as if it had been red-hot. The task, however, was brought to an end without accident of any kind; and when the stores of the *Hansa* were safely deposited in the galleries of the Hive, Lieutenant Procope avowed that he really felt that his mind had been unburdened from a great anxiety.

Captain Servadac gave old Isaac full permission to take up his residence amongst the rest of the community, promised him the entire control over his own property, and altogether showed him so much consideration that, but for his unbounded respect for his master, Ben Zoof would have liked to reprimand him for his courtesy to a man whom he so cordially despised.

Although Hakkabut clamored most vehemently about his goods being carried off "against his will," in his heart he was more than satisfied to see his property transferred to a place of safety, and delighted, moreover, to know that the transport had been effected without a farthing of expense to himself. As soon, then, as he found the tartan empty, he was only too glad to accept the offer that had been made him, and very soon made his way over to the quarters in the gallery where his merchandise had been stored. Here he lived day and night. He supplied himself with what little food he required from his own stock of provisions, a small spirit-lamp sufficing to perform all the operations of his meager cookery. Consequently all intercourse between himself and the rest of the inhabitants was entirely confined to business transactions, when occasion required that some purchase should be made from his stock of commodities. Meanwhile, all the silver and gold of the colony was gradually finding its way to a double-locked drawer, of which the Jew most carefully guarded the key.

The 1st of January was drawing near, the anniversary of the shock which had resulted in the severance of thirty-six human beings from the society of their fellow-men. Hitherto, not one of them was missing. The unvarying calmness of the climate, notwithstanding the cold, had tended to maintain them in good health, and there seemed no reason to doubt that, when Gallia returned to the earth, the total of its little population would still be complete.

The 1st of January, it is true, was not properly "New Year's Day" in Gallia, but Captain Servadac, nevertheless, was very anxious to have it observed as a holiday.

"I do not think," he said to Count Timascheff and Lieutenant Procope, "that we ought to allow our people to lose their interest in the world to which we are all hoping to return; and how can we cement the bond that ought to unite us, better than by celebrating, in common with our fellow-creatures upon earth, a day that awakens afresh the kindliest sentiments of all? Besides," he added, smiling, "I expect that Gallia, although invisible just at present to the naked eye, is being closely watched by the telescopes of our terrestrial friends, and I have no doubt that the newspapers and scientific journals of both hemispheres are full of accounts detailing the movements of the new comet."

"True," asserted the count. "I can quite imagine that we are occasioning no small excitement in all the chief observatories."

"Ay, more than that," said the lieutenant; "our Gallia is certain to be far more than a mere object of scientific interest or curiosity. Why should we doubt that the elements of a comet which has once come into collision with the earth have by this time been accurately calculated? What our friend the professor has done here, has been done likewise on the earth, where, beyond a question, all manner of expedients are being discussed as to the best way of mitigating the violence of a concussion that must occur."

The lieutenant's conjectures were so reasonable that they commanded assent. Gallia could scarcely be otherwise than an object of terror to the inhabitants of the earth, who could by no means be certain that a second collision would be comparatively so harmless as the first. Even to the Gallians themselves, much as they looked forward to the event, the prospect was not unmixed with alarm, and they would rejoice in the invention of any device by which it was likely the impetus of the shock might be deadened.

Christmas arrived, and was marked by appropriate religious observance by everyone in the community, with the exception of the Jew, who made a point of secluding himself more obstinately than ever in the gloomy recesses of his retreat.

To Ben Zoof the last week of the year was full of bustle. The arrangements for the New Year *fête* were entrusted to him, and he was anxious, in spite of the resources of Gallia being so limited, to make the program for the great day as attractive as possible.

It was a matter of debate that night whether the professor should be invited to join the party; it was scarcely likely that he would care to

come, but, on the whole, it was felt to be advisable to ask him. At first
Captain Servadac thought of going in person with the invitation; but,
remembering Rosette's dislike to visitors, he altered his mind, and
sent young Pablo up to the observatory with a formal note, requesting
the pleasure of Professor Rosette's company at the New Year's *fête*.

Frenchmen, Russians, Spaniards, and little Nina, as the representative of
Italy, sat down to a feast.

Pablo was soon back, bringing no answer except that the professor
had told him that "to-day was the 125th of June, and that to-morrow
would be the 1st of July."

Consequently, Servadac and the count took it for granted that Palmyrin Rosette declined their invitation.

An hour after sunrise on New Year's Day, Frenchmen, Russians, Spaniards, and little Nina, as the representative of Italy, sat down to a feast such as never before had been seen in Gallia. Ben Zoof and the Russian cook had quite surpassed themselves. The wines, part of the *Dobryna's* stores, were of excellent quality. Those of the vintages of France and Spain were drunk in toasting their respective countries, and even Russia was honored in a similar way by means of a few bottles of kummel. The company was more than contented—it was as jovial as Ben Zoof could desire; and the ringing cheers that followed the great toast of the day—"A happy return to our Mother Earth," must fairly have startled the professor in the silence of his observatory.

The *dejeuner* over, there still remained three hours of daylight. The sun was approaching the zenith, but so dim and enfeebled were his rays that they were very unlike what had produced the wines of Bordeaux and Burgundy which they had just been enjoying, and it was necessary for all, before starting upon an excursion that would last over nightfall, to envelop themselves in the thickest of clothing.

Full of spirits, the party left the Hive, and chattering and singing as they went, made their way down to the frozen shore, where they fastened on their skates. Once upon the ice, everyone followed his own fancy, and some singly, some in groups, scattered themselves in all directions. Captain Servadac, the count, and the lieutenant were generally seen together. Negrete and the Spaniards, now masters of their novel exercise, wandered fleetly and gracefully hither and thither, occasionally being out of sight completely. The Russian sailors, following a northern custom, skated in file, maintaining their rank by means of a long pole passed under their right arms, and in this way they described a trackway of singular regularity. The two children, blithe as birds, flitted about, now singly, now arm-in-arm, now joining the captain's party, now making a short peregrination by themselves, but always full of life and spirit. As for Ben Zoof, he was here, there, and everywhere, his imperturbable good temper ensuring him a smile of welcome whenever he appeared.

Thus coursing rapidly over the icy plain, the whole party had soon exceeded the line that made the horizon from the shore. First, the rocks of the coast were lost to view; then the white crests of the cliffs were no longer to be seen; and at last, the summit of the volcano, with its corona of vapor, was entirely out of sight. Occasionally the skaters were obliged to stop to recover their breath, but, fearful of frost-bite, they almost instantly resumed their exercise, and proceeded nearly as far as Gourbi Island before they thought about retracing their course.

They looked like graceful Eskimos.

But night was coming on, and the sun was already sinking in the east with the rapidity to which the residents on Gallia were by this time well accustomed. The sunset upon this contracted horizon was very remarkable. There was not a cloud nor a vapor to catch the tints of the declining beams; the surface of the ice did not, as a liquid sea

would, reflect the last green ray of light; but the radiant orb, enlarged
by the effect of refraction, its circumference sharply defined against
the sky, sank abruptly, as though a trap had been opened in the ice
for its reception.

Before the daylight ended. Captain Servadac had cautioned the
party to collect themselves betimes into one group. "Unless you are
sure of your whereabouts before dark," he said, "you will not find it
after. We have come out like a party of skirmishers; let us go back in
full force."

The night would be dark; their moon was in conjunction, and would
not be seen; the stars would only give something of that "pale radiance" which the poet Corneille has described.

Immediately after sunset the torches were lighted, and the long
series of flames, fanned by the rapid motion of their bearers, had much
the appearance of an enormous fiery banner. An hour later, and the
volcano appeared like a dim shadow on the horizon, the light from the
crater shedding a lurid glare upon the surrounding gloom. In time
the glow of the burning lava, reflected in the icy mirror, fell upon the
troop of skaters, and cast their lengthened shadows grotesquely on the
surface of the frozen sea.

Later still, half an hour or more afterwards, the torches were all but
dying out. The shore was close at hand. All at once, Ben Zoof uttered
a startled cry, and pointed with bewildered excitement towards the
mountain. Involuntarily, one and all, they plowed their heels into the
ice and came to a halt. Exclamations of surprise and horror burst from
every lip. The volcano was extinguished! The stream of burning lava
had suddenly ceased to flow!

Speechless with amazement, they stood still for some moments.
There was not one of them that did not realize, more or less, how critical was their position. The sole source of the heat that had enabled
them to brave the rigor of the cold had failed them! death, in the cru-
ellest of all shapes, seemed staring them in the face—death from cold!
Meanwhile, the last torch had flickered out.

It was quite dark.

"Forward!" cried Servadac, firmly.

At the word of command they advanced to the shore; clambered
with no little difficulty up the slippery rocks; gained the mouth of the
gallery; groped their way into the common hall.

How dreary! how chill it seemed!

The fiery cataract no longer spread its glowing covering over the mouth of the grotto. Lieutenant Procope leaned through the aperture. The pool, hitherto kept fluid by its proximity to the lava, was already encrusted with a layer of ice.

Such was the end of the New Year's Day so happily begun.

CHAPTER XIII.

THE BOWELS OF THE COMET

THE whole night was spent in speculating, with gloomy forebodings, upon the chances of the future. The temperature of the hall, now entirely exposed to the outer air, was rapidly falling, and would quickly become unendurable. Far too intense was the cold to allow anyone to remain at the opening, and the moisture on the walls soon resolved itself into icicles. But the mountain was like the body of a dying man, that retains awhile a certain amount of heat at the heart after the extremities have become cold and dead. In the more interior galleries there was still a certain degree of warmth, and hither Servadac and his companions were glad enough to retreat.

Here they found the professor, who, startled by the sudden cold, had been fain to make a precipitate retreat from his observatory. Now would have been the opportunity to demand of the enthusiast whether he would like to prolong his residence indefinitely upon his little comet. It is very likely that he would have declared himself ready to put up with any amount of discomfort to be able to gratify his love of investigation; but all were far too disheartened and distressed to care to banter him upon the subject on which he was so sensitive.

Next morning, Servadac thus addressed his people. "My friends, except from cold, we have nothing to fear. Our provisions are ample— more than enough for the remaining period of our sojourn in this lone world of ours; our preserved meat is already cooked; we shall be able to dispense with all fuel for cooking purposes. All that we require is warmth—warmth for ourselves; let us secure that, and all may be well. Now, I do not entertain a doubt but that the warmth we require is resident in the bowels of this mountain on which we are living; to the depth of those bowels we must penetrate; there we shall obtain the warmth which is indispensable to our very existence."

His tone, quite as much as his words, restored confidence to many of his people, who were already yielding to a feeling of despair. The count and the lieutenant fervently, but silently, grasped his hand.

"Nina," said the captain, "you will not be afraid to go down to the lower depths of the mountain, will you?"

"Not if Pablo goes," replied the child.

"Oh yes, of course, Pablo will go. You are not afraid to go, are you, Pablo?" he said, addressing the boy.

"Anywhere with you, your Excellency," was the boy's prompt reply.

And certain it was that no time must be lost in penetrating below the heart of the volcano; already the most protected of the many ramifications of Nina's Hive were being pervaded by a cold that was insufferable. It was an acknowledged impossibility to get access to the crater by the exterior declivities of the mountain-side; they were far too steep and too slippery to afford a foothold. It must of necessity be entered from the interior.

Lieutenant Procope accordingly undertook the task of exploring all the galleries, and was soon able to report that he had discovered one which he had every reason to believe abutted upon the central funnel. His reason for coming to this conclusion was that the caloric emitted by the rising vapors of the hot lava seemed to be oozing, as it were, out of the tellurium, which had been demonstrated already to be a conductor of heat. Only succeed in piercing through this rock for seven or eight yards, and the lieutenant did not doubt that his way would be opened into the old lava-course, by following which he hoped descent would be easy.

Under the lieutenant's direction the Russian sailors were immediately set to work. Their former experience had convinced them that spades and pick-axes were of no avail, and their sole resource was to proceed by blasting with gunpowder. However skillfully the operation might be carried on, it must necessarily occupy several days, and during that time the sufferings from cold must be very severe.

"If we fail in our object, and cannot get to the depths of the mountain, our little colony is doomed," said Count Timascheff.

"That speech is not like yourself," answered Servadac, smiling. "What has become of the faith which has hitherto carried you so bravely through all our difficulties?"

The count shook his head, as if in despair, and said, sadly, "The Hand that has hitherto been outstretched to help seems now to be withdrawn."

"But only to test our powers of endurance," rejoined the captain, earnestly. "Courage, my friend, courage! Something tells me that this cessation of the eruption is only partial; the internal fire is not all extinct. All is not over yet. It is too soon to give up; never despair!"

Lieutenant Procope quite concurred with the captain. Many causes, he knew, besides the interruption of the influence of the oxygen upon the mineral substances in Gallia's interior, might account for the stoppage of the lava-flow in this one particular spot, and he considered it more than probable that a fresh outlet had been opened in some other part of the surface, and that the eruptive matter had been diverted into the new channel. But at present his business was to prosecute his labors so that a retreat might be immediately effected from their now untenable position.

Restless and agitated, Professor Rosette, if he took any interest in these discussions, certainly took no share in them. He had brought his telescope down from the observatory into the common hall, and there at frequent intervals, by night and by day, he would endeavor to continue his observations; but the intense cold perpetually compelled him to desist, or he would literally have been frozen to death. No sooner, however, did he find himself obliged to retreat from his study of the heavens, than he would begin overwhelming everybody about him with bitter complaints, pouring out his regrets that he had ever quitted his quarters at Formentera.

On the 4th of January, by persevering industry, the process of boring was completed, and the lieutenant could hear that fragments of the blasted rock, as the sailors cleared them away with their spades, were rolling into the funnel of the crater. He noticed, too, that they did not fall perpendicularly, but seemed to slide along, from which he inferred that the sides of the crater were sloping; he had therefore reason to hope that a descent would be found practicable.

Larger and larger grew the orifice; at length it would admit a man's body, and Ben Zoof, carrying a torch, pushed himself through it, followed by the lieutenant and Servadac. Procope's conjecture proved correct. On entering the crater, they found that the sides slanted at the angle of about 4 degrees; moreover, the eruption had evidently been of recent origin, dating probably only from the shock which had invested Gallia with a proportion of the atmosphere of the earth, and beneath the coating of ashes with which they were covered, there were various irregularities in the rock, not yet worn away by the action of the lava, and these afforded a tolerably safe footing.

"Rather a bad staircase!" said Ben Zoof, as they began to make their way down.

Ben Zoof, carrying a torch, pushed himself through it,

In about half an hour, proceeding in a southerly direction, they had descended nearly five hundred feet. From time to time they came upon large excavations that at first sight had all the appearance of

galleries, but by waving his torch, Ben Zoof could always see their
extreme limits, and it was evident that the lower strata of the mountain did not present the same system of ramification that rendered the
Hive above so commodious a residence.

Throwing the gleams of torch-light in all directions.

It was not a time to be fastidious; they must be satisfied with such
accommodation as they could get, provided it was warm. Captain Servadac was only too glad to find that his hopes about the temperature
were to a certain extent realized. The lower they went, the greater was
the diminution in the cold, a diminution that was far more rapid than
that which is experienced in making the descent of terrestrial mines.

In this case it was a volcano, not a colliery, that was the object of exploration, and thankful enough they were to find that it had not become extinct. Although the lava, from some unknown cause, had ceased to rise in the crater, yet plainly it existed somewhere in an incandescent state, and was still transmitting considerable heat to inferior strata.

Lieutenant Procope had brought in his hand a mercurial thermometer, and Servadac carried an aneroid barometer, by means of which he could estimate the depth of their descent below the level of the Gallian Sea. When they were six hundred feet below the orifice the mercury registered a temperature of 6 degrees below zero.

"Six degrees!" said Servadac; "that will not suit us. At this low temperature we could not survive the winter. We must try deeper down. I only hope the ventilation will hold out."

There was, however, nothing to fear on the score of ventilation. The great current of air that rushed into the aperture penetrated everywhere, and made respiration perfectly easy.

The descent was continued for about another three hundred feet, which brought the explorers to a total depth of nine hundred feet from their old quarters. Here the thermometer registered 12 degrees above zero—a temperature which, if only it were permanent, was all they wanted. There was no advantage in proceeding any further along the lava-course; they could already hear the dull rumblings that indicated that they were at no great distance from the central focus.

"Quite near enough for me!" exclaimed Ben Zoof. "Those who are chilly are welcome to go as much lower as they like. For my part, I shall be quite warm enough here."

After throwing the gleams of torch-light in all directions, the explorers seated themselves on a jutting rock, and began to debate whether it was practicable for the colony to make an abode in these lower depths of the mountain. The prospect, it must be owned, was not inviting. The crater, it is true, widened out into a cavern sufficiently large, but here its accommodation ended. Above and below were a few ledges in the rock that would serve as receptacles for provisions; but, with the exception of a small recess that must be reserved for Nina, it was clear that henceforth they must all renounce the idea of having separate apartments. The single cave must be their dining-room, drawing-room, and dormitory, all in one. From living the life of rabbits in a warren, they were reduced to the existence of moles, with the difference that they could not, like them, forget their troubles in a long winter's sleep.

The cavern, however, was quite capable of being lighted by means of lamps and lanterns. Among the stores were several barrels of oil and a considerable quantity of spirits of wine, which might be burned when required for cooking purposes. Moreover, it would be unnecessary for them to confine themselves entirely to the seclusion of their gloomy residence; well wrapped up, there would be nothing to prevent them making occasional excursions both to the Hive and to the sea-shore. A supply of fresh water would be constantly required; ice for this purpose must be perpetually carried in from the coast, and it would be necessary to arrange that everyone in turn should perform this office, as it would be no sinecure to clamber up the sides of the crater for 900 feet, and descend the same distance with a heavy burden.

But the emergency was great, and it was accordingly soon decided that the little colony should forthwith take up its quarters in the cave. After all, they said, they should hardly be much worse off than thousands who annually winter in Arctic regions. On board the whaling-vessels, and in the establishments of the Hudson's Bay Company, such luxuries as separate cabins or sleeping-chambers are never thought of; one large apartment, well heated and ventilated, with as few corners as possible, is considered far more healthy; and on board ship the entire hold, and in forts a single floor, is appropriated to this purpose. The recollection of this fact served to reconcile them, in a great degree, to the change to which they felt it requisite to submit.

Having remounted the ascent, they made the result of their exploration known to the mass of the community, who received the tidings with a sense of relief, and cordially accepted the scheme of the migration.

The first step was to clear the cavern of its accumulation of ashes, and then the labor of removal commenced in earnest. Never was a task undertaken with greater zest. The fear of being to a certainty frozen to death if they remained where they were, was a stimulus that made everyone put forth all his energies. Beds, furniture, cooking utensils—first the stores of the *Dobryna*, then the cargo of the tartan—all were carried down with the greatest alacrity, and the diminished weight combined with the downhill route to make the labor proceed with incredible briskness.

Although Professor Rosette yielded to the pressure of circumstances, and allowed himself to be conducted to the lower regions, nothing would induce him to allow his telescope to be carried underground; and as it was undeniable that it would certainly be of no service deep down in the bowels of the mountain, it was allowed to remain undisturbed upon its tripod in the great hall of Nina's Hive.

As for Isaac Hakkabut, his outcry was beyond description lamentable. Never, in the whole universe, had a merchant met with such reverses; never had such a pitiable series of losses befallen an unfortunate man. Regardless of the ridicule which his abject wretchedness excited, he howled on still, and kept up an unending wail; but meanwhile he kept a keen eye upon every article of his property, and amidst universal laughter insisted on having every item registered in an inventory as it was transferred to its appointed place of safety. Servadac considerately allowed the whole of the cargo to be deposited in a hollow apart by itself, over which the Jew was permitted to keep a watch as vigilant as he pleased.

By the 10th the removal was accomplished. Rescued, at all events, from the exposure to a perilous temperature of 60 degrees below zero, the community was installed in its new home. The large cave was lighted by the *Dobryna's* lamps, while several lanterns, suspended at intervals along the acclivity that led to their deserted quarters above, gave a weird picturesqueness to the scene, that might vie with any of the graphic descriptions of the "Arabian Nights' Entertainments."

"How do you like this, Nina?" said Ben Zoof.

"*Va bene!*" replied the child. "We are only living in the cellars instead of upon the ground floor."

"We will try and make ourselves comfortable," said the orderly.

"Oh yes, we will be happy here," rejoined the child; "it is nice and warm."

Although they were as careful as they could to conceal their misgivings from the rest, Servadac and his two friends could not regard their present situation without distrust. When alone, they would frequently ask each other what would become of them all, if the volcanic heat should really be subsiding, or if some unexpected perturbation should retard the course of the comet, and compel them to an indefinitely prolonged residence in their grim abode. It was scarcely likely that the comet could supply the fuel of which ere long they would be in urgent need. Who could expect to find coal in the bowels of Gallia,—coal, which is the residuum of ancient forests mineralized by the lapse of ages? Would not the lava-cinders exhumed from the extinct volcano be their last poor resource?

"Keep up your spirits, my friends," said Servadac; "we have plenty of time before us at present. Let us hope that as fresh difficulties arise, fresh ways of escape will open. Never despair!"

"True," said the count; "it is an old saying that 'Necessity is the mother of invention.' Besides, I should think it very unlikely that the internal heat will fail us now before the summer."

The lieutenant declared that he entertained the same hope. As the reason of his opinion he alleged that the combustion of the eruptive matter was most probably of quite recent origin, because the comet before its collision with the earth had possessed no atmosphere, and that consequently no oxygen could have penetrated to its interior.

"Most likely you are right," replied the count; "and so far from dreading a failure of the internal heat, I am not quite sure that we may not be exposed to a more terrible calamity still?"

"What?" asked Servadac.

"The calamity of the eruption breaking out suddenly again, and taking us by surprise."

"Heavens!" cried the captain, "we will not think of that."

"The outbreak may happen again," said the lieutenant, calmly; "but it will be our fault, our own lack of vigilance, if we are taken by surprise." And so the conversation dropped.

The 15th of January dawned; and the comet was 220,000,000 leagues from the sun.

Gallia had reached its aphelion.

CHAPTER XIV.

DREARY MONTHS

HENCEFORTH, then, with a velocity ever increasing, Gallia would re-approach the sun.

Except the thirteen Englishmen who had been left at Gibraltar, every living creature had taken refuge in the dark abyss of the volcano's crater.

And with those Englishmen, how had it fared?

"Far better than with ourselves," was the sentiment that would have been universally accepted in Nina's Hive. And there was every reason to conjecture that so it was. The party at Gibraltar, they all agreed, would not, like themselves, have been compelled to have recourse to a stream of lava for their supply of heat; they, no doubt, had had abundance of fuel as well as food; and in their solid casemate, with its substantial walls, they would find ample shelter from the rigor of the cold. The time would have been passed at least in comfort, and perhaps in contentment; and Colonel Murphy and Major Oliphant would have had leisure more than sufficient for solving the most abstruse problems of the chess-board. All of them, too, would be happy in the confidence that when the time should come, England would have full meed of praise to award to the gallant soldiers who had adhered so well and so manfully to their post.

It did, indeed, more than once occur to the minds both of Servadac and his friends that, if their condition should become one of extreme emergency, they might, as a last resource, betake themselves to Gibraltar, and there seek a refuge; but their former reception had not been of the kindest, and they were little disposed to renew an acquaintanceship that was marked by so little cordiality. Not in the least that they would expect to meet with any inhospitable rebuff. Far from that; they knew well enough that Englishmen, whatever their faults, would be the last to abandon their fellow-creatures in the hour of distress.

Nevertheless, except the necessity became far more urgent than it had hitherto proved, they resolved to endeavor to remain in their present quarters. Up till this time no casualties had diminished their original number, but to undertake so long a journey across that unsheltered expanse of ice could scarcely fail to result in the loss of some of their party.

The horses descended in pain.

However great was the desire to find a retreat for every living thing in the deep hollow of the crater, it was found necessary to slaughter almost all the domestic animals before the removal of the community from Nina's Hive. To have stabled them all in the cavern below would have been quite impossible, whilst to have left them in the upper galleries would only have been to abandon them to a cruel death; and since meat could be preserved for an indefinite time in the original store-places, now colder than ever, the expedient of killing the animals seemed to recommend itself as equally prudent and humane.

Naturally the captain and Ben Zoof were most anxious that their favorite horses should be saved, and accordingly, by dint of the greatest care, all difficulties in the way were overcome, and Zephyr and Galette were conducted down the crater, where they were installed in a large hole and provided with forage, which was still abundant.

Counting and recounting his money.

Birds, subsisting only on scraps thrown out to them did not cease
to follow the population in its migration, and so numerous did they
become that multitudes of them had repeatedly to be destroyed.

The general re-arrangement of the new residence was no easy business, and occupied so much time that the end of January arrived before they could be said to be fairly settled. And then began a life of
dreary monotony. Then seemed to creep over everyone a kind of moral
torpor as well as physical lassitude, which Servadac, the count, and
the lieutenant did their best not only to combat in themselves, but
to counteract in the general community. They provided a variety of
intellectual pursuits; they instituted debates in which everybody was
encouraged to take part; they read aloud, and explained extracts from
the elementary manuals of science, or from the books of adventurous
travel which their library supplied; and Russians and Spaniards, day
after day, might be seen gathered round the large table, giving their
best attention to instruction which should send them back to Mother
Earth less ignorant than they had left her.

Selfish and morose, Hakkabut could never be induced to be present at these social gatherings. He was far too much occupied in his
own appropriated corner, either in conning his accounts, or in counting his money. Altogether, with what he had before, he now possessed the round sum of 150,000 francs, half of which was in sterling
gold; but nothing could give him any satisfaction while he knew that
the days were passing, and that he was denied the opportunity of
putting out his capital in advantageous investments, or securing a
proper interest.

Neither did Palmyrin Rosette find leisure to take any share in the
mutual intercourse. His occupation was far too absorbing for him to
suffer it to be interrupted, and to him, living as he did perpetually in
a world of figures, the winter days seemed neither long nor wearisome.
Having ascertained every possible particular about his comet, he was
now devoting himself with equal ardor to the analysis of all the properties of the satellite Nerina, to which he appeared to assert the same
claim of proprietorship.

In order to investigate Nerina it was indispensable that he should
make several actual observations at various points of the orbit; and
for this purpose he repeatedly made his way up to the grotto above,
where, in spite of the extreme severity of the cold, he would persevere

in the use of his telescope till he was all but paralyzed. But what he felt more than anything was the want of some retired apartment, where he could pursue his studies without hindrance or intrusion.

It was about the beginning of February, when the professor brought his complaint to Captain Servadac, and begged him to assign him a chamber, no matter how small, in which he should be free to carry on his task in silence and without molestation. So readily did Servadac promise to do everything in his power to provide him with the accommodation for which he asked, that the professor was put into such a manifest good temper that the captain ventured to speak upon the matter that was ever uppermost in his mind.

"I do not mean," he began timidly, "to cast the least imputation of inaccuracy upon any of your calculations, but would you allow me, my dear professor, to suggest that you should revise your estimate of the duration of Gallia's period of revolution. It is so important, you know, so all important; the difference of one half minute, you know, would so certainly mar the expectation of reunion with the earth—"

And seeing a cloud gathering on Rosette's face, he added:

"I am sure Lieutenant Procope would be only too happy to render you any assistance in the revision."

"Sir," said the professor, bridling up, "I want no assistant; my calculations want no revision. I never make an error. I have made my reckoning as far as Gallia is concerned. I am now making a like estimate of the elements of Nerina."

Conscious how impolitic it would be to press this matter further, the captain casually remarked that he should have supposed that all the elements of Nerina had been calculated long since by astronomers on the earth. It was about as unlucky a speech as he could possibly have made. The professor glared at him fiercely.

"Astounding, sir!" he exclaimed. "Yes! Nerina was a planet then; everything that appertained to the planet was determined; but Nerina is a moon now. And do you not think, sir, that we have a right to know as much about our moon as those *terrestrials*"—and he curled his lip as he spoke with a contemptuous emphasis—"know of theirs?"

"I beg pardon," said the corrected captain.

"Well then, never mind," replied the professor, quickly appeased; "only will you have the goodness to get me a proper place for study?"

"I will, as I promised, do all I can," answered Servadac.

"Very good," said the professor. "No immediate hurry; an hour hence will do."

But in spite of this condescension on the part of the man of science, some hours had to elapse before any place of retreat could be discovered likely to suit his requirements; but at length a little nook was found in the side of the cavern just large enough to hold an armchair and a table, and in this the astronomer was soon ensconced to his entire satisfaction.

900 feet below ground.

Buried thus, nearly 900 feet below ground, the Gallians ought to have had unbounded mental energy to furnish an adequate reaction to the depressing monotony of their existence; but many days would often elapse without any one of them ascending to the surface of the soil, and had it not been for the necessity of obtaining fresh water, it seemed almost probable that there would never have been an effort made to leave the cavern at all.

A few excursions, it is true, were made in the downward direction. The three leaders, with Ben Zoof, made their way to the lower depths of the crater, not with the design of making any further examination as to the nature of the rock—for although it might be true enough that it contained thirty per cent. of gold, it was as valueless to them as granite—but with the intention of ascertaining whether the subterranean fire still retained its activity. Satisfied upon this point, they came to the conclusion that the eruption which had so suddenly ceased in one spot had certainly broken out in another.

February, March, April, May, passed wearily by; but day succeeded to day with such gloomy sameness that it was little wonder that no notice was taken of the lapse of time. The people seemed rather to vegetate than to live, and their want of vigor became at times almost alarming. The readings around the long table ceased to be attractive, and the debates, sustained by few, became utterly wanting in animation. The Spaniards could hardly be roused to quit their beds, and seemed to have scarcely energy enough to eat. The Russians, constitutionally of more enduring temperament, did not give way to the same extent, but the long and drear confinement was beginning to tell upon them all. Servadac, the count, and the lieutenant all knew well enough that it was the want of air and exercise that was the cause of much of this mental depression; but what could they do? The most serious remonstrances on their part were entirely in vain. In fact, they themselves occasionally fell a prey to the same lassitude both of body and mind. Long fits of drowsiness, combined with an utter aversion to food, would come over them. It almost seemed as if their entire nature had become degenerate, and that, like tortoises, they could sleep and fast till the return of summer.

Strange to say, little Nina bore her hardships more bravely than any of them. Flitting about, coaxing one to eat, another to drink, rousing Pablo as often as he seemed yielding to the common languor, the child became the life of the party. Her merry prattle enlivened the gloom of the grim cavern like the sweet notes of a bird; her gay Italian songs broke the monotony of the depressing silence; and almost unconscious as the half-dormant population of Gallia were of her influence, they still would have missed her bright presence sorely. The months still glided on; how, it seemed impossible for the inhabitants of the living tomb to say. There was a dead level of dullness.

At the beginning of June the general torpor appeared slightly to relax its hold upon its victims. This partial revival was probably due to the somewhat increased influence of the sun, still far, far away. During the first half of the Gallian year, Lieutenant Procope had taken careful note of Rosette's monthly announcements of the comet's progress, and he was able now, without reference to the professor, to calculate the rate of advance on its way back towards the sun. He found that Gallia had re-crossed the orbit of Jupiter, but was still at the enormous distance of 197,000,000 leagues from the sun, and he reckoned that in about four months it would have entered the zone of the telescopic planets.

Gradually, but uninterruptedly, life and spirits continued to revive, and by the end of the month Servadac and his little colony had regained most of their ordinary physical and mental energies. Ben Zoof, in particular, roused himself with redoubled vigor, like a giant refreshed from his slumbers. The visits, consequently, to the long-neglected galleries of Nina's Hive became more and more frequent.

One day an excursion was made to the shore. It was still bitterly cold, but the atmosphere had lost nothing of its former stillness, and not a cloud was visible from horizon to zenith. The old footmarks were all as distinct as on the day in which they had been imprinted, and the only portion of the shore where any change was apparent was in the little creek. Here the elevation of the ice had gone on increasing, until the schooner and the tartan had been uplifted to a height of 150 feet, not only rendering them quite inaccessible, but exposing them to all but certain destruction in the event of a thaw.

Isaac Hakkabut, immovable from the personal oversight of his property in the cavern, had not accompanied the party, and consequently was in blissful ignorance of the fate that threatened his vessel. "A good thing the old fellow wasn't there to see," observed Ben Zoof; "he would have screamed like a peacock. What a misfortune it is," he added, speaking to himself, "to have a peacock's voice, without its plumage!"

During the months of July and August, Gallia advanced 164,000,000 leagues along her orbit. At night the cold was still intense, but in the daytime the sun, here full upon the equator, caused an appreciable difference of 20 degrees in the temperature. Like birds, the population spent whole days exposed to its grateful warmth, rarely returning till nightfall to the shade of their gloomy home.

This spring-time, if such it may be called, had a most enlivening influence upon all. Hope and courage revived as day by day the sun's disc expanded in the heavens, and every evening the earth assumed a greater magnitude amongst the fixed stars. It was distant yet, but the goal was cheeringly in view.

"I can't believe that yonder little speck of light contains my mountain of Montmartre," said Ben Zoof, one night, after he had been gazing long and steadily at the far-off world.

"You will, I hope, some day find out that it does," answered his master.

"I hope so," said the orderly, without moving his eye from the distant sphere. After meditating a while, he spoke again. "I suppose Professor Rosette couldn't make his comet go straight back, could he?"

"Hush!" cried Servadac.

Ben Zoof understood the correction.

"No," continued the captain; "it is not for man to disturb the order of the universe. That belongs to a Higher Power than ours!"

CHAPTER XV.

THE PROFESSOR PERPLEXED

ANOTHER month passed away, and it was now September, but it was still impossible to leave the warmth of the subterranean retreat for the more airy and commodious quarters of the Hive, where "the bees" would certainly have been frozen to death in their cells. It was altogether quite as much a matter of congratulation as of regret that the volcano showed no symptoms of resuming its activity; for although a return of the eruption might have rendered their former resort again habitable, any sudden outbreak would have been disastrous to them where they were, the crater being the sole outlet by which the burning lava could escape.

"A wretched time we have had for the last seven months," said the orderly one day to his master; "but what a comfort little Nina has been to us all!"

"Yes, indeed," replied Servadac; "she is a charming little creature. I hardly know how we should have got on without her."

"What is to become of her when we arrive back at the earth?"

"Not much fear, Ben Zoof, but that she will be well taken care of. Perhaps you and I had better adopt her."

"Ay, yes," assented the orderly. "You can be her father, and I can be her mother."

Servadac laughed. "Then you and I shall be man and wife."

"We have been as good as that for a long time," observed Ben Zoof, gravely.

By the beginning of October, the temperature had so far moderated that it could scarcely be said to be intolerable. The comet's distance was scarcely three times as great from the sun as the earth from the sun, so that the thermometer rarely sunk beyond 35 degrees below zero. The whole party began to make almost daily visits to the Hive, and frequently proceeded to the shore, where they resumed their skating exercise, rejoicing in their recovered freedom like prisoners liberated from a dungeon. Whilst the rest were enjoying their recreation, Servadac and the count would hold long conversations with Lieutenant Procope about their present position and future prospects, discussing all manner of speculations as to the results of the anticipated collision with the earth, and wondering whether any measures could be devised for mitigating the violence of a shock which might be terrible in its consequences, even if it did not entail a total annihilation of themselves.

"Have you no parents?"

There was no visitor to the Hive more regular than Rosette. He had already directed his telescope to be moved back to his former observa-

tory, where, as much as the cold would permit him, he persisted in
making his all-absorbing studies of the heavens.

The result of these studies no one ventured to inquire; but it became
generally noticed that something was very seriously disturbing the
professor's equanimity. Not only would he be seen toiling more frequently up the arduous way that lay between his nook below and his
telescope above, but he would be heard muttering in an angry tone that
indicated considerable agitation.

One day, as he was hurrying down to his study, he met Ben Zoof,
who, secretly entertaining a feeling of delight at the professor's manifest discomfiture, made some casual remark about things not being
very straight. The way in which his advance was received the good
orderly never divulged, but henceforward he maintained the firm conviction that there was something very much amiss up in the sky.

To Servadac and his friends this continual disquietude and ill-humor on the part of the professor occasioned no little anxiety. From
what, they asked, could his dissatisfaction arise? They could only conjecture that he had discovered some flaw in his reckonings; and if this
were so, might there not be reason to apprehend that their anticipations of coming into contact with the earth, at the settled time, might
all be falsified?

Day followed day, and still there was no cessation of the professor's
discomposure. He was the most miserable of mortals. If really his calculations and his observations were at variance, this, in a man of his
irritable temperament, would account for his perpetual perturbation.
But he entered into no explanation; he only climbed up to his telescope,
looking haggard and distressed, and when compelled by the frost to
retire, he would make his way back to his study more furious than
ever. At times he was heard giving vent to his vexation. "Confound it!
what does it mean? what is she doing? All behind! Is Newton a fool? Is
the law of universal gravitation the law of universal nonsense?" And
the little man would seize his head in both his hands, and tear away at
the scanty locks which he could ill afford to lose.

Enough was overheard to confirm the suspicion that there was some
irreconcilable discrepancy between the results of his computation and
what he had actually observed; and yet, if he had been called upon to
say, he would have sooner insisted that there was derangement in the
laws of celestial mechanism, than have owned there was the least prob-

ability of error in any of his own calculations. Assuredly, if the poor professor had had any flesh to lose he would have withered away to a shadow.

But this state of things was before long to come to an end. On the 12th, Ben Zoof, who was hanging about outside the great hall of the cavern, heard the professor inside utter a loud cry. Hurrying in to ascertain the cause, he found Rosette in a state of perfect frenzy, in which ecstasy and rage seemed to be struggling for the predominance.

"Eureka! Eureka!" yelled the excited astronomer.

"What, in the name of peace, do you mean?" bawled Ben Zoof, in open-mouthed amazement.

"Eureka!" again shrieked the little man.

"How? What? Where?" roared the bewildered orderly.

"Eureka! I say," repeated Rosette; "and if you don't understand me, you may go to the devil!"

Without availing himself of this polite invitation, Ben Zoof betook himself to his master. "Something has happened to the professor," he said; "he is rushing about like a madman, screeching and yelling 'Eureka!'"

"Eureka?" exclaimed Servadac. "That means he has made a discovery;" and, full of anxiety, he hurried off to meet the professor.

But, however great was his desire to ascertain what this discovery implied, his curiosity was not yet destined to be gratified. The professor kept muttering in incoherent phrases: "Rascal! he shall pay for it yet. I will be even with him! Cheat! Thrown me out!" But he did not vouchsafe any reply to Servadac's inquiries, and withdrew to his study.

From that day Rosette, for some reason at present incomprehensible, quite altered his behavior to Isaac Hakkabut, a man for whom he had always hitherto evinced the greatest repugnance and contempt. All at once he began to show a remarkable interest in the Jew and his affairs, paying several visits to the dark little storehouse, making inquiries as to the state of business and expressing some solicitude about the state of the exchequer.

The wily Jew was taken somewhat by surprise, but came to an immediate conclusion that the professor was contemplating borrowing some money; he was consequently very cautious in all his replies.

It was not Hakkabut's habit ever to advance a loan except at an extravagant rate of interest, or without demanding far more than an adequate security. Count Timascheff, a Russian nobleman, was evidently rich; to him perhaps, for a proper consideration, a loan might be made: Captain Servadac was a Gascon, and Gascons are proverbially poor; it would never do to lend any money to him; but here was a professor, a mere man of science, with circumscribed means; did *he* expect to borrow? Certainly Isaac would as soon think of flying, as of lending money to him. Such were the thoughts that made him receive all Rosette's approaches with a careful reservation.

It was not long, however, before Hakkabut was to be called upon to apply his money to a purpose for which he had not reckoned. In his eagerness to effect sales, he had parted with all the alimentary articles in his cargo without having the precautionary prudence to reserve enough for his own consumption. Amongst other things that failed him was his stock of coffee, and as coffee was a beverage without which he deemed it impossible to exist, he found himself in considerable perplexity.

He pondered the matter over for a long time, and ultimately persuaded himself that, after all, the stores were the common property of all, and that he had as much right to a share as anyone else. Accordingly, he made his way to Ben Zoof, and, in the most amiable tone he could assume, begged as a favor that he would let him have a pound of coffee.

The orderly shook his head dubiously.

"A pound of coffee, old Nathan? I can't say."

"Why not? You have some?" said Isaac.

"Oh yes! plenty—a hundred kilograms."

"Then let me have one pound. I shall be grateful."

"Hang your gratitude!"

"Only one pound! You would not refuse anybody else."

"That's just the very point, old Samuel; if you were anybody else, I should know very well what to do. I must refer the matter to his Excellency."

"Oh, his Excellency will do me justice."

"Perhaps you will find his justice rather too much for you." And with this consoling remark, the orderly went to seek his master.

Rosette meanwhile had been listening to the conversation, and secretly rejoicing that an opportunity for which he had been watching had arrived. "What's the matter, Master Isaac? Have you parted with all your coffee?" he asked, in a sympathizing voice, when Ben Zoof was gone.

"Ah! yes, indeed," groaned Hakkabut, "and now I require some for my own use. In my little black hole I cannot live without my coffee."

"Of course you cannot," agreed the professor.

"And don't you think the governor ought to let me have it?"

"No doubt."

"Oh, I must have coffee," said the Jew again.

"Certainly," the professor assented. "Coffee is nutritious; it warms the blood. How much do you want?"

"A pound. A pound will last me for a long time."

"And who will weigh it for you?" asked Rosette, scarcely able to conceal the eagerness that prompted the question.

"Why, they will weigh it with my steelyard, of course. There is no other balance here." And as the Jew spoke, the professor fancied he could detect the faintest of sighs.

"Good, Master Isaac; all the better for you! You will get your seven pounds instead of one!"

"Yes; well, seven, or thereabouts—thereabouts," stammered the Jew with considerable hesitation.

Rosette scanned his countenance narrowly, and was about to probe him with further questions, when Ben Zoof returned. "And what does his Excellency say?" inquired Hakkabut.

"Why, Nehemiah, he says he shan't give you any."

"Merciful heavens!" began the Jew.

"He says he doesn't mind selling you a little."

"But, by the holy city, why does he make me pay for what anybody else could have for nothing?"

"As I told you before, you are not anybody else; so, come along. You can afford to buy what you want. We should like to see the color of your money."

"Merciful heavens!" the old man whined once more.

"Now, none of that! Yes or no? If you are going to buy, say so at once; if not, I shall shut up shop."

Hakkabut knew well enough that the orderly was not a man to be trifled with, and said, in a tremulous voice, "Yes, I will buy."

The professor, who had been looking on with much interest, betrayed manifest symptoms of satisfaction.

"How much do you want? What will you charge for it?" asked Isaac, mournfully, putting his hand into his pocket and chinking his money.

"Oh, we will deal gently with you. We will not make any profit. You shall have it for the same price that we paid for it. Ten francs a pound, you know."

"Give it a little push, please."

The Jew hesitated.

"Come now, what is the use of your hesitating? Your gold will have no value when you go back to the world."

"What do you mean?" asked Hakkabut, startled.

"You will find out some day," answered Ben Zoof, significantly.

Hakkabut drew out a small piece of gold from his pocket, took it close under the lamp, rolled it over in his hand, and pressed it to his lips. "Shall you weigh me the coffee with my steelyard?" he asked, in a quavering voice that confirmed the professor's suspicions.

"There is nothing else to weigh it with; you know that well enough, old Shechem," said Ben Zoof. The steelyard was then produced; a tray was suspended to the hook, and upon this coffee was thrown until the needle registered the weight of one pound. Of course, it took seven pounds of coffee to do this.

"There you are! There's your coffee, man!" Ben Zoof said.

"Are you sure?" inquired Hakkabut, peering down close to the dial. "Are you quite sure that the needle touches the point?"

"Yes; look and see."

"Give it a little push, please."

"Why?"

"Because—because—"

"Well, because of what?" cried the orderly, impatiently.

"Because I think, perhaps—I am not quite sure—perhaps the steelyard is not quite correct."

The words were not uttered before the professor, fierce as a tiger, had rushed at the Jew, had seized him by the throat, and was shaking him till he was black in the face.

"Help! help!" screamed Hakkabut. "I shall be strangled."

"Rascal! consummate rascal! thief! villain!" the professor reiterated, and continued to shake the Jew furiously.

Ben Zoof looked on and laughed, making no attempt to interfere; he had no sympathy with either of the two.

The sound of the scuffling, however, drew the attention of Servadac, who, followed by his companions, hastened to the scene. The combatants were soon parted. "What is the meaning of all this?" demanded the captain.

As soon as the professor had recovered his breath, exhausted by his exertions, he said, "The old reprobate, the rascal has cheated us! His steelyard is wrong! He is a thief!"

Captain Servadac looked sternly at Hakkabut.

"How is this, Hakkabut? Is this a fact?"

"No, no—yes—no, your Excellency, only—"

"He is a cheat, a thief!" roared the excited astronomer. "His weights deceive!"

"Stop, stop!" interposed Servadac; "let us hear. Tell me, Hakkabut—"

"Help! help!" screamed Hakkabut. "I shall be strangled."

"The steelyard lies! It cheats! it lies!" roared the irrepressible Rosette.

"Tell me, Hakkabut, I say," repeated Servadac.

The Jew only kept on stammering, "Yes—no—I don't know."

But heedless of any interruption, the professor continued, "False weights! That confounded steelyard! It gave a false result! The mass was wrong! The observations contradicted the calculations; they were wrong! She was out of place! Yes, out of place entirely."

"What!" cried Servadac and Procope in a breath, "out of place?"

"Yes, completely," said the professor.

"Gallia out of place?" repeated Servadac, agitated with alarm.

"I did not say Gallia," replied Rosette, stamping his foot impetuously; "I said Nerina."

"Oh, Nerina," answered Servadac. "But what of Gallia?" he inquired, still nervously.

"Gallia, of course, is on her way to the earth. I told you so. But that Jew is a rascal!"

CHAPTER XVI.

A JOURNEY AND A DISAPPOINTMENT

It was as the professor had said. From the day that Isaac Hakkabut had entered upon his mercantile career, his dealings had all been carried on by a system of false weight. That deceitful steelyard had been the mainspring of his fortune. But when it had become his lot to be the purchaser instead of the vendor, his spirit had groaned within him at being compelled to reap the fruits of his own dishonesty. No one who had studied his character could be much surprised at the confession that was extorted from him, that for every supposed kilogram that he had ever sold the true weight was only 750 grams, or just five and twenty per cent. less than it ought to have been.

The professor, however, had ascertained all that he wanted to know. By estimating his comet at a third as much again as its proper weight, he had found that his calculations were always at variance with the observed situation of the satellite, which was immediately influenced by the mass of its primary.

But now, besides enjoying the satisfaction of having punished old Hakkabut, Rosette was able to recommence his calculations with reference to the elements of Nerina upon a correct basis, a task to which he devoted himself with redoubled energy.

It will be easily imagined that Isaac Hakkabut, thus caught in his own trap, was jeered most unmercifully by those whom he had attempted to make his dupes. Ben Zoof, in particular, was never wearied of telling him how on his return to the world he would be prosecuted for using false weights, and would certainly become acquainted with the inside of a prison. Thus badgered, he secluded himself more than ever in his dismal hole, never venturing, except when absolutely obliged, to face the other members of the community.

On the 7th of October the comet re-entered the zone of the telescopic planets, one of which had been captured as a satellite, and the origin of the whole of which is most probably correctly attributed to the disintegration of some large planet that formerly revolved between the orbits of Mars and Jupiter. By the beginning of the following month half of this zone had been traversed, and only two months remained before the collision with the earth was to be expected. The temperature was now rarely below 12 degrees below zero, but that was far too cold to permit the slightest symptoms of a thaw. The surface of the sea remained as frozen as ever, and the two vessels, high up on their icy pedestals, remained unaltered in their critical position.

It was about this time that the question began to be mooted whether it would not be right to reopen some communication with the Englishmen at Gibraltar. Not that any doubt was entertained as to their having been able successfully to cope with the rigors of the winter; but Captain Servadac, in a way that did honor to his generosity, represented that, however uncourteous might have been their former behavior, it was at least due to them that they should be informed of the true condition of things, which they had had no opportunity of learning; and, moreover, that they should be invited to co-operate with the population of Nina's Hive, in the event of any measures being suggested by which the shock of the approaching collision could be mitigated.

The count and the lieutenant both heartily concurred in Servadac's sentiments of humanity and prudence, and all agreed that if the intercourse were to be opened at all, no time could be so suitable as the present, while the surface of the sea presented a smooth and solid footing. After a thaw should set in, neither the yacht nor the tartan could be reckoned on for service, and it would be inexpedient to make use of the steam launch, for which only a few tons of coal had been reserved, just sufficient to convey them to Gourbi Island when the occasion should arise; whilst as to the yawl, which, transformed into a sledge, had performed so successful a trip to Formentera, the absence of wind would make that quite unavailable. It was true that with the return of summer temperature, there would be certain to be a derangement in the atmosphere of Gallia, which would result in wind, but for the present the air was altogether too still for the yawl to have any prospects of making its way to Gibraltar.

The only question remaining was as to the possibility of going on foot. The distance was somewhere about 240 miles. Captain Servadac declared himself quite equal to the undertaking. To skate sixty or seventy miles a day would be nothing, he said, to a practical skater like himself. The whole journey there and back might be performed in eight days. Provided with a compass, a sufficient supply of cold meat, and a spirit lamp, by which he might boil his coffee, he was perfectly sure he should, without the least difficulty, accomplish an enterprise that chimed in so exactly with his adventurous spirit.

Rosette with his head between his hands.

Equally urgent were both the count and the lieutenant to be allowed to accompany him; nay, they even offered to go instead; but Servadac, expressing himself as most grateful for their consideration, declined their offer, and avowed his resolution of taking no other companion than his own orderly.

Highly delighted at his master's decision, Ben Zoof expressed his satisfaction at the prospect of "stretching his legs a bit," declaring that nothing could induce him to permit the captain to go alone. There was no delay. The departure was fixed for the following morning, the 2nd of November.

Although it is not to be questioned that a genuine desire of doing an act of kindness to his fellow-creatures was a leading motive of Servadac's proposed visit to Gibraltar, it must be owned that another idea, confided to nobody, least of all to Count Timascheff, had been conceived in the brain of the worthy Gascon. Ben Zoof had an inkling that his master was "up to some other little game," when, just before starting, he asked him privately whether there was a French tricolor among the stores. "I believe so," said the orderly.

"Then don't say a word to anyone, but fasten it up tight in your knapsack."

Ben Zoof found the flag, and folded it up as he was directed. Before proceeding to explain this somewhat enigmatical conduct of Servadac, it is necessary to refer to a certain physiological fact, coincident but unconnected with celestial phenomena, originating entirely in the frailty of human nature. The nearer that Gallia approached the earth, the more a sort of reserve began to spring up between the captain and Count Timascheff. Though they could not be said to be conscious of it, the remembrance of their former rivalry, so completely buried in oblivion for the last year and ten months, was insensibly recovering its hold upon their minds, and the question was all but coming to the surface as to what would happen if, on their return to earth, the handsome Madame de L—— should still be free. From companions in peril, would they not again be avowed rivals? Conceal it as they would, a coolness was undeniably stealing over an intimacy which, though it could never be called affectionate, had been uniformly friendly and courteous.

Under these circumstances, it was not surprising that Hector Servadac should not have confided to the count a project which, wild as it was, could scarcely have failed to widen the unacknowledged breach that was opening in their friendship.

The project was the annexation of Ceuta to the French dominion. The Englishmen, rightly enough, had continued to occupy the fragment of Gibraltar, and their claim was indisputable. But the island of

Ceuta, which before the shock had commanded the opposite side of the strait, and had been occupied by Spaniards, had since been abandoned, and was therefore free to the first occupant who should lay claim to it. To plant the tricolor upon it, in the name of France, was now the cherished wish of Servadac's heart.

"Who knows," he said to himself, "whether Ceuta, on its return to earth, may not occupy a grand and commanding situation? What a proud thing it would be to have secured its possession to France!"

Next morning, as soon as they had taken their brief farewell of their friends, and were fairly out of sight of the shore, Servadac imparted his design to Ben Zoof, who entered into the project with the greatest zest, and expressed himself delighted, not only at the prospect of adding to the dominions of his beloved country, but of stealing a march upon England.

Both travelers were warmly clad, the orderly's knapsack containing all the necessary provisions. The journey was accomplished without special incident; halts were made at regular intervals, for the purpose of taking food and rest. The temperature by night as well as by day was quite endurable, and on the fourth afternoon after starting, thanks to the straight course which their compass enabled them to maintain, the adventurers found themselves within a few miles of Ceuta.

As soon as Ben Zoof caught sight of the rock on the western horizon, he was all excitement. Just as if he were in a regiment going into action, he talked wildly about "columns" and "squares" and "charges." The captain, although less demonstrative, was hardly less eager to reach the rock. They both pushed forward with all possible speed till they were within a mile and a half of the shore, when Ben Zoof, who had a very keen vision, stopped suddenly, and said that he was sure he could see something moving on the top of the island.

"Never mind, let us hasten on," said Servadac. A few minutes carried them over another mile, when Ben Zoof stopped again.

"What is it, Ben Zoof?" asked the captain.

"It looks to me like a man on a rock, waving his arms in the air," said the orderly.

"Plague on it!" muttered Servadac; "I hope we are not too late." Again they went on; but soon Ben Zoof stopped for the third time.

"It is a semaphore, sir; I see it quite distinctly." And he was not mistaken; it had been a telegraph in motion that had caught his eye.

"Plague on it!" repeated the captain.

"Too late, sir, do you think?" said Ben Zoof.

"Yes, Ben Zoof; if that's a telegraph—and there is no doubt of it—somebody has been before us and erected it; and, moreover, if it is moving, there must be somebody working it now."

He was keenly disappointed. Looking towards the north, he could distinguish Gibraltar faintly visible in the extreme distance, and upon the summit of the rock both Ben Zoof and himself fancied they could make out another semaphore, giving signals, no doubt, in response to the one here.

"Yes, it is only too clear; they have already occupied it, and established their communications," said Servadac.

"And what are we to do, then?" asked Ben Zoof.

"We must pocket our chagrin, and put as good a face on the matter as we can," replied the captain.

"But perhaps there are only four or five Englishmen to protect the place," said Ben Zoof, as if meditating an assault.

"No, no, Ben Zoof," answered Servadac; "we must do nothing rash. We have had our warning, and, unless our representations can induce them to yield their position, we must resign our hope."

Thus discomfited, they had reached the foot of the rock, when all at once, like a "Jack-in-the-box," a sentinel started up before them with the challenge:

"Who goes there?"

"Friends. Vive la France!" cried the captain.

"Hurrah for England!" replied the soldier.

By this time four other men had made their appearance from the upper part of the rock.

"What do you want?" asked one of them, whom Servadac remembered to have seen before at Gibraltar.

"Can I speak to your commanding officer?" Servadac inquired.

"Which?" said the man. "The officer in command of Ceuta?"

"Yes, if there is one."

"I will acquaint him with your arrival," answered the Englishman, and disappeared.

In a few minutes the commanding officer, attired in full uniform, was seen descending to the shore. It was Major Oliphant himself.

Servadac could no longer entertain a doubt that the Englishmen had forestalled him in the occupation of Ceuta. Provisions and fuel had evidently been conveyed thither in the boat from Gibraltar before the sea had frozen, and a solid casemate, hollowed in the rock, had afforded Major Oliphant and his contingent ample protection from the rigor of the winter. The ascending smoke that rose above the rock was sufficient evidence that good fires were still kept up; the soldiers appeared to have thriven well on what, no doubt, had been a generous diet, and the major himself, although he would scarcely have been willing to allow it, was slightly stouter than before.

"Captain, look there!"

Being only about twelve miles distant from Gibraltar, the little garrison at Ceuta had felt itself by no means isolated in its position; but by frequent excursions across the frozen strait, and by the constant use of the telegraph, had kept up their communication with their fellow-countrymen on the other island. Colonel Murphy and the major had not even been forced to forego the pleasures of the chessboard. The game that had been interrupted by Captain Servadac's former visit was not yet concluded; but, like the two American clubs that played their celebrated game in 1846 between Washington and Baltimore, the two gallant officers made use of the semaphore to communicate their well-digested moves.

The major stood waiting for his visitor to speak.

"Major Oliphant, I believe?" said Servadac, with a courteous bow.

"Yes, sir, Major Oliphant, officer in command of the garrison at Ceuta," was the Englishman's reply. "And to whom," he added, "may I have the honor of speaking?"

"To Captain Servadac, the governor general of Gallia."

"Indeed!" said the major, with a supercilious look.

"Allow me to express my surprise," resumed the captain, "at seeing you installed as commanding officer upon what I have always understood to be Spanish soil. May I demand your claim to your position?"

"My claim is that of first occupant."

"But do you not think that the party of Spaniards now resident with me may at some future time assert a prior right to the proprietorship?"

"I think not, Captain Servadac."

"But why not?" persisted the captain.

"Because these very Spaniards have, by formal contract, made over Ceuta, in its integrity, to the British government."

Servadac uttered an exclamation of surprise.

"And as the price of that important cession," continued Major Oliphant, "they have received a fair equivalent in British gold."

"Ah!" cried Ben Zoof, "that accounts for that fellow Negrete and his people having such a lot of money."

Servadac was silent. It had become clear to his mind what had been the object of that secret visit to Ceuta which he had heard of as being made by the two English officers. The arguments that he had intended to use had completely fallen through; all that he had now to do was carefully to prevent any suspicion of his disappointed project.

"May I be allowed to ask, Captain Servadac, to what I am indebted for the honor of this visit?" asked Major Oliphant presently.

"I have come, Major Oliphant, in the hope of doing you and your companions a service," replied Servadac, rousing himself from his reverie.

"Major Oliphant, I believe?" said Servadac, with a courteous bow.

"Ah, indeed!" replied the major, as though he felt himself quite independent of all services from exterior sources.

"I thought, major, that it was not unlikely you were in ignorance of the fact that both Ceuta and Gibraltar have been traversing the solar regions on the surface of a comet."

The major smiled incredulously; but Servadac, nothing daunted, went on to detail the results of the collision between the comet and the earth, adding that, as there was the almost immediate prospect of another concussion, it had occurred to him that it might be advisable for the whole population of Gallia to unite in taking precautionary measures for the common welfare.

"In fact, Major Oliphant," he said in conclusion, "I am here to inquire whether you and your friends would be disposed to join us in our present quarters."

"I am obliged to you, Captain Servadac," answered the major stiffly; "but we have not the slightest intention of abandoning our post. We have received no government orders to that effect; indeed, we have received no orders at all. Our own dispatch to the First Lord of the Admiralty still awaits the mail."

"But allow me to repeat," insisted Servadac, "that we are no longer on the earth, although we expect to come in contact with it again in about eight weeks."

"I have no doubt," the major answered, "that England will make every effort to reclaim us."

Servadac felt perplexed. It was quite evident that Major Oliphant had not been convinced of the truth of one syllable of what he had been saying.

"Then I am to understand that you are determined to retain your two garrisons here and at Gibraltar?" asked Servadac, with one last effort at persuasion.

"Certainly; these two posts command the entrance of the Mediterranean."

"But supposing there is no longer any Mediterranean?" retorted the captain, growing impatient.

"Oh, England will always take care of that," was Major Oliphant's cool reply. "But excuse me," he added presently; "I see that Colonel Murphy has just telegraphed his next move. Allow me to wish you good-afternoon."

And without further parley, followed by his soldiers, he retired into the casemate, leaving Captain Servadac gnawing his mustache with mingled rage and mortification.

"A fine piece of business we have made of this!" said Ben Zoof, when he found himself alone with his master.

"We will make our way back at once," replied Captain Servadac.

"Yes, the sooner the better, with our tails between our legs," rejoined the orderly, who this time felt no inclination to start off to the march of the Algerian zephyrs. And so the French tricolor returned as it had set out—in Ben Zoof's knapsack.

On the eighth evening after starting, the travelers again set foot on the volcanic promontory just in time to witness a great commotion.

Palmyrin Rosette was in a furious rage. He had completed all his calculations about Nerina, but that perfidious satellite had totally disappeared. The astronomer was frantic at the loss of his moon. Captured probably by some larger body, it was revolving in its proper zone of the minor planets.

CHAPTER XVII.

A BOLD PROPOSITION

On his return Servadac communicated to the count the result of his expedition, and, though perfectly silent on the subject of his personal project, did not conceal the fact that the Spaniards, without the smallest right, had sold Ceuta to the English.

Having refused to quit their post, the Englishmen had virtually excluded themselves from any further consideration; they had had their warning, and must now take the consequences of their own incredulity.

Although it had proved that not a single creature either at Gourbi Island, Gibraltar, Ceuta, Madalena, or Formentera had received any injury whatever at the time of the first concussion, there was nothing in the least to make it certain that a like immunity from harm would attend the second. The previous escape was doubtless owing to some slight, though unaccountable, modification in the rate of motion; but whether the inhabitants of the earth had fared so fortunately, was a question that had still to be determined.

The day following Servadac's return, he and the count and Lieutenant Procope met by agreement in the cave, formally to discuss what would be the most advisable method of proceeding under their present prospects. Ben Zoof was, as a matter of course, allowed to be present, and Professor Rosette had been asked to attend; but he declined on the plea of taking no interest in the matter. Indeed, the disappearance of his moon had utterly disconcerted him, and the probability that he should soon lose his comet also, plunged him into an excess of grief which he preferred to bear in solitude.

Although the barrier of cool reserve was secretly increasing between the captain and the count, they scrupulously concealed any outward token of their inner feelings, and without any personal bias applied their best energies to the discussion of the question which was of such mutual, nay, of such universal interest.

Servadac was the first to speak. "In fifty-one days, if Professor Rosette has made no error in his calculations, there is to be a recurrence
of collision between this comet and the earth. The inquiry that we have
now to make is whether we are prepared for the coming shock. I ask
myself, and I ask you, whether it is in our power, by any means, to
avert the evil consequences that are only too likely to follow?"

Count Timascheff, in a voice that seemed to thrill with solemnity,
said: "In such events we are at the disposal of an over-ruling Providence; human precautions cannot sway the Divine will."

"But with the most profound reverence for the will of Providence,"
replied the captain, "I beg to submit that it is our duty to devise whatever means we can to escape the threatening mischief. Heaven helps
them that help themselves."

"And what means have you to suggest, may I ask?" said the count,
with a faint accent of satire.

Servadac was forced to acknowledge that nothing tangible had
hitherto presented itself to his mind.

"I don't want to intrude," observed Ben Zoof, "but I don't understand why such learned gentlemen as you cannot make the comet go
where you want it to go."

"You are mistaken, Ben Zoof, about our learning," said the captain;
"even Professor Rosette, with all his learning, has not a shadow of power
to prevent the comet and the earth from knocking against each other."

"Then I cannot see what is the use of all this learning," the orderly
replied.

"One great use of learning," said Count Timascheff with a smile,
"is to make us know our own ignorance."

While this conversation had been going on, Lieutenant Procope
had been sitting in thoughtful silence. Looking up, he now said, "Incident to this expected shock, there may be a variety of dangers. If,
gentlemen, you will allow me, I will enumerate them; and we shall,
perhaps, by taking them *seriatim*, be in a better position to judge
whether we can successfully grapple with them, or in any way mitigate their consequences."

There was a general attitude of attention. It was surprising how
calmly they proceeded to discuss the circumstances that looked so
threatening and ominous.

"First of all," resumed the lieutenant, "we will specify the different
ways in which the shock may happen."

"And the prime fact to be remembered," interposed Servadac, "is that the combined velocity of the two bodies will be about 21,000 miles an hour."

"Express speed, and no mistake!" muttered Ben Zoof.

"Just so," assented Procope. "Now, the two bodies may impinge either directly or obliquely. If the impact is sufficiently oblique, Gallia may do precisely what she did before: she may graze the earth; she may, or she may not, carry off a portion of the earth's atmosphere and substance, and so she may float away again into space; but her orbit would undoubtedly be deranged, and if we survive the shock, we shall have small chance of ever returning to the world of our fellow-creatures."

"Professor Rosette, I suppose," Ben Zoof remarked, "would pretty soon find out all about that."

"But we will leave this hypothesis," said the lieutenant; "our own experience has sufficiently shown us its advantages and its disadvantages. We will proceed to consider the infinitely more serious alternative of direct impact; of a shock that would hurl the comet straight on to the earth, to which it would become attached."

"A great wart upon her face!" said Ben Zoof, laughing.

The captain held up his finger to his orderly, making him understand that he should hold his tongue.

"It is, I presume, to be taken for granted," continued Lieutenant Procope, "that the mass of the earth is comparatively so large that, in the event of a direct collision, her own motion would not be sensibly retarded, and that she would carry the comet along with her, as part of herself."

"Very little question of that, I should think," said Servadac.

"Well, then," the lieutenant went on, "what part of this comet of ours will be the part to come into collision with the earth? It may be the equator, where we are; it may be at the exactly opposite point, at our antipodes; or it may be at either pole. In any case, it seems hard to foresee whence there is to come the faintest chance of deliverance."

"Is the case so desperate?" asked Servadac.

"I will tell you why it seems so. If the side of the comet on which we are resident impinges on the earth, it stands to reason that we must be crushed to atoms by the violence of the concussion."

"Regular mincemeat!" said Ben Zoof, whom no admonitions could quite reduce to silence.

"And if," said the lieutenant, after a moment's pause, and the slight-est possible frown at the interruption—"and if the collision should occur at our antipodes, the sudden check to the velocity of the comet would be quite equivalent to a shock *in situ*; and, another thing, we should run the risk of being suffocated, for all our comet's atmosphere would be assimilated with the terrestrial atmosphere, and we, suppos-ing we were not dashed to atoms, should be left as it were upon the summit of an enormous mountain (for such to all intents and purposes Gallia would be), 450 miles above the level of the surface of the globe, without a particle of air to breathe."

He talked to the Count.

"But would not our chances of escape be considerably better," asked Count Timascheff, "in the event of either of the comet's poles being the point of contact?"

"Taking the combined velocity into account," answered the lieutenant, "I confess that I fear the violence of the shock will be too great to permit our destruction to be averted."

A general silence ensued, which was broken by the lieutenant himself. "Even if none of these contingencies occur in the way we have contemplated, I am driven to the suspicion that we shall be burnt alive."

"Burnt alive!" they all exclaimed in a chorus of horror.

"Yes. If the deductions of modern science be true, the speed of the comet, when suddenly checked, will be transmuted into heat, and that heat will be so intense that the temperature of the comet will be raised to some millions of degrees."

No one having anything definite to allege in reply to Lieutenant Procope's forebodings, they all relapsed into silence. Presently Ben Zoof asked whether it was not possible for the comet to fall into the middle of the Atlantic.

Procope shook his head. "Even so, we should only be adding the fate of drowning to the list of our other perils."

"Then, as I understand," said Captain Servadac, "in whatever way or in whatever place the concussion occurs, we must be either crushed, suffocated, roasted, or drowned. Is that your conclusion, lieutenant?"

"I confess I see no other alternative," answered Procope, calmly.

"But isn't there another thing to be done?" said Ben Zoof.

"What do you mean?" his master asked.

"Why, to get off the comet before the shock comes."

"How could you get off Gallia?"

"That I can't say," replied the orderly.

"I am not sure that that could not be accomplished," said the lieutenant.

All eyes in a moment were riveted upon him, as, with his head resting on his hands, he was manifestly cogitating a new idea. "Yes, I think it could be accomplished," he repeated. "The project may appear extravagant, but I do not know why it should be impossible. Ben Zoof has hit the right nail on the head; we must try and leave Gallia before the shock."

"Leave Gallia! How?" said Count Timascheff.

The lieutenant did not at once reply. He continued pondering for a time, and at last said, slowly and distinctly, "By making a balloon!"

Servadac's heart sank.

"A balloon!" he exclaimed. "Out of the question! Balloons are exploded things. You hardly find them in novels. Balloon, indeed!"

"Listen to me," replied Procope. "Perhaps I can convince you that my idea is not so chimerical as you imagine." And, knitting his brow, he proceeded to establish the feasibility of his plan. "If we can ascertain the precise moment when the shock is to happen, and can succeed in launching ourselves a sufficient time beforehand into Gallia's atmosphere, I believe it will transpire that this atmosphere will amalgamate with that of the earth, and that a balloon whirled along by the combined velocity would glide into the mingled atmosphere and remain suspended in mid-air until the shock of the collision is overpast."

Count Timascheff reflected for a minute, and said, "I think, lieutenant, I understand your project. The scheme seems tenable; and I shall be ready to co-operate with you, to the best of my power, in putting it into execution."

"Only, remember," continued Procope, "there are many chances to one against our success. One instant's obstruction and stoppage in our passage, and our balloon is burnt to ashes. Still, reluctant as I am to acknowledge it, I confess that I feel our sole hope of safety rests in our getting free from this comet."

"If the chances were ten thousand to one against us," said Servadac, "I think the attempt ought to be made."

"But have we hydrogen enough to inflate a balloon?" asked the count.

"Hot air will be all that we shall require," the lieutenant answered; "we are only contemplating about an hour's journey."

"Ah, a fire-balloon! A montgolfier!" cried Servadac. "But what are you going to do for a casing?"

"I have thought of that. We must cut it out of the sails of the *Dobryna*; they are both light and strong," rejoined the lieutenant. Count Timascheff complimented the lieutenant upon his ingenuity, and Ben Zoof could not resist bringing the meeting to a conclusion by a ringing cheer.

Truly daring was the plan of which Lieutenant Procope had thus become the originator; but the very existence of them all was at stake, and the design must be executed resolutely. For the success of the enterprise it was absolutely necessary to know, almost to a minute, the precise time at which the collision would occur, and Captain Servadac undertook the task, by gentle means or by stern, of extracting the secret from the professor.

To Lieutenant Procope himself was entrusted the superintendence of the construction of the montgolfier, and the work was begun at once. It was to be large enough to carry the whole of the twenty-three residents in the volcano, and, in order to provide the means of floating aloft long enough to give time for selecting a proper place for descent, the lieutenant was anxious to make it carry enough hay or straw to maintain combustion for a while, and keep up the necessary supply of heated air.

The sails of the *Dobryna*, which had all been carefully stowed away in the Hive, were of a texture unusually close, and quite capable of being made airtight by means of a varnish, the ingredients of which were rummaged out of the promiscuous stores of the tartan. The lieutenant himself traced out the pattern and cut out the strips, and all hands were employed in seaming them together. It was hardly the work for little fingers, but Nina persisted in accomplishing her own share of it. The Russians were quite at home at occupation of this sort, and having initiated the Spaniards into its mysteries, the task of joining together the casing was soon complete. Isaac Hakkabut and the professor were the only two members of the community who took no part in this somewhat tedious proceeding.

A month passed away, but Servadac found no opportunity of getting at the information he had pledged himself to gain. On the sole occasion when he had ventured to broach the subject with the astronomer, he had received for answer that as there was no hurry to get back to the earth, there need be no concern about any dangers of transit.

Indeed, as time passed on, the professor seemed to become more and more inaccessible. A pleasant temperature enabled him to live entirely in his observatory, from which intruders were rigidly shut out. But Servadac bided his time. He grew more and more impressed with the importance of finding out the exact moment at which the impact would take place, but was content to wait for a promising opportunity to put any fresh questions on the subject to the too reticent astronomer.

Meanwhile, the earth's disc was daily increasing in magnitude; the comet traveled 50,000,000 leagues during the month, at the close of which it was not more than 78,000,000 leagues from the sun.

A thaw had now fairly set in. The breaking up of the frozen ocean was a magnificent spectacle, and "the great voice of the sea," as the whalers graphically describe it, was heard in all its solemnity. Little streams of water began to trickle down the declivities of the mountain and along the shelving shore, only to be transformed, as the melting of the snow continued, into torrents or cascades. Light vapors gathered on the horizon, and clouds were formed and carried rapidly along by breezes to which the Gallian atmosphere had long been unaccustomed. All these were doubtless but the prelude to atmospheric disturbances of a more startling character; but as indications of returning spring, they were greeted with a welcome which no apprehensions for the future could prevent being glad and hearty.

A double disaster was the inevitable consequence of the thaw. Both the schooner and the tartan were entirely destroyed. The basement of the icy pedestal on which the ships had been upheaved was gradually undermined, like the icebergs of the Arctic Ocean, by warm currents of water, and on the night of the 12th the huge block collapsed *en masse*, so that on the following morning nothing remained of the *Dobryna* and the *Hansa* except the fragments scattered on the shore.

Although certainly expected, the catastrophe could not fail to cause a sense of general depression. Well-nigh one of their last ties to Mother Earth had been broken; the ships were gone, and they had only a balloon to replace them!

To describe Isaac Hakkabut's rage at the destruction of the tartan would be impossible. His oaths were simply dreadful; his imprecations on the accursed race were full of wrath. He swore that Servadac and his people were responsible for his loss; he vowed that they should be sued and made to pay him damages; he asserted that he had been brought from Gourbi Island only to be plundered; in fact, he became so intolerably abusive, that Servadac threatened to put him into irons unless he conducted himself properly; whereupon the Jew, finding that the captain was in earnest, and would not hesitate to carry the threat into effect, was fain to hold his tongue, and slunk back into his dim hole.

By the 14th the balloon was finished, and, carefully sewn and well varnished as it had been, it was really a very substantial structure. It was covered with a network that had been made from the light rigging of the yacht, and the car, composed of wicker-work that had formed partitions in the hold of the *Hansa*, was quite commodious enough to hold the twenty-three passengers it was intended to convey. No thought had been bestowed upon comfort or convenience, as the ascent was to last for so short a time, merely long enough for making the transit from atmosphere to atmosphere.

The necessity was becoming more and more urgent to get at the true hour of the approaching contact, but the professor seemed to grow more obstinate than ever in his resolution to keep his secret.

On the 15th the comet crossed the orbit of Mars, at the safe distance of 56,000,000 leagues; but during that night the community thought that their last hour had taken them unawares. The volcano rocked and trembled with the convulsions of internal disturbance, and Servadac and his companions, convinced that the mountain was doomed to some sudden disruption, rushed into the open air.

The first object that caught their attention as they emerged upon the open rocks was the unfortunate professor, who was scrambling down the mountain-side, piteously displaying a fragment of his shattered telescope.

It was no time for condolence.

A new marvel arrested every eye. A fresh satellite, in the gloom of night, was shining conspicuously before them.

That satellite was a part of Gallia itself!

By the expansive action of the inner heat, Gallia, like Gambart's comet, had been severed in twain; an enormous fragment had been detached and launched into space!

The fragment included Ceuta and Gibraltar, with the two English garrisons!

CHAPTER XVIII.

THE VENTURE MADE

WHAT would be the consequences of this sudden and complete disruption, Servadac and his people hardly dared to think.

The first change that came under their observation was the rapidity of the sun's appearances and disappearances, forcing them to the conviction that although the comet still rotated on its axis from east to west, yet the period of its rotation had been diminished by about one-half. Only six hours instead of twelve elapsed between sunrise and sunrise; three hours after rising in the west the sun was sinking again in the east.

"We are coming to something!" exclaimed Servadac. "We have got a year of something like 2,880 days."

"I shouldn't think it would be an easy matter to find saints enough for such a calendar as that!" said Ben Zoof.

Servadac laughed, and remarked that they should have the professor talking about the 238th of June, and the 325th of December.

It soon became evident that the detached portion was not revolving round the comet, but was gradually retreating into space. Whether it had carried with it any portion of atmosphere, whether it possessed any other condition for supporting life, and whether it was likely ever again to approach to the earth, were all questions that there were no means of determining. For themselves the all-important problem was—what effect would the rending asunder of the comet have upon its rate of progress? and as they were already conscious of a further increase of muscular power, and a fresh diminution of specific gravity, Servadac and his associates could not but wonder whether the alteration in the mass of the comet would not result in its missing the expected coincidence with the earth altogether.

Although he professed himself incompetent to pronounce a decided opinion, Lieutenant Procope manifestly inclined to the belief that no alteration would ensue in the rate of Gallia's velocity; but Rosette, no doubt, could answer the question directly, and the time had now arrived in which he must be compelled to divulge the precise moment of collision.

But the professor was in the worst of tempers. Generally taciturn and morose, he was more than usually uncivil whenever any one ventured to speak to him. The loss of his telescope had doubtless a great deal to do with his ill-humor; but the captain drew the most favorable conclusions from Rosette's continued irritation. Had the comet been in any way projected from its course, so as to be likely to fail in coming into contact with the earth, the professor would have been quite unable to conceal his satisfaction. But they required to know more than the general truth, and felt that they had no time to lose in getting at the exact details.

The opportunity that was wanted soon came.

On the 18th, Rosette was overheard in furious altercation with Ben Zoof. The orderly had been taunting the astronomer with the mutilation of his little comet. A fine thing, he said, to split in two like a child's toy. It had cracked like a dry nut; and mightn't one as well live upon an exploding bomb?—with much more to the same effect. The professor, by way of retaliation, had commenced sneering at the "prodigious" mountain of Montmartre, and the dispute was beginning to look serious when Servadac entered.

Thinking he could turn the wrangling to some good account, so as to arrive at the information he was so anxiously seeking, the captain pretended to espouse the views of his orderly; he consequently brought upon himself the full force of the professor's wrath.

Rosette's language became more and more violent, till Servadac, feigning to be provoked beyond endurance, cried:

"You forget, sir, that you are addressing the Governor-General of Gallia."

"Governor-General! humbug!" roared Rosette. "Gallia is my comet!"

"I deny it," said Servadac. "Gallia has lost its chance of getting back to the earth. Gallia has nothing to do with you. Gallia is mine; and you must submit to the government which I please to ordain."

"And who told you that Gallia is not going back to the earth?" asked the professor, with a look of withering scorn.

"Why, isn't her mass diminished? Isn't she split in half? Isn't her velocity all altered?" demanded the captain.

"And pray who told you this?" again said the professor, with a sneer.

"Everybody. Everybody knows it, of course," replied Servadac.

"Everybody is very clever. And you always were a very clever scholar too. We remember that of old, don't we?"

The captain spoke.

"Sir!"

"You nearly mastered the first elements of science, didn't you?"

"Sir!"

"A credit to your class!"

"Hold your tongue, sir!" bellowed the captain again, as if his anger was uncontrollable.

"Not I," said the professor.

"Hold your tongue!" repeated Servadac.

"Just because the mass is altered you think the velocity is altered?"

"Hold your tongue!" cried the captain, louder than ever.

"What has mass to do with the orbit? Of how many comets do you know the mass, and yet you know their movements? Ignorance!" shouted Rosette.

"Ah! bad student."

"Insolence!" retorted Servadac.

Ben Zoof, really thinking that his master was angry, made a threatening movement towards the professor.

"Touch me if you dare!" screamed Rosette, drawing himself up to the fullest height his diminutive figure would allow. "You shall answer for your conduct before a court of justice!"

"Where? On Gallia?" asked the captain.

"No; on the earth."

"The earth! Pshaw! You know we shall never get there; our velocity is changed."

"On the earth," repeated the professor, with decision.

"Trash!" cried Ben Zoof. "The earth will be too far off!"

"Not too far off for us to come across her orbit at 42 minutes and 35.6 seconds past two o'clock on the morning of this coming 1st of January."

"Thanks, my dear professor—many thanks. You have given me all the information I required;" and, with a low bow and a gracious smile, the captain withdrew. The orderly made an equally polite bow, and followed his master. The professor, completely nonplussed, was left alone.

Thirteen days, then—twenty-six of the original Gallian days, fifty-two of the present—was all the time for preparation that now remained. Every preliminary arrangement was hurried on with the greatest earnestness.

There was a general eagerness to be quit of Gallia. Indifferent to the dangers that must necessarily attend a balloon ascent under such unparalleled circumstances, and heedless of Lieutenant Procope's warning that the slightest check in their progress would result in instantaneous combustion, they all seemed to conclude that it must be the simplest thing possible to glide from one atmosphere to another, so that they were quite sanguine as to the successful issue of their enterprise. Captain Servadac made a point of showing himself quite enthusiastic in his anticipations, and to Ben Zoof the going up in a balloon was the supreme height of his ambition. The count and the lieutenant, of colder and less demonstrative temperament, alike seemed to realize the possible perils of the undertaking, but even they were determined to put a bold face upon every difficulty.

The sea had now become navigable, and three voyages were made to Gourbi Island in the steam launch, consuming the last of their little reserve of coal.

The first voyage had been made by Servadac with several of the sailors. They found the gourbi and the adjacent building quite uninjured by the severity of the winter; numbers of little rivulets intersected the pasture-land; new plants were springing up under the influence of the equatorial sun, and the luxuriant foliage was tenanted by the birds which had flown back from the volcano. Summer had almost abruptly succeeded to winter, and the days, though only three hours long, were intensely hot.

Another of the voyages to the island had been to collect the dry grass and straw which was necessary for inflating the balloon. Had the balloon been less cumbersome it would have been conveyed to the island, whence the start would have been effected; but as it was, it was more convenient to bring the combustible material to the balloon.

The last of the coal having been consumed, the fragments of the shipwrecked vessels had to be used day by day for fuel. Hakkabut began making a great hubbub when he found that they were burning some of the spars of the *Hansa*; but he was effectually silenced by Ben Zoof, who told him that if he made any more fuss, he should be compelled to pay 50,000 francs for a balloon-ticket, or else he should be left behind.

By Christmas Day everything was in readiness for immediate departure. The festival was observed with a solemnity still more marked than the anniversary of the preceding year. Every one looked forward to spending New Year's Day in another sphere altogether, and Ben Zoof had already promised Pablo and Nina all sorts of New Year's gifts.

It may seem strange, but the nearer the critical moment approached, the less Hector Servadac and Count Timascheff had to say to each other on the subject. Their mutual reserve became more apparent; the experiences of the last two years were fading from their minds like a dream; and the fair image that had been the cause of their original rivalry was ever rising, as a vision, between them.

The captain's thoughts began to turn to his unfinished rondo; in his leisure moments, rhymes suitable and unsuitable, possible and impossible, were perpetually jingling in his imagination. He labored under the conviction that he had a work of genius to complete. A poet he had left the earth, and a poet he must return.

Count Timascheff's desire to return to the world was quite equaled by Lieutenant Procope's. The Russian sailors' only thought was to follow their master, wherever he went. The Spaniards, though they

would have been unconcerned to know that they were to remain upon
Gallia, were nevertheless looking forward with some degree of pleasure
to revisiting the plains of Andalusia; and Nina and Pablo were only
too delighted at the prospect of accompanying their kind protectors on
any fresh excursion whatever.

Everyone worked on the balloon.

The only malcontent was Palmyrin Rosette. Day and night he persevered in his astronomical pursuits, declared his intention of never
abandoning his comet, and swore positively that nothing should induce him to set foot in the car of the balloon.

The misfortune that had befallen his telescope was a never-ending
theme of complaint; and just now, when Gallia was entering the nar-

row zone of shooting-stars, and new discoveries might have been within his reach, his loss made him more inconsolable than ever. In sheer desperation, he endeavored to increase the intensity of his vision by applying to his eyes some belladonna which he found in the *Dobryna's* medicine chest; with heroic fortitude he endured the tortures of the experiment, and gazed up into the sky until he was nearly blind. But all in vain; not a single fresh discovery rewarded his sufferings.

No one was quite exempt from the feverish excitement which prevailed during the last days of December. Lieutenant Procope superintended his final arrangements. The two low masts of the schooner had been erected firmly on the shore, and formed supports for the montgolfier, which had been duly covered with the netting, and was ready at any moment to be inflated. The car was close at hand. Some inflated skins had been attached to its sides, so that the balloon might float for a time, in the event of its descending in the sea at a short distance from the shore. If unfortunately, it should come down in mid-ocean, nothing but the happy chance of some passing vessel could save them all from the certain fate of being drowned.

The 31st came. Twenty-four hours hence and the balloon, with its large living freight, would be high in the air. The atmosphere was less buoyant than that of the earth, but no difficulty in ascending was to be apprehended.

Gallia was now within 96,000,000 miles of the sun, consequently not much more than 4,000,000 miles from the earth; and this interval was being diminished at the rate of nearly 208,000 miles an hour, the speed of the earth being about 70,000 miles, that of the comet being little less than 138,000 miles an hour.

It was determined to make the start at two o'clock, three-quarters of an hour, or, to speak correctly 42 minutes 35.6 seconds, before the time predicted by the professor as the instant of collision. The modified rotation of the comet caused it to be daylight at the time.

An hour previously the balloon was inflated with perfect success, and the car was securely attached to the network. It only awaited the stowage of the passengers.

Isaac Hakkabut was the first to take his place in the car. But scarcely had he done so, when Servadac noticed that his waist was encompassed by an enormous girdle that bulged out to a very extraordinary extent. "What's all this, Hakkabut?" he asked.

"It's only my little bit of money, your Excellency; my modest little fortune—a mere bagatelle," said the Jew.

"And what may your little fortune weigh?" inquired the captain.

"Only about sixty-six pounds!" said Isaac.

"Sixty-six pounds!" cried Servadac. "We haven't reckoned for this."

"Merciful heavens!" began the Jew.

He was taken and put quietly down at the bottom of the car.

"Sixty-six pounds!" repeated Servadac. "We can hardly carry ourselves; we can't have any dead weight here. Pitch it out, man, pitch it out!"

"God of Israel!" whined Hakkabut.

"Out with it, I say!" cried Servadac.

"What, all my money, which I have saved so long, and toiled for so hard?"

"It can't be helped," said the captain, unmoved.

"Oh, your Excellency!" cried the Jew.

"Now, old Nicodemus, listen to me," interposed Ben Zoof; "you just get rid of that pouch of yours, or we will get rid of you. Take your choice. Quick, or out you go!"

The avaricious old man was found to value his life above his money; he made a lamentable outcry about it, but he unfastened his girdle at last, and put it out of the car.

Very different was the case with Palmyrin Rosette. He avowed over and over again his intention of never quitting the nucleus of his comet. Why should he trust himself to a balloon, that would blaze up like a piece of paper? Why should he leave the comet? Why should he not go once again upon its surface into the far-off realms of space?

His volubility was brought to a sudden check by Servadac's bidding two of the sailors, without more ado, to take him in their arms and put him quietly down at the bottom of the car.

To the great regret of their owners, the two horses and Nina's pet goat were obliged to be left behind. The only creature for which there was found a place was the carrier-pigeon that had brought the professor's message to the Hive. Servadac thought it might probably be of service in carrying some communication to the earth.

When every one, except the captain and his orderly, had taken their places, Servadac said, "Get in, Ben Zoof."

"After you, sir," said Ben Zoof, respectfully.

"No, no!" insisted Servadac; "the captain must be the last to leave the ship!"

A moment's hesitation and the orderly clambered over the side of the car. Servadac followed. The cords were cut. The balloon rose with stately calmness into the air.

CHAPTER XIX.

WHEN the balloon had reached an elevation of about 2,500 yards, Lieutenant Procope determined to maintain it at that level. A wire-work stove, suspended below the casing, and filled with lighted hay, served to keep the air in the interior at a proper temperature.

Beneath their feet was extended the basin of the Gallian Sea. An inconsiderable speck to the north marked the site of Gourbi Island. Ceuta and Gibraltar, which might have been expected in the west, had utterly disappeared. On the south rose the volcano, the extremity of the promontory that jutted out from the continent that formed the framework of the sea; whilst in every direction the strange soil, with its commixture of tellurium and gold, gleamed under the sun's rays with a perpetual iridescence.

Apparently rising with them in their ascent, the horizon was well-defined. The sky above them was perfectly clear; but away in the northwest, in opposition to the sun, floated a new sphere, so small that it could not be an asteroid, but like a dim meteor. It was the fragment that the internal convulsion had rent from the surface of the comet, and which was now many thousands of leagues away, pursuing the new orbit into which it had been projected. During the hours of daylight it was far from distinct, but after nightfall it would assume a definite luster.

The object, however, of supreme interest was the great expanse of the terrestrial disc, which was rapidly drawing down obliquely towards them. It totally eclipsed an enormous portion of the firmament above, and approaching with an ever-increasing velocity, was now within half its average distance from the moon. So close was it, that the two poles could not be embraced in one focus. Irregular patches of greater or less brilliancy alternated on its surface, the brighter betokening the continents, the more somber indicating the oceans that absorbed the solar rays. Above, there were broad white bands, darkened on the side averted from the sun, exhibiting a slow but unintermittent movement; these were the vapors that pervaded the terrestrial atmosphere.

But as the aeronauts were being hurried on at a speed of 70 miles a second, this vague aspect of the earth soon developed itself into definite outlines. Mountains and plains were no longer confused, the distinction between sea and shore was more plainly identified, and instead of being, as it were, depicted on a map, the surface of the earth appeared as though modelled in relief.

"Europe! Russia! France!" shout Procope, the count, and Servadac, almost in a breath.

Twenty-seven minutes past two, and Gallia is only 72,000 miles from the terrestrial sphere; quicker and quicker is the velocity; ten minutes later, and they are only 36,000 miles apart!

The whole configuration of the earth is clear.

"Europe! Russia! France!" shout Procope, the count, and Servadac, almost in a breath.

And they are not mistaken. The eastern hemisphere lies before them in the full blaze of light, and there is no possibility of error in distinguishing continent from continent.

The surprise only kindled their emotion to yet keener intensity, and it would be hard to describe the excitement with which they gazed at the panorama that was before them. The crisis of peril was close at hand, but imagination overleaped all consideration of danger; and everything was absorbed in the one idea that they were again within reach of that circle of humanity from which they had supposed themselves severed forever.

And, truly, if they could have paused to study it, that panorama of the states of Europe which was outstretched before their eyes, was conspicuous for the fantastic resemblances with which Nature on the one hand, and international relations on the other, have associated them. There was England, marching like some stately dame towards the east, trailing her ample skirts and coroneted with the cluster of her little islets; Sweden and Norway, with their bristling spine of mountains, seemed like a splendid lion eager to spring down from the bosom of the ice-bound north; Russia, a gigantic polar bear, stood with its head towards Asia, its left paw resting upon Turkey, its right upon Mount Caucasus; Austria resembled a huge cat curled up and sleeping a watchful sleep; Spain, with Portugal as a pennant, like an unfurled banner, floated from the extremity of the continent; Turkey, like an insolent cock, appeared to clutch the shores of Asia with the one claw, and the land of Greece with the other; Italy, as it were a foot and leg encased in a tight-fitting boot, was juggling deftly with the islands of Sicily, Sardinia, and Corsica; Prussia, a formidable hatchet imbedded in the heart of Germany, its edge just grazing the frontiers of France; whilst France itself suggested a vigorous torso with Paris at its breast.

All at once Ben Zoof breaks the silence: "Montmartre! I see Montmartre!" And, smile at the absurdity as others might, nothing could induce the worthy orderly to surrender his belief that he could actually make out the features of his beloved home.

The only individual whose soul seemed unstirred by the approaching earth was Palmyrin Rosette. Leaning over the side of the car, he kept his eyes fixed upon the abandoned comet, now floating about a mile and a half below him, bright in the general irradiation which was flooding the surrounding space.

Chronometer in hand, Lieutenant Procope stood marking the minutes and seconds as they fled; and the stillness which had once again fallen upon them all was only broken by his order to replenish the stove, that the montgolfier might retain its necessary level. Servadac and the count continued to gaze upon the earth with an eagerness that almost amounted to awe. The balloon was slightly in the rear of Gallia, a circumstance that augured somewhat favorably, because it might be presumed that if the comet preceded the balloon in its contact with the earth, there would be a break in the suddenness of transfer from one atmosphere to the other.

The next question of anxiety was, where would the balloon alight? If upon *terra firma*, would it be in a place where adequate resources for safety would be at hand? If upon the ocean, would any passing vessel be within hail to rescue them from their critical position? Truly, as the count observed to his comrades, none but a Divine Pilot could steer them now.

"Forty-two minutes past!" said the lieutenant, and his voice seemed to thrill through the silence of expectation.

There were not 20,000 miles between the comet and the earth!

The calculated time of impact was 2 hours 47 minutes 35.6 seconds. Five minutes more and collision must ensue!

But was it so? Just at this moment, Lieutenant Procope observed that the comet deviated sensibly in an oblique course. Was it possible that after all collision would not occur?

The deviation, however, was not great; it did not justify any anticipation that Gallia would merely graze the earth, as it had done before; it left it certain that the two bodies would inevitably impinge.

"No doubt," said Ben Zoof, "this time we shall stick together."

Another thought occurred. Was it not only too likely that, in the fusion of the two atmospheres, the balloon itself, in which they were being conveyed, would be rent into ribbons, and every one of its passengers hurled into destruction, so that not a Gallian should survive to tell the tale of their strange peregrinations?

Moments were precious; but Hector Servadac resolved that he would adopt a device to secure that at least some record of their excursion in solar distances should survive themselves.

Tearing a leaf from his note-book, he wrote down the name of the comet, the list of the fragments of the earth it had carried off, the names of his companions, and the date of the comet's aphelion; and having subscribed it with his signature, turned to Nina and told her he must have the carrier-pigeon which was nestling in her bosom.

The child's eyes filled with tears; she did not say a word, but imprinting a kiss upon its soft plumage, she surrendered it at once, and the message was hurriedly fastened to its neck. The bird wheeled round and round in a few circles that widened in their diameter, and quickly sunk to an altitude in the comet's atmosphere much inferior to the balloon.

Some minutes more were thus consumed and the interval of distance was reduced to less than 8,000 miles.

The velocity became inconceivably great, but the increased rate of motion was in no way perceptible; there was nothing to disturb the equilibrium of the car in which they were making their aerial adventure.

"Forty-six minutes!" announced the lieutenant.

The glowing expanse of the earth's disc seemed like a vast funnel, yawning to receive the comet and its atmosphere, balloon and all, into its open mouth.

"Forty-seven!" cried Procope.

There was half a minute yet. A thrill ran through every vein. A vibration quivered through the atmosphere. The montgolfier, elongated to its utmost stretch, was manifestly being sucked into a vortex. Every passenger in the quivering car involuntarily clung spasmodically to its sides, and as the two atmospheres amalgamated, clouds accumulated in heavy masses, involving all around in dense obscurity, while flashes of lurid flame threw a weird glimmer on the scene.

In a mystery every one found himself upon the earth again. They could not explain it, but here they were once more upon terrestrial soil; in a swoon they had left the earth, and in a similar swoon they had come back!

Of the balloon not a vestige remained, and contrary to previous computation, the comet had merely grazed the earth, and was traversing the regions of space, again far away!

CHAPTER XX.

BACK AGAIN

"In Algeria, captain?"

"Yes, Ben Zoof, in Algeria; and not far from Mostaganem." Such were the first words which, after their return to consciousness, were exchanged between Servadac and his orderly.

They had resided so long in the province that they could not for a moment be mistaken as to their whereabouts, and although they were incapable of clearing up the mysteries that shrouded the miracle, yet they were convinced at the first glance that they had been returned to the earth at the very identical spot where they had quitted it.

In fact, they were scarcely more than a mile from Mostaganem, and in the course of an hour, when they had all recovered from the bewilderment occasioned by the shock, they started off in a body and made their way to the town. It was a matter of extreme surprise to find no symptom of the least excitement anywhere as they went along. The population was perfectly calm; every one was pursuing his ordinary avocation; the cattle were browsing quietly upon the pastures that were moist with the dew of an ordinary January morning. It was about eight o'clock; the sun was rising in the east; nothing could be noticed to indicate that any abnormal incident had either transpired or been expected by the inhabitants. As to a collision with a comet, there was not the faintest trace of any such phenomenon crossing men's minds, and awakening, as it surely would, a panic little short of the certified approach of the millennium.

"Nobody expects us," said Servadac; "that is very certain."

"No, indeed," answered Ben Zoof, with a sigh; he was manifestly disappointed that his return to Mostaganem was not welcomed with a triumphal reception.

They reached the Mascara gate. The first persons that Servadac recognized were the two friends that he had invited to be his seconds in the duel two years ago, the colonel of the 2nd Fusiliers and the captain of the 8th Artillery. In return to his somewhat hesitating salutation, the colonel greeted him heartily, "Ah! Servadac, old fellow! is it you?"

"I, myself," said the captain.

"Where on earth have you been to all this time? In the name of peace, what have you been doing with yourself?"

"You would never believe me, colonel," answered Servadac, "if I were to tell you; so on that point I had better hold my tongue."

"Hang your mysteries!" said the colonel; "tell me, where have you been?"

"No, my friend, excuse me," replied Servadac; "but shake hands with me in earnest, that I may be sure I am not dreaming." Hector Servadac had made up his mind, and no amount of persuasion could induce him to divulge his incredible experiences.

Anxious to turn the subject, Servadac took the earliest opportunity of asking, "And what about Madame de L——?"

"Madame de L——!" exclaimed the colonel, taking the words out of his mouth; "the lady is married long ago; you did not suppose that she was going to wait for you. 'Out of sight, out of mind,' you know."

"True," replied Servadac; and turning to the count he said, "Do you hear that? We shall not have to fight our duel after all."

"Most happy to be excused," rejoined the count. The rivals took each other by the hand, and were united henceforth in the bonds of a sincere and confiding friendship.

"An immense relief," said Servadac to himself, "that I have no occasion to finish that confounded rondo!"

It was agreed between the captain and the count that it would be desirable in every way to maintain the most rigid silence upon the subject of the inexplicable phenomena which had come within their experience. It was to them both a subject of the greatest perplexity to find that the shores of the Mediterranean had undergone no change, but they coincided in the opinion that it was prudent to keep their bewilderment entirely to themselves. Nothing induced them to break their reserve.

The very next day the small community was broken up.

The *Dobryna's* crew, with the count and the lieutenant, started for Russia, and the Spaniards, provided, by the count's liberality, with a competency that ensured them from want, were despatched to their native shores. The leave taking was accompanied by genuine tokens of regard and goodwill.

For Isaac Hakkabut alone there was no feeling of regret. Doubly ruined by the loss of his tartan, and by the abandonment of his fortune, he disappeared entirely from the scene. It is needless to say that no one troubled himself to institute a search after him, and, as Ben Zoof sententiously remarked, "Perhaps old Jehoram is making money in America by exhibiting himself as the latest arrival from a comet!"

But however great was the reserve which Captain Servadac might make on his part, nothing could induce Professor Rosette to conceal his experiences. In spite of the denial which astronomer after astronomer gave to the appearance of such a comet as Gallia at all, and of its being refused admission to the catalogue, he published a voluminous treatise, not only detailing his own adventures, but setting forth, with the most elaborate precision, all the elements which settled its period and its orbit. Discussions arose in scientific circles; an overwhelming majority decided against the representations of the professor; an unimportant minority declared themselves in his favor, and a pamphlet obtained some degree of notice, ridiculing the whole debate under the title of "The History of an Hypothesis." In reply to this impertinent criticism of his labors, Rosette issued a rejoinder full with the most vehement expressions of indignation, and reiterating his asseveration that a fragment of Gibraltar was still traversing the regions of space, carrying thirteen Englishmen upon its surface, and concluding by saying that it was the great disappointment of his life that he had not been taken with them.

Pablo and little Nina were adopted, the one by Servadac, the other by the count, and under the supervision of their guardians, were well educated and cared for. Some years later, Colonel, no longer Captain, Servadac, his hair slightly streaked with grey, had the pleasure of seeing the handsome young Spaniard united in marriage to the Italian, now grown into a charming girl, upon whom the count bestowed an ample dowry; the young people's happiness in no way marred by the fact that they had not been destined, as once seemed likely, to be the Adam and Eve of a new world.

The career of the comet was ever a mystery which neither Servadac nor his orderly could eliminate from the regions of doubt. Anyhow, they were firmer and more confiding friends than ever.

One day, in the environs of Montmartre, where they were secure from eavesdroppers, Ben Zoof incidentally referred to the experiences in the depths of Nina's Hive; but stopped short and said, "However, those things never happened, sir, did they?"

His master could only reply, "Confound it, Ben Zoof! What is a man to believe?"

THE END

FROM THE FRENCH EDITION

Made in United States
North Haven, CT
24 March 2023

34507849R00221